PRIMARY TARGET

(THE FORGING OF LUKE STONE—BOOK 1)

JACK MARS

ISBN: 978-1-64029-472-1

CHAPTER ONE

March 16, 2005
2:45 p.m. Afghanistan Time (5:15 a.m. Eastern Daylight Time)
Bagram Air Base
Parwan Province, Afghanistan

"Luke, you don't have to do this," Colonel Don Morris said.

Sergeant First Class Luke Stone stood at ease inside Don's office. The office itself was inside a glorified corrugated metal Quonset hut, not far from where the new runway was going in.

The air base was a wonderland of constant sound—there were earth movers digging and paving, there were construction workers hammering together hundreds of plywood B-huts to replace the tents that troops stationed here had previously lived in, and if that wasn't enough, there were Taliban rocket attacks from the surrounding mountains and suicide bombers on motorcycles blowing themselves up at the front gates.

Luke shrugged. His hair was longer than military guidance. He had a three-day growth of beard on his face. He wore a flight suit with no indication of rank on it.

"I'm just following orders, sir."

Don shook his head. His own flattop haircut was black, shot through with gray and white. His face could have been carved from granite. Indeed, his entire body could have been. His blue eyes were deep-set and intense. The color of his hair and the lines on his face were the only signs that Don Morris had been alive on Earth for more than fifty-five years.

Don was packing the meager contents of his office into boxes. One of the legendary founders of Delta Force was retiring from the United States Army. He had been handpicked to launch and manage a small intelligence agency in Washington, DC, a semi-autonomous group within the FBI. Don was referring to it as a civilian Delta Force.

"Don't you dare call me sir," he said. "And if you're following orders today, then follow this one: decline the mission."

1

Luke smiled. "I'm afraid you're no longer my commanding officer. Your orders don't carry a lot of weight these days. Sir."

Don's eyes met Luke's. He kept them there for a long moment.

"It's a deathtrap, son. Two years after the fall of Baghdad, the war effort in Iraq is a total balls-up. Here in God's country, we control to the perimeter of this base, the Kandahar airport, downtown Kabul, and not a whole lot else. Amnesty International and the Red Cross and the European press are all screaming about black sites and torture prisons, including right here, three hundred yards from where we're standing. The brass just want to change the narrative. They need a win in capital letters. And Heath wants a feather in his cap. That's all he ever wants. None of that is worth dying over."

"Lieutenant Colonel Heath has decided to lead the raid personally," Luke said. "I was informed less than an hour ago."

Don's shoulders slumped. Then he nodded.

"No surprise there," he said. "You know what we used to call Heath? Captain Ahab. He gets fixated on something, some whale of a thing, and he will chase it to the bottom of the sea. And he'll be happy to take all his men with him."

Don paused. He sighed.

"Listen, Stone, you have nothing to prove to me, or to anyone. You've earned a free pass. You can decline this mission. Hell, in a couple of months, you could leave the Army if you want and come join me in DC. I'd like that."

Now Luke nearly laughed. "Don, not everybody around here is middle-aged. I'm thirty-one years old. I don't think a suit and tie, and lunch at my desk, is quite my speed just yet."

Don held a framed photograph in his hands. It hovered above an open box. He stared down at it. Luke knew the photo well. It was a faded color snapshot of four shirtless young men, Green Berets, mugging for the camera before a mission in Vietnam. Don was the only one of those men who was still alive.

"Me neither," Don said.

He looked at Luke again.

"Don't die out there tonight."

"I don't plan to."

Don glanced at the photo again. "No one ever does," he said.

For a moment, he stared out the window at the snowcapped peaks of the Hindu Kush rising all around them. He shook his head. His broad chest rose and fell. "Man, I'm going to miss this place."

* * *

"Gentlemen, this mission is suicide," the man at the front of the room said. "And that's why they send men like us."

Luke sat in a folding chair in the drab cinderblock briefing room, twenty-two other men sitting in the chairs around him. They were all Delta Force operators, the best of the best. And the mission, as Luke understood it, was difficult—but not necessarily suicide.

The man giving this final briefing was Lieutenant Colonel Morgan Heath, as hands-on and gung-ho a commander as there was. Not yet forty years old, it was clear that Delta was not the end of the line for Heath. He had rocketed up to his current rank, and his ambitions seemed to point toward a higher profile. Politics, maybe a book deal, maybe a stint on TV as a military expert.

Heath was handsome, very fit, and over-the-top eager. That wasn't unusual for a Delta operator. But he also talked a lot. And that wasn't Delta at all.

Luke had watched him a week earlier, giving an interview to a reporter and a photographer from *Rolling Stone* magazine, and walking the guys through the advanced stealth and navigational capabilities of an MH-53J helicopter—not necessarily classified information, but definitely not the kind of thing you want to share with everyone.

Stone almost called him on it. But didn't.

He didn't, not because Heath outranked him—that didn't matter in Delta, or shouldn't—but because he could imagine ahead of time Heath's response: "You think the Taliban read American pop magazines, Sergeant?"

Now, Heath's presentation was up-to-the-minute technology for ten years earlier, PowerPoint on a white backdrop. A young man in a turban and with a dark beard appeared on the screen.

"You all know your man," Heath said. "Abu Mustafa Faraj al-Jihadi was born sometime around 1970 among a tribe of nomads in eastern Afghanistan or the tribal regions of western Pakistan. He probably had no formal education to speak of, and his family probably crisscrossed the border like it wasn't even there. Al Qaeda runs in his veins. When the Soviets invaded Afghanistan in 1979, by all accounts he joined the resistance as a child soldier, possibly as young as eight or nine years old. All this time later, decades of nonstop war, and somehow he's still breathing. Heck, he's still rocking and rolling. We believe he's responsible for organizing at least two dozen major terror attacks, including last October's suicide attacks in Mumbai, and the bombing of the USS *Sarasota* at Port of Aden, in which seventeen American sailors died."

Heath paused for effect. He eyed everyone in the room.

"This guy is bad news. Getting him will be the next best thing to taking down Osama bin Laden. You guys want to be heroes? This is your night."

Heath clicked a button in his hand. The photo on the screen changed. Now it was a split image—on one side of the vertical border was an aerial shot of al-Jihadi's compound just outside a small village; on the other side was a 3-D rendering of what was believed to be al-Jihadi's house. The house was two stories, made of stone, and built against a steep hill—Luke knew it was possible that the back of the house emptied into a tunnel complex.

Heath launched into a description of how the mission would go. Two choppers, twelve men on each. The choppers would set down in a field just outside the walls of the compound, unload the men, then take off again and provide aerial support.

The twelve men of A-Team—Luke and Heath's team—would breach the walls, enter the house, and assassinate al-Jihadi. If possible, they would carry the body out on a stretcher and return it to base. If not, they would photograph it for later identification. B-Team would hold the walls and the approach to the compound from the village.

The choppers would then touch down again and extract both teams. If for any reason the choppers could not land again, the two teams would make their way to an old abandoned American forward fire base on a rocky hillside less than half a mile outside the village. Extraction would take place there, or the teams would hold the former base until extraction could occur. Luke knew all this by heart. But he didn't like the idea of a rendezvous at that old fire base.

"What if that fire base is compromised?" he said.

"Compromised in what way?" Heath said.

Luke shrugged. "I don't know. You tell me. Booby-trapped. Staffed up by Taliban snipers. Used by sheepherders as a place to gather their flock."

Around the room, a few people laughed.

"Well," Heath said, "our most recent satellite images show the place empty. If there are sheep up there, then there'll be nice bedding and plenty to eat. Don't worry, Sergeant Stone. This is going to be a precision decapitation strike. In and out, gone almost before they realize we're there. We're not going to need the old fire base."

"*Madre de Dios*, Stone," Robby Martinez said. "I got a bad feeling about this one, man. Look at that night out there. No moon, cold, howling winds. We're going to catch some dust, for sure. We're going to catch hell tonight. I know it."

Martinez was small, slim, razor sharp. There was not a wasted ounce of meat on his body. When he worked out in shorts and no shirt, he looked like a drawing of the human anatomy, each muscle group carefully delineated.

Luke was checking and rechecking his pack and his weapons.

"You always got a bad feeling, Martinez," Wayne Hendricks said. He was sitting next to Luke. "The way you talk, a man would think you never saw combat before."

Hendricks was Luke's best buddy in the military. He was a big, thick-bodied hunk from the redneck wilds of north central Florida who had grown up hunting boar with his dad. He was missing his right front tooth—punched out in a bar fight in Jacksonville when he was seventeen, and never replaced. He and Luke had almost nothing in common except football—Luke had been the quarterback on his varsity squad, Wayne had played tight end. Even so, they had clicked the minute they first discovered each other in the 75th Rangers.

It seemed like they did everything together.

Wayne's wife was eight months pregnant. Luke's wife, Rebecca, was seven months along. Wayne had a girl coming, and had asked Luke to be her godfather. Luke had a boy coming, and had asked Wayne to be the boy's godfather. One night, while drunk at a bar outside Fort Bragg, Luke and Wayne had cut open their right palms with a serrated knife, and shaken hands.

Blood brothers.

Martinez shook his head. "You know where I been, Hendricks. You know what I've seen. I wasn't talking to you, anyway."

Luke glanced out the open bay door. Martinez was right. The night was cold and windy. Frigid dust blew across the pad as the choppers prepared for takeoff. Clouds skidded across the sky. It was going to be a bad night for flying.

All the same, Luke felt confident. They had what they needed to win this. The helicopters were MH-53J Pave Lows, the most advanced and most powerful transport choppers in the United States arsenal.

They had state-of-the-art terrain-following radar, which meant they could fly very low. They had infrared sensors so they could fly in bad weather, and they could reach a top speed of 165 miles per hour. They were armor plated, to shrug off all but the heaviest ordnance the enemy might have. And they were flown by the US Army 160th Special Operations Aviation Regiment, code name Nightstalkers, the Delta Force of helicopter pilots—probably the best chopper pilots in the world.

The raid was scheduled for a night with no moonlight so the helicopters could enter the operation area low to the ground and undetected. The choppers were going to use hilly terrain and nap-of-the-earth techniques to reach the compound without appearing on radar and alerting any unfriendlies—especially the Pakistani military and intelligence services, who were suspected to be cooperating with the Taliban in hiding the target.

With friends like the Pakistanis…

The low-slung buildings of the air base and the larger flight control tower squatted against the staggering backdrop of the snow-capped mountains. As Luke stared out the bay door, two fighter jets took off a quarter mile away, the scream of their engines nearly deafening. A moment later, the jets reached the sound barrier somewhere in the distance. The takeoffs were loud, but the sonic booms were muted by the wind at high altitude.

The chopper's engine whined into life. The rotor blades began to turn, slowly at first, then with increasing speed. Luke glanced along the line. Ten men in jumpsuits and helmets, not including himself, were all compulsively checking and rechecking their gear. The twelfth, Lieutenant Colonel Heath, was leaning into the cockpit at the front of the chopper, talking to the pilots.

"I'm telling you, Stone," Martinez said.

"I heard you the first time, Martinez."

"Good luck don't last forever, man. One fine day it runs out."

"I don't worry because it ain't luck in my case," Wayne said. "It's skill."

Martinez sneered at that.

"A big fat bastard like you? You're lucky every time a bullet *doesn't* hit you. You're the biggest, slowest thing out here."

Luke suppressed a laugh and went back to his gear. His weapons included an HK416 assault rifle and an MP5 for close quarter fighting. The guns were loaded and he had extra magazines stuffed in his pockets. He had a SIG P226 sidearm, four grenades, a cutting and breaching tool, and night vision goggles. This particular night vision device was the GPNVG-18, far more advanced and with a much better field of view than the standard night vision goggles offered to typical servicemen.

He was ready to rock.

Luke felt the chopper taking off. He glanced up. They were on the move. To their left, he saw the second helicopter, also leaving its pad.

"You guys are the luckiest men alive, as far as I'm concerned," he said.

"Oh yeah?" Martinez said. "Why's that?"

Luke shrugged and smiled. "You're riding with me."

* * *

The chopper flew low and fast.

The rocky hills buzzed by below them, maybe two hundred feet down, almost close enough to touch. Luke watched the inky darkness through the window. He guessed they were moving at over a hundred miles per hour.

The night was black, and they were flying without lights. He couldn't even see the second helicopter out there.

He blinked and saw Rebecca instead. She was something to behold. It wasn't so much the physical details of her face and body, which were indeed beautiful. It was the essence of her. In the years they'd been together, he had come to see past the physical. But time was passing so fast. The last time he had seen her—when was that, two months ago?—her pregnancy had just been beginning to show.

I need to get back there.

Luke glanced down—his MP5 was across his lap. For a split second, it almost seemed alive, like it might suddenly decide to start firing on its own. What was he doing with this thing? He had a child on the way.

"Gentlemen!" a voice shouted. Luke nearly jumped out of his skin. He looked up, and Heath stood in front of the group. "We are approaching target, ETA approximately ten minutes. I just got a report from base. The high winds have kicked up a bunch of dust. We're going to hit some weather between here and the target."

"Terrific," Martinez said. He looked at Luke, all the meaning in his eyes.

"What's that supposed to mean, Martinez?" Heath said.

"I love weather, sir!" Martinez shouted.

"Oh yeah?" Heath said. "Why's that?"

"It ramps the pucker factor up to twelve. Makes life more exciting."

7

Heath nodded. "Good man. You want excitement? It looks like we might be landing in zero-zero conditions."

Luke didn't like the sound of that. Zero-zero meant zero ceiling, zero visibility. The pilots would be forced to let the chopper's navigation system do the sighting for them. That was okay. What was worse was the dust. Here in Afghanistan it was so fine that it flowed almost like water. It could come through the tiniest cracks. It could get into gearboxes, and into weapons. Clouds of dust could cause brownouts, completely obscuring any unfriendly obstacles that might be waiting in the landing zone.

Dust storms stalked the nightmares of every airborne soldier in Afghanistan.

As if on cue, the chopper shuddered and got hit with a blast of sideways wind. And just like that, they were inside the dust storm. The sound outside the chopper changed—a moment ago the loud whirr of the rotors and the roar of the wind was all you could hear. Now the sound of the spitting dust hitting the outside of the chopper competed with the other two sounds. It sounded almost like rain.

"Call the dust!" Heath shouted.

Men were at the windows, peering outside at the boiling cloud.

"Dust at the tailwheel!" someone shouted.

"Dust at the cargo door!" Martinez said.

"Dust at the landing gear!"

"Dust at the cockpit door!"

Within seconds, the chopper was engulfed. Heath repeated each call out into his headset. They were flying blind now, the chopper pushing through a thick, dark sky.

Luke stared out at the sand hitting the windows. It was hard to believe they were still airborne.

Heath touched a hand to his helmet.

"Pirate 2, Pirate 2... yes, copy. Go ahead, Pirate 2."

Heath had radio contact with all aspects of the mission inside his helmet. Apparently, the second helicopter was calling him about the storm.

He listened.

"Negative on return to base, Pirate 2. Continue as planned."

Martinez's eyes met Luke's again. He shook his head. The chopper bucked and swayed. Luke looked down the line of men. These were hardened fighters, but not one of them looked eager to continue this mission.

"Negative on set-down, Pirate 2. We need you on this..."

Heath stopped and listened again.

"Mayday? Already?"

He waited. Now he looked at Luke. His eyes were narrow and hard. He didn't seem frightened. He seemed frustrated.

"I lost them. That's our support. Can any of you guys see them out there?"

Martinez looked out the window. He grunted. It wasn't even night anymore. There was nothing to see out there but brown dust.

"Pirate 2, Pirate 2, can you read me?" Heath said.

He waited a beat.

"Come in, Pirate 2. Pirate 2, Pirate 2."

Heath paused. Now he listened.

"Pirate 2, status report. Status…"

He shook his head and looked at Luke again.

"They crashed."

He listened again. "Minor injuries only. Helicopter disabled. Engines dead."

Suddenly, Heath punched the wall near his head.

"Dammit!"

He glared at Luke. "Son of a bitch. The cowards. They ditched. I know they did. It just so happens their instrumentation failed, they got lost in the storm, and they crashed seven miles from a Tenth Mountain Division bivouac. How convenient. They're going to *walk* there."

He paused. A breath of air escaped him. "Doesn't that beat all? I never thought I'd see a Delta Force unit DD a mission."

Luke watched him. DD meant *done deal*. It meant disappearing, laying low, bowing out. Heath suspected that Pirate 2 had pulled the plug on the operation themselves. Maybe they had, maybe they hadn't. But it might be the right thing to do.

"Sir, I think we should turn around," Luke said. "Or maybe we should set this thing down. We have no support unit, and I don't think I've ever seen a storm…"

Heath shook his head. "Negative, Stone. We continue with minor edits. Six-man team raids the house. Six-man team holds the village approaches."

"Sir, with all due respect, how is this chopper going to land and take off again?"

"No landing," Heath said. "We'll fast rope down. Then the chopper can go vertical and find the top of this storm, wherever it is. They can come back when we have the target secured."

"Morgan…" Luke began, addressing his superior officer by his first name, a convention he could only get away with in a few places, one of them being Delta Force.

Heath shook his head. "No, Stone. I want al-Jihadi, and I'm going to have him. This storm doubles our element of surprise—they'll never expect us to come out of the sky on a night like this. Mark my words. We're going to be legends after this."

He paused, staring directly into Stone's eyes. "ETA five minutes. Make sure you have your men ready, Sergeant."

* * *

"Okay, okay," Luke shouted over the roar of the engines and the chopper blades and the sand spitting against the windows.

"Listen up!" The two lines of men stared at him, in jumpsuit and helmets, weapons at the ready. Heath watched him from the far end. These were Luke's men and Heath knew it. Without Luke's leadership and cooperation, Heath could quickly have a mutiny on his hands. For a split second, Luke remembered what Don had said:

We used to call him Captain Ahab.

"Mission plan has changed. Pirate 2 is one hundred percent SNAFU. We are pressing forward with Plan B. Martinez, Hendricks, Colley, Simmons. You're with me and Lieutenant Colonel Heath. We are A-Team. We will move into the house, eliminate any opposition, acquire the target, and terminate. We are going to be moving very fast. Go mode. Understood?"

Martinez, as always: "Stone, how you plan to make this a twelve-man assault? It's a twenty-four-man—"

Luke stared at him. "I said *understood?*"

Various grunts and growls indicated they understood.

"No one resists us," Luke said. "Someone shoots, someone so much as shows a weapon, they're out of the game. Copy?"

He glanced through the windows. The chopper fought through a brown shit storm, moving fast, but well below its max airspeed. Visibility out there was zero. Less than zero. The chopper shuddered and lurched as if to confirm that assessment.

"Copy," the men around him said. "Copy that."

"Packard, Hastings, Morrison, Dobbs, Murphy, Bailey. You are B-Team. B-team, you support and cover us. When we drop, two of you hold the drop spot, two hold the perimeter near the gates of the compound. When we go inside, two move forward and hold the front of the house. You're also the last men out. Eyes sharp, heads on a swivel. Nobody moves against us. Eliminate all resistance, and any possible resistance. This place is bound to be hotter than hell. Your job is to make it cold."

He looked at them all.

"Are we clear?"

A chorus of voices followed, each of differing depth and timbre.

"Clear."

"Clear."

"Clear."

Luke crouched on a low-slung bench in the personnel hold. He felt that old trickle of fear, of adrenaline, of excitement. He had swallowed a Dexedrine right after takeoff, and it was starting to kick in. Suddenly he felt sharper and more alert than before.

He knew the drug's effects. His heart rate was up. His pupils were dilating, letting in more light and making his vision better. His hearing was more acute. He had more energy, more stamina, and he could remain awake for a long time.

Luke's men sat forward on their benches, eyes on him. His thoughts were racing ahead of his ability to speak.

"Children," he said. "Watch for them. We know there are women and children in the compound, some of them family members of the target. We are not shooting women and children tonight. Copy?"

Resigned voices answered.

"Copy that."

"Copy."

It was an inevitability of these assignments. The target always lived among women and children. The missions always happened at night. There was always confusion. Children tended to do unpredictable things. Luke had seen men hesitate to kill children and then pay the price when the children turned out to be soldiers who didn't hesitate to kill them. To make matters worse, their teammates would then kill the child soldiers, ten seconds too late.

People died in war. They died suddenly and often for the craziest reasons—like not wanting to kill children, who were dead a minute later anyway.

"That said, don't die out there tonight. And don't let your brothers die."

The chopper rolled on, blasting through the spitting, shrieking darkness. Luke's body swayed and bounced with the helicopter. Outside, there was flying dirt and grit all around them. They were going to be out there a few moments from now.

"If we catch these guys napping, we might have an easy time of this. They're sure not expecting us tonight. I want to drop in, acquire the target inside ten minutes, and load back up within fifteen minutes."

The chopper rocked and bucked. It fought to remain in the air.

Luke paused and took a breath.

"Do not hesitate! Seize the initiative and keep it. Push them and push them. Make them afraid. Do what comes naturally."

This after just telling them to watch for children. He was sending mixed messages, he knew that. He had to get on script, but it was hard. A dark night, an insane dust storm, one chopper down before the mission even started, and a commanding officer who would not turn around.

A thought went through his mind, laser fast, so fast he almost didn't recognize it.

Abort. Abort this mission.

He looked at the two lines of men. They looked back at him. The normal enthusiasm these guys would show was sorely lacking. A couple of sets of eyes glanced out the windows.

Sand was spraying against the helicopter. It was like the chopper was a submarine under water, except the water was made out of dust.

Luke could abort the mission. He could overrule Heath. These guys would follow him over Heath—they were his guys, not Heath's. The payback would be hell, of course. Heath would come for him. Don would try to protect Luke.

But Don would be a civilian.

The charges would be insubordination at best, mutiny at worst. A court martial was practically guaranteed. Luke knew the precedents—a lunatic, suicidal order was not necessarily an unlawful order. He would lose any court martial case.

He was still staring at the men. They were still staring at him. He could see it in their eyes, or thought he could:

Call it off.

Luke shook that away.

He looked at Wayne. Wayne raised his eyebrows, gave a slight shrug.

Up to you.

"All right, boys," Luke said. "Hit hard and fast tonight. No screwing around. We go in, we do our jobs, and we get right back out again. Trust me. This won't hurt a bit."

CHAPTER TWO

10:01 p.m. Afghanistan Time (1:01 p.m. Eastern Daylight Time)
Near the Pakistan Border
Kamdesh District
Nuristan Province, Afghanistan

"Go!" Luke shouted. "Go! Go! Go!"

Two thick ropes descended from the bay door of the chopper. Men dropped down them, then disappeared into the swirling dust. They could be a thousand feet in the air, or ten feet above the playground.

The wind howled. Biting sand and dirt sprayed in. Luke's face was covered by a ventilator mask. He and Heath were the last ones out the door. Heath wore a similar mask—they looked like two survivors of a nuclear war.

Heath looked at Luke. His mouth moved beneath his mask.

"We're gonna be legends, Stone!"

Luke hit the green START button on his stopwatch. This had better be quick.

He glanced below him. He couldn't see a damn thing down there, or anywhere. It was all on faith. He went over the side and fell through bleak darkness. Two seconds later, maybe three, he touched down hard on the ground. The landing sent a shockwave up his legs.

He released the rope and looked around, trying to get his bearings.

Heath landed a second later.

Men in masks appeared out of the gloom. Martinez, Hendricks. Hendricks gestured behind him.

"There's the wall!"

Something large loomed back there. Okay, that was the wall to the compound. A couple of dim lights shone on top of it.

Hendricks was saying something, but Luke couldn't hear it.

"What?"

"They know!"

They know? Who? Knew what?

Above their heads, the sound of the chopper's engines changed as it began to rise away. Suddenly, a bright light flashed from on top of the wall.

Something zipped by, screaming as it did.

Mortar.

"Incoming!" Luke screamed. "Incoming!"

All around him, vague shadows threw themselves to the ground.

Two more flashes of light launched.

Then another.

Then another.

How did they know?

In the black darkness of the sky, something exploded. It blew up in muted orange and red. In the sandstorm, the explosion sounded like the crackling of distant thunder. The chopper. It was hit.

From his vantage point on the ground, Luke watched it circle in the sky, an orange streak against the black. It looped toward the right, spinning now. Its engines screamed, and Luke thought he could hear the sound of its blades.

Whump. Whump. Whump. Whump.

It seemed to move in slow motion, sideways and down. It lit up the night like a tracer as it passed over the stone wall of the compound.

BOOOM!

It exploded on the other side of the wall, inside the compound. A fireball went up, two or three stories high. For an instant, Luke imagined it was all over. Chopper down, pilots dead. Support chopper inoperable. They were trapped here, and the Taliban seemed to have known they were coming.

But that helicopter just blew apart inside the compound.

Like a bomb.

And that might give them the initiative.

Several men in masks lay nearby.

Martinez, Hendricks, Colley, Simmons. His team.

Heath had to be around here somewhere.

"Up!" Luke shouted. "Up! Let's go!"

He jumped to his feet, dragging the nearest person with him. In an instant, they were all up and running, a dozen men, moving fast. Night vision was useless. Lights were useless, and would draw fire. They simply ran in total, spinning darkness.

In ten seconds, they reached the wall. Luke guessed left, and moved that way, hugging the stone. Within a few seconds, he came to the opening. There was the chopper, an apocalypse. A few silhouettes ran in the light from the flames, pulling wounded away from it.

Luke didn't hesitate. He ran through the opening, his MP5 out now. He gave them a burst from the gun, a blat of automatic fire. Now the silhouettes were running away, back toward another looming shadow, lights beckoning in the chaos.

The house.

His men were running with him.

Up ahead, the silhouettes of the retreating men sprinted up the small flight of stairs to the stone house. Luke sprinted up the stairs behind them.

Two men faced the doorway, pulling automatic weapons down from their shoulders. They wore the long beards and headwraps of the Taliban.

POP! POP! POP! POP! POP!

Luke fired without thinking about it. The two men fell.

Suddenly, there was an explosion behind him. He glanced back—it was impossible to see what was going on. He moved into the house. An instant later, four more men appeared next to him—his A-Team. They took up firing positions in the stone foyer, facing in toward the rest of the house.

They removed their ventilator masks simultaneously, almost as if they were one person. Martinez went to the downed Taliban and shot each one in the head. He didn't touch either one of them.

"Dead!" he said.

It was quieter here.

"B-Team leader," Luke said into his helmet mic. "Status?"

Heath came running into the house out of the darkness.

"B-Team leader…"

"We're holding the front gate," a voice said inside Luke's helmet. It was Murphy. His Bronx accent was unmistakable. "Stone! This don't look good. That was an ambush! They were waiting for us!"

"Just hold the gate, Murph. We'll be out in a couple of minutes."

"You better hurry, man. Somebody knew we were coming. Won't be long before there's more of them, and I can't see ten feet in front of my nose."

Luke's team had already moved further into the house. Heat went in right behind them.

"Hang in there. We're inside."

"Make it quick," Murphy's voice said. "I don't know if we're still going to be here."

"Murphy! Hold that gate! We'll be right out."

"Aye, aye," Murphy said.

Luke turned toward the darkened corridor.

Another man appeared—a big man in a white robe. He managed to reach his trigger, but he fired wildly. Luke kneeled, drew a bead on the man.

POP! A dark red circle appeared on his chest.

He seemed surprised, but then slid bonelessly to the floor.

Now Luke moved through the dark hallways, listening for sounds up ahead. He didn't have to listen long.

BANG!

A flashbang went off, then another.

BANG!

There was shouting and gunfire up ahead. Luke moved slowly toward it, snaking along the wall. Now there were sounds behind him, out on the grounds—automatic fire and explosions.

Luke checked his stopwatch. They'd been on the ground for less than four minutes, and the whole mission was already FUBAR.

"Stone!"

Murphy's voice again. "Trouble. Barbarians at the gates. I repeat: front gates under attack. Unfriendlies converging. Men down. Hastings down. Bailey down. We are falling back to the house."

"Uh, negative, B-Team. Hold those gates!"

"There's nothing to hold," Murphy said. "They're ripping it up! They got an anti-tank gun out there."

"Hold it anyway. It's our only way out of here."

"Dammit, Stone!"

"Murphy! Hold those gates!"

Luke ran further into the house.

There was screaming just ahead of him. He ran through a doorway, crossed the threshold…

And came upon a scene of total chaos.

There were at least fifteen people in a large back room. The floors were covered in thick, overlapping carpets. The walls were hung with carpets—ornate, richly colored carpets depicting vast landscapes—deserts, mountains, jungles, waterfalls.

Simmons was dead. He lay on his back, his body splayed, his eyes open and staring. His helmet was off and a chunk of his head above the eyes was gone. Two women were also dead. A small child, a boy, was dead. Three men in robes and turbans were dead.

It was a massacre in here. There were guns, and blood, all over the floor.

At the very back, near a closed door, a mass of people stood. A crowd of men in robes and turbans held children in front of them, and pointed rifles outward. Behind the men, another man lurked— he was hidden enough that Luke could barely see him.

He must be the target.

All around the chamber, Luke's team crouched or kneeled, still as statues, their guns trained on the group, looking for a shot. Lieutenant Colonel Heath stood in the center of the room, his MP5 machine gun pointed into the crowd.

"Okay," Luke said. "It's okay. Nobody do any—"

"Drop those weapons!" Heath shouted in English. His eyes were wild. He was focused on one thing—getting that whale.

"Heath!" Luke said. "Relax. There's children. We can—"

"I see the children, Stone."

"So let's just—"

Heath fired, a burst of full auto.

Instantly Luke hit the ground as gunfire broke out in all directions. He covered his head, curled into a ball, and turned his back to the action.

The shooting lasted several seconds. Even after it stopped, a few shots continued, one every few seconds, like the last of the popcorn popping. When it was finally over, Luke picked his head up. The knot of people by the closed door lay in a writhing pile.

Heath was down. Luke didn't care about that. Heath was the cause of this nightmare.

Another of Luke's men was down, over in the corner. God, what a mess. Three men down. An unknown number of civilians dead.

Luke climbed to his feet. Two other men stood at the same time. One was Martinez. The other was Colley. Martinez and Colley converged on the pile of people near the back, moving slowly, guns still drawn.

Luke glanced around the room. There were corpses everywhere. Simmons was dead. Heath... a large hole had been punched through his head where his face had been. The man had no face. Luke felt nothing about that. This was Heath's mission. It had gone as wrong as possible. Now Heath was dead.

And one more man was down.

It seemed like a complicated math problem, but really, it was simple subtraction that anyone could do. Luke's mind was not working correctly. He recognized that. Six men had come in here.

Heath and Simmons were dead. Martinez, Colley, and Stone were still in the game. That meant the last man down could only be…

Luke ran to the man. Yes, it was. It was Hendricks. Wayne.

WAYNE.

He was still moving.

Luke kneeled by him and pulled off his helmet.

Wayne's arms and legs were moving slowly, almost like he was treading water.

"Wayne! Wayne! Where are you hit?"

Wayne's eyes rolled. They found Luke. He shook his head. He began to cry. He was breathing heavily, almost gasping for air.

"Oh, buddy…" Wayne said.

"Wayne! Talk to me."

Feverishly, Luke began to unfasten Wayne's ballistic vest.

"Medic!" he screamed. "Medic!"

An instant later, Colley was there, kneeling behind him. "Simpson was the medic. I'm the backup."

Wayne was hit in the chest. Somehow shrapnel had gotten under his vest. Luke's hands searched him. He was also shot high in the leg. That was worse than the chest, by a lot. His pants were saturated with blood. His femoral artery must be hit. Luke's hand came away dripping red. There was blood everywhere. There was a lake of it under Wayne's body. It was a miracle he was still alive.

"Tell Katie," Wayne said.

"Shut up!" Luke said. "You're going to tell her yourself."

Wayne's voice was barely above a whisper.

"Tell her…"

Wayne seemed to be looking at something far away. He gazed, and then did a double take, as if confused by what he was seeing. An instant later, his eyes became still.

He stared at Luke. His mouth was slack. Nobody was home.

"Oh God, Wayne. No."

Luke looked at Colley. It was as if he were seeing Colley for the first time. Colley looked young—like barely old enough to shave. That couldn't be, of course. The man was in Delta Force. He was a trained killer. He was a consummate pro. But his neck looked about as thick as Luke's forearm. He seemed to be swimming in his clothes.

"Check him," Luke said, though he already knew what Colley would say. He fell back into a cross-legged position, and sat that way for a long moment. They had a day off during Ranger School one time. A bunch of guys held a pick-up game of football. It was a hot day, and the game was shirts versus skins. Luke spent the game throwing laser strikes to this big, thick, foul-mouthed redneck with a front tooth missing.

"Wayne."

"He's gone," Colley said.

Just like that, Wayne was dead. Luke's blood brother. The godfather of Luke's unborn son. A long, helpless breath went out of Luke.

In war, Luke knew, that's how it went. One second, your friend—or your sister, or your wife, or your child—was alive. The next second, they were gone. There was no way to turn back that clock, not even one second.

Wayne was dead. They were a long way from home. And this night was just getting started.

"Stone!" Martinez said.

Luke pulled himself to his feet once again. Martinez stood by the pile of corpses that had once protected the target. All of them appeared to be dead, all but one, the man who had stood at the back. He was tall, still youthful, with a long black beard speckled with a little gray. He lay among the fallen—shot full of holes, but alive.

Martinez pointed a pistol down at him.

"What's the guy's name? The one we're looking for?"

"Abu Mustafa Faraj al-Jihadi?" Luke said. It wasn't really a question. It wasn't anything, just a string of syllables.

The man nodded. He didn't say anything. He looked like he was in some pain.

Luke took a small digital camera from inside his vest. The camera was encased in hard rubber. You could bounce it off the floor and it wouldn't break. He fidgeted with it for a second, and then took a few snaps of the man. He checked the images before he turned the camera off. They were fine—not exactly professional quality, but Luke didn't work for *National Geographic*. All he needed was evidence. He looked down at the terrorist leader.

"Gotcha," Luke said. "Thanks for playing."

BANG!

Martinez fired once, and the man's head came apart.

"Mission accomplished," Martinez said. He shook his head and walked away.

Luke's radio crackled.

"Stone! Where are you?"

"Murphy. What's the status?"

Murphy's voice cut in and out. "It's a bloodbath out here. I lost three men. But we commandeered one of their big guns, and we cut an opening. If we want to get out of here, we need to go RIGHT NOW."

"We'll be out in a minute."

"I wouldn't take that long," Murphy said. "Not if you want to live."

* * *

Six men ran through the village.

After all that fighting, the place was like a ghost town. At any second, Luke was expecting gunshots or rockets to come screaming out of the tiny homes. But nothing happened. There didn't even seem to be any people left here.

Back the way they had come, smoke rose. The walls of the compound were destroyed. The helicopter still burned, the flames crackling in the eerie quiet.

Luke could hear the heavy breathing of the other men, running uphill with gear and weapons. In ten minutes, they made it to the old forward operating base on the rocky hillside outside the village.

To Luke's surprise, the place was okay. There were no supplies cached there, of course—but the sandbags were still in place, and the location gave a commanding view of the surrounding area. Luke could see lights on in the homes, and the chopper on fire.

"Martinez, see if you can raise Bagram on the radio. We need an extraction. Hide and seek is over. Tell them to send overwhelming force. We need to get back inside that compound and bring our men out."

Martinez nodded. "I told you, man. Luck runs out for everybody."

"Don't tell me, Martinez. Just get us out of here, okay?"

"All right, Stone."

It was a dark night. The sandstorm had passed. They still had weapons. Along the sandbagged rampart, his men were loading up ammo and checking gear.

It wasn't out of the question that….

"Murphy, send a flare up," he said. "I want to get a look at what we're dealing with."

"And give away our position?" Murphy said.

"I think they probably know where we are," Luke said.

Murphy shrugged and popped one into the night.

The flare moved slowly across the sky, casting eerie shadows on the rocky terrain below. The ground almost appeared to be boiling. Luke stared and stared, trying to make sense of what he was seeing. There was so much activity down there, it was like an ant farm, or a swarm of rats.

It was men. Hundreds of men were methodically moving themselves, their gear, and their weapons into position.

"I guess you're right," Murphy said. "They know we're here."

Luke looked at Martinez.

"Martinez, what's the status on that extraction?"

Martinez shook his head. "They say it's a no go. Nothing but wicked sandstorms between base and here. Zero visibility. They can't even put the choppers in the air. They say hold out till morning. The wind's supposed to die down after sunrise."

Luke stared at him. "They have to do better than that."

Martinez shrugged. "They can't. If the choppers won't fly, the choppers won't fly. I wish those storms had come in before we left."

Luke stared out at the seething mass of Taliban on the hillsides below them. He turned back to Martinez.

Martinez opened his mouth as if to speak.

Luke pointed at him. "Don't say it. Just get ready to fight."

"I'm always ready to fight," Martinez said.

The shooting started moments later.

* * *

Martinez was screaming.

"They're coming through on all sides!"

His eyes were wide. His guns were gone. He had taken an AK-47 from a Taliban, and was bayoneting everyone who came over the wall. Luke watched him in horror. Martinez was an island, a small boat in a sea of Taliban fighters.

And he was going under. Then he was gone, under a pile.

They were just trying to live until daybreak, but the sun refused to rise. The ammunition had run out. It was cold, and Luke's shirt was off. He had ripped it off in the heat of combat.

Turbaned, bearded Taliban fighters poured over the walls of the outpost. Men screamed all around him.

A man came over the wall with a metal hatchet.

Luke shot him in the face. The man lay dead against the sandbags. Now Luke had the hatchet. He waded into the fighters surrounding Martinez, swinging wildly. Blood spattered. He chopped at them, sliced them.

Martinez reappeared, back on his feet, stabbing with the bayonet.

Luke buried the hatchet in a man's skull. It was deep. He couldn't pull it out. Even with the adrenaline raging through his system, he didn't have the strength left. He looked at Martinez.

"You okay?"

Martinez shrugged. He gestured at the bodies all around them. "I been better than this before. I'll tell you that."

There was an AK-47 at Luke's feet. He picked it up and checked the magazine. Empty. Luke tossed it away and pulled his handgun. He fired down the trench—it was overrun with enemies. A line of them were running this way. More came sliding, falling, jumping over the wall.

Where were his guys? Was anyone else still alive?

He killed the closest man with a shot to the face. The head exploded like a cherry tomato. He grabbed the man by his tunic and held him up as a shield. The headless man was light—it was if the corpse was an empty suit of clothes.

He killed four men with four shots. He kept firing.

Then he was out of bullets. Again.

A Taliban charged with an AK-47, bayonet attached. Luke pushed the corpse at him, then threw his gun like a tomahawk. It bounced off the man's head, distracting him for a second. Luke used that time. He stepped into the attack, sliding along the edge of the bayonet. He plunged two fingers deep into the man's eyes, and pulled.

The man screamed. His hands went to his face. Now Luke had the AK. He bayoneted his enemy in the chest, two, three, four times. He pushed it in deep.

The man breathed his last right into Luke's face.

Luke's hands roamed the man's body. The fresh corpse had a grenade in its breast pocket. Luke took it, pulled it, and tossed it over the rampart into the oncoming hordes.

He hit the deck.

BOOOM.

The explosion was *right there*, spraying dirt and rock and blood and bone. The sandbagged wall half collapsed on top of him.

Luke clawed his way to his feet, deaf now, his ears ringing. He checked the AK. Empty. But he still had the bayonet.

"Come on, you bastards!" he screamed. "Come on!"

More men came over the wall, and he stabbed them in a frenzy. He ripped and tore at them with his bare hands. He shot them with their own guns.

A man came over what was left of the wall. He wasn't a man—he was a boy. He had no beard. He had no need of a razor. His skin was smooth and dark. His brown eyes were round in terror. He clutched his hands to his chest.

Luke faced off with this child—the kid was maybe fourteen. There were more coming behind him. They slid and crashed over the barrier. The passageway was choked with corpses.

Why are his hands like that?

Luke knew why. He was a suicide bomber.

"Grenade!" Luke shouted, even if no one was alive to hear him.

He dove backward, digging under one body, then another. There were so many, he crawled and crawled, burrowing toward the center of the Earth, putting a blanket of dead men between him and the boy.

BOOOM!

He heard the explosion, muffled by the bodies, and he felt the heat wave. He heard the shrieks of the next wave of dying. But then another explosion came, and another.

And another.

Luke was fading from the concussions. Maybe he was hit. Maybe he was dying. If this was to die, it wasn't so bad. There was no pain.

He thought of the kid—skinny teenager, wide around the middle like a barrel-chested man. The kid was wearing a suicide vest.

He thought of Rebecca, round with child.

Darkness took him.

* * *

At some point, the sun had risen, but there was no warmth in it. The fighting had stopped somehow—he couldn't remember when, or how, it had ended. The ground was rugged and hard. There were dead bodies everywhere. Skinny, bearded men lay all over the ground, with eyes wide and staring.

Luke. His name was Luke.

He was sitting on a pile of bodies. He had awakened beneath them, and he had crawled out from under them like a snake.

They were piled here like cordwood. He didn't like sitting on them, but it was convenient. It was high enough that it gave him a view down the hillside through the remains of the sandbag wall, but it kept him low enough that no one but a very good sniper could probably get a shot at him.

The Taliban didn't have a lot of very good snipers. Some, but not many, and most of the Taliban around here appeared to be dead now.

Nearby, he spotted one crawling back down the hill, trailing a line of blood like the trail of slime that follows a snail. He should really go out there and kill that guy, but he didn't want to risk being in the open.

Luke glanced down at himself. He didn't look good. His chest was painted red. He was soaked in the blood of dead men. His body trembled from hunger, and from exhaustion. He stared out at the surrounding mountains, just coming into view as the day brightened. It was really a pretty day. This was beautiful country.

How many more were out there? How long before they came?

He shook his head. He didn't know. It didn't really matter. Any at all would probably be too many.

Martinez was sprawled on his back nearby, low in the trench. He was crying. He couldn't move his legs. He'd had enough. He wanted to die. Luke realized he had been tuning out Martinez for a while now.

"Stone," he said. "Hey, Stone. Hey! Kill me, man. Just kill me. Hey, Stone! Listen to me, man!"

Luke was numb.

"I'm not going to kill you, Martinez. You're gonna be all right. We're going to get out of here, and the docs are gonna patch you up. So give it a rest… okay?"

Nearby, Murphy was sitting on an outcropping of rock, staring into space. He wasn't even trying to take cover.

"Murph! Get down here. You want a sniper to put a bullet in your head?"

Murphy turned and looked at Luke. His eyes were just… gone. He shook his head. An exhalation of air escaped from him. It sounded almost like laughter. He stayed right where he was.

As Luke watched, Murphy took out a pistol. It was incredible that he still had a gun on him. Luke had been fighting with his bare hands, rocks, and sharp objects for…

He didn't know how long.

Murphy put the barrel of the gun to the side of his head, eyes on Luke the entire time. He pulled the trigger.

Click.

He pulled the trigger several more times.

Click, click, click, click… click.

"Out," he said.

He threw the gun away. It clattered down the hillside.

24

Luke watched the gun bounce away. It seemed to go on for longer than he would ever expect. Eventually, it slid to a stop in a scree of loose rocks. He looked at Murphy again. Murphy just sat there, looking at nothing.

If more Taliban came, they were done. Neither one of these guys had much fight left in them, and the only weapon Stone still had was the bent bayonet in his hand. For a moment, he thought idly about picking through some of these dead guys for weapons. He didn't know if he had the strength left to stand. He might have to crawl instead.

A line of black insects appeared in the sky far away. He knew what they were in an instant. Helicopters. United States military helicopters, probably Black Hawks. The cavalry was coming. Luke didn't feel good about that, or bad.

He felt nothing at all.

CHAPTER THREE

March 19
Night
An airplane over Europe

"Are you men comfortable?"

"Yes, sir," Luke said.

Murphy didn't respond. He sat in a recliner across the narrow aisle from Luke, staring out the window at blank darkness. They were in a small jet that was set up almost like someone's living room. Luke and Murphy sat at the back, facing forward. In the front were three men, including a Delta Force colonel and a three-star general from the Pentagon. There was also a man in civilian clothes.

Behind the men were two green berets, standing at attention.

"Specialist Murphy?" the general said. "Are you comfortable?"

Murphy slid the window shade down. "Yeah. I'm fine."

"Murphy, do you know how to address a superior officer?" the colonel said.

Murphy turned away from the window. He looked directly at the men for the first time.

"I'm not in your army anymore."

"Why are you on this plane, in that case?"

Murphy shrugged. "Someone offered me a ride. There aren't a lot of commercial flights out of Afghanistan these days. So I figured I'd better take this one."

The man in civilian clothes glanced at the cabin door.

"If you're not in the military, I suppose we could always ask you to leave. Of course, it's a long way to the ground."

Murphy followed the man's eyes.

"Do it. I promise you'll come with me."

Luke shook his head. If this were a playground, he would almost smile. But this wasn't a playground, and these men were deadly serious.

"Okay, Murph," he said. "Take it down a notch. I was on that hill with you. Nobody on this plane put us there."

Murphy shrugged. "All right, Stone." He looked at the general. "Yes, I'm comfortable, sir. Very comfortable. Thank you."

The general glanced down at some paperwork in front of him.

"Thank you, gentlemen, for your service. Specialist Murphy, if you are interested in being discharged early from your obligations, I suggest you take that up with your commanding officer when you return to Fort Bragg."

"Okay," Murphy said.

The general looked up. "As you know, this was a difficult mission which did not go exactly as planned. I'd like to take the opportunity to familiarize myself with the facts of the situation. I have the records from the mission debrief when you both returned to Bagram. I gather from the testimony, and the photographic evidence, that the overall mission was a success. Would you agree with that, Sergeant Stone?"

"Uh… if by the overall mission, you mean to find and assassinate Abu Mustafa Faraj, then yes sir. I suppose it was a success."

"That is what I meant, Sergeant. Faraj was a dangerous terrorist, and the world is a better place now that he's gone. Specialist Murphy?"

Murphy stared at the general. It was clear to Luke that Murphy was no longer all there. He was better than he was the morning after the battle, but not by much.

"Yes?" he said.

The general gritted his teeth. He glanced at the men to his left and his right.

"What is your assessment of the mission, please?"

Murphy nodded. "Oh. The one we just did?"

"Yes, Specialist Murphy."

Murphy didn't answer for several seconds. He seemed to be thinking about it.

"Well, we lost nine Delta guys and two chopper pilots. Martinez is alive, but he's scrambled eggs. Also, we killed a bunch of children, so I'm told, and at least a few women. There were piles of dead guys on the ground. I mean hundreds of dead guys. And I guess there was a famous terrorist there too, but I never saw him. So… about par for the course, I guess you'd say. It's kind of how these things go. This wasn't my first rodeo, if you know what I mean."

He looked across the aisle at Luke.

"Stone looks okay. And speaking just for myself, I didn't get a scratch on me. So sure, I'd say it went fine."

The officers stared at Murphy.

"Sir," Luke said. "I think what Specialist Murphy is trying to say, and you'll see from my testimony that I agree, is the mission was poorly conceived and probably ill advised. Lieutenant Colonel Heath was a brave man, sir, but maybe not a very good strategist or tactician. After the first chopper crashed, I requested that he abort the mission, and he refused. He was also personally responsible for the deaths of a number of civilians, and likely for the death of Corporal Wayne Hendricks."

Absurdly, saying the name of his friend nearly brought Luke to tears. He choked them back. This wasn't the time or the place.

The general glanced down at his paperwork again. "And yet you do agree that the mission was a success? The object of the mission was achieved?"

Luke thought about that for a long moment. In the narrowest military sense, they had achieved the mission goal. That was true. They had killed a wanted terrorist, and perhaps somewhere down the line, that was going to save lives. It might even save many more lives than were lost.

That was how these men wanted to define success.

"Sergeant Stone?"

"Yes, sir. I do agree."

The general nodded. So did the colonel. The man in civilian clothes made no response at all.

The general gathered his papers together and handed them to the colonel.

"Good," he said. "We're going to be landing in Germany soon, gentlemen, and then I'll take my leave of you. Before I do, I want to impress upon you that I believe you've done a great thing, and you should be very proud. You're obviously courageous men, and very skilled at your jobs. Your country owes you a debt of gratitude, one that will never be repaid adequately. It will also never be acknowledged publicly."

He paused.

"Please recognize that the mission to kill Abu Mustafa Faraj al-Jihadi, while successful, did not take place. It does not exist in any recordkeeping, nor will it ever exist. The men who lost their lives as part of this mission died in a training accident during a sandstorm."

He looked at them, his eyes hard now.

"Is that understood?"

"Yes sir," Luke said, without hesitation. The fact that they were disappearing this mission didn't surprise him in the least. He would disappear it too, if he could.

"Specialist Murphy?"

Murphy raised a hand and shrugged. "It's your deal, man. I don't think I've ever been on a mission that did exist."

CHAPTER FOUR

March 23
4:35 p.m.
United States Army Special Operations Command
Fort Bragg
Fayetteville, North Carolina

"Can I bring you a cup of tea?"

Luke nodded. "Thank you."

Wayne's wife, Katie, was a pretty blonde, small, quite a bit younger than Wayne. Luke thought she was maybe twenty-four. She was pregnant with their daughter—eight months—and she was huge.

She was living in base housing, half a mile from Luke and Becca. The house was a tiny, three-room bungalow in a neighborhood of exactly identical houses. Wayne was dead. She was there because she had nowhere else to go.

She brought Luke his tea in a small ornate cup, the adult version of the cups little girls use when they have imaginary tea parties. She sat down across from him. The living room was spare. The couch was a futon that could fold out into a double bed for guests.

Luke had met Katie twice before, both times for five minutes or less. He hadn't seen her since before she was pregnant.

"You were Wayne's good friend," she said.

"Yes. I was."

She stared into her teacup, as if maybe Wayne was floating at the bottom.

"And you were on the mission where he died." It wasn't a question.

"Yes."

"Did you see it? Did you see him die?"

Already, Luke didn't like where these questions were headed. How to answer a question like that? Luke had missed the shots that killed Wayne, but he had seen him die, all right. He would give almost anything to unsee it.

"Yes."

"How did he die?" she said.

"He died like a man. Like a soldier."

She nodded, but said nothing. Maybe that wasn't the answer she was looking for. But Luke didn't want to go any further.

"Was he in pain?" she said.

Luke shook his head. "No."

She looked into his eyes. Her eyes were red and rimmed with tears. There was a terrible sadness there. "How can you know that?"

"I spoke to him. He told me to tell you that he loved you."

It was a lie, of course. Wayne hadn't managed to utter a complete sentence. But it was a white lie. Luke believed that Wayne would have said it, if he could have.

"Is that why you came here, Sergeant Stone?" she said. "To tell me that?"

Luke took a breath.

"Before he died, Wayne asked me to be your daughter's godfather," Luke said. "I agreed, and I'm here to honor that commitment. Your daughter will be born soon, and I want to help you through this situation in any way I can."

There was a long, silent pause between them. It stretched longer and longer.

Finally, Katie shook her head, just a tiny amount. She spoke softly.

"I could never have a man like you be my daughter's godfather. Wayne is dead because of men like you. My girl will never have a father because of men like you. Do you understand? I'm here because I still have the healthcare, and so my baby will be born here. But after that? I'm going to run as far away from the Army, and from people like you, as I can. Wayne was stupid to be involved in this, and I was stupid to go along with it. You don't have to worry, Sergeant Stone. You have no responsibility to me. You're not my baby's godfather."

Luke couldn't think of a single thing to say. He looked in his cup and saw that he had already finished his tea. He put the teacup down on the table. She picked it up and moved her bulk to the door of the tiny house. She opened the door and held it open.

"Good day, Sergeant Stone."

He stared at her.

She began to cry. Her voice was as soft as ever.

"Please. Get out of my house. Get out of my life."

* * *

Dinner was dreary and sad.

They sat across the table from each other, not speaking. She had made stuffed chicken and asparagus, and it was good. She had opened a beer for him and poured it into a glass. She had done nice things.

They were eating quietly, almost as though things were normal.

But he couldn't bring himself to look at her.

There was a black matte Glock nine-millimeter on the table near his right hand. It was loaded.

"Luke, are you okay?"

He nodded. "Yeah. I'm fine." He took a sip of his beer.

"Why is your gun on the table?"

Finally, he looked up at her. She was beautiful, of course, and he loved her. She was pregnant with his child, and she wore a flower-print maternity blouse. He could almost cry at her beauty, and at the power of his love for her. He felt it intensely, like a wave crashing against the rocks.

"Uh, it's just there in case I need it, babe."

"Why would you need it? We're just eating dinner. We're on the base. We're safe here. No one can…"

"Does it bother you?" he said.

She shrugged. She slid a small forkful of chicken into her mouth. Becca was a slow and careful eater. She ate little bites, and it often took her a long time to finish her dinner. She didn't strap the ol' feedbag on like some people did. Luke loved that about her. It was one of their differences. He tended to inhale his food.

He watched her chew her food in slow motion. Her teeth were large. She had bunny teeth. It was cute. It was endearing.

"Yeah, a little," she said. "You've never done that before. Are you afraid that…"

Luke shook his head. "I'm not afraid of anything. We have a child on the way, all right? It's important that we keep our child safe from harm. It's our responsibility. It's a dangerous world, Becca, in case you didn't know that."

Luke nodded at the truth of what he was saying. More and more, he was beginning to notice hazards all around them. There were sharp dinner knives in the kitchen drawer. There were carving knives and a big meat cleaver in a wooden block on the counter. There were scissors in the cabinet behind the bathroom mirror.

The car had brakes, and someone could easily cut the brake lines. If Luke knew how to do it, then a lot of people knew. And there were a lot of people out there who might want to settle a score with Luke Stone.

It almost seemed like…

Becca was crying. She pushed her chair away from the table and stood up. Her face had turned crimson in the past ten seconds.

"Babe? What's wrong?"

"You," she said, the tears streaming down her face. "There's something wrong with you. You've never come home like this before. You've barely said hello to me. You haven't touched me at all. I feel like I'm invisible. You stay up all night. You don't seem like you've slept at all since you got here. Now you've got a gun on the dinner table. I'm a little bit afraid, Luke. I'm afraid there's something very, very wrong."

He stood, and she took a step back. Her eyes went wide.

That look. It was the look of a woman who was afraid of a man. And he was that man. It horrified him. It was if he had snapped suddenly awake. He never imagined she would ever look at him that way. He never wanted her to look that way again, not at him, not at anyone, not for any reason.

He glanced at the table. He had placed a loaded gun there during dinner. Now why would he do that? Suddenly, he was ashamed of that gun. It was square and squat and ugly. He wanted to cover it with a napkin, but it was too late. She had already seen it.

He looked at her again.

She stood across from, abject, like a child, her shoulders hunched, her face crinkled up, the tears streaming down her cheeks.

"I love you," she said. "But I'm so worried right now."

Luke nodded. The next thing he said surprised him.

"I think I might need to go away for a little while."

CHAPTER FIVE

April 14
9:45 a.m. Eastern Daylight Time
Fayetteville Department of Veteran Affairs (VA) Health Care
Center
Fayetteville, North Carolina

"Why are you here, Stone?"

The voice shook Luke from whatever reverie he had become lost in. He often wandered alone through his thoughts and his memories these days, and afterward he couldn't remember what he had been thinking about.

He glanced up.

He was sitting in a folding chair among a group of eight men. Most of the men sat in folding chairs. Two were in wheelchairs. The group took up a corner of a large but dreary open room. Windows against the far wall showed that it was a sunny, early spring day. Somehow the light from outside didn't seem to reach into the room.

The group was positioned in a semicircle, facing a middle-aged bearded man with a large stomach. The man wore corduroy pants and a red flannel shirt. The stomach protruded outward almost like a beach ball was hiding under the shirt, except the face of it was flat, like air was leaking out. Luke suspected that if he punched that stomach, it would be as hard as an iron skillet. The man was tall, and he leaned way back in his chair, his thin legs out in a straight line in front of him.

"Excuse me?" Luke said.

The man smiled, but there was no humor in it.

"Why... are... you... here?" he said again. He said it slowly this time, as if talking to a small child, or an imbecile.

Luke looked around at the men. This was group therapy for war veterans.

It was a fair question. Luke didn't belong here. These guys were wrecked. Physically disabled. Traumatized.

A few of them didn't seem like they were ever coming back. The guy named Chambers was probably the worst. He had lost an arm and both his legs. His face was disfigured. The left half was covered by bandages, a large metal plate protruding from under there, stabilizing what was left of the facial bones on that side. He had lost his left eye, and they hadn't replaced it yet. At some point, after they finished rebuilding his orbital socket, they were going to give him a nice new fake eye.

Chambers had been riding in a Humvee that ran over an IED in Iraq. The device was a surprise innovation—a shaped charge that penetrated straight up through the undercarriage of the vehicle, and then straight through Chambers, taking him apart from the bottom up. The military was retrofitting the old Humvees with heavy underside armor, and redesigning the new ones, to guard against these sorts of attacks in the future. But that wasn't going to help Chambers.

Luke didn't like to look at Chambers.

"Why are you here?" the leader said yet again.

Luke shrugged. "I don't know, Riggs. Why are you here?"

"I'm trying to help men get their lives back," Riggs said. He said it without missing a beat. Either it was a canned answer he kept for when people confronted him, or he actually believed it. "How about you?"

Luke said nothing, but everyone was staring at him now. He rarely said anything in this group. He would just as soon not attend. He didn't think it was helping him. Truth be told, he thought the whole thing was a waste of time.

"Are you afraid?" Riggs said. "Is that why you're here?"

"Riggs, if you think that, then you don't know me very well."

"Ah," Riggs said, and raised his meaty hands just a bit. "Now we're getting somewhere. You're a hardcase. We know that already. So do it. Step up. Tell us all about Sergeant First Class Luke Stone of the United States Army Special Forces. Delta, am I right? Neck deep in the shit, right? One of the guys who went on that botched mission to kill the Al Qaeda guy, the guy who supposedly did the USS *Sarasota* bombing?"

"Riggs, I wouldn't know anything about any mission like that. A mission like that would be classified information, which would mean that if either of us knew anything about it, we wouldn't be at liberty…"

Riggs smiled and made a spinning wheel motion with his hand. "To discuss such a high-level and crucial targeted assassination that never existed in the first place. Yeah, yeah, yeah. We all know the talk. We've heard it before. Believe me, Stone, you're not that important. Every man in this group has seen combat. Every man in this group is intimately aware of the—"

"What kind of combat have you seen, Riggs?" Luke said. "You were in the Navy. On a destroyer. In the middle of the ocean. You've been riding a desk in this hospital for the past fifteen years."

"This isn't about me, Stone. It's about you. You're in a VA hospital, in the psych ward. Right? I'm not in the psych ward. You are. I work in the psych ward, and you live there. But you're not committed. You're voluntary. You can walk out of here any time you want. Right in the middle of this session, if you like. Fort Bragg is five or six miles from here. All your old buddies are over there, waiting for you. Don't you want to get back together with them? They're waiting for you, man. Rock and roll. There's always another classified FUBAR mission to go on."

Luke said nothing. He just stared at Riggs. The man was out of his mind. He was the crazy one. He wasn't even slowing down.

"Stone, I see you Delta guys come through here from time to time. You never have a scratch on you. You guys are like, supernatural. The bullets always miss you somehow. But you're freaked out. You're burnt out. You've seen too much. You've killed too many people. You've got their blood all over you. It's invisible, but it's there."

Riggs nodded to himself.

"We had a Delta guy come through here back in oh-three, about your age, insisted he was fine. He had just come back from a top secret mission in Afghanistan. It was a slaughterhouse. Of course it was. But he didn't need all this talk. Sound like anybody we know? When he left here, he went home, killed his wife, his three-year-old daughter, and then put a bullet in his own brain."

A pause drew out between Luke and Riggs. None of the other men said a word. The guy was a button pusher. For some reason, he saw that as his job. It was important that Luke stay cool and not let Riggs get under his skin. But Luke didn't like this kind of thing. He felt a surge building inside him. Riggs was moving into dangerous territory.

"Is that what you're scared of?" Riggs said. "You're worried you're gonna go home and blow your wife's brains all over the—"

Luke was up from his chair and across the space between him and Riggs in less than a second. Before he knew what had happened, he had grabbed Riggs, kicked his chair out from under him, and thrown him to the floor like a rag doll. Riggs's head banged off the stone tile.

Luke crouched over him and reared back his fist.

Riggs's eyes were wide, and for a split second fear flashed across his face. Then his calm demeanor returned.

"That's what I like to see," he said. "A little enthusiasm."

Luke took a deep breath and let his fist relax. He looked around at the other men. None of them had made a move. They just stared dispassionately as if a patient attacking his therapist was a normal part of their day.

No. That wasn't it. They stared like they didn't care what happened, like they were beyond caring.

"I know what you're trying to do," Luke said.

"I'm trying to break you out of your shell, Stone. And it looks like it's finally starting to work."

* * *

"I don't want you here," Martinez said.

Luke sat in a wooden chair next to Martinez's bed. The chair was surprisingly uncomfortable, as if it had been designed to discourage loitering.

Luke was doing the thing he had avoided for weeks—he was visiting Martinez. The man was in a different building of the hospital, yes. But it was all of a twelve-minute walk from Luke's own room. Luke hadn't been able to face that walk until now.

Martinez was on a long road, a road that he seemed to have no interest in traveling. His legs had been shredded, and could not be saved. One was gone at his pelvis, one below the knee. He still had the use of his arms, but he was paralyzed from just below his ribcage down.

Before Luke came in here, a nurse whispered to him that Martinez spent most of his time crying. He also spent a lot of time sleeping—he was on a heavy dose of sedatives.

"I just came to say goodbye," Luke said.

Martinez had been staring out the window at the bright day. Now he turned to look at Luke. His face was fine. He had always been a handsome guy, and he still was. God, or the Devil, or whoever was in charge of these things, had spared the man his face.

"Hello and goodbye, right? Good for you, Stone. You're all in one piece, you gonna walk right out of here, probably get a promotion, some kind of citation. Never see another minute of combat because you were in the psych ward. Ride a desk, make more money, send other guys in. Good for you, man."

Luke sat quietly. He folded one leg over the other. He didn't say a word.

"Murphy stopped by here a couple of weeks ago, did you know that? I asked if he was going to see you, but he said no. He didn't want to see you. Stone? Stone's a suck-up to the brass. Why should he see Stone? Murphy said he's gonna ride the freight trains across the country, like a hobo. That's his plan. You know what I think? I think he's gonna shoot himself in the head."

"I'm sorry about what happened," Luke said.

But Martinez wasn't listening.

"How's your wife, man? Pregnancy coming along good? Little Luke junior on the way? That's real nice, Stone. I'm happy for you."

"Robby, did I do something to you?" Luke said.

Tears began to stream down Martinez's face. He pounded the bed with his fists. "Look at me, man! I have no legs! I'm gonna be pissing and shitting in a bag the rest of my life, okay? I can't walk. I'm never gonna walk. I can't…"

He shook his head. "I can't…"

Now Martinez began to weep.

"I didn't do it," Luke said. His voice sounded small and weak, like a child's voice.

"Yes! You did it! You did this. It was you. It was your mission. We were your guys. Now we're dead. All but you."

Luke shook his head. "No. It was Heath's mission. I was just—"

"You bastard! You were just following orders. But you could have said no."

Luke said nothing. Martinez breathed deeply.

"I told you to kill me." He gritted his teeth. "I told you… to… kill… me. Now look at this… this mess. You were the one." He shook his head. "You could have done it. Nobody would know."

Luke stared at him. "I couldn't kill you. You're my friend."

"Don't say that!" Martinez said. "I'm not your friend."

He turned his head to face the wall. "Get out of my room."

"Robby…"

"How many men you killed, Stone? How many, huh? A hundred? Two hundred?"

Luke spoke barely above a whisper. He answered honestly. "I don't know. I stopped counting."

"You couldn't kill one man as a favor? A favor to your so-called friend?"

Luke didn't speak. Such a thing had never occurred to him before. Kill his own man? But he realized now that it was possible.

For a split second, he was back on that hillside on that cold morning. He saw Martinez sprawled on his back, crying. Luke walked over to him. There was no ammo left. All Luke had was the twisted bayonet in his hand. He crouched down next to Martinez, the bayonet protruding from his fist like a spike. He reached up with it, above Martinez's heart, and…

"I don't want you here," Martinez said now. "I want you out of my room. Get out, okay, Stone? Get out right now."

Suddenly, Martinez started screaming. He took the nurse call button from his bedside and began ramming it with his thumb.

"I want you out! Get out! Out!"

Luke stood. He raised his hands. "Okay, Robby. Okay."

"OUT!"

Luke headed for the door.

"I hope you die, Stone. I hope your baby dies."

Then Luke was out in the hall. Two nurses were coming toward him, walking but moving fast.

"Is he okay?" the first one said.

"Did you hear me, Stone? I hope your…"

But Luke had already covered his ears and was running down the hall. He ran through the building, sprinting now, gasping for air. He saw the EXIT sign, turned toward it, and burst through the double doors. Then he was running across the grounds along a concrete pathway. Here and there, people turned to look, but Luke kept running. He ran until his lungs began to burn.

A man was coming the other way. The man was older, but broad and strong. He walked upright with military bearing, but wore blue jeans and a leather jacket. Luke was almost on top of him before he realized he knew him.

"Luke," the man said. "Where you running to, son?"

Luke stopped. He bent over and put his hands on his knees. His breath came in harsh rasps. He fought for big lungfuls.

"Don," he said. "Oh man, Don. I'm out of shape."

He stood up. He reached out to shake Don Morris's hand, but Don pulled him into a bear hug instead. It felt… Luke didn't have words for it. Don was like a father to him. Feelings surged. It felt safe. It felt like a relief. It felt like for so long, he had been holding so many things inside of him, things Don knew intuitively, without having to be told. Being hugged by Don Morris felt like being home.

After a long moment, they parted.

"What are you doing here?" Luke said.

He imagined Don was down from Washington to meet with the brass at Fort Bragg, but Don dispelled that notion in just a few words.

"I came to get you," he said.

* * *

"It's a good deal," Don said. "The best you're going to get."

They were driving through the tree-lined cobblestone streets of downtown Fayetteville in a nondescript rental sedan. Don was at the wheel, Luke in the passenger seat. People sat in open air coffee shops and restaurants along the sidewalks. It was a military city—a lot of the people who were out and about were upright and fit.

But in addition to being healthy, they also looked happy. At this moment, Luke couldn't imagine what that felt like.

"Tell me again," he said.

"You go out at the rank of Master Sergeant. Honorable discharge, effective at the end of this calendar year, though you can go on indefinite leave as early as this afternoon. The new pay goes into effect immediately, and carries on until discharge. Your service record is intact, and your wartime veteran's pension and all other benefits are in place."

It sounded like a good deal. But Luke hadn't considered leaving the Army until this minute. The entire time he was in the hospital, he had been hoping to rejoin his unit. Meanwhile, behind the scenes, Don had been negotiating an exit for him.

"And if I want to stay in?" he said.

Don shrugged. "You've been in the hospital for nearly a month. The records I've seen suggest you've made little or no progress in therapy, and are considered an uncooperative patient."

He sighed. "They're not going to take you back, Luke. They think you're damaged goods. If you refuse the package I just described, they plan to send you out with an involuntary psychiatric discharge at your current rank and pay, with a diagnosis of post-traumatic stress disorder. I'm sure I don't have to tell you the sort of prospects faced by men with a discharge under those circumstances."

Luke supposed that none of this was a very big surprise, but it was still painful to hear. He knew the deal. The Army didn't even formally acknowledge the existence of Delta Force. The mission was classified—it never happened. So it wasn't as if he hoped to receive a medal during a public ceremony. In Delta, you didn't do it for the glory.

Even so, while he expected to be ignored, he didn't expect to be thrown on the scrap heap. He had given a lot of himself to the Army, and they were ready to dump him after one bad mission. True, the mission was more than bad. It was a disaster, a debacle, but that wasn't his fault.

"They're kicking me out either way," he said. "I can go quietly or I can go kicking and screaming."

"That's right," Don said.

Luke sighed heavily. He watched the old town roll past. They passed out of the historic district and into a more modern roadway with strip malls. They came to the end of a long block and Don turned left into a Burger King parking lot.

Civilian life was coming, whether Luke liked it or not. It was a world he had left fourteen years before. He had never expected to see it again. What went on in that world?

He watched an overweight young couple waddle toward the door of the restaurant.

"What am I going to do?" Luke said. "After the end of this year? What kind of civilian job can I possibly get?"

"That's easy," Don said. "You're going to come work for me."

Luke looked at him.

Don pulled into a spot near the back. There were no other cars here. "The Special Response Team is ready to go. While you've been lying in bed and examining your navel, I've been wrestling with bureaucrats and drawing up paperwork. I've got funding cemented in place, at least through the end of the year. I've got a small headquarters in the Virginia suburbs, not far from the CIA. They're stenciling the letters on the door as we speak. I've got the ear of the FBI director. And I spoke on the phone—briefly, I might add—with the President of the United States."

Don turned off the car and looked at Luke.

"I'm ready to hire my first agent. You're it."

He gestured with his head at a large sign near the front of the parking lot. Luke glanced where Don indicated. Just beneath the Burger King logo was a series of black letters on a white background. Taken together, the letters spelled out a bleak message.

Now Hiring. Inquire Within.

"If you don't want to join me, I'll bet there are plenty of other opportunities out there for you."

Luke shook his head. Then he laughed.

"This has been a strange day," he said.

Don nodded. "Well, it's about to get even stranger. Here's another surprise. This one's a gift. I didn't want to give it to you at the hospital because hospitals are awful places. Especially VA hospitals."

Standing in front of the car was a beautiful young woman with long brown hair. She looked in at Luke, tears in her eyes. She wore a light jacket, open to reveal a mommy shirt. The woman was very pregnant.

With Luke's son.

It took Luke a split second to recognize her—something he would never reveal to anyone, not even under pain of torture. His mind hadn't been working right these past weeks, and she was out of place in this wasteland of a parking lot. He didn't expect to see her here. Her presence was unreal, otherworldly.

Rebecca.

"Oh my God," Luke said.

"Yeah," Don said. "You might want to go say hello before she finds someone better. Around here? It won't take long."

"Why… why did you bring her here?"

Don shrugged. He looked around at the Burger King parking lot.

"It's more romantic than meeting her back at the base."

Then Luke was out of the car. He seemed to float to her. They embraced, and he held her for a long time. Endlessly. He never wanted to let go of her.

For the first time, Luke felt tears streaming down his own face. He breathed deeply. It felt so good to hold her. He didn't speak. He couldn't think of a single word to say.

She looked up at him and rubbed the tears away from his face.

"Isn't it great?" she said. "Don said you're going to work for him."

Luke nodded. He still didn't speak. It seemed like it was settled, then. Don and Becca had made the decision for him.

"I love you so much, Luke," she said. "I'm so glad this military life is over."

CHAPTER SIX

May 3
7:15 a.m. Eastern Daylight Time
Headquarters of the Special Response Team
McLean, Virginia—Suburbs of Washington, DC

"I think I might have something for you," Don Morris said.

They were sitting in Don's new office. The place was starting to take shape. There were photos of his wife and kids on the desk, framed ribbons and proclamations on the walls. The desk itself was a wide expanse of gleaming oak. On top of it sat a telephone console, a computer monitor, a cell phone, a satellite phone, and not much else. Don wasn't a big believer in paperwork.

"Something to get you out in the field a bit. You've seemed a little antsy since you came here. This might cure that."

Luke stared at him. It was almost as if Don had just read his mind. Don had done him a favor by giving him this job. Luke knew that. It was a lifeline thrown to a drowning man. But Luke was already inching toward the door. It had been weeks of sitting and talking so far. Luke was bored. That was okay. The danger was that if it went on too long, he would start to go crazy. Desk-bound intelligence work was not for him. That was beginning to become abundantly clear.

"I'm all ears," Luke said.

Don gestured back out the open door to his office. "Let's go down the hall."

Luke followed Don along the narrow hallway to the brightly lit conference room at the other end. This small office complex had been a satellite office for the Bureau of Housing and Urban Development until six months ago. Don was working to drag the building into the twenty-first century a little bit.

With that in mind, a tall young guy with a ponytail and wearing strange wraparound aviator glasses was hanging a flat-panel display on one wall. Another display was already on the far wall, wires running to a control panel on the long conference table. The guy was wearing a red, white, and blue T-shirt, jeans and red Converse All-Star high-top sneakers.

Luke barely looked at him. He assumed that he was a technician from a government contractor agency, or possibly some techie buried deep inside the FBI.

"Luke, have you met Mark Swann?" Don said, casually blowing those thoughts out of the water. "He's our new systems designer and operator, in charge of our intelligence networks, Internet, satellite connections… Mark's going to wear a lot of hats, at least for a little while. Mark Swann, this is Agent Luke Stone. Luke is our first field agent, although we are about to add a couple more."

The guy turned around. He was skinny. He had stovepipe legs. The front of his American flag shirt read "We're Number 31!"

The guy's eyes met Luke's. Luke sized him up quickly. He was young, maybe early twenties—he looked even younger than that. He was confident bordering on arrogant. He was smart. He had probably been a computer geek in high school. He and Luke were going to be in different departments. This guy's thing was equipment—taking it apart, putting it back together, making it hum. He had probably never participated in a moment of violence in his life, and might not have witnessed any such moments.

They shook hands.

"We're number thirty-one, are we?" Luke said. "What are we number thirty-one at?"

The guy shrugged and smiled.

"I don't know, man. Maybe you can guess."

Luke nearly laughed.

"I can't guess," he said. "Maybe you can just help me out a little."

"Healthcare," the guy said. "We're number thirty-one in healthcare, according to the World Health Organization. We're number one in healthcare expenditures, though, if you're looking for something to be proud about."

Luke was still holding the guy's hand.

"I'd be proud to break a few of your bones, and see what a good job American doctors do putting them back together. But you'd probably prefer to get them fixed in Mexico."

Swann took his hand back. "Cuba, maybe. Or Canada."

"Very nice, Mark," Don said. "I'm sure Agent Stone is glad to discover that he's been risking his neck all these years for a country with such a mediocre healthcare performance."

Don gestured with his head at the audiovisual set-up. "How's it coming?"

Mark nodded. "The first display is ready to go. High-definition, high-speed connection. You can pull that keyboard up on the table there, and that small screen, and access any of your own files just by using your login. You can choose whatever you want to share and it'll come up on the big screen. I can easily make that ability available to anyone in the building—I just wanted you to take it for a test drive first, see how you like it."

Don nodded. "Very cool. What about visitors? Also, what about sharing information with other venues?"

The kid Mark Swann raised his hands as if to say *Don't shoot!* "It's coming. But we're going to want airtight encryption before we start broadcasting intelligence outside the building. You can email anything you want. But in terms of putting up video imagery or data that appear elsewhere, or bringing broadcasts in here? That'll happen on a case-by-case basis with each partner. CIA, NSA, the White House if it comes to that, even FBI headquarters. They've all got their own procedures and we're going to be following their leads."

Don nodded. "Okay, Mark. I like it already. Can you give Agent Stone and me about twenty, maybe thirty minutes? And send Trudy Wellington in here?"

Swann nodded. "Sure."

When he left, Don looked at Luke.

"Funny kid," Luke said.

"Whiz kid," Don said. "My goal here is to hire the best. And when it comes to that, it isn't always the guy who fits the suit the best. In terms of technology, usually it isn't. We're cowboys in here, Luke. We're the kids who color outside the lines. That's what they want from us. The FBI director said that himself."

"I'm with you," Luke said.

"You should be. You're one of the best special operators I've seen in my long career, and in terms of coloring outside the lines... well..."

Suddenly a young woman appeared in the doorway. If anything, she was even younger than the guy who just left. Don was staffing this place up with children. This child, however, was beautiful. She had long, curly brown hair. She wore a dress shirt and slacks that hugged her curves. She wore big red eyeglasses that gave her a slight owlish appearance.

"Don?"

"Trudy, come in. I want you to meet Luke Stone. He's the man I told you about. Luke, this is Trudy Wellington. She is our new intel officer. She's another whiz kid, graduated MIT as a teenager, spent a couple of years in CIA listening stations. Now she's with us, ready to take a quantum leap to the next level of spycraft."

Luke shook hands with the young woman. She was a little sheepish, wouldn't quite meet his eyes. Hell, she was still a kid.

Luke glanced back and forth between Don and Trudy. Something about the body language...

Nah, it was impossible. Don had been married for thirty years. He had a daughter and a son who were older than this Trudy person.

"Trudy's going to brief us on the mission we have on deck."

Trudy sat right down at the conference table. Luke and Don did the same. She immediately took the keyboard, pulled the small monitor forward, and typed in her information. Her office computer's desktop appeared on the large flat-panel display on the wall.

"You already know how to use this?" Don said.

"Yeah, well... We had AV stuff like this at MIT, of course. Not so much at CIA that I saw, but I imagine they have it somewhere. Swann gave me access earlier. I think he was showing off."

"Anyway, it's pretty cool," Don said.

Luke nodded. He almost laughed again. He pictured steel-eyed Don as he had known him these past several years—parachuting into combat zones, commanding men in the field, remorselessly killing bad guys. He seemed almost absurdly proud of his little agency, its office gizmos, and the young civilians who manipulated them with such ease. Well, good for him.

On the screen, a United States Marine Corps ID appeared. It showed a soldier with a flattop haircut, a broad jaw, and a threatening gaze. He seemed sarcastic, irritated, and ready to murder someone all at once. He looked like the kind of guy who would do his combat service overseas, then come home and spend his time getting in bar fights during R&R. A rough customer.

Luke had seen a lot of guys like that. As a matter of fact, he had knocked a few of them unconscious.

"I'm going to assume that neither of you have prior knowledge of the subject, or the task at hand," Trudy said. "It might make this conversation a little longer than necessary, it might not. But it tends to guarantee we're all on the same page. Sound okay?"

"Good," Don said.

"Sounds okay to me," Luke said.

She nodded. "Then let's begin. The man on the screen is former Marine Corps Sergeant Edwin Lee Parr. Thirty-seven years old, raised in Kentucky, south of Lexington. Combat veteran, who

45

saw action in both the invasion of Panama in 1989, and the Gulf War. He was also deployed in a peacekeeping role at the end of the Kosovo War. Purple Heart and a Bronze Star for meritorious service during the invasion of Panama. Honorable discharge December 1999, after twelve years of service.

"Parr came home and kicked around the country for a year and a half after that, doing security work. He had a concealed carry license, and was mostly a personal bodyguard, mostly for businessmen, often for diamond dealers. He worked for a firm called White Knight Security, and bounced between New York, Miami, Chicago, Los Angeles, and San Francisco. A few documented trips to Tokyo, Hong Kong, and London, though it isn't clear how the firearm regulations were handled in those cases."

Luke stared into the man's angry eyes. It didn't seem like bad work for a combat veteran. Not much action, but plenty of movement. It might even appeal to a man like…

"Then September eleven happened," Trudy said.

"Did he reenlist?" Luke said.

She shook her head. "No. Within a short period of time, there was enormous demand for experienced military contractors. White Knight Security spun off a whole new division called White Knight Consultants. Edwin Parr was one of their first available combat zone experts. He did a tour in Afghanistan, and has now been in Iraq for twenty-five straight months."

Luke was beginning to wish she would get to the point. The thought of Edwin Lee Parr in a combat theater, beholden to little or no chain of command, and making ten times the money of normal soldiers irritated Luke. To put it mildly.

"Twenty-five months?" Luke said. "What's he doing over there? I mean, besides padding his bank account?"

"Edwin Parr appears to have gone rogue," Trudy said.

She paused and looked away from the keyboard and mouse for a moment. "The next images are graphic."

Luke stared at her.

"I think we can handle it," Don said.

Trudy nodded. "Parr was fired by White Knight four months ago, despite having a five-year relationship with them. White Knight disavows knowledge of his activities or whereabouts. They disclaim responsibility for his actions."

A new image appeared on the screen. It showed perhaps a dozen bodies strewn about some sort of market square. The bodies were almost not recognizable as human—they had been torn apart by a bomb or some type of high-caliber repeating weapon.

"Parr is operating in northwest Iraq, in what is known as the Sunni Triangle, beyond the reach of coalition troops. He has anywhere up to a dozen former or possibly present-tense contractors operating with him, as well as what we believe are one or two Marine Corps deserters. He is believed to be responsible for ordering a civilian massacre that took place in this Fallujah open air market, and it is believed that this is an image of the aftermath of that massacre. As many as forty people may have died in the attack."

Luke was interested. "Why would he do that?"

A new image appeared on the screen. It showed two burned and headless torsos hanging from a bridge overpass.

"The bodies you see here have been identified as the remains of former American military contractors Thomas Calence, age thirty-one, and Vladimir Garcia, age thirty-nine. Their jeep was attacked by Sunni insurgents. They were captured, beheaded, and set on fire. When this happened, neither man was on any payroll as a military contractor. The massacre in the previous image appears to have been payback for the deaths of Calence and Garcia, as part of an escalating series of tit for tat attacks. Calence and Garcia had been operating with Parr."

"What were they doing?" Luke said.

A new image appeared, a map of the so-called Sunni Triangle.

"The Sunni Triangle was Saddam Hussein's stronghold in Iraq. The south of the country is primarily Shiite, and Saddam took great pains to suppress the Shiites, including frequent massacres. The north is primarily Kurdish, and if anything, the Kurds got even worse treatment than the Shiites. But north-central and northwest Iraq is Sunni. Saddam was born there, and the people there are his loyalists. It has been very difficult for the American military to tame this region, and much of it is still a no-go zone. We believe that Parr operates out there because this is where the bulk of Saddam's wealth is hidden.

"It seems that Parr has been systematically uncovering secret caches of money, weapons, diamonds, gold, and other precious metals, as well as luxury cars. He is finding this stuff through the use of torture and murder of Saddam's former lieutenants and intimidation of the local population. The locals hate Parr, and they are actively trying to kill him.

"But Parr has put together a small army of tough hombres—military consultants, several of them former special operators, and as I already indicated, possibly two Marine Corps deserters. All his men are battle-hardened, and Parr is making them rich, as long as they can stay alive. On that score, they are taking increasingly extreme measures to make sure they do so. Currently, they are kidnapping women and girls from the local tribes. We believe they are holding them as human shields. It's also possible they are selling some of them to Al Qaeda, and to Shiite tribesmen from the south."

Trudy paused.

"He is looting Saddam's buried treasure as fast as he can, and he is not letting anyone get in his way."

"What's our role in this?" Luke said.

Don shrugged. "We're the FBI, son. We're going to go in there, rescue anyone being held against their will, and arrest Edwin Lee Parr for kidnapping and for murder."

"Arrest him…" Luke said. "For murder. In a war zone. Where hundreds of thousands of people have already died."

He let his mind chew on that one for a minute.

Don nodded. "That's correct. Then we're going to bring him back here, try him, and lock him away. This man Parr is a mess, and he needs to be cleaned up. He's a murderer, a liar, and a thief. He's out there beyond anyone's reach, operating under no one's command, and has become a law unto himself. He is committing atrocities that the Iraqi people are blaming on Americans. If he keeps on, he is going to cause an international incident, one that will give our entire effort in Iraq, in Afghanistan, and around the world, a black eye."

Luke took a deep breath. "How do you picture this going?"

Don and Trudy stared at him.

Trudy spoke. "If you take the case, the CIA will provide you with an identity as a corrupt military contractor on the make," she said. "You and a partner will proceed alone to the Sunni Triangle, find Parr's headquarters from half a dozen suspected locations, infiltrate his team, arrest him, and then call for a helicopter extraction."

Luke grunted. He nearly laughed. He looked at young, lovely Trudy, graduate of an elite East Coast university. For some reason, he focused on her hands. They were tiny, immaculate, even beautiful. He doubted they had ever held a gun. They looked like they had never lifted anything heavier than a pencil, or been sullied by an ounce of dirt, in their lives. Her hands should be on a commercial for Palmolive. Her hands should have their own TV show.

"That sounds good," he said. "Did you come up with that? I can tell you that my last helicopter extraction went pretty well. My

48

best friend died, my commanding officer died, pretty much everybody died, actually. The only people who didn't die were me, a guy who lost his mind, and another guy who lost both his legs *and* his mind. And… you know, his ability to…"

Luke trailed off. He didn't want to finish that sentence.

"That guy won't speak to me anymore because he asked me to kill him, and I declined."

Trudy stared at Luke with those big, pretty eyes. The glasses made her eyes seem bigger than they really were. She looked, at this moment, like a scientist staring through a microscope at an insect.

"That's awkward," she said.

"It's old news," Don said. "You either climb back on the horse, or you don't."

Luke nodded. He raised his hands. "I know. I'm sorry. I know that. Okay? So let's say I go in. What if Parr doesn't want to come quietly? What if spending the rest of his life in prison doesn't exactly appeal to him?"

Don shrugged. "If he resists arrest, then you terminate his command, and terminate his group's ability to operate, by whatever means available to you at that time."

"You realize we're talking about Americans?" Luke said.

They both just looked at him. Neither one answered. A long moment passed. It was a silly question. Of course they realized.

"Do you want it?" Don said.

It took a minute before Luke spoke. Did he want it? Of course he wanted it. What choice did he have? What else was he going to do? Sit in this office building and go crazy? Sit here and turn down missions until Don finally got the message and let him go? This was what he had been hired for. Compared to the things he had done previously, it wasn't even much of a mission. It was practically a weekend getaway.

An image of Rebecca, very pregnant now, out at her family's cabin, flashed across the screen in his mind. His son was growing inside her. He would be here soon. Despite this desk job, despite the long commute, despite the fact that he was gone all day five days a week, the past month was about the happiest they had ever been together.

What was Becca going to think about this?

"Luke?" Don said.

Luke nodded. "Yeah. I want it."

CHAPTER SEVEN

6:15 p.m. Eastern Daylight Time
Queen Anne's County, Maryland—Eastern Shore of
Chesapeake Bay

"You look beautiful," Luke said.

He had just arrived. He had ripped off his shirt and tie and changed into jeans and a T-shirt as soon as he walked in the door. Now he had a can of beer in his hand. The beer was ice cold and delicious.

The traffic was insane. It was a ninety-minute drive from DC, through Annapolis, across the Chesapeake Bay Bridge, and on to the Eastern Shore. But none of that mattered because he was home now.

He and Becca were staying at her family's cabin in Queen Anne's County. The cabin was an ancient, rustic place sitting on a small bluff right above the bay. It was two floors, wooden everything, with creaks and squeaks everywhere you stepped. There was a screened-in porch facing the water and a kitchen door that slammed shut with enthusiasm.

The living room furniture was generations old. The beds were old metal skeletons on springs; the bed in the master bedroom was almost long enough, but not quite, for Luke to sleep comfortably on it. By far the sturdiest thing in the house was the stone fireplace in the living room. It was almost as if the grand old fireplace had been there already, and someone with a sense of humor had built a clapboard shack all around it.

To hear tell of it, the house had been in the family for a hundred years. Some of Becca's earliest memories happened in that house.

It really was a beautiful place. Luke loved it there.

They were sitting on the back patio, enjoying the late afternoon as the sun slowly went west over the vast sweep of water. It was a breezy day, and white sails were everywhere out there. Luke almost wished that time would stop and he could just sit right in this spot forever. The setting was amazing, and Becca did look beautiful. Luke wasn't lying about that.

She was pretty as ever, and almost as petite. Their son was a basketball she was smuggling under her shirt. She had spent part of the afternoon digging a bit in her garden, and she was a little bit sweaty and flushed. She wore a big floppy sun hat and was drinking a big glass of ice water.

She smiled. "You don't look too bad yourself."

A long pause drew out between them.

"How did your day go?" she said.

Luke took another sip of his beer. He believed that when trouble was brewing, the thing to do was to get right to it. Beating around the bush was not normally his style. And Becca deserved to hear it right away.

"Well, it was different. Don is staffing the place up. And he dropped a project in my lap today."

"Well, that's good," Becca said. "It's good news, right? Something to sink your teeth into? I know you've been feeling a little bored by the job, and frustrated by the commute."

Luke nodded. "Sure, it's good. It could be. It's police work, I guess you'd say. We're the FBI, right? That's what we do. The downside is, if I'm going to take the assignment—and really, I don't have a lot of choice since it is my job—then I need to go out of town for a few days."

Luke could hear himself hemming and hawing. He didn't like the sound of it. Go out of town? Was it a joke? Don wasn't sending him to Pittsburgh.

Now Becca sipped her water. Her eyes watched him over the top of the glass. They were wary eyes. "Where do you have to go?"

Here it came. Might as well put it out there.

"Iraq."

Her shoulders slumped. "Oh, Luke. Come on." She sighed heavily. "He wants you to go to Iraq? You just came from Afghanistan, and you nearly got killed. Doesn't he realize we're about to have a baby? I mean, he knows this, right?"

Luke nodded. "He saw you, babe. Remember? He brought you down to see me."

"Then how can he even think of this? I hope you told him no."

Luke took another sip of his beer. It was a touch warmer now. Not quite as delicious as a moment ago.

"Luke? You told him no, right?"

"Sweetheart, it's my job. There aren't a lot of jobs like this available to me. Don threw me a rope and saved my neck. The Army was going to say I had PTSD and put me out on my butt. That didn't happen because of Don. I don't have a lot of room to tell him no right now. And as things go, this is a pretty easy assignment."

"An easy assignment in a war zone," Becca said. "What's the job? Assassinate Osama bin Laden?"

Luke shook his head. "No."

"What is it then?"

"There's an American military contractor over there that's out of control. He's looting old Saddam Hussein hideouts and stealing cash, artwork, gold, diamonds… They want me and a partner to arrest him. It's not a military operation at all. It's a police job."

"Who's the partner?" she said. He could see in her eyes she was thinking about what happened to his last partner.

"I haven't met him yet."

"Why don't they just have the military police do this?"

Luke shook his head. "It's not an issue for the military. Like I said, it's a police matter. The contractor is technically a civilian. They want to make the difference clear."

Luke thought of all the things he was leaving out. The restive nature of the region, and the fierce fighting going on there. The atrocities Parr had committed. The team of badass operators and remorseless killers he had accumulated around himself. The desperation they must feel right now to get out alive, unscathed, with all their loot, and without being captured by the law. The dead men, decapitated and burned, and hanging from a bridge.

Abruptly, Becca started crying. Luke put the beer down and went to her. He kneeled by her chair and hugged her.

"Oh God, Luke. Tell me this isn't going to start up again. I don't think I can bear it. Our son is coming."

"I know," he said. "I know that. It's not going to be like before. It's not a deployment. I'll be gone three days, maybe four. I arrest a guy, I bring him home."

"What if you die?" she said.

"I'm not going to die. I'm going to be very careful. I probably won't even have to draw my gun."

He almost couldn't believe the things he was telling her.

She was shaking now from the tears.

"I don't want you to go," she said.

"I know, honey. I know. But I have to. It'll be very quick. I will call you every night. You can stay with your folks. And then I'll be right back. It'll be like I never even left."

She shook her head, the tears coming harder now. "Please," she said. "Please tell me it's going to be okay."

Luke squeezed her tight, mindful of the baby growing inside her. "It's going to be okay. It's going to be fine. I know it is."

CHAPTER EIGHT

May 5
3:45 p.m. Eastern Daylight Time
Joint Base Andrews
Prince George's County, Maryland

"You're the boss," Don said.

He was a couple of inches taller than Luke, and quite a bit broader. With Don's gray hair, and his size, and his age, and his experience... well, Luke always felt a little bit like a child next to Don.

"Don't let them forget who's in charge. I'd be coming with you, but I'm stuck in meetings. You're my representative. As far as this trip is concerned, you are me."

Luke nodded. "Okay, Don."

They were walking a long, wide corridor through the terminal. Swarms of people, mostly in uniforms of various kinds, milled about, moving to and fro. People were standing and eating at Taco Bell and Subway. Men and women were hugging. Piles of baggage were going by on carts. The place was busy. There were two wars on at once, and all across the armed services, personnel were on the move.

"We've got a new guy joining you. He's your partner, but you're the senior partner. His name is Ed Newsam. I like him. He's big, he's cocky as hell, and he's young. I plucked him out of Delta, even though he's only been there a year."

"A year? Don..."

"In a year, he's already acquitted himself very admirably. Believe me, you're going to be happy I acquired this guy. He's a stud. He's an animal, like you were at that age."

At thirty-two, Luke was already beginning to feel old. He had been back in the gym the past few weeks, and it was suddenly an uphill climb to get in shape. That was a rude awakening. He had let himself go during his stay in the hospital.

"Trudy and Swann are traveling with you, but they won't go into theater with you. They will stay in the Green Zone where it's safe, and offer you guidance and intelligence from there. Under no circumstances should you put them in harm's way. They are not military personnel, nor have they been."

Luke nodded. "Understood."

Don stopped. He turned to face Luke. His hard eyes softened a touch. It was like he was Luke's dad—the father he never had. Don was just a big, gray-haired, broad-chested, face-like-a-granite-cliff dad.

"You're going to do fine, son. You've held command positions before. You've been in war zones before. You've been on difficult missions before, impossible missions. This isn't like that. This one's got a glass jaw, okay? Big Daddy Cronin is going to be running this operation on the ground. He's got your back and he's going to make sure you have the people you need in the air above you, and one step behind you."

Luke was glad to hear that. Bill Cronin was a CIA Special Agent. He had been around the block a few times, had a lot of Middle East experience. Luke had served under him twice before—once while on loan from Delta Force to the CIA, and once during a joint special op.

Don went on. "I fully expect you guys to walk in there and for Parr to drop his weapon and throw his hands in the air. He'll be relieved you're not Al Qaeda. We need an early win to show the congressmen we mean business, so I padded your comeback schedule with an easy knockout. But don't tell the others that. They think this is the most serious thing ever."

Luke smiled and shook his head. "Okay, Dad."

"I'd ruffle your hair, but you're too old," Don said.

Up ahead was a small waiting area for their gate. Three rows of five seats each were clustered in front of a desk, and behind the desk, the door to the tarmac. The desk was abandoned, and no one sat in the chairs. This was an empty area of the terminal.

Through the large windows, Luke could see a small blue State Department jet plane parked and waiting outside. A rollaway staircase led up to the open cabin door of the plane.

A group of three people milled around at the gate. Two of them were Trudy Wellington and Mark Swann. Trudy was tiny, and looked every inch of it. Swann was tall and thin, but was positively dwarfed by the third member of their party, a black guy in jeans and a leather jacket. The black guy stood by himself, a little bit away from Trudy and Swann. He had a green rucksack on the floor at his feet.

"That the guy?" Luke said. "Newsam?"

Don nodded. "That's the guy.

Luke soaked him in as they approached. He looked to be six foot, five inches tall. His shoulders were broad, as was his chest. Beneath his leather jacket he wore a white T-shirt that clung to his massive frame. It looked like someone had painted it on there. His arms were covered by his jacket, but his fists were huge. He wore yellow work boots on his big feet. He looked like a cartoon rendering of a superhero.

Except for his face—it was as arrogant and as young as that of any kid in high school. There wasn't a line on it.

"This guy has seen combat before?" Luke said.

Don nodded again. "Oh yeah."

"Okay. You're the boss."

"Yes I am."

They reached the group. The three of them turned. Trudy's and Swann's eyes were focused on Don, their boss. The newcomer, Newsam, stared at Luke.

"Thanks for coming out, everyone. Trudy and Mark, you've had the opportunity to meet Luke Stone, your commander on this trip. Luke was one of the best special operators I had the pleasure to serve with in the United States Army. Luke, this is Ed Newsam, who I didn't serve with, but who I've heard spectacular things about."

The two men shook hands. Luke looked into the eyes of the larger man. Newsam didn't do anything overt—he didn't, for example, try to crush Luke's hand in his own. But his eyes said it all: *You don't command me.*

Luke begged to differ. But this wasn't the time or the place to worry about it. If they were going to work together, though, especially in a combat zone, the time would almost certainly come.

Don said a few words of encouragement to send the group off. But Luke wasn't listening anymore. He just watched those hard young eyes, as they watched him.

CHAPTER NINE

11:15 p.m. Central European Summer Time (5:15 p.m. Eastern Daylight Time)
Institut Le Rosey
Rolle, Switzerland

It was the most famous school in the world.

Well, it was the most expensive, anyway.

But really, it was just very boring, and she didn't want to be here. Her mom and dad had sent her here for a year of "finishing" before she went to college. And it had been the dreariest, loneliest year of her life. Maybe things would get better now that it was almost over. She was accepted to Yale for the fall.

Of course she was. Her father was one of Yale's most well-known alumni, so why wouldn't they accept her? She was Elizabeth Barrett, younger daughter of David P. Barrett, the current President of the United States.

In fact, she was finishing up on the telephone with her dad right now.

"Well, sweetheart, are there any positives that you can take away from this year?"

That was her father, always talking about "positives." Was it even a real word? He said words and phrases like that all the time—there were always positives, and takeaways, and we were always moving forward, and climbing the ladder, and building something great. She had begun to suspect that he wasn't nearly as optimistic as he talked. The whole act was a fake, a fraud. He just said these things because he knew that in his life, there was always someone listening.

She hated that part of it. She hated the security detail from the Secret Service that hovered nearby twenty-four hours a day. She liked some of the agents themselves, but she hated the fact of it, that it was necessary, that her life was stilted and thwarted at every turn because of it. They were listening to this phone call, of course, and they were never far away—a man stood out in the hall all night while she slept.

"I don't know, Dad," she said. "I just don't know. I'll be glad to get out of here."

57

"Well, you got to go skiing in the Swiss Alps, right? You met people from all over the world."

"I liked our Colorado trips better when I was a kid," she said. "And the people I met? Yeah, great. Kids from Russia whose dads are the gangsters that stole all the industries when the Soviet Union collapsed. Kids from Saudi Arabia and Dubai whose dads are all princes or whatever. Is everybody in Saudi Arabia a prince? I think that's the big takeaway, Dad. Everybody in Saudi Arabia belongs to the royal family."

Her dad the President laughed. It made her smile. She hadn't heard that from him in a long, long while. And it made her think about how things used to be, back when her dad worked in the family oil business and co-owned a pro football team. He had been a fun dad, once upon a time.

When they used to have family barbecues, he would wear a chef's apron that said *World's Funnest Dad* on it. That seemed like a long time ago now.

"Well, honey," he said, "I'm pretty sure not everybody in Saudi Arabia is in the royal family."

"I know," she said. "Some people are servants and slaves."

"Elizabeth!" he said, but he wasn't angry. He was having fun with her. She was always the one to say the outrageous things, even when she was young.

"The truth hurts, Dad."

"Elizabeth? That's very funny. But I've got to run. Do this for me, will you? You've got just a week left to go there. Try to make the best of it. Take advantage of the opportunities presented, and do something that excites you, okay?"

"I don't know what that would be," she said, except now she was lying to him. "But I'll do my best."

"Good. You're beautiful, hon. Your mom and I love you. Grandpa and Grandma send their love. And call your sister, will you?"

"Okay," Elizabeth said. "I love you too, Dad."

She hung up the telephone. In her mind, she imagined all the people who were hanging up at the same time. Her dad certainly, probably in the Oval Office. But also Secret Service people listening on other phones in the Oval Office—two or three of them, hanging up as one. Also, people sitting at computer screens in the CIA building, or the FBI headquarters. Also, her personal bodyguard standing out in the hall, with the wire going to his ear. Was he on the phone call? She bet he was.

Also, the Russian and Chinese spy agencies. You knew they were listening. And the billionaire Russian gangsters who sent their uncouth lout children to this expensive school. Were they listening? Probably.

Also, the security office here at the school. Of course they were listening. Providing security was a big part of the babysitting service here, and the school advertised to parents about how "seamlessly the school's security apparatus can dovetail with your own to safeguard every moment of your child's learning experience."

She felt like screaming.

She sat for a moment on her bed. Outside the window, it was night in Switzerland. She could see the lights of boats on Lake Geneva from here, and the darkness of the mountains towering on the other side of the lake. She could even see the twinkling lights of villages high on the hillsides.

For a moment, she looked at herself in the full-length mirror across from her bed. She was pretty. She knew that. She had long brown hair and a very nice body, even if she had to say so herself. But she was eighteen years old, and she had barely even kissed a boy in her life. No boy could get through the security cordon around her.

She was bored! She was trapped! She was going to die a virgin!

She could not believe that this was her life. She couldn't say a word without people listening in. She couldn't go anywhere without large men following her, encircling her, protecting her.

And really, she couldn't go anywhere at all. Everyplace she wanted to go was a security risk.

Well, she would see about that, wouldn't she?

She got up and walked through her apartment to the bathroom that she shared with her suitemate. She crossed through the room with its heated tile floors, its rain shower and five-foot-wide vanity and mirror—it was a nice bathroom, she had to admit. Her family was old money—they didn't believe in luxurious things—and she had never had a bathroom like this one before.

She knocked on the adjoining door.

"Come in!" a voice said.

Elizabeth opened the door and entered. Suddenly, she was in another world—the apartment of Rita Chadwick. The apartments were the same generic layout—bedroom, small kitchen, and living area—but Rita had personalized hers. She had a sense of bohemian hippie culture, and the place was hung with drapes and beads and Tibetan prayer flags. On one wall was a giant poster called

"Earthrise," showing planet Earth as it supposedly looked from the moon. On another was a life-sized poster of the rapper Eminem on stage, wearing a T-shirt and dripping sweat.

Rita wore bell-bottom jeans and a flowered shirt. She was darkly pretty, and had straight black hair tied back with a purple headwrap.

Allowing Elizabeth to have a suitemate was the one nod to normalcy that her dad, the Secret Service, and the school would give her. Even that was hardly normal. Elizabeth and Rita were suitemates and friends, but they led very different lives.

Rita's family had owned magazines and newspapers for two centuries. She had wealth, but no security to speak of—her family was fine with the level of security provided by the school. It was nothing for Rita to hire a car service to take her the twenty miles into Geneva on weekend nights. She would eat in the restaurants and party in the dance clubs until the early hours of the morning, then take a car back here, arriving home around dawn.

Or sometimes not at all.

Sometimes on weekend nights, after participating in whatever lame group activities were on offer here on campus, Elizabeth would wake up in the early hours before sunrise and listen to see if Rita had come home that night.

Rita had freedom, and lots of it—and Elizabeth had none. The Secret Service had vetted Rita and found her not to be a threat, mostly because there was no way to smuggle anyone on campus. People she knew in Geneva could visit her, but only during the daytime, and they couldn't come into the building at all. After they passed through security, they had to sit out on the campus grounds.

Rita was sitting on her bed, making a drawing on a pad with a thick black pencil. "Hey, babe," she said, without looking up.

"Hey, babe," Elizabeth said.

Hey, babe—that was their thing. They called each other babe.

Elizabeth's friendship with Rita was one of the few good things that had come out of this school year. Rita was going to Brown next year, in Providence, Rhode Island, just up the road from Yale. Elizabeth was hopeful that they would stay in touch, and stay friends. But you never could tell. A lot of these so-called friendships fell apart after you weren't in the same space anymore.

"How's your dad?" Rita said.

"You know," Elizabeth said.

Rita nodded. "I know. He's President, and that's a big job."

"That's right."

Rita flipped the page in her drawing pad. Now she was writing something instead of drawing.

"I imagine he's busy doing Presidential things."

"He's very busy acting Presidential," Elizabeth said.

It was dummy talk. Over time, they had evolved a system of communication that the Secret Service couldn't overhear or intercept. They would continue to talk normally, about this or that, like dizzy high school girls. All the while, they would pass written messages back and forth, which they would later rip up and throw out in the dining hall garbage cans.

Rita turned the pad around and showed Elizabeth what she had written.

Do you still want to go for it? Escape Mode?

Escape Mode was a plan that Rita had invented for Elizabeth, a way to break her out of the prison she was in and give her a chance to experience a little adventure, a little excitement, and what little nightlife the city of Geneva had to offer.

The plan was daring, to say the least. Breathtaking. Audacious. If it worked, it would only work once. So any attempt at it was a one-time chance, a desperate grab for all the marbles.

Their rooms were two stories above the ground, but their windows opened to a rooftop that sloped downward to the edge. According to Rita, there was a rain gutter out there made of a hard metal, like steel or iron. It was not flimsy. She knew this because she had climbed down it on a couple of occasions during the middle of the night to visit a boy in one of the other dorms.

Escape Mode involved Rita preparing to go to Geneva on a weekend night. Meanwhile, Elizabeth would pretend to turn in early—while also preparing for a night out. Rita would call for a car service to pick her up. When the car came, Rita would go downstairs like she always did. Elizabeth would sit inside with the TV set on, loud. Elizabeth had been watching the TV with the sound way up for months, on the off chance she would ever get the guts to try Escape Mode.

With the TV on, Elizabeth would then slide out the window she had opened earlier, cross the roof silently, shimmy down the rain gutter, drop to the ground, then run for the driveway turnaround where the car would be parked.

Once she was inside the car, they would head for the gates of the school. The car's windows would be blacked, and according to Rita, security on the way out of campus was cursory—a wave-through—compared to how it was on the way in.

If they made it through the gates, for once in her life Elizabeth would be free. Rita would take her to Club Baroque, where the dance music DJs played, and they would dance to house music in a packed nightclub until the place closed. Then they would go for food and coffee, and get back here at dawn.

It was the crime of the century. There were boys who lived in Geneva—their families were in banking—whom Rita hung out with. Sometimes they came to campus during visiting hours. One of them was a very handsome young guy from Turkey named Ahmet. He was thin, with curly black hair and skin the shade of coffee— light and sweet, Rita called it. He wore American-style clothes. He spoke English. He was normal—not like a lot of Arab guys, who were religious fanatics.

Were Turkish guys Arabs? Elizabeth wasn't sure about that. But Rita had told Elizabeth that Ahmet thought she was cute.

Rita handed Elizabeth the pencil. She tapped the words *Escape Mode?* Elizabeth made a quick scrawl in response.

Yes.

"Well, you know," Rita said, "when you're leader of the free world, you have a lot to worry about. Wars going on everywhere, fingers on the button, Yuri's dad cutting off natural gas supplies to Europe."

Yuri was an idiotic fourteen-year-old boy from Moscow who went to school here, and who delighted in telling anyone who would listen that his father controlled the natural gas pipeline running from Russia to Germany. Yuri hadn't gotten his growth spurt yet. He wasn't even five feet tall.

Elizabeth handed the pencil back.

"That's all Yuri has, natural gas," she said.

Clock's ticking, Rita wrote. *School year's over. Friday night?*

"And he blows it up everybody's ass," Rita said.

Elizabeth took the pencil and circled the original *Yes.*

Sure? Rita wrote.

Elizabeth circled the word again. Now it was *Yes* in two big black circles.

They both laughed at poor little Yuri. Silly boy.

Good, Rita wrote. *It'll be fun.*

Elizabeth nodded. "Fun," she said. It was a weird thing to say, since it didn't quite follow what Rita had said, but it was all Elizabeth could think of.

Fun.

And that was all it was to Rita, who took her vast freedom for granted. Her nights in Geneva, her occasional side trips to London and Paris and Milan. But to Elizabeth, it was something else again. It was huge, it was energizing, it was terrifying. Her entire body tingled when she thought about it. Her breath caught in her throat.

Would she be able to go through with it?

Would she be able to make herself climb through the window and shimmy down the rain gutter? Then what? A drive through the countryside to the city. A crowded club with lights flaring, music pumping, bodies pressed together. Drinks? Sure, she would have a drink, even though she was technically too young. Just a long hoped for night of adventure. The chance to be anonymous, among anonymous people, and maybe have some real fun for once.

Well, her dad told her to do something exciting, didn't he?

Who was she kidding? Her parents would kill her if they found out, and they were definitely going to find out. Escape Mode only went in one direction. There was no plan for coming back in. There was no way to shimmy back up the rain gutter. She would just have to reenter the campus, and the building, the old-fashioned way.

By then, the Secret Service man outside her door would have probably grown suspicious of the TV playing all night and let himself in. The alarm would be raised. There might even be an international incident.

Elizabeth felt herself ramping up with anxiety. She took a deep breath to try to calm herself down. After this, she was going to be grounded until she was forty.

Rita wrote something new. She turned it around so Elizabeth could see.

Ahmet will be there.

CHAPTER TEN

6:15 p.m. Eastern Daylight Time
The Skies over the Atlantic Ocean

The small blue jet with the US Department of State logo streaked north and east across the sky, dark water below them.

Inside the plane, Luke and his new team moved tentatively toward working together for the first time—they used the front four passenger seats as their meeting area. They stowed their luggage, and their gear, in the seats at the back.

Luke glanced around.

This was the young team. They looked like some kind of youth group going for their first overnight.

Trudy Wellington sat directly across from Luke, occasionally tossing her curly brown hair out of her face. She was slim and attractive in a green sweatshirt and blue jeans. Her blue eyes hid behind her big, red-rimmed owl glasses.

Across from Luke and to the left, facing him, was Mark Swann. He stretched his long bird legs out into the aisle, an old pair of ripped jeans and a pair of red Chuck Taylor sneakers there for anyone to trip over. His aviator glasses were tinted yellow. He wore a black Ramones T-shirt, covered by a red flannel shirt.

In the seat next to Luke sat Ed Newsam. His jacket was off now, demonstrating his rippling upper body. He was steely-eyed, huge, a bear of a man. He wore a precisely trimmed beard, his hair shaved to the skin on the sides with about an inch on top. Both his beard and his hair were jet black.

All three of these people were staring hard at Luke. None of them looked friendly. Trudy and Swann seemed edgy, skittish almost, as though their lack of confidence in Luke made them nervous. Newsam didn't seem nervous at all. He sat back in his seat as though he might fall asleep at any moment.

"So what's the story, boss man?" he said.

Luke smiled. He and this big kid were going to get tangled up. He could see that already. "Boss man, huh?"

"Would you prefer if I call you Hot Rod?" Newsam said.

"Why don't you call me Luke? Or you can also try Mr. Stone."

Newsam grunted at that.

Luke glanced out his window. It was a bright day, but the sun was already behind them. In a little while, as they moved further east, the sky would begin to darken. Iraq was a long way, so far that they'd have to stop in Germany to refuel.

"Trudy?"

She nodded, her eyes going wider than before. Luke had suddenly thrust her on stage. "Yes?"

"You're the intelligence officer, right?"

"Yes."

Luke shrugged. "Well, we all know something about this case, but you probably know the most. I imagine you have some paperwork on all this, don't you?"

She nodded again. "Of course. Sure."

"Why don't you fill us in?"

There was a thick file folder on the seat next to her. She picked it up and opened it. On one side was a slim three-ring binder. On the other side was a sleeve holding loose documents. She opened the binder several pages from the beginning.

"Okay," she said. "I'm going to assume that none of you have any prior knowledge of the events, the people involved, or the strategies we plan to take."

"Sounds good to me," Luke said. "Boys?"

"Good," Swann said.

"Let's hear it," Ed said. He eased back into his seat.

"It's a lot of information," Trudy said. "It might take a little while."

Luke shrugged. "It's a long flight," he said. "We've got all the time in the world."

He listened for a bit as she went through her paperwork, describing for the others, and for Luke, the past and present of Edwin Lee Parr. Gradually, Luke drifted. He thought of Rebecca alone at her family's country house, waiting for him to return.

He could picture her standing on the back patio, framed by the sunset, her belly large with their child. He wanted, more than anything, for this trip to happen fast. He knew that past the eighth month, that baby could come anytime. Due dates were more like suggestions or guidelines than a hard and fast schedule.

He thought of her eating dinner at her parents' big stone house in the Virginia suburbs, maybe sleeping over. *Probably* sleeping over. Her parents were wealthy, and as far as Luke knew, had never worked a day in their lives. They didn't think much of Luke, he knew. Elite special operations units did not impress them. People who joined the military were a different class of people from them, from their daughter, from their grandchild. He wasn't sure what worried them more—that he would die during a deployment, or that he would come home alive.

"…Luke?" Trudy had said.

"Yeah, I'm sorry. What was that again?"

Beside him, Ed Newsam released a sort of sneering laugh.

"Do you want me to go over the operation plan?" she said.

"Sure. Let's hear it."

She riffled through some papers. She pointed at him. "Luke, your name is Edward King. They made your identity easy to remember. You're thirty-two years old, the same age you are now. You were in the Seventy-fifth Army Rangers, which you were, in fact, in. You used to work for Blackstone Corporation, and that's how you came to be in Iraq, but they fired you for insubordination. Now you're on your own, looking to make a score."

She turned to Newsam. "Ed, your name is David Dell. People call you DD. Also easy to remember. You're twenty-five years old and you were once in the Eighty-seventh Airborne. You also worked for Blackstone, but your contract was not renewed. You and Ed King are now partners."

"Okay," Newsam said. "That's fine. But how do the big guy and I infiltrate?"

Big guy. Newsam was trying to be a comedian. Luke didn't like comedians.

"Easy enough," Trudy said. "There's an informant. I don't have his identity because that's protected information. He was detained and arrested by a squad of Marines at a checkpoint outside of the city of Fallujah. He was riding in a Range Rover with three young Iraqi women. It wasn't clear how an American came to be riding with three Iraqi women, but they were apparently in some distress. What little understanding I have of the situation is that the girls were teenagers, and he may have bought them, from their families or possibly from someone else, for a nominal amount of money."

"He's a pimp," Newsam said.

Trudy was noncommittal. "I don't have any information on what he was doing or intended to do. All we know is whoever he is, he was with Parr up until very recently. He is now in the custody of the CIA, and has been interrogated by Bill Cronin."

Luke inwardly winced at the idea of someone being interrogated by Bill Cronin. The guy who got picked up probably had a rough night with Bill. Well, good for him. People like Bill Cronin existed for a reason, and they didn't come to see you unless you had strayed way off the path.

"He is a cooperating witness now," Trudy said, telling Luke something he already knew. Men in the custody of Big Daddy Cronin were invariably cooperating witnesses. If they were still alive, they were eager to cooperate. "He is on Parr's team, and the plan is that he will take you back into Sunni-controlled territory and lead you directly to Parr."

"How long has he been in custody?" Luke said.

She referred to a sheet of paper. "Uh, approximately seventy-two hours as of this moment. By the time he leads you back to Parr's hideout, figure more like four days."

"So they're going to be suspicious of him," Luke said.

She nodded. "Probably. The story goes that he was picked up by a patrol, spent a few days in jail, then was released with the two of you."

Ed Newsam shook his head. "That story is going to last exactly—"

"It only needs to last long enough to get you to Parr's hideout and in the door," Trudy said.

"Then what?" Newsam said.

"Then you arrest him."

Newsam stared at her, the faintest echo of a grin on his face. But he didn't say anything. Luke silently commended him for that. When Trudy had first pitched Luke the idea for this mission, he hadn't been able to keep quiet about it.

"All three of you are going to be wearing GPS units," Mark Swann said. "The car you ride in will have a strobing transponder embedded on the roof—it'll be visible from the sky by our guys, but not on the ground by Parr's guys."

"Unless he has command of a satellite or a drone," Newsam said.

Swann shook his head. "I highly doubt it. The guy has gone all the way outlaw. The US military controls those skies. Parr is trying to stay invisible. He's not flying anything."

"Two Black Hawks with Ranger squads on each are going to be trailing you," Trudy continued. "Also, if need be, there will be an Apache gunship on call. You can call in reinforcements or a heavy airstrike at any time."

"So the whole game…" Luke began.

She nodded. "Yes. You're following the informant down the rabbit hole, and confirming that he has led you to Parr. Once in Parr's presence, you make the positive ID on him. At that point, Parr can surrender to you or he can die. The choice will be his to make."

"And we're dangled there in front of him like fresh meat," Newsam said.

"Well, not in so many words," Trudy said. "But…"

"Yes," Mark Swann said.

CHAPTER ELEVEN

May 6
11:05 a.m. Arabian Standard Time (4:05 a.m. Eastern Daylight Time)
The Embassy of the United States in Iraq (aka the Republican Palace)
The International Zone (aka the Green Zone)
Karkh District
Baghdad, Iraq

"How was the trip in from the airport?" Big Daddy Bill Cronin said.

He was a bear of a man. Tall, with a thick body, big shoulders and arms, and a bushy red beard maybe softening now and going a bit gray. Luke had known Big Daddy for a few years. Two years ago, Big Daddy had been his CIA handler when Luke went deep undercover here in Iraq.

"Fine," Luke said.

And it had been fine. If fine meant riding at high speed in a convoy of armored Humvees, each one with passengers packed in like sardines, heavily armed soldiers hanging out the windows, aiming their guns at anything and everything every inch of the way, and screaming curses in Arabic at any and all human beings they passed.

The convoy didn't take any enemy fire on the trip, and that was fine.

"And the landing? How was that?"

"The pilots stuck the landing, to coin a phrase," Luke said. "A few people puked, but we came in safe and sound." The second leg of their trip had been a flight from Germany aboard a medium-sized passenger jet. The plane had come down to the Baghdad airport in corkscrew fashion, banking hard left and dropping fast the entire way, to thwart any rocket attacks from the ground. When the plane hit the runway, the pilots braked hard, bringing the plane to an abrupt stop.

"Very nice," Bill Cronin said. He looked at the rest of Luke's crew.

"Did you guys enjoy your first Baghdad special?"

"I was one of the people who puked," Trudy said.

"So was I," Swann said.

Cronin smiled. "It's a rite of passage. I've done it a couple of times myself." He looked at big Ed Newsam.

"You?"

Newsam shook his head and smiled. "I don't puke, man."

Cronin shook his head. "You don't know what you're missing, buddy."

Bill Cronin wore khaki slacks, shiny black shoes, and an open-throated dress shirt, which at this time of the morning was beginning to soak through with sweat. There was no air conditioning in Saddam Hussein's former Republican Palace.

He walked briskly, leading them down a series of wide marble hallways, all of them teeming with people. Crowds of people zigged and zagged, squeezing past each other in each direction. People sat in wheeled office chairs at makeshift desks pushed up against the stone walls, typing into computer keyboards or jabbering into telephones, their voices echoing off the twenty-foot-high rounded and tiled ceilings. Wires snaked across the floors, or ran along the walls, bundled with heavy black duct tape. People in various stages of sweaty undress tried to catch a few minutes or hours of sleep on military-issue cots, the cots lining stretches of hallway in single file like ants.

Here and there, areas were sectioned off with plywood, some hung with canvas drapes or tarps, making instant offices or maybe bedrooms. The plywood boards were spray painted with series of letters and numbers. Luke was tired from the trip, but he figured the designations would make sense to him if he stopped for a moment to think about them. A couple of the plywood walls were adorned with American flags.

"The old place is looking good," Luke said. "Like Calcutta."

He had spent several days here in an earlier time, soon after the building had been abandoned, and then looted. In those days, barely anyone was here, there was no electricity, and a handful of international troops held the approaches against all comers.

The area that had coalesced into the Green Zone had once been the wealthiest neighborhood in Baghdad. Saddam had lived here in the Republican Palace, of course. But the whole district had been filled with mansions of varying sizes, upscale apartment houses, fashionable restaurants and shops. When the American invasion came and the bombing started, the residents all left with whatever they could carry.

When Luke first arrived in Baghdad in 2003, few people understood that all these places were up for grabs. You could move right in, on a first-come first-served basis, if you had the right mindset and the firepower to protect yourself. Combat units on patrol took over several of the mansions.

A couple of units even took the Palace. Since it was among the easier places to fortify and protect, within short order it became the bizarre, grandiose, and yet rudimentary and rustic headquarters of the Coalition Provisional Government. No electricity, no air conditioning, no running water, portable lights only, and nearly constant mortar attacks. It looked like things had settled down some since then.

Big Daddy shrugged and shook his head. "It's gotten crowded, for sure. What can I say? It's the safest place in town. Almost nobody can get into the Green Zone who doesn't belong here. Fanatics smuggle a bomb or a grenade in once in a while, and people still blow themselves up at the checkpoints on a regular basis, but if you don't happen to be standing outside the gates when it happens, then you're fine. We still take mortar fire sometimes, but it usually doesn't reach, and the walls are ten feet thick anyway. Also, the swimming pool in the back has water in it now, and it's open for business. Everybody wants to be here, and never mind the crowds."

They passed a gaggle of people taking notes as a tall jarhead captain lectured them about something or other.

"I've got a conference room reserved up ahead here, so we should be fine," Bill said. "We can get away from all this noise."

He turned down a short, narrow corridor. At the end was a heavy wooden door which he opened without a key. The room was dimly lit by battery-operated lamps sitting on a table made from a thick wood slab sitting on two sawhorses. There were no windows. Instead, the walls were covered in a tiled mosaic showing a desert oasis scene, possibly from a time at the dawn of civilization.

Two men sat at the table. Both stood when Bill Cronin, Luke, and the team came in. The first, a tall man with close-cropped gray hair, stood ramrod straight in a United States Army camouflage uniform with no identifying marks. Luke knew right away what that meant. The second man was smaller, younger, with sandy hair, a haggard, doughy face and a bit of a paunch. His skin was pale despite being in the middle of a desert—he looked like he didn't get outside much. He was smoking a cigarette and sweating profusely. The climate didn't seem to agree with him.

"Agent Luke Stone, this is Colonel Radis of Joint Special Operations Command. This is Mr. Montgomery from the British Embassy." Cronin made a funny bird's feet gesture with his fingers when he said the words *British Embassy.* Luke also knew what that meant. The man didn't work for the British Embassy.

He introduced his young team to the two men.

"Won't you all sit down?" Colonel Radis said. "We've got water for everyone."

Luke and his group sat. Bill Cronin remained standing. Eight or nine generic plastic bottles of water were on the table in front of them. Trudy and Swann reached for bottles. Ed Newsam was apparently too cool for that. Luke reached and took one.

"We know you just came in, and you must be eager to get to your accommodations, so we'll go through this as quickly as we can," Radis said.

"I think we know most of the details of the operation," Luke said. "Trudy received a great deal of information before we left, and she briefed us on the flight."

Radis nodded. "Good. We've got some classified material here that may not have been transmitted to you because of its delicate nature. The fewer eyes with the opportunity to see this information, the better. And I believe it will increase your understanding of the situation."

"Okay," Luke said. "Hit us."

Montgomery put a series of photographs on the table in a row, one at a time. Luke picked one up, glanced at it, and handed it to Trudy. Then he picked up another one. They were photos of abandoned palaces, similar in nature to the one they were in, but in worse shape. Walls were pockmarked with bullet holes or half destroyed by mortar fire. Fixtures were ripped out and missing. Trashed furniture and equipment lay heaped in piles. Pyramid-shaped rock slides of rubble lay against ruined walls. Burnt-out skeletons of trucks and cars sat side by side in parking lots. In one photo, a bust of Saddam Hussein wore a medieval equestrian combat helmet on his head—as though Saddam had been a horseback warrior during the Golden Age of Islam.

Luke smiled at that one. Saddam looked like a child playing make-believe.

"As you may know, Saddam was in power here for nearly twenty-four years," Montgomery said. He spoke with a clipped, upper-crust English accent. He had an oddly high-pitched voice. He seemed like an odd man in many ways. Spooks often were.

"And during that time, he built between eighty and one hundred palaces for his own private use, as well as the use of his family, Baath party officials, friends and business partners of his, and his many mistresses. He wasn't shy about looting Iraq's treasury, stockpiling priceless antiquities looted from his own country, from Iran during the war in the early 1980s, and from Kuwait during his occupation there in 1990. Unmarked cash, much of it in American dollars, cars, gold, diamonds, anything you can imagine.

"He moved much of this hoard to banks outside the country, but some of it is still right here, hidden in his palaces, but also in old weapons depots, in underground bunkers and caves. We believe the value of his secret fortune runs into the many billions of dollars. Indeed, Saddam was probably one of the richest men on Earth."

"And this widely known fact is classified because why?" Ed Newsam said.

Montgomery raised an index finger. "It isn't as widely known as you may believe. There are hundreds of thousands of troops— American and coalition—not to mention reporters, aid workers, and international observers tramping through this country right now. There are millions of Iraqis, many of them in unsanctioned militias. If everyone knew the size of this fortune, the war would become more of a free-for-all money hunt than it is currently."

"Wouldn't want that," Newsam said. "Would we?"

"Our soldiers have a mission here," Radis said. "And it isn't looting and grabbing."

Ed smiled his arrogant young smile. His teeth gleamed white.

"No? What is it then?"

"Show them the other pictures."

Montgomery came out with a new pile of photographs. He placed these on the table, one by one, in a grid, as he had done with the others. Luke picked up the first of these and winced.

It showed what looked like a five-year-old girl, ripped apart by machine gun fire.

"These are disturbing," Colonel Radis said.

The next one showed a pile of bodies, women and children, their robes soaked with blood. The wall behind them was pockmarked, as though it was being used by a firing squad.

"We believe this is the work of Parr and his group," Montgomery said. "All of these photos were taken in the past few days."

"Why is he doing this?" Luke said.

"Edwin Lee Parr has gone insane," Radis said.

"Clearly insane," Mark Swann said. He was looking at the photos from behind his hand, his fingers opened half an inch.

"Parr and his group have been working with Sunni informants, some of whom were former officials in Saddam's regime, and some of whom were in the Iraqi military. This is how he's been so successful in discovering Saddam's hidden treasure. Our intelligence suggests that Parr and his group currently have hundreds of millions in American dollars alone in their possession, and possibly hundreds of millions more in gold and silver bars, and diamonds. The local people are now well aware of what he's doing and what he has. Parr is trapped in the Sunni Triangle with no way out of the country. But the country is awash in weaponry, and Parr has obtained his share of it. With no way out, he is holding his own and maintaining control by increasingly harsh means. He has been targeting women and children, especially the women and children of local elders who stand up to him. More and more, he is taking the women hostage and using them as human shields."

Luke felt his heart sink. This was supposed to be an arrest. He was the police now. But he had a young partner who showed him no respect, and the man he was supposed to arrest was a psychotic committing atrocities against a civilian population.

Terrific.

"We are concerned that Parr is going to attempt a run for the Syrian border."

"What good will that do?" Luke said.

"If he makes it that far, it's possible that corrupt border guards and the Syrian military will accept payoffs from him, and smuggle him and his men to the Turkish border. Perhaps they can obtain new identities along the way. If they make it to Turkey with some of their millions, and with new identities, then they might as well be in Europe at that point."

Luke looked at Bill. "What are the chances of that happening?"

Bill shrugged. "He's been pretty good so far. My guess is he could make it, but it would take a lot of bloodletting to pull it off."

"How many human shields does he have?" Ed Newsam said. It seemed like the first serious comment or question he had made since Luke met him.

"We think probably at least fifty," Montgomery said. "And he will certainly kill all of them if he has to. He's desperate, he's shown no compunction about killing, and if anything, he seems to have, shall we say, an increasing appetite for it."

"So what's next?" Luke said.

"You guys get some rest and some decent food in your stomachs," Radis said. "We'll get our informant cleaned up a bit—that will probably take a few hours. He's had a couple of long question and answer sessions he's sleeping off."

Luke glanced at Bill again. Big Daddy made a face to indicate disapproval, or possibly disgust. Big Daddy was known as an unpleasant interrogator. Among that group, most were dispassionate, almost like scientists carrying out experiments on rodents. In Luke's experience, Bill seemed to take an active dislike of his subjects. The more he hurt them, the more he started to hate them.

"The informant believes he knows exactly where Parr is," Montgomery said. "That was another fact we didn't want to transmit. Tomorrow morning, before first light, we would like you gentlemen to go in there."

"Arrest Parr?" Luke said.

Big Daddy did a small head shake.

"If he'll see reason," Radis said. "Sure, arrest him if you like. We'll take it from there." Briefly, Luke thought of the CIA black site that existed at Bagram air base in Afghanistan. Something told him that the justice Parr was going to see wasn't going to involve a judge and jury back in the United States.

"Edwin Lee Parr is beyond reason," Montgomery said.

* * *

Trudy Wellington riffled through some papers on the desk.

"The man we're about to see is Davis Cole, thirty-six years old. Ex-Marine with combat experience in several theaters. Ex-convict who served thirty months in the New York State prison system for manslaughter. The case apparently involved a fist fight that started in a Manhattan bar—the result of an argument over the results of a professional hockey game."

"I guess he won that argument," Ed Newsam said.

The four of them were sitting at a table in a small room. In front of them was a glass partition which Bill Cronin had said was one-way glass. On the other side was another wooden table—with one chair. When Cole came in, they would be able to see him, but he wouldn't be able to see them. Also, the interrogation room was mic'd—Cole's voice would carry into this room, but he wouldn't be able to hear them.

"Cole grew up in Philadelphia," Trudy said. "Apparently, it was a game between the New York Rangers and the Philadelphia Flyers."

"That explains everything," Mark Swann said.

Luke was silent. This was the man who was supposed to get them in to see Edwin Parr. Luke didn't mind the banter about him, but he also wanted to get to the meat of it.

"What is he doing here?" he said.

Trudy looked as the dossier. "He's a former military contractor with Triple Canopy. How they hired him with his record is still an open question."

"It's a war zone," Newsam said. "Always room for more killers."

"Triple Canopy let him go in February of this year," Trudy said. "He has been operating in Iraq under no one's supervision for the past few months. It is possible that they released him because they discovered he was working with Parr."

"Why don't we know these things?" Luke said. "We don't talk to the contracting companies? They don't answer us? It seems like they might want to respond to inquiries from the government, if they want to keep their contracts."

"Cole's not arrested," Trudy said. "Officially, he's not here. No one has any reason to inquire about his employment history with Triple Canopy, because no one has him in custody."

Luke nodded. "Ah. That makes sense."

On the other side of the glass partition, a side door opened and a big man walked in. He was perfectly bald. He was shirtless and wore camouflage pants and combat boots. His upper body was huge—with a massive chest and shoulders, and a neck like the stump of an oak tree. Oddly, Cole had what looked like a metal collar around his neck. He also had one black eye—it was half shut and turning various shades of purple and sickly yellow. His lower lip had been busted open on the left side—it was swollen to three or four times its normal size, and someone had been kind enough to stitch it up for him. That seemed to be the only damage he had sustained.

Luke knew that Big Daddy Cronin preferred to leave the scars on the inside.

Big Daddy himself followed the man in. Cole wasn't restrained in any way, and he was bigger than Cronin. Although they were about five years apart in age, Cole also seemed much younger than Big Daddy. Cole was muscle everywhere, muscles stacked on top of muscles, with hardly an ounce of fat on his body. Big Daddy was not.

"Have a seat," Big Daddy said.

Cole sat in the chair at the table. On his left pectoral muscle, near his heart, was a tattoo of a Confederate flag. Well faded now, it looked like it had been bright full color at one time. Luke had also caught a glimpse of a black prison tattoo swastika on the guy's right shoulder.

Luke glanced at Newsam, but Newsam made no sign he'd seen any of it.

"State your name," Big Daddy said.

"Davis Michael Cole," the man said automatically in a deep voice. "First Marines Expeditionary—"

Big Daddy slapped him hard across the back of his bald head. Cole flinched at the slap.

"Shut up," Big Daddy said. "You're not in the Marines."

Cole's mouth closed with a snap.

Big Daddy pointed at the Confederate flag tattoo. Then he turned Cole's arm toward the window to show the swastika tattoo. "You guys seeing this?"

He shook his head. He looked down at Cole and took a deep breath.

"You know something, Cole? You know what I'm going to tell you, right? I hate tattoos like that. I hate *things* like that. I HATE IT. It makes me hate you. No, that's not true. I don't hate you. I have a very strong urge to help you. To correct your thinking, even if that means I have to kill you to do it."

Big Daddy took a deep, slow breath. "Let me ask you a question. What country's military were you supposedly in?"

"The American military," Cole said, his voice flat and automatic.

"And the Confederates were what to the United States of America?"

Cole didn't answer.

Suddenly Big Daddy punched him in the back of the head.

"You better say it."

He punched Cole again.

Cole gritted his teeth.

Then Big Daddy had a gun in his hand—it appeared there as though he was a magician and making a gun appear was one of his easier tricks. It was a smallish .38 caliber revolver, like police officers carried once upon a time. He opened the gun and slid a single bullet into a chamber.

Then he closed it and gave the wheel a spin.

Trudy moved as if to stand up from her seat, but Luke put a hand on her shoulder.

"Wait a minute," he said.

Big Daddy put the gun to Cole's head.

"Okay, so we're going to play a little game here," he said. "It's called the history game. I'll ask you a question about American history, and you answer it. Ready? Here goes. What were the Confederates?"

Cole closed his eyes.

Big Daddy pulled the trigger.

Click.

Cole's entire body jerked, almost as if a bullet had gone through his head.

"Where are you right now, Cole?"

"Nowhere."

Big Daddy nodded. "Nowhere, that's right. You're not in American custody, are you? Or anyone's custody?"

Cole shook his head. "No."

"You could just die and no one would ever know, couldn't you?"

Cole nodded. His entire body was shaking now. "Yes."

Big Daddy placed the gun against Cole's head again.

"So what were the Confederates?"

"You son of a bitch!" Cole shouted. But he made no move to stand up or defend himself. Tears began to stream down his face.

Big Daddy didn't seem excited or even all that interested. He calmly pulled the trigger again.

Click.

Cole made a moaning sound.

"It's coming, Cole. It's going to be in there. I've already pulled that trigger twice. The odds are going south for you. The next chamber has the round, I can feel it. For the last time, what were the Confederates?"

He put the muzzle to Cole's temple. "Here it comes. What were the—"

"Traitors!" Cole screamed. "They were traitors!"

"Traitors, what?" Big Daddy said.

"Traitors, sir," Cole said. He took a deep breath.

"You dumb bastard. If you were in the United States Marine Corps like you claim, what in God's name are you doing with the flag of traitors on your chest?"

Cole shook his head. "I don't know... sir."

Big Daddy's shoulders slumped, as though he was a teacher dealing with a particularly frustrating student. He looked through the glass wall at the observers and sighed. He shrugged.

"It's like pulling teeth sometimes. You know that? We're not even going to get into what the Nazis were. We don't have time for that lesson today."

The gun disappeared into wherever it had come from—a magic trick in reverse.

"Good job, Cole," Big Daddy said. "The Confederates were indeed traitors to America. They were the defenders of chattel slavery. They fought against the American military, and they invaded sovereign American territory. The American military defeated them, and humiliated them, and slaughtered them, in a victory for the United States of America, and for everything that is good and decent and right."

He smacked Cole across the top of the head again. Cole barely moved this time. He was *resigned* to this, Luke realized. In just a few days, Cronin had made this big, fierce killer resigned to this mistreatment.

Big Daddy paused for a moment. "And what are you?" he said.

"A dirtbag mercenary," Cole said. He offered that answer without any hesitation at all. Davis Cole seemed to care more about what the Confederacy was than what he himself might be.

"Good," Big Daddy said. "What else?"

Cole shrugged. "A pimp. A rapist."

"And?"

"A disgrace to the American flag," Cole said.

Big Daddy sighed again, and then smiled. "Okay, now we're getting somewhere. What are you going to do tomorrow morning?"

Cole took a deep breath. "I'm going to drive two guys into Edwin Parr's compound."

"Where is Parr's compound, as far as you know?"

"When I left, it was inside Al-Arabi Palace in Tikrit. The place is well protected, comfortable, and I have no reason to believe he's moved during the past several days. Logistically, it would be very hard to do so because the locals are hostile to him, and they can't reach him there. But if he leaves…" Cole shrugged. "He'll be up for grabs."

"When you get those two guys inside, what are you going to do then?"

"I'm going to assist them in arresting Parr, or killing him, whichever the case may be. Then I'm going to help them get out again."

"And if you don't cooperate, or if you hesitate in carrying out your assigned tasks, or if you do anything funny at all?"

"I'll be killed."

"Good. And if you try to escape?"

"I'll be killed."

"What's that around your neck?" Big Daddy said.

Cole's big hand reached up and reflexively touched the metal collar. His fingers followed it around in a circle.

"It's a GPS unit so you know where I am at all times."

"Very good. What else is it?"

"It's a bomb."

Trudy audibly gasped.

"Your friend is a psychopath," she said to Luke.

Luke nodded. "Big Daddy? Yeah, maybe. I think so."

Big Daddy patted Cole on top of the head. "Good dog. It's a small incendiary, with a remote detonator, isn't it? It won't make much of an explosion, just enough to take your head right off your shoulders. And who decides if that bomb goes off or not?"

"You do."

Now Big Daddy's grin was very wide. He looked into the mirrored window again. He put a proprietary hand on top of Cole's head.

"I predict that this very able combat veteran is going to make one heck of a good, cooperative guide for you guys tomorrow. He will give his very life to ensure the success of the operation. This is because he knows that if the operation fails, and he's somehow alive afterwards, I'm going to kill him anyway."

He looked down at Cole's face.

"With pleasure."

CHAPTER TWELVE

8:45 p.m. Central European Summer Time (2:45 p.m. Eastern Daylight Time)
Bourg-de-Four-Square
Old Town
Geneva, Switzerland

It's happening, the text message read.

The message was from his dear friend Rita Chadwick, the black sheep of a very old and very wealthy publishing family.

Ahmet looked up from his flip cell phone at the action all around him. Night had come to the oldest place in Geneva. Legend had it that Romans had first built this place and that it had been an open air market for cattle trading.

He sat at an outdoor café in the ancient square, nursing a cup of coffee. The night was cool, and the lights of the town, combined with the splashing of the medieval fountains and the cooing of the rich young lovers, made for a lovely setting. He was alone, just as he liked it.

His tiny flat was a few blocks from here, along the narrow cobblestone streets of the Old Town. It befit the son of a banker that he lived in one of the most expensive neighborhoods, in one of the most expensive cities on the planet.

His name was not Ahmet, although during the past year of living here, he had nearly forgotten that. He was not from Turkey, nor was he the son of a banker, or anything remotely like that. He was not twenty-one years old, as his friends believed. He was twenty-five, and his youthful good looks, his high degree of physical fitness (but not muscularity, no—muscularity was threatening, and Ahmet was anything but a threat) combined with fantastically subtle cosmetic surgery, gave him the impression of being a younger man.

Also, his friends were not his friends. He had no friends here. Or, more accurately, there were people here who thought of him as a friend. They were his friends, but he was not their friend. To Ahmet, friends were a means to an end, a form of currency. They were also a tool of war.

He was here for work, and for no other reason. But he was a convincing actor, and the people around him believed he was a rich young Turk, just hanging out here in Geneva, killing time and partying with the adult children of the global elite.

No. That wasn't him.

He had been placed here when it became known, about a year ago, that the daughter of the President of the United States would attend one year of school at the Institut Le Rosey, just twenty miles outside the city.

His job was to accomplish the impossible. He was somehow to meet the girl, Elizabeth Barrett, and despite the layers of security around her, he was to charm her, seduce her, and lure her off the campus and away from her security detail. That was his entire job—others would do the rest.

He was to accomplish this without arousing suspicion or risking his cover story. Better for the operation to be a complete failure, and for him to waste an entire year hanging around in clubs and shops in Geneva, than to call any attention to himself. His job was to be a fisherman—cast his line and wait to see if the fish would bite.

For a long time, it seemed that it would never happen. Indeed, the entire student body and faculty of the school relocated to Gstaad for three months during the winter. But Ahmet stayed here. Fishermen were not camp followers.

In carrying out this task, the girl Rita had been very helpful. She was on a list he had been given early in this mission. He had targeted her, of course, and built up her trust over time. She was a rich party girl, a hedonist, and she had slept with two of Ahmet's friends, who were not his friends. She would have almost certainly slept with Ahmet, but Ahmet was a gentleman, and did not think of Rita in that way. However, during a visit to the school's campus, he caught sight of Rita's friend Elizabeth.

"She is so beautiful! I must meet her. Who is she?"

"Oh," Rita said. "I'm afraid she's out of your reach, lover boy."

"She can't be out of my reach. Who is she?"

"She's Elizabeth Barrett."

Ahmet made a face showing his confusion. The name meant nothing to him.

"A celebrity of some kind in your country?"

Rita nodded. "You might say that. She's the daughter of the President."

"Still, if I can meet her... somewhere quiet, where we can talk... maybe she would like me."

"I think she'd fall head over heels for you, but you'd have to pry her out of the grip of the Secret Service."

"I might have some ideas about that."

Over time, he and Rita had concocted a plan. Rita would help Elizabeth escape the clutches of the school, and her security detail, for just one night. One night of fun, one night of talk, and dancing, and laughter. Ahmet and Elizabeth would get this one chance to meet, away from the prying eyes of the world.

But time passed, and the school year was coming to a close. Soon, the students would all leave for their next carefully scripted and curated adventures. It seemed that young Elizabeth was not brave enough to carry out the plan. And that was where everything stood, in a holding pattern, until this very moment.

He took a deep breath, and remained calm.

Escape mode? he typed into his phone, and pressed SEND.

He sipped his coffee and gazed out at the people in light jackets walking arm in arm through the square.

A few moments passed, then his phone beeped with the reply.

Yes.

For several minutes, he stared down at that word. His breath seemed to have caught in his throat. Was it even possible?

I don't believe it. When?

An eternity passed before Rita wrote him again.

Believe it or not. Tomorrow night.

Ahmet felt his heart beating in his chest. Tomorrow night was very soon. His handlers had long ago become skeptical of his ability to carry out this operation. Now they would have to overcome their skepticism.

They needed to act fast. Men needed to be brought into the city from far-flung places. Of course, there was a plan. There had always been a plan. But the plan had to be set in motion immediately, practically this instant.

He knocked back the last of his coffee and threw some money on the table. Then he was up and moving through the square toward his flat. He had to get a coded message out, and hope that they could act in time. He also had to hope against hope that Rita was correct, and beautiful Elizabeth really was planning to make her escape.

He typed into his phone as he walked.

I'm very excited.

CHAPTER THIRTEEN

May 7
5:35 a.m. Arabian Standard Time
Al-Arabi Palace
Tikrit
Saladin Governorate, Iraq

"You gotta get that guy off my back," Davis Cole said. "He wants to kill me."

"Don't worry, I'll talk to him," Luke said.

It was just before sunrise. They drove quickly through the dusty, early morning streets of Tikrit, passing block after block of low stone buildings, many of them damaged, even half-destroyed, from combat.

Few people were out. Here and there, they passed the silhouettes of skinny people moving through the darkness. They could be ghosts.

This was Saddam Hussein country. Saddam had been born and raised here. The people were loyal to him, and many of his highest-ranking officials had been Tikritis. Earlier in the year, Saddam himself had been captured hiding in a hole in the ground on a farm not far outside town. The Americans still considered this hostile territory.

Cole was driving the car, a beat-up black Mercedes. It was draped in after-market armor, and had smoked bulletproof glass. It wouldn't stop a rocket attack, but garden-variety gunshots would bounce off it. Luke rode in the front passenger seat, MP5 submachine gun on his lap. Ed Newsam rode in the back, armed with another MP5 and an M-79 grenade launcher.

Luke wasn't sure about that grenade launcher, but the man had insisted on it, so…

The cover story went that when Cole was arrested, the Americans seized his Humvee and freed his girls. After three days of stonewalling his interrogators—during which time he had received the black eye and busted lip—he was released. Then he met Luke and Ed in a bar inside the Green Zone. Luke and Ed had been contractors until they realized freelancing was more lucrative. They had carjacked this Mercedes three weeks ago from a

Jordanian businessman and were tooling around in it, looking to make a score.

"No, I mean it," Cole said. "This thing around my neck... He could drop me anytime he wants."

Luke noted that Cole was wearing a buttoned-up shirt that came nearly to his chin. The metal collar he wore was hidden from sight. That was probably for the best. It could be hard to explain a thing like that.

"I've known the guy for a few years," Luke said. "You might not believe this, but he actually likes you. If he really wanted to kill you, you'd already be dead."

"He's torturing me, man. Don't you get that? This is torture. It's against the laws of war. This thing on my neck..."

A deep voice intruded on the conversation. It was Ed Newsam, calm but annoyed. "Hey, man. You better shut up with that talk. I don't want to hear it. Stone don't want to hear it. We don't care about your problems. You got a job to do. Do the job, and we'll give the man a good report on you."

Cole shook his head. "That guy's got a problem with me. He wants to kill me. I don't know if a good report—"

"Whose fault is that? Mine? Stone's? Shut up or I'll call your master right now. Tell him you're not cooperating."

"My master?"

"The man owns you, don't he?" Ed Newsam said. Luke didn't bother to look back at him. Instead, he watched the passing city, and the road up ahead. "Call a thing what it is. That's my philosophy."

They turned onto a wide boulevard. It had been a grand concourse at one time, lined with trees on either side. Most of the trees had been chopped down to the stumps. Burnt out cars and military trucks lined the curbs. The road itself was pockmarked and pitted, as though it had been bombed from the air.

At the far end, maybe a mile in the distance, a tall palace seemed to float in the sky, with minarets on either side. As they approached, Luke could see that it was surrounded by high stone walls and a checkpoint gate. It was hard to tell in the early morning gloom what the checkpoint was constructed from.

"This is when it gets serious," Cole said.

"You know these guys, right?" Luke said.

Cole laughed. "Oh yeah. Straight up cowboys, every one of them."

"Well, you just convince them that we're on the level," Ed said.

"I'll do my best."

"Do better than that, and maybe you'll live through this day."

The walls of the palace loomed just ahead. Everything was clearer now. The high wall was topped with looped razor wire. Guard towers stood twenty feet above the wall every fifty yards or so. The windows were gone—replaced by sheet metal with firing slots cut out of them. It was impossible to tell which towers had men in them and which didn't.

Closer to the ground, the gate was more of a wall than a gate. Luke looked closely. It was a large passenger bus, maybe from the 1960s, its side hung with more sheet metal. Opening the gate meant driving the bus out of the way. Outside the gate, flanking it on either side, were two wrecked armored troop carriers. These were the guard posts.

As the Mercedes pulled up, men with automatic weapons appeared from behind the demolished trucks. At first there were two men, then four, then five. Two men appeared on top of the bus. All of the men had their weapons trained on the Mercedes.

"Calm," Cole said. "Don't do anything stupid."

He powered his window down. Instantly, the muzzle of an AK-47 poked inside the car. The man wielding it wore a green balaclava covering his face.

Cole shook his head. "Watts, you better get that gun out of my face before I get irritated."

The guy pulled his face covering up to the top of his head, revealing his face. He had a narrow jawline, covered with recent stubble. His eyes were blue. "Cole? What the hell are you doing, man? We heard you got busted. Nobody knew if you were alive or dead. How did you know it was me?"

Cole looked at him. "Because you look like a kid playing Spider-Man, Watts. That's why. You're the biggest ten-year-old boy in Iraq. And yes, I'm alive. Took my lumps like a man and didn't say a word."

Watts half-nodded, then shook his head. He took in Cole's face, with the sickly black and yellow shiner and the busted lip. Then he broke into a smile. "Yeah, you look like, uh... you look good, Cole. It's an improvement."

Luke noticed there were still two guns pointed at the car on the passenger side. He didn't power his own window down.

"So I'm alive, I'm back, and I'm ready for action. You gonna open the gate or what?"

Watts gestured with his chin. "Who are your friends?"

"These guys? Couple of hotshots I picked up in Baghdad. They got cut loose from Blackstone a while back. These are their wheels. Mine got impounded. They're looking for work, they heard about

Parr. Word gets around. I told them I'd take them to see the man himself. He can decide to take them on, or not. If not, they're walking home. Or riding a camel."

Watts laughed. "You," he said, looking at Luke. "You got ID on you?"

Luke nodded. "Yeah."

"Roll your window down and hand it to the man standing there."

Luke powered his window down, reached inside his shirt, and came out with his contractor identification card. He handed it to the shaggy-haired gunman outside his window.

"What's your date of birth?" Watts said.

Luke didn't hesitate. "April 23, 1974."

Watts looked at the man holding the ID card. The man nodded.

"What's your sign?" Watts said.

"My sign?"

"Yeah. Your astrology sign."

"Why? You looking for a boyfriend?"

All around them, the gunmen laughed.

"Funny guy," Watts said. "Everybody knows their sign, even if they never read the horoscopes. Except for you, apparently."

"Taurus," Luke said. "The bull."

Ed Newsam had also handed his ID to the men outside his window.

"You there," Watts said. "Where did you grow up?"

"It doesn't say it on my ID."

"Play along, anyway. Just for fun."

Ed shrugged. "East New York."

Watts laughed. "East New York? What's that? Like East St. Louis?"

"It's a neighborhood. In Brooklyn."

"Yeah? What's it like there?"

Ed leveled his gaze at Watts. "It's the pits. Like Tikrit, except the people are tougher, and there's more gunfire."

"You must feel right at home, then."

Ed shrugged again, didn't say anything.

"All right, gentlemen. The gate will open for you now. Cole, your two buddies will surrender their weapons once inside. Parr's getting a little paranoid in his old age. He doesn't like people he doesn't know carrying guns around the house."

"Fair enough," Cole said.

It made sense, certainly. Luke could see the logic in it from their point of view, and it would raise suspicion if he tried to argue against it. But it was also going to make this arrest a bit more complicated.

Just ahead of them, the engine of the bus roared into life with a belch and blat of black smoke, and the old beast pulled slowly forward. The gate was open.

"Here we go, boys," Cole said.

* * *

They left their guns with two men in the courtyard beyond the gate. One of them wore a white skull mask. The other wore a black mask that covered everything but his eyes, like a Ninja warrior.

"Hey, McDonough," Cole said to the man in the skull mask. "How are you doing?"

"Cole," the guy said. "I heard you died."

"Well, I'm back from the dead," Cole said.

The guys in this crew were going insane. To Luke, that much was clear. They no longer tried to present themselves as soldiers, or even military contractors. As their position became more tenuous, and the violence necessary to maintain that position became more extreme, their mode of dress became more bizarre. They were beginning to look like a gang from a *Mad Max* movie.

Weaponless now, Luke and Ed followed Cole through wide marble hallways, open to the air. Luke glanced through the tall, minaret-shaped window openings—the dark Tigris River flowed by. The palace was built right on the river.

"Step lively past those windows, gentlemen," Cole said. He had an AK-47 slung over his shoulder and a handgun strapped at his waist—his friends had let him keep his weapons. "Snipers on the outside sometimes take pot shots at heads they see walking by. I'd hate to see either of you get hurt, for obvious reasons."

His voice echoed off the stonework.

"Cole," Luke said.

Cole glanced back at him.

Luke spoke very low because of the echoes. His voice was barely louder than a hiss. "When I tell you to look at your shoelaces, I want your sidearm in my hand. Do you understand?"

Cole turned around again.

"Cole," Luke said again.

Cole raised a hand. "I got you."

"Fast," Luke said. "Your life depends on it. So do ours."

"Do me a favor," Ed Newsam said.

"Yeah?"

88

"Give me a little heads-up before you do that. I don't want to get caught in the middle of your crossfire."

Luke nodded. "Okay."

"I mean it. Don't do the white man thing and hang me out to dry. I've been down that road before. I don't like it."

"I got you, Ed. I heard you the first time."

They passed through a rotunda with a giant hanging chandelier. The lights were out, but Luke could see a colorful tile mosaic on the ceiling. It looked like moons and stars, but he wasn't quite sure. The pillars in the rotunda were black marble. A wrecked white grand piano sat half on the floor in a corner.

They moved into another room. The ceiling was three stories above their heads. To their right was a large swimming pool filled with shimmering turquoise water. To their left was an older Rolls Royce Silver Shadow, just parked there. It looked like it was still in good shape—at least cosmetically, the war hadn't touched it.

At the far end of the pool was a sort of throne—a wide sofa at the top of three steps, shaped like Aladdin's lamp. Each armrest had a lion's head protruding from its face. The throne could comfortably seat four.

As Luke's eyes became accustomed to the dim light in the room, he noticed a man sitting on the throne—slouching on it was a more accurate description. He had a machine gun draped across his lap.

Edwin Lee Parr.

Parr had red hair, which he had let grow into a ponytail. He also had a long red beard—he no longer looked anything like his USMC or contractor photos. He wore camouflage pants, heavy boots, and a light gray T-shirt. He was long and thin, like a strip of beef jerky—not the massive, muscle-bound freak look so popular among both soldiers and mercenaries these days.

Well, not everybody could hang that kind of muscle on themselves.

There were several other men, sprawled in various chairs around the room. And there was a man floating on his back in the swimming pool. None of them made a move or a sign at the approaching guests. None of them seemed to care.

This must be the headquarters, the throne room of the king. And these other men were his various courtiers and jesters.

"Well, Cole. Back from the dead, I see," the man on the throne said. His voice revealed a slight lilt, almost like a Southern gentleman.

89

"That's what they keep telling me," Cole said. "But it wasn't as bad as all that."

The man nodded, didn't respond.

"I brought you company," Cole said.

"I see," Parr said. "Uninvited company ain't my favorite thing. Popovers, my mama used to call it. People who just popped over were never welcome in our house, I can tell you that." He shook his head and smiled. "Never mind. Who do you have here?"

"Friends, that's the famous Edwin Lee Parr," Cole said, doing his job and identifying the subject. He glanced around the large echoing room at the other men. "Edwin Parr, this here's Ed King and David Dell. Couple of fellas looking to make a little money while they're here in God's country."

"Make a little money, huh?" Parr said. "That what you guys are hoping to do?"

"We heard you're the man to see," Luke said.

Parr shook his head gently. "Not quite. If all you're looking to do is make a little money, I suggest you go back to the Green Zone and visit Uncle Sam at a Marine Corps recruiting station. We're out here making a lot of money. More money than you ever saw in your young lives, and maybe more money than you ever imagined. But you'll risk your lives to get it."

"Sounds good to me," Ed Newsam said. "I've been risking my life for chump change."

Parr pushed himself into a standing position. Was he stoned? Drunk? Hung over? Luke couldn't tell.

"Why should I trust you?" he said.

Luke shrugged. "You shouldn't. You should ask around and find out about us. We're in no hurry. We'll wait. You'll find out we're the real deal."

Parr smiled. "I go on instinct. It's worked for me all this time."

One of the men sprawled in the chairs pushed himself up and followed, an Uzi cradled in his arms. The guy was short and thick, shaped like a thumb. His arms were immense. His neck was like the stump of an oak tree. A tattoo circled it, which looked like a necklace of thorns. He wore a white wife-beater T-shirt, camo pants, and boots. He was bald except for a low, three-inch-wide strip of Mohawk on top of his head. A scar ran down the side of his face.

"Is this guy part of your instinct?" Luke said.

"That's Roger," Parr said. "He's what keeps you honest. I trust you, but I'm a trusting soul. Not Roger. If you try anything stupid, he's gonna kill you. And another thing. You see that door back there?"

Parr pointed to a rounded doorway in the back of the chamber.

"Yeah."

"We're about to pass through that thing. That's the point of no return. You can turn around right now, and go back out onto the street. Find your way home, or wherever you want to go. No harm, no foul. But once you pass through that door there, and you witness the secrets of this palace, there's no coming back. You're either in or you're out after that. And if you're not in, you're dead."

He raised his hands, palms upward, as if to say "Sorry!"

He looked at them for a long moment. His eyes were so bloodshot they seemed to glow in the dim light of the room.

"So what's it gonna be, boys? In or out?"

Ed and Luke looked at each other.

"I'm in, man. I'm sick of being thrown to the wolves for nickels and dimes. This close to millions, I'm not turning back."

Parr nodded. "Good man." He looked at Luke.

"You?"

Luke nodded. "I'm in."

Parr smiled. "Follow the yellow brick road, boys, and I'll show you what I'm talking about. Come along and learn something."

* * *

Parr led them through the door.

Now there was a small entourage moving through the marble hallways. Parr, his bodyguard Roger, Cole, Luke, and Ed. Luke and Ed were the only ones who were not armed.

"We're running a business here," Parr said. "And we treat it like a business. Which means there's a pyramid structure and a chain of command, with me at the top and newbies at the bottom. We do percentage deals. That means if you want to earn, you gotta put in work. What I'm about to show you? You haven't earned any of it, understood?"

He stopped and looked at them both.

"You put in your work, you bring in swag, and then you get a piece of the action. That's how this goes. Also, if I see you putting in work and I like what you're doing, I might see fit to throw you a bonus from the stash that came before you. But as of now? Nada. That's what you're starting with. Zero."

"Fine," Luke said. "I'm good."

"Cool with me," Ed said. "You'll come to find out I'm a go-getter. I don't want anything I didn't get."

Parr raised a finger. His eyes were tired. "Son, when you see what we got here, you might change your mind about that. But be careful. Every man in this building knows his percentage. And they'll kill you if you try to take it."

They came to a solid wooden door. It was round, and inlaid with intricate painted carvings. The knob looked like it might be solid gold.

"This is door number one," Parr said. "Let's see what's behind it, shall we?"

He opened the door and the group followed him into the room. It was a long and low stone chamber, lit by recessed lights in the ceiling. The most obvious feature of the room were the piles of money loaded onto wooden pallets. The piles were nearly man-high, ten-foot-by-ten-foot squares. The money was sectioned into bricks, each brick double-wrapped by rubber bands.

Parr picked up a brick from the first pile.

"American dollars," he said. "The real thing, I think. Each brick is a hundred grand. There's what…" He looked at the bodyguard with the Mohawk. "How many bricks in that pile, Roger?"

The guy shrugged. His voice was low and mellow. "I think they said four hundred. Something like that."

Parr tossed the brick back onto the pile. "You can do the math on that. Never was my strong spot."

They passed another pile of dollars, then another. Both were about the same size as the first one. Then they came to a fourth pile—about the same size as the others, but this time a different currency. Parr picked up a brick.

"British pounds," he said. "They tell me that each pound is worth about two dollars these days. Ain't that something? You'd think it would be the other way around. But the world's been stood on its head just recently."

He moved onto the next pile.

"Euros," he said, without stopping. "They tell me it's about a dollar thirty-five to a euro. Personally, I think that's a disgrace."

They passed another pallet of euros. Quick calculations told Luke that if what Parr was saying was true, there were at least a couple hundred million dollars' worth of stolen currency in this room alone.

He followed Parr to the far end of the chamber. Here was something amazing to see. Pyramids of gold bars, half a dozen of them, all of them four or five feet high.

"We found these underneath a country estate," Parr said. "Cemented behind a false wall down in the wine cellar. Most of the wine was skunked, but some of it was still pretty good. Sorry. We drank it. These people aren't even supposed to have wine. It's against their religion."

"Who lived there?" Luke said.

Parr shrugged. "Rich folks, I guess, maybe friends of Saddam. Must have run off when the bombs started dropping."

The man Roger giggled at that statement. Parr's eyes flashed a warning to him.

"It gets messy out there, kids."

"We've seen it," Ed said.

Parr nodded. "Yeah. I imagine you have. But have you done it? Have you made the mess?"

He turned to face the gold bars again. He waved a hand at them.

"I don't know what to tell you. Five-pound bars, solid gold... at what? Eight hundred, nine hundred dollars an ounce? A couple thousand of them here."

"How are you planning to get all this stuff out of here?" Luke said.

Parr sighed. "Son, you ain't seen nothing yet. We got about thirty-five vintage, cherry luxury cars parked inside this complex. Rolls Royces, Lambos, old race cars from the Monaco days, old James Bond kind of cars... I've never seen anything like it. We've got millions of dollars in old Soviet weaponry. We could take jet airliners down from here. We got rooms full of old pottery and statues, and I mean thousands of years old. Who knows what that stuff is worth? We got paintings—a guy told me he thinks we have a real Pablo Picasso in one of these rooms. Looks like it to him. Me, I couldn't say."

"And you're totally surrounded by enemies," Luke said.

"Yeah," Parr said. "We are. But we do have one card up our sleeve."

They followed Parr through another doorway and down another long, narrow hall. At the end was a metal door.

"Saddam and his people always kept prisoners in these palaces," Parr said. "I guess for when they got bored and decided they wanted to have a little fun."

He opened the door.

Immediately there came a small scream—the sound a startled animal might make—followed by low, muted crying and moaning.

Behind the door was a chamber. It was dim in there. There were no windows, and only one pale yellow light on the ceiling. On both sides of the chamber were several cells—rounded doors hung with vertical iron bars. Luke quickly counted them. There were seven on each side, fourteen in total.

Luke peered inside a cell. The cell had a low ceiling, and four or five women and girls were in there. They cowered toward the back, the women crouched in front of the girls, evidently trying to protect them. He looked up the row. There appeared to be people in every cell.

"Who are they?" Luke said.

Parr shrugged. "Locals. Wives and daughters of imams and big shots. I don't know who they all are. I don't even care. All I know is before we started taking hostages, the bad boys were attacking this place every day. Now they know we got their women, and they come looking to negotiate. Nothing's come of it so far, but these little chickadees could be our ticket out of here."

"What do you tell the husbands?" Ed Newsam said. "You're gonna sell their women to Al Qaeda?"

Parr shook his head. He smiled. "Nah. This is Sunni country around here. Half these guys like Al Qaeda, or are in Al Qaeda. We tell them we're gonna sell their women to the Shiites."

Luke glanced at Cole. Cole had been arrested with a truck full of women and girls. Big Daddy had taught him to say that he was a pimp and a rapist.

"You do anything to them yet?" Luke said.

Parr put a finger to his lips. "Sshhhh. Don't ever talk like that. If the men outside these walls thought for one minute that these girls were ruined, or whatever these barbaric Arab concepts are, they'd blow us all apart in an afternoon. Us, the girls, the wives... we'd all be dead and they wouldn't care. Because of the shame. And they could do it, too. These walls are thick, but our neighbors have anti-tank weapons. The only thing keeping us alive right now is we have hostages, and the men outside think they are safe and intact."

They left the jail and Parr closed the door behind him. He moved ahead down the hallway. They passed into a wide chamber with a two-story ceiling.

"You're trapped in here, Parr," Luke said.

Parr nodded, but didn't bother to turn around. "Yeah. You could say that."

Luke decided that this was as good a time as any. He and Ed were in here with Parr and one other man. They might not get an opportunity like this again. From what Luke had seen, Parr's little army was past it. Their vulnerability had finally dawned on them. If Parr gave up, the rest of them probably would, too.

"Even if you could somehow bargain your way past the local Sunnis, you'll never manage to get all this stuff out of the country. Border guards, Al Qaeda, American military checkpoints, satellites, drones, helicopters… forget it."

Parr simply stood. He still didn't turn.

"You got any ideas?" he said. "I mean, now that you've seen it, you're in. Just like I told you. I can't exactly let you walk out of here."

Luke turned to Cole.

"Cole, look at your shoelace."

It happened fast. But not fast enough.

Was there the slightest hesitation on Cole's part? Maybe.

Worse, he unclipped his gun and flipped it across the five feet to Luke, but his aim was just bad enough that Luke had to step forward and snatch it out of the air. He spun it around and held it in a two-handed grip. He pointed it at Parr.

But Parr's bodyguard Roger already had his own gun down and drew it. Ed Newsam stood between Roger and Luke. Now Roger's Uzi was pointed directly into Ed's broad chest. Ed looked at Luke.

"Dammit! You were supposed to give me a heads-up."

Luke sighed. He was right. "Okay. I know. My bad."

Ed shook his head. "*Your* bad? The man is pointing an Uzi at my chest. This is exactly what I didn't want to happen. I told you that ahead of time, and you did it anyway. I notice no one is pointing a gun at you. This isn't a TV show, man. The black guy is not expendable."

"I made a mistake, Ed."

"Yeah, you did. You made a big mistake."

"Roger, if you shoot that man," Luke said, "I'll blow Parr's brains out."

"If he shoots me… that's terrific, Stone."

Roger shrugged. "I'm not even sure if I care about Parr that much."

Parr turned around.

"What's going on here, sweethearts?"

"Edwin Lee Parr," Luke said, "my name is Agent Luke Stone. I work for the FBI Special Response Team. You are under arrest for murder, kidnapping, crimes against humanity, looting, theft of

95

antiquities, and a host of other felonies. You have the right to remain silent. You should know that if you forfeit this right, anything you say can and will be used against you in a court of law. You have the right to an attorney. If you can't afford an attorney, one will be…"

At that point, Parr began to laugh.

"Son, did you happen to notice that I live in a palace? I'm a wealthy man. Do you think I can't afford an attorney?"

Luke shook his head. "I think you'll be forfeiting most of your wealth."

Parr's smile faded. His face became pained. "You're gonna arrest me for murder? In a place like this? Don't that beat all?"

From the corner of his eye, Luke noticed that Cole had pulled his AK-47 down from his shoulder. He had it ready, but wasn't pointing it at anyone in particular.

"It's over, Parr," Luke said. "There's no way out of here. We're your only chance. You surrender to us, and they'll send you back to the States. You'll get a trial. You'll go to prison." He shrugged. "Maybe there's some defense—fog of war, temporary insanity. Maybe you'll see daylight again one day. But if you stay here…"

Luke shook his head.

"These people are going to cut your heart out."

Parr looked at Cole.

"You did this to me, Cole? You brought these guys in here? You knew about this?"

Cole shrugged. "The CIA had me. They tortured me, Parr. They were gonna kill me. They still might."

Parr gritted his teeth. He shook his head. "You punk traitor. You don't have to wait for the CIA. Roger, kill that man."

Roger had a perfect angle on Cole. He turned his Uzi two feet to his left and fired a short spray. The ugly blat of automatic gunfire was deafening in the rounded chamber, echoing off the walls and ceilings.

Ed Newsam's entire body jerked, almost as if he had taken the bullets instead.

Cole turned just in time to take the shots in his chest. It knocked him backward—he was wearing body armor under his clothes. Cole stumbled but stayed on his feet. Roger hosed him again. This one took Cole's head off above his eyebrows. Bone and blood and brains spewed backward. The shots ricocheted around the room.

Luke's ears were ringing now.

He turned toward Roger. Big Ed's back was in the way.

Ed!" he shouted. "Duck!"

Ed dropped like a trapdoor had opened beneath him.

Luke fired a single shot from his handgun. BANG! It hit Roger directly in the face, punching his features inward. Roger dropped, his Uzi clattering across the floor.

Luke turned back toward Parr.

Parr had his own sidearm out. He raised it to point it at Luke.

Luke pointed his own gun at Parr.

"Drop it!" Luke said.

Parr shook his head. "You drop it."

"Parr…"

"You're stupid, man," Parr said. "This whole thing is stupid."

The two guns came closer. They were inches apart now, and the maw at the end of Parr's gun was like a tunnel, like a cave, like the abyss itself. Luke had been at the point of a gun before, many times. It never got easier.

"Drop that gun!" Luke shouted.

Parr's hands were shaking. Luke saw Parr's gun in a blown-out close-up, like it was a giant poster on a wall. Parr's finger put pressure on the trigger. The gun inched closer, and now the two guns were so close they could almost touch. They were like two nervous lovers, coming together for their first kiss.

BANG!

Luke pulled his trigger and the sound was loud in his ears, deafening. His ears rang and it was like his head was inside a helmet stuffed with cotton. The only sound was the ringing. It went on and on, as if someone had hit a bell with a hammer and then let the vibrations play out, like ripples on a pond.

The shot had hit Parr in the center of his chest.

No body armor for Parr. He was the king of this castle, and he probably hadn't planned on going outside today. A spot of blood appeared on his shirt, then began to spread. Soon it became a lake.

He looked at his chest, then looked at Luke. His left hand reached up and touched the blood on his shirt. His fingers came away red. His jaw hung slack. His eyes were wide with surprise.

His gun was still pointed at Luke.

"Don't you dare pull that trigger," Luke said.

Parr looked at the gun in his hand.

Ed Newsam was standing again. He suddenly walked over and took the gun away. Parr stared at him for a second and then fell to the floor. His head made a noise as it connected with the stonework.

To Luke, it seemed as if he could almost feel the impact through his feet.

Ed turned and pointed Parr's gun at Luke's head. It was a large caliber handgun. The end of the barrel was a gaping maw, a tunnel you could drive a truck through.

He did it so quickly and without hesitation that for a split second Luke really thought Ed was going to shoot him.

"How's it feel, man? You like that?"

Now they pointed their guns at each other, Parr on the floor between them.

Luke gestured with his head at Parr. "Check him."

"I can't believe you just did that," Newsam said. "Are you crazy? First you didn't signal me in any way that you were going to make the arrest, even though I asked you to. You put my life at risk. Then you nearly shot me in the head. I felt the breeze go past my scalp. I'm not a piece of furniture, okay? You want to risk someone's life during an operation, risk your own life."

Luke looked at him. He lowered his own gun. If Ed wanted to shoot him, so be it.

"Check the subject," he said. "Tell me if he's dead or not."

The gun wavered.

"Do *something*. Check him or shoot me. I don't care."

Newsam kneeled and checked Parr's pulse. He shook his head.

"He's gone." He looked up at Luke. "But you and I need to talk."

Luke was already kneeling, sliding his right boot off and ripping the tiny radio transmitter out of the side compartment where it was sewn in. He clicked the button, opened the transmitter to its full length, and held the thin metal antenna to his mouth.

"Swann, you with me?"

Swann's deep voice came across the airwaves. It sounded tinny, like Swann was speaking to him from the bottom of a soup can.

"Stone? I'll be damned. This thing works. We're right here. You guys alive?"

Luke looked at Ed.

"We're alive. We're fine. No injuries. Parr is dead. Cole is dead. Newsam and I have the hostages secured and can protect them. Bring in the choppers. If they ride the loudspeaker and let everybody know what's up, I'll bet they can take this place in about five minutes flat. They should take out the main gate first, which is actually a bus. Once that's gone, these guys can't protect themselves. They'll be looking for friendlies to surrender to."

"Awesome, Luke. Here comes the cavalry. Over."

"Thank you. Over and out."

Luke folded the antenna closed. He looked at Newsam again.

Newsam's eyes were hard. "You and me are gonna talk about this. We get back to base, we're gonna talk for real. We're not in the service anymore. We don't need to worry about rank."

Luke nearly smiled, but then didn't. He thought at first that the guy was putting him on, but now he could see that he wasn't. He was honestly mad.

The operation had been a total success. Parr was dead. In a little while, the 1st Cavalry was going to storm this palace, and the women and girls would be returned to their families. The money and stolen antiquities would be recovered.

Okay, Luke had made a mistake. It put Ed in a dangerous position for a moment. But it had worked out fine.

"What's your problem?" Luke said.

Ed pointed at him. "You're my problem. Rock stars like you. You could have gotten me killed. But the mission would have been a success anyway. I've seen a lot of that in my time. We did what we were sent to do, but oh yeah, spear carrier third from left got wasted. Oh well. Tragic, really, but they're going to bury him at Arlington and his mama's gonna hold the flag."

Luke shook his head. "What do you want me to do? Say I'm sorry?"

Ed's fierce eyes stared. "No. I've heard about you, man. And I'm going to demonstrate to you that I'm not the one you drop in a hole on your way to glory."

"Buddy, you know what they say when you're picking a dancing partner, don't you?"

Ed shook his head. "No. Why don't you tell me?"

Luke nodded. "They say, *Choose wisely.*"

"Is that supposed to scare me? Why, because technically you're my boss? Because you're gonna go above my head and get me in trouble? Because you're gonna threaten my job?"

"No," Luke said. "Because I'm gonna kick your ass."

Ed half-smiled and shook his head. "I can't wait."

"Well, while you savor the anticipation, do you mind if we finish up the mission in the meantime?"

* * *

"Good job, boys. Your mothers will be proud."

The man was talking to Ed and Luke.

99

"This is exactly the kind of trash that needs cleaning up. They're ruining my war zone. I don't like that."

He was a tall, ramrod straight colonel from the 1st Cavalry. He had stepped off a Black Hawk in the wide palace courtyard, wearing a cowboy hat, snakeskin boots, and wraparound sunglasses. He lit up a victory cigar and smiled.

Luke had been right. As soon as the choppers announced over the loudspeakers that Parr was dead, his little ragtag army had rolled over. They hadn't fired a shot. There were less than twenty of them, and they wanted no part of a fight against Black Hawks and Apaches. They were tired. They just wanted to go home and do their time. Maybe they could cop some kind of plea deal, and see daylight again before they were old men.

Then again, maybe not.

Luke watched a group of them being loaded into a chopper. They were daisy-chained together, manacled at the ankles and wrists. Bearded, muscled-up, with long hair or Mohawks, wearing crazy clothes and with tattoos all over them. It had been a game to them. They were stars in a movie only they could see.

Now, they were abject in defeat. Their shoulders were slumped, their heads down. Clean-cut 1st Cav guys moved them along, none too gently.

"What goes up must come down," Ed Newsam said. He said it loud enough for the men in chains to hear him. One of them, a big guy with a thick beard and long blond hair, turned and glared at Ed.

"Yeah, man. I'm talking to you. Enjoy those thirty years inside. I'll be thinking about you when I'm sipping rum and Coke in Barbados."

Just then, the first group of women and girls were brought outside. They squinted in the bright sunlight. It was unfortunate timing. The girls were afraid of the 1st Cav soldiers, as it was. But they cowered when they saw the remains of Parr's militia.

All but one.

An older woman in a long black robe and black headscarf broke off from the group.

"Ma'am?" said one of the young soldiers escorting them. "Ma'am!"

She walked up to Ed's blond friend and spit in his face. She shouted something in Arabic at him. She waved her hand in his face. Two other women came up and pulled her gently by the shoulders. She let them lead her back to the group.

The big blond's hands were pinned at his sides. He had no way to wipe off the woman's spit. The guy chained behind him leaned in and whispered something to him. The blond shook his head.

Ed laughed and nodded. "That guy's having a day." He raised his voice and addressed the guy again. "Having fun, Blondie?"

The guy looked at Ed again. He said something under his breath. It sounded like "Shove it."

Ed's grin was wider than ever. He raised his arms, turned his face to the sun, and took a deep breath. "Light of day, baby. The breath of freedom. It's gonna be a long time before you see or taste either one again."

The 1st Cavalry colonel looked at Luke and Ed.

"You boys need a ride home?"

Luke looked at Ed. "You ready, big man? Or you want to catcall these guys a little more before we go?"

Ed shrugged. "Ready when you are, boss."

CHAPTER FOURTEEN

1:35 p.m. Arabian Standard Time (6:35 a.m. Eastern Daylight Time)
The Embassy of the United States in Iraq (aka the Republican Palace)
The International Zone (aka the Green Zone)
Karkh District
Baghdad, Iraq

It was hot out.

The bright sun, and the heat, went straight to your head.

Luke had changed into khaki pants, boots, and a T-shirt. He needed the upper body freedom that the T-shirt gave him, but he still wanted the kick that the boots would give him. This was a big guy and it was going to take a lot of oomph to finish him.

"Listen," Mark Swann said. "This is ridiculous. You guys don't have to do this."

Luke gestured with his head. "Talk to him."

They were standing in a small stone courtyard. A fountain had once been in this courtyard, but at some point the Americans had ripped it out and paved it over with cement. That seemed a shame, but now it made a perfect little fighting square.

Across the courtyard was Ed Newsam. From here, he looked almost impossibly large, formidable, as invulnerable as a mountain. It would be hard to take him down. He was dressed just the same as Luke—khakis, boots, and a T-shirt.

"This has to be done," Newsam said. "The man nearly got me shot. Then he nearly took my head off himself. You don't know it, because you don't live in that world, but he's got a little reputation for getting people killed, shrugging it off, and moving on. A boss is one thing, and that's fine, but everybody deserves respect. I'm not dying for Hot Rod's next promotion. We're just gonna make that clear."

Luke heard the words coming out of Ed's mouth, but had trouble connecting them to himself. An image of Martinez, paralyzed, missing body parts, and crying flashed through Luke's mind.

We were your guys. Now we're dead. All but you.

Luke shoved that away. He was in a fight. If he didn't dial in, this big man was going to take his head off.

"I'm going to call Don Morris," Trudy said.

"Go ahead," Newsam said. "He'll know I'm right."

Luke and Ed began to circle each other. They moved closer, closer… Somehow, word must have gotten out that a fight was underway. People, mostly men, wandered out of the embassy building. Several soldiers in uniform began to coalesce around the outside of the square. This was old hat to them—fights happened sometimes. They used their bodies to obscure the view of people further away, especially people in authority who might stop the fight prematurely.

Luke glanced at them. A couple of them were MPs.

"Come on, little man," Ed said. "Throw a punch and give these people a show."

"It's your fight," Luke said. "Not mine."

Ed shrugged. "Okay."

He charged, moving like lightning for a man so large. His left fist pinioned out, a jab. Luke slipped it, darted inside, and landed his own jab directly to Ed's face. Then he bounced backward again, out of Ed's reach. He immediately circled to his right.

A small cheer went up from the crowd. David had struck Goliath a blow.

But Luke saw Ed's eyes. That hadn't hurt him a bit. Surprised him? Yes. Frustrated him? Sure. Annoyed him? You bet. But hurt him? Not a chance.

"That all you got?" Ed said.

This was going to be a long war.

Suddenly, someone was clapping their hands. The sound was LOUD. A man's voice came.

"Uh, dummies?"

The crowd was turning toward the man. Luke didn't take his own eyes off Ed, not for a split second. That would be a recipe for disaster. He'd probably wake up on the plane ride home.

"No, not you guys. Them. Those dummies. The tough guys. The rest of you idiots, don't you have someplace to be?"

Luke and Ed continued to circle.

"Stone!" the man shouted, and Luke knew who it was without having to look.

Ed glanced that way, and Luke took the opportunity to back up. He looked to his right. Big Daddy Cronin stood there.

"Don't make me come in there. I'll kill you both dead."

They stared at him.

Now he smiled.

"Nice work this morning, boys. Beautiful. Fast, clean, no collateral damage, makes us look like the good guys for a change. I like that. Even better, it opened up a previously unknown lead."

Luke noticed that he didn't mention Davis Cole at all.

Big Daddy held up a fist. His index finger extended from the top of it and beckoned to them.

"Come with me. We have a visitor."

* * *

Luke and Ed followed Big Daddy through the echoing hallways. Luke was so intent on keeping his eye on Ed, that they were entering a room before he noticed that Swann and Trudy had come with them.

Big Daddy looked at Swann and Trudy in surprise.

"It's okay, Bill," Luke said. "They're with me."

They entered the room. It was a very small chamber, different from the one before, with solid stone walls.

The British intelligence agent Montgomery was here, standing in the corner.

A man sat a wooden table. He wore white robes and a black and white checkered headdress. His beard was black and gray, trending toward white, and he wore thick glasses, which made his eyes seem like fish swimming in twin fishbowls. He stood when the group entered.

He glanced at Big Daddy.

"These are the men?" he said in perfect English.

Big Daddy nodded. "Yes. These are the men who saved your nieces this morning."

He turned to Luke and Ed and extended a hand to each of them. The man's hands were old and frail, but had a firm grip. They stood in an awkward triangle for a moment, holding hands. The man couldn't possibly know that Luke and Ed had just come from a fistfight in the courtyard—a fight resulting from the same mission that saved his family members.

The man squeezed their hands tightly. A tear appeared on one cheek.

"Gentlemen, this is Imam Muhammad al-Barak. He is a tribal elder and religious council leader in the city of Tikrit and the surrounding area. He came here today at great risk to himself and his family."

"The situation is very complicated," he said. "Many in my region are supporters of Saddam. They would like to see the Americans ousted and the government restored. Many others are extremists of the type that would like to see Saddam executed, the Americans ousted, and a Sunni religious government installed."

Luke shrugged. The man was still gripping their hands. "Not a lot of fans of the Americans around."

The man shook his head in all seriousness, missing the irony in Luke's statement. "None," he said simply. "The rabid dogs that you killed this morning did nothing to help the American cause. My sister…"

The man shut his eyes. Now tears streamed freely.

After a moment, he composed himself and spoke again.

"My sister thought her beloved daughters were lost to her. So many young ones were taken. So many in the community thought that those animals… And yet, it seemed impossible to act against them. And the American government would do nothing."

Big Daddy raised a hand. "Well, let's be clear a minute. These guys work for the American government. And so do I."

The imam cast a baleful eye at Big Daddy.

"We petitioned your embassy and your military leaders for months. We described the priceless artifacts being stolen, the people being murdered at will, the complete disregard for human life by these American soldiers—contractors, you call them. The embassy told us it was out of their hands. But these men came, just two men, and ended the disaster in a single morning. And the leader of this carnage is dead. Praise Allah."

The man finally let go of their hands. He gestured at a slim manila envelope that sat on the table.

"In that envelope is my gift to you… and you." He pointed to Luke and Ed in turn. "I ask, in all sincerity, that only you men open it, and only you men make use of what is inside. I consider it a goodwill gesture, and believe me when I say I will know what happens and who is involved."

What was the man offering them—a check? Two tickets on a cruise liner? Plane tickets to a Red Sea resort? For a moment, Luke pictured himself and angry Ed Newsam lying back on lounge chairs side by side, sipping drinks and looking out at the water. It was an odd meeting.

"Oh, we can't accept tips," Luke almost said, but didn't.

"What is it?" he said instead.

"It is a map to a location in the western desert," the man said. "It is a lawless territory, and the people are openly hostile to your government and its plans. The location is a camp, and people are trained there for what you would call terrorism."

"There are many kinds of terrorism," Ed Newsam said.

The man nodded. "Yes."

"Do you want us to bomb the site?" Luke said.

"No. You must go there. There are plans afoot. I have heard rumors. Something is going to happen. The organizers are there, or were. Some of the people involved were trained there in the past— trained to withstand pain, boredom, extremes of heat and cold, physical and psychological torture."

Luke stared at the man. "What are they going to do?"

The imam shook his head. "I don't know. I cannot find out, and if I were to press for details, my life would be forfeit. The things I have already told you, and the map I have left for you, are already enough to see me hung in a public place and bled white."

"And only we can go there?" Luke said.

The man nodded. "That is my request. This was my gift to you. It is a gift of thanks and of common brotherhood. I ask that you honor it in that way."

He stared at them a long moment.

"Your comrades are common dogs to me. Worse than dogs. I would see this entire complex bombed to dust and all its denizens set aflame to die in agony, if Allah would permit it. May it happen this very day. But you are men of honor. You have my undying gratitude, and that of my people."

He looked at Big Daddy again.

"Thank you. I must go."

* * *

"You all heard the man," Montgomery said in his clipped British accent. He was leaning back in a chair, smoking a sweet-smelling cigarette.

He looked at Big Daddy. "This was intelligence offered to these chaps and no one else. If we're to send men into that desert, then I say let it be them. Barak said he would know who went there, and I believe him. There will almost certainly be video feeds or captures which show who infiltrated the camp. He will take it as an insult if the wrong men go."

They were all sitting in yet another room—this one served as Big Daddy and Montgomery's joint intelligence office. It was a haphazard place, with thick plywood as walls, lined with soft egg crate soundproofing. There were three desks, all covered with papers and folders and various vending machine wrappers and empty Coke cans. There were two Toughbook laptops, and wires snaking everywhere.

"Is this really where you hold your top secret meetings?" Mark Swann said. "I mean, look at this place. Nothing about this says Your Eyes Only. I can hear people typing on old IBM Selectric typewriters two makeshift doors away. Is it even safe to talk here?"

Big Daddy shrugged. "Normally we hold secret talks on a windy bridge south of Baghdad where the Madhi Army dumps the dismembered corpses of its enemies into the Tigris River. Would you rather go there?"

Swann shrugged. "Nah. I was teasing you. This'll be fine."

Luke was leaning back. He pulled the images from the envelope closer. They were satellite photos taken from a distance that showed the location of the camp superimposed on a map of Iraq, then progressively zoomed in to show more topographical detail, and finally more detail of the camp itself.

The camp wasn't much to look at—a cluster of tents, a couple of low stone houses, and some corrugated aluminum buildings in a barren desert north and west of the Sunni Triangle. There looked to be a firing range. There was a helipad and an old airstrip—the airstrip was narrow, short, and in a state of disrepair that suggested only very small and light planes could get in there, flown by people who weren't too picky about whether they lived or died.

"The place looks abandoned," Luke said. "I don't see a single car or truck. I don't see any movement. I don't see an active roadway. I don't see evidence of garbage burns, or recent activity on that firing range. I don't think there's anybody there."

Luke didn't like to look at the photos. He didn't like them because he had carried out the mission he had been assigned, and he had done it quickly. He had killed two men this morning, and he didn't enjoy killing. They had been here a little over twenty-four hours, and he wanted to go home. His wife was pregnant with their first child. He wanted to get back to her, hug her, and reassure her that he loved her and wanted to be with her always.

He also didn't like to look at them because he knew what was going to happen next. He and Ed Newsam were going to helicopter out to the desert, probably this very afternoon, and they were going to arrive at that camp before sundown.

What were they going to find there? If Luke had to guess, he'd say they were going to find dead bodies in those tents, decomposing in the baking heat of the desert, swarming with flies.

This was the gift the grateful imam had given him—the opportunity to find a pile of corpses of militants who had become expendable, and whatever mystery that solved or made more complicated for people like Big Daddy Cronin.

"What do you think, boys?" Big Daddy said. "You could go out there, check the place out, grab anything interesting, and be home for supper. Tomorrow morning you can be on your way home to the States. Monty's right. It's on you. The man offered it to you as gift."

"I've gotten better gifts," Newsam said.

* * *

The phone was ringing half a world away.

Luke sat at a makeshift desk carrel—like everything around here, it had been built with raw plywood. There was a bank of a dozen such carrels in a row, lined up in an echoing marble hallway. A person sat at every single one of them.

There was an office telephone console on the desk in front of Luke, and after several tries, he had managed to dial out to an international operator, who had put the call through. The handset was pressed to his right ear, and he inserted a finger in his left ear to drown out the clatter and buzz of typing, conversations, laughter, and just plain noise all around him.

His heart skipped a beat.

Pick it up.

The ringing stopped.

"Hello?"

It was her. Becca. Amazingly, she sounded clear, as if she were sitting right in front of him. He pictured her standing, or actually, more likely sitting, in the kitchen of the country house, the old phone mounted on the wall, the handset attached to a long, curly black wire.

"How you doing, baby?" he said.

"Luke?"

"The very same."

She breathed heavily. "Oh my God. I've been so worried about you."

"It's okay," he said. "Everything's okay. This is the first chance I've had to call."

There was trepidation in her voice. "Did you go on your mission yet?"

"Yeah. It's all set. We did it this morning. It went off without a hitch. We were back here by lunchtime, had a couple of debriefings, and… you know."

The air seemed to leak out of her. "That's a relief. When are you coming home?"

"As soon as we can. Tomorrow, maybe. Hopefully tomorrow."

"Good. I can't wait to see you."

"Me too," he said. "I can't wait to see you." He meant every word of it. He couldn't wait to see his wife. He couldn't wait to get out of here. He wanted nothing more than to get on a plane. He would do it right now, if he could.

A shadow passed across his mind—in an hour, he and Ed Newsam were supposed to get on a helicopter to the western desert and investigate that camp. He had a bad feeling about that. Everything seemed to give him a bad feeling these days. He wondered if there would ever be a return to the time before the Afghanistan mission, a time before this terrible feeling of dread that seemed to follow him everywhere.

"How are you feeling?" he said to Becca.

"Honey, I am very, very pregnant now. It just seemed to hit me after you left. I feel like I've gained ten pounds in the past day. I'm eating like crazy. I think this is going to be a very big boy."

"But no labor pains?"

The thought of Becca going into labor while he was away was another point of dread for him. He wanted to be there when his son was born. He wanted to be with her and support her, and he wanted to witness the miracle himself.

He had seen a lot of death in the past fourteen years. It would be a very nice change to watch life begin.

"Uh, you know… I don't think so."

"You don't *think* so?"

"I'm a little uncomfortable, but it's nothing I'd call labor pains."

More fear. The idea of her going into labor out there at the house, alone, in the middle of the Eastern Shore countryside… that did not appeal to him. He wanted that baby born at a major medical center in the city, with all the technology, and the best doctors on duty. Some country doctor at a medical clinic…

He shook his head and took a deep breath. Okay, it's okay. People have been coming into this world for a long time. Country doctors have delivered a lot of babies.

"Honey, if you think you might be going into labor, or that it might happen in the next day or two, why don't you drive over to your mom and dad's place? You'll be close to the hospital then. I can meet you there."

"Okay, Luke. If I feel that way, I will. I was waiting for you to be here."

"Okay. Well, let's not wait until you feel that way. Let's anticipate and let's act before the thing happens. If you wait until you go into labor to make that move, then it's already too late."

He hated the tone of his voice. He hated the worst-case scenario planning that his mind went to naturally, and imposed on everyone and everything, including his personal life. It had kept him alive all this time, but...

"Luke..."

"Yeah, babe, I'm just trying to—"

"I love you, honey. Everything is all right. I'm not in labor."

He stopped.

"Okay. I know that. I love you, too. I love hearing the sound of your voice."

Someone tapped him on the shoulder. He glanced behind him. It was Mark Swann. Swann was a big grinning stork, a doofus in yellow-tinted aviator glasses and a ponytail, standing there.

Behind Swann, a line of people were waiting for the telephone.

"How is it there?" Luke said.

"How is it?" she said.

"Yeah. What does it look like?"

"Well," she said. "It's really beautiful. Spring is in full bloom. I'm sitting at the kitchen table, looking out at Chesapeake Bay, which is sort of sun-dappled, I guess you'd say. There's a big colorful sailboat out there with twin masts."

He closed his eyes and pictured it.

Swann tapped him again. If he did it a third time, Luke was going to break his hand off. At the elbow.

"Honey, I've still got to take care of a couple of things related to the mission before the day is over," he said. "You know, tying up loose ends. I've got people tapping me on the shoulder right now."

He was about to fly into disputed territory, possible combat, and he was not telling her this. He shook his head. He hated this part. He was lying, not directly, but by omission, in the same way he hadn't told her that he killed two men this morning.

She knew so little about what he did. Would she welcome a bloodstained killer back into her arms?

"Okay, sweetie," she said. "You run. I'm glad you're safe. I'm so happy to hear your voice. I hope they let you out of there tomorrow."

"Me, too," he said.

"I love you," she said.

"I love you."

After they hung up, he looked at Swann.

"What?"

Swann's dopey grin faltered for a second. Was the man high? He could picture that easily. Swann looked exactly like someone who probably went out for smoke breaks, and smoked dope instead of a cigarette.

"They sent me to get you," he said. "They're ready for this mission to roll ASAP."

CHAPTER FIFTEEN

5:50 p.m. Arabian Standard Time (10:50 a.m. Eastern Daylight Time)
The Hamad Desert
Western Iraq

They called it the Little Bird. Sometimes they called it the Flying Egg.

It was the MH-6 helicopter—fast and light, highly maneuverable, the kind of chopper that didn't need room to land. It could come down on small rooftops, and on narrow roadways in crowded neighborhoods. It was the chopper most beloved by special operations forces. Luke and Ed rode in one out into the stark high desert of western Iraq.

The surreal, undulating desert landscape below them was orange-yellow with vast blackened, sunblasted regions. Parts of it looked like parking lot blacktop. The sky was pale blue, with the giant orange orb of the sun moving toward the horizon. It was an alien landscape. Hot winds blew in through the open bay doors.

Luke knew they were being followed by two Apache helicopter gunships—armored and armed to the teeth with thirty-millimeter miniguns and Hydra rockets. The Apaches were flying high above them, and well to the south. But they were outfitted with state of the art radar and ground video systems. They could see well enough.

Luke and Ed were not talking.

Ed's bulk slouched beside him in the cramped compartment. They both wore flight suits and helmets. Luke wore a heavy tactical vest, as did Ed. The weight had settled onto Luke, making him feel as if gravity had doubled. His pants were lined with lightweight armor.

Luke was armed with his MP5 submachine gun and a Remington pump-action shotgun. He felt the heft of both guns. They were heavy. The weight was reassuring. The MP5 was loaded with armor-piercing rounds. If there were bad guys here, those rounds should punch through most body armor they could be wearing. Luke had half a dozen magazines fully loaded, just in case he needed them.

In Delta, they let you carry what you wanted—what you felt would be effective. Don kept that tradition intact.

The sounds of the chopper blades and the winds were nearly deafening, but he and Ed could talk if they wanted to. So far, they hadn't. But Luke felt he should try to mend fences a little bit. It was hard to go into combat sitting next to a man who hated him.

"Ed!" Luke shouted.

Ed nodded, but didn't say anything.

"You got a problem with me? That's fine! But don't get me killed out here! Okay?"

Ed looked at him with squinted eyes. "What do you take me for, man?"

"An angry kid!"

"I'm a professional," Ed said. He raised a big, gloved fist. "I'll hurt you with this. But I ain't gonna let these men out here hurt you. Ruin my enjoyment?"

He shook his head.

"Unh-uh."

Luke nodded.

"Good enough. Just remember who's in charge."

The pilot's voice appeared inside Luke's headset.

"Guys! ETA two minutes. Two minutes to the drop site. This is a touch and go, just like we said in the briefing. So when I set it down, do your thing, or you'll be hanging off my rails. Two minutes."

Luke and Ed grabbed their weapons and clambered out onto the wooden side-mounted bench seats, their legs dangling in the air. The chopper adjusted to the redistribution of weight.

They came in low over the camp, just above a cluster of tents, their entry flaps blowing in the wind. The camp was bigger than it had looked in the satellite photos—much of it had been deliberately obscured by sand-colored tarps. Still, the place seemed like a ghost town. No one was out.

The Little Bird pilot hit the old helipad directly in the middle. He touched down and both men slid out onto the hard-packed desert gravel. Three seconds later, the chopper was back in the air.

Luke and Ed ran across the dusty campsite, holing up in the shade of a low cinderblock outbuilding. The chopper banked hard to the right, turning toward the north and east, out of harm's way. Within seconds, it was a speck moving higher and now turning toward the south. It would circle at a safe distance until they called it back.

"Okay," Ed said. "You're the boss. What first?"

Luke gestured with his head. "Those large tents in the middle there. I'd say that is, or was, the headquarters."

"What about these buildings?" Ed said.

"Food storage and weapons storage, if I had to guess."

Ed nodded, then shrugged, as if he wasn't sure.

"What do you think they are?" Luke said.

"I have no idea, white man. They pay you to do the thinking."

"Don't think in that case," Luke said. "Guess."

Ed peered around the corner at the tents blowing in the wind. "Those tents are half-collapsed, look like they been sitting out here in the weather by themselves for days, if not weeks. My guess? If we don't find dead people inside them, they're decoys. From the air, they make this place look abandoned, or like somebody wiped it out. If the place is still active, then at least one of these buildings is the entrance to a bunker, or underground complex. If I was a bad guy right now, I'd be playing dead, and doing it where nobody could see me. You can't hide this camp from satellites, but you can make it look like nobody's home."

Luke nodded. "Okay. I like that. What do you say we cross over there, see what we find in the tents? Maybe what we're looking for is there."

Ed gazed across the open terrain toward the tents. "You gonna get me killed out there?"

Luke shook his head. "You cover me. I'll go first."

Ed smiled, just a bit. "See what I mean? A little respect, that's all I ask. Recognize that I'm alive too."

Luke didn't touch any of that. "On your go," he said.

Ed waited a beat. He took a breath. "Go."

Luke took off. The sky was huge above him. His feet pounded and arms pumped as he dashed across the open space, totally exposed. The main tent seemed like it was miles away. A second later, he was there. He burst through the entryway and inside.

Inside, it was darker and cooler than outside.

Luke lay on the floor, breathing hard for a few seconds. He looked around. There was nothing in the tent. Nothing at all.

He moved to the opening, took out his gun, and got ready to lay covering fire.

Ed ran across the fifty-yard gap. No one took a shot. Nothing moved.

Ed crouched near him. His big face was red and sweaty. It was hot out there.

"Uh-oh," Luke said. "Looks like you might be a little…"

Suddenly, a tracer ripped through the thick canvas of the tent, a few feet above their heads. It tore a hole out the other side as it went.

"Dammit!" Luke shouted. "Down! Get down!"

Ed hit the ground.

An instant later, gunfire was strafing the air just above their heads. There was no sense even trying to fight back. They lay in place. Their one saving grace was the bad guys couldn't see them and didn't know exactly where they were. But if they stayed here very long, they would be dead men. Luke pulled out his radio.

"Viper One, Viper One, come in," he said, calling the name of the lead Apache helicopter.

A Texas drawl answered him. "Viper One, over."

"We got problems down here!" Luke shouted.

"We see it," the Texas drawl said. "We are en route to your position."

"What does it look like?" Luke said.

"Uh, about twenty... scratch that. Thirty fighters or thereabouts, emerging from two stone buildings, and converging on a cluster of tents."

"We're in those tents!" Luke shouted.

"Roger that. Keep your heads down, boys. It's about to get hot down there."

"Watch the tents!" Ed screamed.

A few seconds later, a sound came. It was low at first, building and becoming louder, a whistling sound. Then it was a shriek, still coming, impossibly loud.

Still coming. It split the day apart. Luke tore his helmet off and covered his ears.

It screamed by overhead. Somewhere nearby, an explosion rent the air.

BA-BOOOOM.

A blast of heat roiled the air inside the tent.

Luke crawled like a worm toward the edge of the tent. He pulled a canvas flap up an inch from the ground.

Outside, men were running. One of the low outbuildings was on fire. The bad guys were no longer interested in Luke and Ed. They knew what was above their heads, and they knew how bad it was. There was nowhere to run, but they tried anyway.

The sound of a chopper's rotor blades beat the ground as it made a low pass. An ugly blat of automatic gunfire ripped the sky as its mini-gun opened up. Luke saw men come apart as they ran, arms, legs, and heads flying in different directions, foundations spraying blood before falling to the ground.

He looked away.

Another Hydra rocket sounded, the missile whistling, then shrieking.

Luke rolled away from the tent edge and curled into a ball. He saw that Ed had already done so.

BA-BOOOOOM.

Now another mini-gun opened up.

The choppers were up there, just above them, clearing this space. He prayed they didn't clear this tent by accident.

Luke went into a vague state of mind. It almost seemed like he was dreaming. Somewhere, Becca lay on an operating table, giving birth to his son. Somewhere, Martinez lay in a hospital bed, begging Luke to kill him. Somewhere, Captain Ahab's ship was sunk by a gigantic white whale.

At some point, the shooting and bombing stopped.

Quiet descended, and Luke could hear the sound of the desert wind again. Outside, it was evening, and the sky was dark, and it was also red, yellow, and orange. He could hear the crackling of flames.

"Ground Hog..." the radio said. "Come in, Ground Hog. This is Viper One. Viper One, calling Ground Hog. Stone, are you alive? Stone!"

Luke crawled to the radio.

Across the way, Ed was still curled into a ball, staring at him. Ed was smart. He still had his helmet on.

Luke picked up the radio.

"Viper One, this is Ground Hog. We are alive and well."

"Ground Hog, this is Viper One," the drawl said. "Your zone is cleared of enemy. We are on patrol above your location, and are unopposed. We have a relayed message from the King. If you are operational, then conduct your search."

"Copy," Luke said.

He looked at Ed.

"I told you, man," Ed said. "These tents were a decoy."

They walked out into the night desert air. Much of the camp was on fire. Bodies of enemy fighters lay all across the ground, many of them ripped to shreds. For a moment, Luke remembered that morning in eastern Afghanistan, but that wasn't like this. Most of those Taliban had died in close quarter fighting and from small arms fire. Their bodies were largely intact. These men had been eviscerated by the Apaches.

116

A couple of the outbuildings must have been weapons storage—they had blown apart when hit by the rockets, and now black, oily smoke was pouring into the sky.

"Didn't leave us much to search, did they?"

Luke and Ed walked to a corrugated steel hut that had barely been hit in the fighting. It was pockmarked with fist-sized holes from the mini-guns, but beyond that, it was in good shape. A padlock held the door shut.

Ed smashed the lock off with his rifle.

They slid the door back. Both Luke and Ed went to their headlamps. They shined their lights around the room inside. It took Luke's eyes a moment to adjust to the lighting. Then he couldn't quite believe what he was looking at.

"What is this stuff doing here?"

CHAPTER SIXTEEN

10:45 p.m. Central European Summer Time (4:45 p.m. Eastern Daylight Time)
Institut Le Rosey
Rolle, Switzerland

"Good night, babe," Rita said, loud enough to be heard.

"Good night, babe," Elizabeth called. "Have fun."

"You too," Rita said.

"Yeah," Elizabeth said. "Fun as always."

Elizabeth almost couldn't believe she was going through with it.

Rita had called for the car service, and it had just passed through the front gates of the school. She was dressed and headed out the door. She wore a tight minidress that hugged her curves. Her long hair hung straight down. She wore heavy makeup with black eyeliner, black lipstick and sparkly glitter, torn stockings, and black high heels. She looked sexy, and trashy, like she was going to a monster ball.

She held up a piece of paper just before she pulled open the front door of her suite.

YOU CAN DO THIS

Then she crumbled up the paper and stuck it in her tiny, glittery purse.

"Night," she said, and opened the door.

Elizabeth went back through the bathroom and into her own suite of rooms. She almost couldn't breathe, she was so excited. Excited, nervous, terrified. The walls of the suite seemed to close in, then expand, almost as if the place itself was breathing.

She checked her preparations. At the moment, she was wearing a pair of gray sweatpants and a long-sleeved T-shirt. The T-shirt was made out of long-john-type material—the nights were still chilly here in the mountains. She had sneakers on her feet.

She had a bookbag packed with her own minidress, high heels, makeup, and cell phone. The TV in her living area was on, loud, like she had been playing it for months—loud enough for the man out in the hall to hear it. Her window out to the roof was already open.

She was in the habit of ignoring her Secret Service man at night, and just going to bed without telling him. The way she played it, she would turn off the lights and leave the TV set on. Then she would watch in the dark. It was a perfectly normal thing to do.

She did that now.

She sat for a moment in the eerie glow of the TV, and the night. A show was on an American satellite station—a show about New Jersey mobsters she had long enjoyed—but she couldn't focus on it right now.

It was now or never. Rita was going to wait five extra minutes, then go.

If it was going to happen, it was all on Elizabeth's shoulders. As it should be. This wasn't Rita's problem. This wasn't Rita's part. She had helped Elizabeth concoct the plan, but Elizabeth had to seize the freedom for herself.

One night. One crazy night of fun, madness, daring, and rebellion, and she would never be able to do this again. From now on, her security would be so tight, she'd be lucky to be able to move from room to room without a big man in a suit, with an earpiece, looking over her shoulder.

Okay. Let's do this.

She stood silently and picked up her bookbag.

She moved toward the window. She still didn't have to do it. She hadn't committed yet. She could turn back at any moment. If the Secret Service man suddenly burst in, she could still explain it away. She was just… standing by the window… breathing in the night air… with a bookbag in her hand.

And in the bookbag were clothes to go out clubbing.

Stop it! Just go!

So she did. She raised a leg and stuck it out the window. The roof was below floor level here, so she had to sit up on the windowsill for a second. She dropped down to the roof with a light *thump.*

Oh God! Did he hear that?

She crouched down and looked back through the window at the front door to her apartment. There was light under the door from the hallway. She felt like she could almost see the shadow of her bodyguard standing out there.

No one came. The man didn't knock or make any move to open her door.

She shrugged to herself, turned, and moved quickly and quietly across the slate roof. It was angled slightly downward. In a moment, she reached the corner. She got down on her knees and felt underneath. The rain gutter was there, just as Rita said it would be.

Elizabeth looked across lawn, and there, maybe a hundred yards away, a black car was parked in the turnaround, its headlights on, waiting. At night, there was a second Secret Service man stationed at the front door of the dormitory, and she knew that every thirty minutes or so he would take a walk around the building.

Let's hope that walk doesn't happen now.

She slipped the backpack over her shoulders. Now here came the tricky part. She reached both hands under the roof, then swung her entire body over. Her legs followed her torso and hit the stucco wall hard, scraping her knee.

That hurt, but she held on—the remnants of her gymnastics training as a young girl were still with her. Now she shimmied down, holding the pipe with her hands, her feet walking down the wall. It was easy.

Near the ground, she dropped and rolled backward onto her butt on the wet grass. She lay there for a moment, breathing deeply.

Holy moly! She had just done that. That was some James Bond stuff.

Then it occurred to her that Rita had already done the same thing at least twice. Okay. She jumped up, turned, and ran across the lawn to the waiting car.

It seemed to take forever to reach it.

The rear door popped open as she approached. She practically dove inside.

Rita was there, inside the luxurious black car. She smiled. There was a piece of paper on her lap.

DON'T TALK ABOUT IT

Elizabeth nodded, pulled the door shut, and smiled. Now they were inside the car and behind smoked glass. No one could see them in here.

"You ready?" Rita said.

Elizabeth was out of breath, but tried to speak calmly. "Finally."

The car rolled slowly across campus. Elizabeth looked at the driver behind the glass partition. He was piloting the car with extreme caution—he probably didn't want to run over the child of a Russian gangster. He was a blond-haired guy, middle-aged, and didn't seem the slightest bit interested in either Elizabeth or Rita.

They approached the gate and the guardhouse. Elizabeth held her breath.

The guard on duty barely glanced at them. He was inside the lighted guardhouse, doing something with paperwork. He looked up and raised a hand. The wrought iron gate slid open.

They were out!

As they pulled away from the campus, Rita squeezed Elizabeth's hand.

The driver opened his window a crack and lit a cigarette.

"Next stop, Geneva," he said over the car's intercom.

Rita looked at Elizabeth.

"This is going to be a fun night," she said.

CHAPTER SEVENTEEN

11:55 p.m. Arabian Standard Time (4:55 p.m. Eastern Daylight Time)
The Embassy of the United States in Iraq (aka the Republican Palace)
The International Zone (aka the Green Zone)
Karkh District
Baghdad, Iraq

"It's a very strange thing."

Luke shook his head. "I know it."

He was sitting across the plywood conference table from Trudy Wellington and Mark Swann. In the center of the table was a black plastic octopus that up until a few moments ago had been speaking as though it was Don Morris. It was a speakerphone, and Don had patched through on a call from the United States.

The meeting had just broken up. Ed Newsam had been here, but after the meeting was over, he had left in a huff. He and Luke had been in combat together twice now, had completed two successful missions, and were still no closer to friends. Big Daddy Cronin and his British alter-ego, Montgomery, had been here as well, but they had slid away to whisper together about possibilities.

That left Luke leaning back in an old wooden office chair, picking the brains of the young intelligence agents still in the room with him.

The corrugated hut at the desert camp had been full of clothes. Not just clothes, but Western-style clothes—the type of clothes that young people would wear in rich Western democracies. European fashions, American jeans and T-shirt ensembles, leather jackets and boots, sunglasses and jewelry. The jewelry might be very convincing costume jewelry, or it might be the real thing—it was all being investigated, and Luke hadn't heard anything about it yet. Knowing Iraq, and from what he had seen this morning, he guessed the jewelry was real gold, real diamonds.

There had also been laptop computers in the hut, along with cell phones, MP3 players, video cameras, and personal digital assistants. There were stacks of maps—in particular maps of downtowns and nightclub districts in places like New York, San

Francisco, Berlin, Paris, Madrid, and London, along with a host of more minor cities like Geneva, Bruges, Liverpool, Dublin, and Prague.

"It's not that strange," Swann said.

"Good, I'm glad to hear it," Luke said. "What is it?"

Swann shrugged. "It's infiltration. Like I've been saying all along. The one laptop I got a chance to look at was loaded with language software. French, Dutch, German, English. From beginner to level five conversational proficiency. Like Don and Big Daddy said, when the second team went down below, one of the rooms still intact in the bunker was set up as a classroom. They were training people to assimilate. They were going to, or already have, sent people to Europe and the United States, pretending to be exchange students, native speakers, world travelers, whatever you like."

Luke believed that was true. "I think that part is obvious on its face. But what about the codes?"

Much of the paperwork, and the computer files, were written in complex codes that, at least in the past several hours, no one had been able to break. The concern was, of course, that moles had been sent out into Western countries to prepare for an attack of some kind, or a series of attacks.

As it was, the camp had been quarantined soon after Luke and Ed secured the place. They had been rushed out of there, and a forensic team brought in. Nearly all the materials onsite had been confiscated and disappeared. Luke assumed that the CIA or NSA had the stuff now. If Big Daddy knew anything about it, he wasn't saying.

For his part, Don had commended his team on a job well done, and told them to come on home on the first plane.

That was good enough for Luke. Nearly dying twice was plenty for one day.

Swann stood up, as if to go. He shrugged. "The codes explain the operation—they give the aliases and locations of the infiltrators, and the instructions for where and when to launch the attack. Maybe. Or maybe they're the recipes for killer tabbouleh. Who knows? I guess that's not our department now. And I'm happy to let the big brains upstairs try to puzzle it out. I'm going to go curl up on a cot in a corner somewhere and get some sleep."

He paused just before leaving. He looked down at Trudy and grinned.

"Care to join me?"

She smiled. "On your cot?"

"I'll find us a nice comfy one."

She shook her head. "Sadly, I don't think there will be enough room for you, me, and your legs."

Swann shrugged. His grin faltered only the tiniest amount.

"Your loss," he said, and went out.

Now Luke and Trudy were alone. He stared at her for a bit. She looked like someone who had no business being here in Baghdad. She was very pretty, thin, with big eyes behind her owl-like glasses. She was young, just out of her teens, even though she had graduated from MIT a few years before. Luke knew Don thought highly of her. Don felt that she had the potential to be one of the best intelligence analysts in the business. Actually, Don felt that she had the potential to be one of the best whatever she decided she wanted to be. Luke suspected that Don was a little bit smitten with her, and more than in just a daughterly way.

Luke could see it. If you looked at her long enough, you began to fall into her deep blue eyes. There was a mystery in there.

"What about you?" he said.

"What about me?"

"What do you think about the camp? Strange place to train young metrosexuals to hang out in Paris nightclubs. No?"

She paused for a moment, as if gathering her thoughts. She had barely spoken during the meeting. She was the youngest person in the room, and the only woman. Don had prodded her a bit, but still hadn't gotten much from her. Big Daddy and Montgomery didn't seem interested in her opinion.

"Well, yes and no," she said. "Let's suppose that camp existed during Saddam's reign. It was well built, with an extensive tunnel system, air conditioning to protect the computer equipment, and lodging for the trainees. No one built all that on the fly since the war started."

True enough. Luke nodded. "Seems fair."

"Okay, then that suggests it was Saddam's government that organized the camp, and that they were training spies, or maybe sleeper cells to carry out terrorist attacks or assassinations in Europe or the United States. It looks like they recruited young people— from the clothes, mostly young men. Maybe they chose them for their intelligence level, or their proficiency with language, or their athletic ability, or maybe even just their looks or their fashion sense. So they bring them to a camp well away from the rest of the society, in the far-flung, inhospitable desert. Why?"

Luke shrugged and smiled. "You tell me."

"Cross training, for one. They can spend most of their time learning to look, speak, and act like Westerners or rich kids from upper-class Arab families. But they can also train with heavy weapons in the desert, far from any prying eyes. They can do survival and extreme climate training. The Western party kid is a cover story, anyway. When push comes to shove, they're probably going to be called upon to kill people, and be killed, or continue to function while uncomfortable, or wounded and in terrible pain. What better place to be uncomfortable or in pain?"

Luke raised a finger. "Good. I like it. You said cross training for one. What else?"

She shrugged and smiled. "Easy. That camp is pretty far from civilization. Far enough away for the trainees to maintain their focus. But it's a four-and-a-half-hour drive from here—close enough that the trainees can go home and see mom and dad during breaks."

Luke returned the smile. "I can see what Don sees in you."

A blush crept up Trudy's face. She shook her head. Then she looked up and stared right at Luke.

"You want to see if there's any place still open to get a drink around here?"

"Are you old enough to drink?" he said.

Now her blush deepened. "You bet I am, buster."

For a split second, Luke entertained the idea. A drink with a beautiful young woman in a far-flung and dangerous place. In another life, he wouldn't mind seeing where such a drink might lead. But it was after midnight here in Iraq, which meant it was mid-afternoon on the Eastern Shore of Maryland.

"I'd love to get a drink with you," he said. "But I need to call my wife before I go to bed. She's going to give birth to our son pretty soon, and I want to remind her to wait until I get there."

Trudy shrugged and smiled, just as Swann had done.

"Your loss," she said.

CHAPTER EIGHTEEN

May 8
12:30 a.m. Central European Summer Time (6:30 p.m. Eastern
Daylight Time, May 7)
The Baroque Club
Rue du Rhone
Geneva, Switzerland

The night glittered.

The car nosed slowly through the crowded streets of Rue du Rhone—the street level stores, now closed, a paradise of the most famous and desirable brands on Earth. Louis Vuitton was here, and Prada, and Omega watches, and Tiffany jewelers. There were chocolatiers and coffee shops, and all the beautiful people, walking and mingling and laughing in sweaters and scarves wrapped around their necks.

Of course, Elizabeth had visited this street before, but never at night. They were a block from where Lake Geneva emptied into the Rhone River, and she kept catching glimpses of it down alleyways and side streets.

"They know me here," Rita was saying. "Just stick close, arm in arm. Act naturally, and follow me in. The sea will part for us, and if you act like it's the most normal thing in the world, we won't have any problems."

Elizabeth had already stripped down to her underwear and changed her clothes in front of the driver, who pretended he wasn't looking, but kept taking glances in the rearview mirror. After that little adventure, following Rita into a club should be a snap.

"They don't care about our age?" Elizabeth said. She already knew the answer because Rita must have explained it to her on a dozen occasions, but she wanted to hear it one last time. It might help to calm her nerves.

Supposedly, the age required to enter these bars was twenty-one.

Rita shrugged. "Age is for the peasants. We are the elite. We do what we want, and we go where we want. The normal rules do not apply."

Elizabeth nodded at the truth of this. The idea was disturbing and exciting and troubling and freeing all at once. Millions of people—billions of people!—were leading their normal, average, everyday lives. But Rita was the granddaughter of publishing billionaires. And Elizabeth was the daughter of the President of the United States. Nothing about them was normal, or average.

They were like exotic birds, flying high above the crowds below.

The car pulled up across the street from the club. Elizabeth stared out the window at it. There must have been a hundred people waiting to get inside, all lined up along the wall, separated from the street by a red velvet rope.

"Rita, there's a lot of…"

Rita put a finger to her lips. "Trust," she said.

The partition between them and the driver slid down. The smell of his cigarette smoke entered their section. Rita handed the man a stack of cash. He didn't bother to count it—he must know it was more than generous.

"I will call you," she told the man. "Maybe four a.m.? Maybe later."

He shrugged and nodded. "Is okay. Anytime. I'll be around."

"We'll leave this bag with you," Rita said, handing Elizabeth's knapsack through the opening. The man took it without expression.

"It's safe with me."

"My ID's in there," Elizabeth said. Her school identification card, her Texas driver's license, her passport—they were all in the bag.

"Better if you don't have it on you," Rita said. "There'll be less questions that way. Come on!"

"Have fun, little girls," the driver said.

They crossed the street, arm-in-arm, just as Rita instructed.

"Laugh like we're already drunk!" she shouted, as though she was drunk and having a great time.

Elizabeth did her best to match Rita's exuberance. They approached the velvet rope. A big man by the front door to the club saw them coming. He pulled the rope aside. Just before they crossed the threshold, Rita turned and pulled three young guys off the line. As Elizabeth looked on, she suddenly realized that one of the guys was Ahmet.

He wore a black leather jacket and jeans. He had a blue scarf around his neck. He looked at her, then quickly looked away as if he was shy. Then he looked at her again and smiled.

Elizabeth laughed.

Suddenly they were through the door and inside the club, a group of five young people, three guys and two girls. The lighting inside the club was purple. Everything was gleaming—the bar, the dance floor, the metal railings. The floor was crowded, people barely dancing, but standing nearly cheek to cheek.

Loud music pounded, the bass pumping below their feet, the lights pulsating.

Elizabeth pressed through the crowd, following Rita toward the back. There was a room back there, with tables and sofas, a VIP section, purple lights swirling. That's where they were headed—to their own private table.

It was an amazing night already. Everything about it was incredible, impossible, just the most... she didn't even have words for it. She was having the time of her life. Her mom and dad were going to kill her. She would be lucky if this little adventure didn't make the newspapers.

Relax... relax... have fun.

She tried to remember to *breathe.*

* * *

A bottle of vodka came, along with a bottle of champagne.

Rita always spent money like water.

Ahmet poured drinks for everyone, including, most of all, for himself. Ahmet needed alcohol to calm his nerves. As soon as he had the glass of vodka and ice in his fist, he took a large gulp of it. The fire roared down his throat and into his belly. He took another gulp. Instantly, it sent its fingers into his brain, unlocking the machinery that had seized up. He became dizzy for a moment, and then he became himself.

It was against his parents' religion, and against every tenet of how he was raised, of course. But those things didn't matter when you were sent abroad. Westerners drank alcohol. Westerners partied. So to fit in, that's what you did.

And Ahmet liked alcohol. It made him feel relaxed. It made him feel more like Ahmet, if that was possible. It was as if he had been trying to be Ahmet his whole life, but never quite succeeding. And then voila! Just like that, some alcohol would hit his bloodstream, and suddenly:

Here's Ahmet! The one we've been missing.

Witty, confident, handsome, compelling, a very good conversationalist, and an excellent dancer. Ahmet came into his own when he drank. And just a little was enough to perform the trick.

Waiting in the line outside, he had found himself gasping for air. He had almost become desperate for a drink—he should have taken one before he left the flat. This night... it was the culmination of a year of effort, a year of lies. It was the culmination of a year of training before that. It was the moment he had been born for—all of his potential was to be realized now, tonight. He could not let it slip through his fingers.

The daughter of the President of the United States was sitting three feet away from him. And almost no one knew she was here.

She was pretty, maybe even beautiful, in the big, well-fed, perfect-teeth blonde way of the United States. But her looks did not matter to him. He did not love her. He did not want to marry her or date her. He might try to kiss her, but only to put her at her ease, and lull her into a sense of security.

But he had to act fast! She and Rita had slipped away from the security protecting her. How long could that last? Another hour? Another five minutes?

When the security discovered her missing, they were going to come with the full weight of the imperialists. The entire country would be locked down. The city would be closed. The borders would be closed. There would be no way out, and then the house-to-house searches would begin.

If necessary, the bloodbath would begin.

Now. He had to move on this now. Everything depended on it.

When he had poured her glass of champagne, he had slipped a little something extra into it. He had practiced just such a move his entire time here in Geneva, and it went effortlessly. It was just a tiny pill—it fell out of his sleeve, into his hand, and then into her champagne flute. It wouldn't make her sleep, or pass out. It would simply multiply the effects of the drink, make her feel spaced out, and help her enjoy herself a little more. She might become a little confused. She might become more trusting than she otherwise would be.

He tapped her shoulder, very lightly. It was the first time he had touched her. She turned to him as if she had been waiting for this all along. He leaned close to her, but did not touch her. She took a sip from the flute of champagne.

"Do you want to dance?" he said, not shouting, but loud enough for her to hear over the thump of the music and the chatter of the crowd.

She nodded.

"Yes."

He held a hand out to her and she took it. Her skin was white and her hand was soft in his. He stood and led her away from the table.

He waded into the crowd of strangers toward the dance floor, the President's daughter holding his hand.

* * *

The champagne had gone to her head.

It was just a few sips, half a glass, but she was not a drinker. It hit her like BOOM. She kind of liked the feeling it gave her. She still had the glass in her hand. She took another sip.

They went out to the dance floor, where the crowd was thickest. People crowded in on all sides, some dancing with drinks and entire bottles of champagne in their hands. It could be New Year's Eve. The bass pumped, making the shimmering purple dance floor tremble. She and Ahmet began to dance, moving just a little, still more than a foot apart.

Ha! The feeling was getting stronger. It surprised her. She was flying. She had never felt like this before.

Ahmet moved gracefully for a man. He started to break it open, arms and legs moving. He could dance! He was a show-off!

She laughed. Maybe he would twirl her.

Suddenly, a black light began to strobe, and people would seem to stop in a freeze frame, then disappear. Dancing, dancing, STOP, then disappear again.

Women in the crowd screamed and raised their drinks in the air each time it happened.

Elizabeth was about to do the same. But then she looked at Ahmet.

Something about him had changed.

The crowd moved around and behind him, STOPPED, then disappeared into the dark. Another scream went up, and a second later, the people materialized out of nowhere again.

Ahmet was holding his head. His handsome face seemed anguished, in pain.

He STOPPED, then disappeared.

The screams were louder this time. The music was becoming more frenzied.

When Ahmet reappeared, he was stumbling away toward the back of the club. His drink was gone. He was leaning over and holding his head. He went down a back hallway toward the bathrooms. He turned and spotted her. He waved her over.

Elizabeth followed. Was he sick? Was he having some kind of health problem? He looked like he was about to throw up.

She had just met him a few moments ago. They had hardly even talked. They had only just started dancing. Everything was going great. Now this.

What was wrong?

Ahead of him in the dark hallway was a lit up exit sign. It was red, showing a male figure going through a doorway.

SORTIE D'URGENCE

Emergency exit.

Was he having an emergency?

Elizabeth put her drink down on a wooden railing and went after him. She moved down the narrow hall. She caught up to him.

His face was stricken.

"Ahmet! What's going on?"

"I don't feel well."

"Should I call someone?"

He shook his head. "I need fresh air, that's all. Please join me outside, just for a few moments."

He pushed his way out the emergency exit and stumbled off to his right.

No alarm sounded.

Elizabeth looked back at the dance floor. The people bobbed and moved, packed into the small space. She still felt high as a kite. She wanted to dance. But a new feeling was washing over her. She suddenly felt confident, and larger than life, like she was Ahmet's protector. He shouldn't be out in the alleyway, sick, by himself.

She would be the strong one. She followed him out into the night.

Behind her, the exit door slammed shut. There was no knob or handle on the outside. The door simply closed flush with the wall of the building. Maybe she could pry it back open with her nails, maybe she couldn't. There was no time to worry about that. Ahmet was still ahead, stumbling down the alley, holding himself up by using the walls around him.

There were garbage cans and dumpsters back here. It was a long, windowless alley between buildings, and it smelled like rotting food. Circular fans blew steam out the back of restaurants.

"Ahmet?" Elizabeth shouted. "Are you all right?"

He raised a hand to her.

She came closer.

"Ahmet?"

He stood upright and turned to face her. He seemed to be crying. His eyes were red. His mouth hung slack.

"I'm sorry," he said. "I get migraines. Do you know what this is?"

She nodded. She kind of knew what a migraine was, she kind of didn't.

"Headaches?" she said.

He nodded and took a deep breath. "Yes. Severe. They can last for hours. I get dizzy. Sometimes I throw up. Pain pills do nothing. The black light... I wasn't expecting it." He shook his head. "I'm very sorry."

"It's okay," she said. "As long as you're all right."

"I can't go back in there. I will walk you around to the front again. We can send a message in to Rita. She will make sure you are readmitted."

Elizabeth nodded. "Okay." It was a bizarre and disappointing end to her little date with Ahmet, she must admit. But maybe something good could still happen.

"Maybe you will feel better in a little while," she said.

He nodded. He seemed weakened, and drained of all energy. "Maybe. I don't know. It usually lasts for some time. Come. Let's walk. Let's get out of this alleyway and back onto the street. It's better."

"Okay. But I think in a few minutes, you're going to start feeling better."

If nothing else, the one thing Elizabeth had gotten from her dad, and her entire family, was optimism. She could picture Ahmet coming back around in no time. She felt a momentary pang when she considered her family. Had they realized she was gone yet? Man, there was going to be hell to pay.

"I think we can get this night started again," she said anyway.

Ahmet half-smiled. "I hope so."

He gestured to her. "This way."

She had taken several steps before it occurred to her that he was moving deeper into the alley, and not back toward the street. The alley was dark back here—several of the lights seemed to be out.

"Is this the right way?" she said. She couldn't tell where the entrance to the club had been. They had gone through the entire club and into the VIP section. Then they had come back to the dance floor, and then down a hallway...

"Yes. The street's up ahead."

Suddenly a man stepped out of an alcove to her right. He was a tall man, and dark. He looked very strong. He reached for her. Ahmet was several feet away, and didn't seem to notice. He was still a little hunched over.

"Ahmet!"

Ahmet turned, his eyes wide.

Now there was another man, this one behind her. She couldn't see him, but she felt his hands. He tried to put a cloth to her face. She ducked away and squirmed out of their grasp. A third man came from an opening on the left. He was dressed in black pants and a black long-sleeve shirt. All three of the men were dressed in black.

She was tangled up with them, kicking at them.

"Ahmet!" she screamed.

She caught a glimpse of him, staring at her, his face a grimace—of pain, of fear, of sickness, she couldn't tell.

Why didn't he help her?

Now she punched and kicked. She scratched at them. She tore at them.

She had taken women's self-defense for an entire year. Her dad had insisted on it. She was good at it, one of the best in the class. She went for the men's weak spots—their eyes, their throats, their balls.

She and her three attackers moved down the alley as one, arms and legs flailing like a giant octopus.

"Help! Help! HELP!"

It occurred to her suddenly the thing you were supposed to scream when you truly needed help. Passersby often ignored cries for help, but they never ignored this one word. She hoped someone was around to hear it.

"FIRE!"

The man tried to put the foul-smelling rag to her face again. She ducked again, but she was running out of strength. Where was Ahmet? Now she couldn't see him at all—maybe he was behind them.

She put in one final burst—her last, desperate gasp...

...and somehow broke away.

Now she was running down the alley, three big men just behind her. Her shoes had come off in the struggle—that was good. She ran over the rough ground in stockinged feet. She could hear the men, their heavy breathing practically in her ear. She could hear their footfalls on the pavement.

"FIRE!" she screamed again.

Up ahead, a dark car pulled across the mouth of the alley.

Oh, thank God!

She ran for it. The men ran after her, hands grasping at her.

The car door opened.

It was coming fast. Now the men were all around her again. They seized her arms. They moved with her momentum, letting it carry the whole group along. They were running her straight toward that open door.

Wait!

They all crashed as one into the car. She tumbled onto the seat, one man with her. He was the one with the rag. He lay on top of her, using his size to imprison her, suffocate her, weigh her down. Still she fought him.

A man in the front seat was yelling something in a language she could not understand. She barely noticed. She scratched and clawed at the man on top of her.

The man pressed the rag to her face. It smelled foul, and sweet. She tried to turn away, but couldn't. Now the rag was across her face like a mask. She breathed it in. Darkness crept in from the corners of her vision.

She was losing the ability to struggle. Her limbs felt heavy.

The man on top of her cooed something to her in that strange language, gently now, as if he was a mother putting a baby to sleep.

She could barely see him anymore.

She tried to push him away, but he was fading. He pressed the rag to her face again.

Everything went black.

* * *

"Ah, holy hell!"

"Go, man! Can't you go any faster?"

"It's the curves. Just take it easy."

His name was Stephen Mostel, and his career was on the line. Sixteen years in the Secret Service, all of it going down the drain right before his eyes. Seven years on First Family assignments, and nothing remotely like this had ever happened before.

He punched the steering wheel.

"Dammit!"

He had gotten lulled to sleep on this job. Elizabeth Barrett was a girl who stayed home. She went from her dorm room to her classes, to the dining room, sometimes to the movie theater, and then back to the dorm. Sometimes she went shopping in Geneva on

134

the weekends. He would never have dreamed—not in one million years—that she would pull something like this.

"It's all right," his partner, Glenn, said. "It's all right. We know who she's with, we know where they went. The driver said the Chadwick girl always goes to the same place, practically every weekend. The local cops and the other agents are converging there as we speak. This is going to be a big nothing. It's going to be okay."

The Secret Service agents worked eight-hour shifts, two men per shift. When they weren't on duty, they all had apartments in Geneva. Every one of them—eight other men—would be at the Baroque Club in minutes, if they weren't already there.

"It's not your neck on the line," Mostel said.

"It is my neck," Glenn said. "I was on door duty. I should have been listening. I didn't hear anything."

"I was on *grounds*, man! They're going to crucify me for this. I'm supposed to see anything that happens outside her window. Somehow she got past me."

"Can't you go any faster?" Glenn said.

Mostel shook his head.

"It's the car."

The car was a Volkswagen, built for the European market. It hugged the curves of the mountain roads just fine, and it was zippy, but it had no zoom.

"Floor it."

Mostel floored the accelerator pedal and the car picked up a little steam. They raced downhill and through a red light. A car coming from the right laid on the horn. They were passing into the outskirts of the city. He had to be careful. Even though it was late, this was where traffic picked up.

His jaw was tight. He was so angry. He was angry at himself for being slow-witted and checked out. He was angry at himself for kicking back and relying on the school's security system. He was angry at the other agents for treating this assignment like a low-key vacation.

But mostly he was angry at Elizabeth. How had she done this to him? He had been assigned to her for over two years. She seemed like a good kid. He was even somewhat friendly with her, as friendly as the job would allow.

Now this.

She had decided to have Elizabeth's Big Adventure at his expense.

"I could just kill her," he said.

It didn't matter what the man's name was. It didn't matter where he came from, or where he was going next.

He was no one, from nowhere.

He moved through the nightclub, crazy pink and purple lights pulsing all around him. The music pumped and thumped. Behind him, on the dance floor, people cheered and shouted. He was headed toward the VIP section.

He was young, he dressed well, he was tall and blond. He looked like a big, healthy, rich northern European, a man who liked to ski in the winters and spend the summers on the beach. He wasn't that, but it didn't matter what he was.

He was here for only one reason.

The girl Elizabeth had been taken. She was gone. The operation was a success. Now his job was to sever the last tie between Elizabeth and the rest of world. That tie was straight ahead of him.

She was a young woman named Rita Chadwick, a very rich and spoiled girl. She had a made a terrible mistake and sent her friend to certain death. She didn't even know this yet. Look at her! She was sitting at a table in the VIP area, pouring champagne and laughing with a group of her admirers.

She was pretty, with long black hair, but the way she opened her mouth when she laughed made the man think of a shark.

As he walked, he removed from his pocket a ten-gram syringe, pre-loaded with sodium pentobarbital in liquid form. It was a high dose, and would kill her in moments, either from paralysis of the diaphragm or from cardiac arrhythmia. He pulled the paper wrapper from it.

His intention was to simply walk up to the railing behind her, pop the syringe into her neck, and depress the plunger as far as it would go. He had administered injections many times in the past, and he didn't need to deliver the entire ten grams to kill her. She was small. Ten grams would kill her several times over.

After the injection, he would simply leave the building through the nearest emergency exit, not twenty meters past her. Her friends would see him, yes, they would. But they were all drunk, and his work would be done before they could move.

Later, they would describe him to the police. Only by then, he would no longer appear as they described them.

Ah. Here was Rita. He was moving close to her now. People were milling around very nearby. That was fine.

Rita would never speak to anyone about her friendship with Elizabeth Barrett.

She would never speak to anyone about her friend Ahmet and how they met.

She would never speak to anyone about how Ahmet and she dreamed up a plan to help Elizabeth Barrett escape from her confinement.

She would never speak to anyone… again.

He looked at the syringe in his hand. He had it right out in the open. Such was the environment in discos that a man could stand in a crowd, brandishing a poison injection, and testing the plunger just a bit.

Rita and her shapely, beautiful neck were just in front of him now. She was all neck to him, like a goose, or even a swan. A vein pulsed there.

He reached for her.

BANG!

Suddenly, to his left, the emergency door burst open. Large men surged in. The police! They pushed people to the ground, screaming and cursing. More and more of them came—five, ten, fifteen. A few had their nightsticks out, wielding them but not hitting anyone.

Across the club, another group stormed in through the front entrance.

Rita turned to see the commotion. Amazing! They were looking for her! Three policemen climbed over the barrier and into the VIP area.

Rita had moved away from the railing. The police were shouting at her.

The man dropped his syringe to the floor.

Mission aborted.

He kicked it under a table.

Suddenly the police were on him, surging past him, shoving him to the wall and out of their way.

The music stopped. The lights came on.

The man allowed himself to be pushed and shoved along, his hands in the air to show they were empty. He was one of many, a face in the crowd, someone who was simply here for a night of good times, no threat to anyone.

* * *

She did not know where she was.

For a long time, Elizabeth drifted in darkness, but then her thoughts started climbing up and out of the abyss.

They were confused thoughts, a mad jumble of images and ideas, and sensations and disembodied voices, all superimposed on each other. She recovered slowly. She felt how her lungs were filling with air, and then she began to do it consciously and with pleasure. She was breathing!

More clearly now she heard the car engine, and mingled with that, the sound of unfamiliar voices. Several men were speaking in a language she did not understand. She tried to open her eyes. Her eyelids seemed glued firmly shut. They were so heavy it was almost unnatural to lift them.

In the first moments, her vision was out of focus. It was like a photograph taken at night, through a rainy, foggy window. Everything was smeared and hazy and very dark. But with each successive moment of consciousness, her wounded brain began to put all the puzzle pieces together. Soon enough, the picture became clearer—resolving itself, slowly and inexorably, into something she did not want to see.

She found herself in a car full of strangers, driving through the night.

Inky darkness flew along outside her window, shadowy landscapes that were formless and empty. The car moved too quickly over rutted and pitted roads, shuddering and banging the entire time. She could make out nothing about where she was. The car seemed to be passing through an unpopulated countryside— there were no lights out there at all. She was in the back seat of the car. The full horror of it began to sink in.

What happened?

Where are they taking me?

Who are these men?

As if on cue, that question was answered. Ahmet was in the front passenger seat. He turned and looked back at her. He stared at her for a moment, as if she were some kind of insect, or an animal about to be dissected.

Her whole body had gone numb. Now she noticed her tongue. It felt thick in her mouth. She made a sound, like a shout, but also like the horrible groaning of an animal.

The men ignored her. They talked incessantly, excitedly, almost in a panic. Their language seemed like the language of a lost jungle tribe.

A sudden attack of fear surged within her.

I can't do this! I do not want to go anywhere with these people!

She wanted to go home. She wanted to go back! Her heart beat at a furious pace, and the blood pounded inside her temples. She pictured her mother and father—the terror they would feel. How stupid she had been!

Someone said something she did not understand. Maybe they were speaking in Turkish, since Ahmet was a Turk.

Is he really a Turk?

She realized she knew nothing about him, only what Rita had told her. He could be anyone from anywhere. Terror suddenly took hold of her.

He could be anyone.

She wanted to run away so badly, to run away and forget all of this. She wanted out.

"I need to go to the bathroom," she said.

Nobody seemed to pay attention.

What if they don't speak English?

But it couldn't be. She knew for sure that Ahmet spoke English.

"I need to go to the bathroom," she said again.

The man behind the wheel said something in the foreign language. Ahmet pulled a bottle from his leather jacket. It was filled with a dark liquid. Ahmet stretched out his arm to give Elizabeth the bottle.

"Drink this."

His eyes sparkled at her. He looked like a demon.

She shook her head. "No. I won't."

The big man who was sitting quietly to her right all this time suddenly turned toward her, and with only his left hand, he pressed her entire body against the seat. The man held down her body with his terrible strength, and at the same time, he opened her mouth with his other hand, compressing her cheeks together, his fingers painfully pushing into her skin.

Ahmet stretched back from the front seat, held the bottle above her head, and poured the alcohol into her mouth—it burned like wildfire.

The flaming liquid fell onto her tongue and flowed down her throat. The nasty liquid warmed her from the inside. A surge of heat suddenly enveloped her like a cozy blanket.

The voices faded and started drifting somewhere far away. She felt much better. Strange waves of sensation were already carrying her into the darkness.

Again.

* * *

They were alien to her—men with blurred faces, framed by dark hair and beards. She did not understand what they were saying, and she did not care—she was beyond caring. She felt herself floating in the air like a balloon—so light and indifferent.

She could no longer think, or feel. She did not belong to herself. Her life was to be decided by strange and scary people. She could not resist anything. She could not say anything. She could not speak at all.

One of the blurry faces spoke to her in English. His voice seemed to echo from far away. "We're going to be in the open for a moment," he said. "Don't cry out or say a word. No one will help you."

Was she hallucinating? The men all seemed to have the same facial features. They were just blank faces, washed out, pixelated, devoid of any specific characteristics, as if they did not have faces at all. The dark framing of their hair and their thick beards made their heads seem disproportionately large. They were men with gigantic heads, and faces that all looked identical.

She was out of the car now.

Suddenly, the darkness enveloped her again. But this new darkness was different. It was not the kind of darkness into which you fall instantly, and disappear into a deep abyss, and which doesn't give you a chance to get scared for even a split second. It was not the same kind of darkness that she had already experienced.

This time it was a darkness where you realize that the worst is just moments or even seconds away. It was the kind of darkness the condemned man experiences when he is brought to the scaffold to be executed.

They had covered her head with a black hood.

One of the men carried her. She felt herself become like some boneless deep sea creature, a jellyfish, but a jellyfish made of bread dough, malleable and light. Her breathing slowed down, her heart was barely beating, her muscles became limp and formless, and her body was slung over someone's shoulder like a bag of rice.

She knew it was the beginning of the end. Soon she would be killed. There would be no explanation of anything—just darkness, confusion, and then death.

She saw her father again, looking for her, very scared.

Her father...

The President of the United States.

She would tell them. It was all a mistake. They had taken the daughter of the President. They were going to be in big trouble.

Of course, they knew that already. That was the whole point of this. The weight of knowledge landed on her with a nearly audible thud. This wasn't a mistake. It was a kidnapping, and had been planned long before.

Rita. Rita had done this to her.

Where was she now? Was she in on it?

It was cold out, and she felt them crossing a gap, an empty space, a threshold of some kind. Then she was sprawled on a padded seat, and her face was uncovered.

They were moving once again. She looked out and saw that they were on a boat, the boat racing, bounding, no lights on, across vast and open water.

CHAPTER NINETEEN

May 8
3:15 a.m. Arabian Standard Time (2:15 a.m. Central European
Summer Time; 8:15 p.m. Eastern Daylight Time, May 7)
Al-Fallujah
45 miles west of Baghdad
Iraq

The street where they met was wrecked.

The Americans had taken the city in brutal house-to-house fighting six months before. All this time later, nothing had been rebuilt. Buildings were mere rubble, or were pockmarked with bullet holes. Scrap metal littered the streets and alleyways. Fresh water was brought in on trucks. The sewage system was destroyed. Half the city still had no electricity.

The locals called it punishment. The Americans called it justice.

The man called himself Abu the Martyr. He was forty-three years old and long ago had started turning gray. His beard was shot through with gray and white. His vision, once so acute, was beginning to fail. When reading the Holy Quran in the evenings, he was forced to hold it as far from his face as his arms would allow. Soon, someone would have to hold it up for him from across the room.

He had been trying to martyr himself for more than twenty years. He was willing, but Allah had chosen not to take him.

"His will, not mine, be done," the Martyr whispered.

He quietly smoked a cigarette and stood in the doorway of an abandoned building. The front façade of the building was intact. The rear of the building was open air and a pile of shattered bricks. A missile or rocket had hit this place, a very typical residential building in what had once been a poor, crowded, but very typical residential neighborhood.

Up the street, a car appeared, its headlights off. It rolled slowly through the ripped up asphalt that littered the road. It descended into a shallow missile crater, then came up the other side.

Now the Martyr could see it more clearly. An old black armored Mercedes, windows smoked, metal rutted and pitted and banged in from use in a war zone. The man was here, just as he announced he would be. How he managed to cross back and forth through the American military checkpoints was a mystery, the answer known only to him.

How he managed to openly cross territory held by Sunni militias was not a mystery—the man was an untouchable.

The car pulled up to the doorway. The window powered down.

The man was white, with sandy-blond hair and an English accent. He was a little overweight, but not sloppy. The extra weight he carried probably came from his love affair with drink, not with food, and certainly not with sedentary behavior. He was a man frequently on the move. Rumor had it that he was a British spy. What else could he be? He had access to intelligence that no one else seemed to have.

His blue eyes were piercing, even in the dark of night.

The Martyr didn't move from the doorway, not right away. Instead, he scanned up and down the street. It was always possible that the Brit had been followed. More than possible—it was probably guaranteed. The man stuck out in these parts like a green plant on the surface of the moon.

"God is great, eh?" the Martyr said.

Indeed, the news of the kidnapping was now circling the entire world. It was a giant blow to the Great Satan, one that would give hope to people of faith everywhere.

"Not my god," the man said in his cultured English accent. "And anyway, I suppose I wouldn't celebrate too soon if I were you."

The Martyr nearly smiled. "No? Why not? The deed is done."

The Brit scanned the roadway ahead for a moment.

"There could be a problem," he said.

"Oh?" the Martyr said. "What problem is that?"

"Do you have the money?" the Brit said.

"Of course."

"Then give it to me and I will describe the problem to you."

The Martyr leaned back into the dark shadows of the doorway. Tucked just down the hall, inside an alcove, was a leather satchel. The bag contained untraceable cash in various denominations and three different currencies—American dollars, euros, and British pounds. The money was worth roughly half a million dollars all told.

The man was expensive, but over time he had proven to be well worth the high price. The Martyr darted across open space, carrying the bag between the doorway and the car. He didn't enjoy being exposed on the street like this.

"The back door is open," the Brit said. "Put the bag on the floor."

The Martyr opened the back door and slid the bag onto the floor behind the driver's side. He slammed the car door and returned to the shelter of his doorway.

"Don't you want to count it?"

The Brit shook his head. "No. I trust you. How can men work together without a little bit of trust?"

"Also, you will have me killed if the money is wrong," the Martyr said.

The Brit nodded. "Yes."

"So what's the problem then?"

"A small group of American operatives is on a trail that is warm, and may soon grow warmer. A Sunni tribal elder from outside Tikrit has been quite forthcoming with information, I'm afraid."

"The camp that was raided?"

The Brit nodded again. "Yes."

"The name of the elder?"

There was a long pause while the Brit sat quietly. He was hesitant, of course, because the brothers would show no mercy to this so-called elder. And they would seek to erase any information the elder might have shared with others, including his family and clan.

"It is no help unless we have the name," the Martyr said.

"Imam Muhammad al-Barak," the Brit said. "God have mercy on him."

"Thank you, Mr. Montgomery," the Martyr said.

The Brit looked at him, his eyes harder than ever. There was something in those eyes that gave the Martyr pause. It was a coldness, as though the Brit could kill the Martyr slowly, and without emotion. It was a coldness like the cold of deep space. Or perhaps it was just an emptiness. Perhaps it was more that something was missing than that something was there.

But within seconds, the Martyr had recovered himself.

"Oh, yes," he said. "I know more than I seem to."

The Brit's cold gaze never wavered. "There are things in this world that you're better off not knowing. If I were you, I'd forget some of the things that you think you know. In fact, I'd start working on that project right now."

The window powered up and the car slowly pulled away.

The Martyr took a long, shaky drag on his cigarette. The Brit didn't frighten him. No man did. He had given himself to Allah more than twenty years ago. He was trying to martyr himself, and Allah just hadn't claimed him yet. It was good to remind himself of that from time to time.

"Your god may have mercy on al-Barak," he said to no one. "But we won't."

CHAPTER TWENTY

May 7
10:05 p.m. Eastern Daylight Time (4:05 a.m. Central European Summer Time, May 8)
The Situation Room
The White House, Washington, DC

His worst nightmare had come true.

David Barrett, President of the United States, strode the halls of the West Wing toward the elevator that would take him down to the Situation Room.

A phalanx of people strode with him, ahead of him, behind him, all around him—aides, interns, Secret Service men, staff of various kinds. He had no idea who half these people were. Everyone was much shorter than he was—many were a head shorter or more. His Chief of Staff, Lawrence Keller, walked by his side.

He looked down at Keller—he was a short, slim man, nearly totally bald. David knew that Lawrence was a long-distance runner. He was late-fifties, divorced, had a couple of kids. He had been around Washington forever, and was a consummate political player. He was the proverbial hot knife cutting through butter. Lawrence Keller was the only comforting fact of this entire disaster—there was someone nearby whom David Barrett could trust.

Everyone was talking at once.

"The Turkish prime minister sends his deepest condolences, and wants you to know that if any Turkish national was involved in this crime, the penalty will be death."

"French commandos are on standby—awaiting our orders. The entire country is on lockdown."

"House to house searches have begun in Geneva, Zurich, and Bern, as well as smaller Swiss cities and towns."

House to house searches had *begun*? What in God's name had taken them so long? He realized he must be in shock. The voices around him were becoming an increasingly strange Babel—impossible to understand. Bits and pieces of nonsensical information flowed past him.

"The British Prime Minister has gone on TV to say..."

"China has offered the use of spy satellites and surveillance…"

"Vladimir Putin is being briefed as we…"

"CIA, NSA, and all intelligence listening stations…"

"Shut up!" he shouted, before he knew he was going to. "Everyone just shut up, and stop talking. I can't stand it anymore."

He turned to Lawrence Keller. "Lawrence, who is going to be briefing us now?"

"General Richard Stark from the Pentagon," Keller said. "I'm told he has up to the minute information, and all intelligence is being fed to, and vetted through, his office."

Barrett nodded. "I need you, Lawrence. I'm lost right now. I need you to stay on these people. I need this to happen at twice the speed it's happening right now. I need to hammer every target on Earth. I don't care what needs to be done or whose toes are stepped on, or frankly, who gets killed. I don't care if entire countries become parking lots. I want my daughter back."

Keller nodded. "I am going to move heaven and earth for you, David. This is my promise."

"Thank you."

The entire phalanx of people moved into the elevator. Barrett stood in the middle of the crowd. He closed his eyes. He saw Elizabeth as a small girl, at a family barbecue at the old family house in Newport, running to him, the sea in the background. He could see every detail of her—the flower dress she wore, her floppy green sunhat, her sandals that buckled at the ankle, her blonde hair, her huge smile, one front tooth missing.

He didn't know if he was going to scream or pass out.

He took a deep breath instead. It would be unseemly to pass out in front of so many strangers. A Barrett did not show weakness.

He had gotten off the phone with his father just minutes ago. His father, eighty-nine-year-old Sylvester Barrett, had spent his life growing the family oil business that his own father had founded. He was a tough man.

"Bury them," his father said. "Make them pay. Every stinking last one of them."

She's my daughter, Dad.

That's what he wanted to say. Couldn't he understand that? His daughter had been kidnapped. He loved her so much—it was like a piece of himself had been taken. If he could be taken in her stead, he would do it. In a heartbeat. No hesitation at all.

I love her. I am dying inside.

But you didn't say things like that to Sylvester Barrett.

If anything, the conversation with his wife had gone even worse. She simply wept over the phone line, and he couldn't think of a single thing to say that might comfort her. He stood there with a lump in his throat, his face turning red as the woman he loved began shrieking at him.

"I'm going to get her back," he croaked, before hanging up the phone. It was the only thing he could think of.

The elevator opened into the egg-shaped Situation Room. It was super-modern, set up for maximum use of the space, with large screens embedded in the walls every couple of feet, and a giant projection screen on the far wall at the end of the table.

Except for David's own seat, every plush leather seat at the table was occupied—overweight men in suits, thin and ramrod-straight military men in uniform. A man in a dress uniform stood at the far head of the table. Richard Stark.

David didn't care for Richard Stark. But right now, he didn't care much for anyone. Maybe Stark would throw him a lifeline in this desperate moment—stranger things had happened.

He sat down in the chair reserved for the President.

The room suddenly went quiet. David knew that he was renowned for his anger and his tirades—many of his closest aides didn't like him. He knew that about himself, and it was another thing he had never cared about. He was a Barrett, after all. If they all quieted down right now, it was because they were afraid of what he would say if they didn't. A crisis was on, and he was inches from an all-consuming rage.

"Okay, Richard," he said. "Never mind the introductions, never mind the niceties and the preliminaries. Just tell me some good news."

Stark slipped a pair of black reading glasses onto his face. He looked down at the sheets of paper in his hand.

"We are developing intelligence along several lines. The roommate, Rita Chadwick, is still in CIA custody, and is cooperating. Her family is insisting she be released pending the arrival of a legal team from New York. We told them no. The lead kidnapper has been identified as Ahmet Kaya of Istanbul, twenty-one years old. It is clear that this is an alias, and we are tracking—"

"Richard!"

There was not a sound in the room. The President of the United States was beginning to shout. In a moment, he might throw one of his trademark temper tantrums.

No. He took a deep breath. He wasn't going to do that.

He spoke in an even, level tone.

148

"Tell me what you have," he said. "Not what you are developing."

Stark nodded. He took his glasses off. He didn't need to look at the papers in his hand. "Okay, David. Your daughter was kidnapped, as you know. Our intelligence suggests that she was taken from Geneva by car, then was loaded onto a boat, which crossed Lake Geneva into France without passing through any border control. We are searching satellite footage to confirm this, though it may be difficult to confirm if the boat was small enough, and operated without lights. After the boat landed, we believe she was taken into the French countryside."

David suddenly felt very subdued.

"And then?" he said.

General Stark shook his head. "We have no idea."

"You don't know where my daughter is?"

"I'm going to be honest with you, David. This happened hours ago. It was clearly planned well ahead of time, and they got a sizeable head start on us. If they made it into France—and we believe they did—and then reached one of the many small airfields in that region…"

President Barrett wanted to cover his ears against the words he knew must come next.

"They could have taken her anywhere."

CHAPTER TWENTY ONE

May 8
6:35 a.m. Arabian Standard Time (10:35 p.m. Eastern Daylight Time, May 7)
The Embassy of the United States in Iraq (aka the Republican Palace)
The International Zone (aka the Green Zone)
Karkh District
Baghdad, Iraq

In the night, he had waited for an attack.

He was lying on a cot, in a gray Go Army T-shirt and boxers, in a sweltering office, surrounded by other people doing more or less the same. No air conditioning, no air at all. He had noise-canceling foam plugs in his ears, and a strapped eyeshade covering his face. The eyeshade was a good one—not too tight, and it left him no peripheral vision at all. He was in a world of total darkness, exactly where he wanted to be.

During the early hours, there had been a sudden flurry of movement, people coming and going, people talking in hushed tones.

Luke didn't care. He had completed his mission—two missions, in fact—and was going home tomorrow. His body was sore, and his brain was tired. He was wrung out. If the embassy was bombed, or overrun by suicide fighters, he assumed someone would wake him up to let him know.

"Luke! Luke Stone! Wake up!"

He took the nightshade off his face, and light flooded in. It was daytime.

Trudy Wellington stood over him. Her hair was mussed. She wore a light blue T-shirt and cotton athletic shorts. Her clothes had practically sweated through. She looked like she had just woken up herself. She looked like breakfast.

Good thing he had turned down that drink.

Luke took his ear plugs out and blinked. The cots around him were all empty.

"Trudy. Good morning."

"I've been looking all over for you," she said. "We need to come up with a better system for where our people are sleeping. It's ridiculous to walk all over this palace looking for everybody."

It seemed a bit late for coming up with a system. They were on their way out of here. A system for cot assignments was going to be unnecessary at best. Okay, Trudy was a little annoyed. That's all it was. She could design a system on the flight home, if she wanted.

"Are we leaving now?" Luke said.

She shook her head. Her hair bounced with it. "No. We have a meeting. You, me, Ed, Mark Swann, Big Daddy, and Don on the phone. As soon as you can claw your way out of bed."

"A meeting? I thought we were done. We're going home today."

Her big eyes blinked at him. She stared at him quizzically.

"You haven't heard?"

He shook his head. "Heard what? No, I guess I haven't."

"We're not going home."

"I'm going home," Luke said. "I have a baby on the way. You guys can stay here if you want." He looked around at all the wooden fold-up cots in the barren room with bare plywood walls. "I mean, it's nice here, so I don't blame you for wanting to stay, but—"

"Luke," she said, her voice suddenly stern. "No one is leaving. All military and intelligence assets are ordered to stay in place and on call until further notice."

"Why? Are we at war?" Luke said, realizing instantly how silly the question sounded. Were they at war? Yes, obviously they were at war. What he meant was…

"There's a problem," Trudy said. "And we've got a meeting right now. As soon as you're ready."

* * *

The young girl wore a bright orange jumpsuit.

She kneeled at the front of the jittery video, her hands behind her back—probably bound. Her hair was tied back under a simple black headscarf.

Behind her, five men stood, all of them wearing black masks across their faces. They were dressed in the manner of a guerrilla army, with heavy ballistic vests, ammo belts across their chests, many-pocketed cargo pants, and combat boots. Four of the men carried AK-47 rifles. They stood in front of a black banner with white lettering in Arabic.

The fifth, a man wearing the black hood of an executioner, carried a long heavy knife, like a machete. He held it aloft, and at times, gestured with it.

The imagery made Luke sick—sick with anger, with rage, with a helpless feeling. Inside of him, there was an animal trapped in a cage, a brute, wanting very badly to kick its way out. If it got out, God help every man in that video, and anyone who worked with them or aided them in any way. God help entire regions and an entire religion.

He glanced at Ed Newsam. The man's huge right fist was clenched. His jaw was set. He stood by the table in what could be mistaken for a relaxed posture—except his entire body was alive with electricity.

Luke took a deep breath.

"My father is an imperialist and a crusader," the girl was saying. Her eyes darted, looking at something off screen. Clearly, it was the script she was being forced to read.

"He is... he is a nitwit, and a dupe of the Western ruling classes... who... use and degrade women, and who... who deliberately corrupt the morals of the youth in the entire world. They are in league with Satan, and my father..."

Here she turned her head and began to cry. Within seconds, she was weeping abjectly, utterly unable to continue. The video jumped, and cut. Now she was facing forward again.

"They cut it to give her time to compose herself," Mark Swann said.

"And my father is their willing servant," the girl said. "He is a coward and a running dog who has used the might of the West to make war on Allah's faithful people, even while in his youth he used his wealth to escape his own military responsibilities, and his country's dirty wars."

"Jesus," Luke said.

"Do not cry for me," she said now. "I am young, but was not naïve. I willfully ignored the suffering my father and his ilk have inflicted on masses of the faithful throughout the world. I am the spawn of evil, and I am not..."

She began to cry again.

"I am not innocent."

She lost it again. She could not speak. She kneeled there, head hanging, face obscured, her entire body shaking with sobs.

The screen jumped again, revealing yet another artless cut. She was kneeling up straight again. She was no longer crying.

"My capture and punishment is a glory to the prophet, and confirmation to Allah's people that their faith is rewarded. I go to my…"

She stopped and took a deep breath.

"I go to my death knowing that I am as guilty of these terrible crimes as any crusader in Iraq, Afghanistan, Africa, or the Holy Land. May the people rejoice at this act of justice, and in time may Allah bring an even greater reckoning upon my father, my family, and my people."

The video jumped again. The girl was still on her knees, but now she was blindfolded. The man in the hood moved to front and center. He jabbed his knife at the screen and his mouth moved, while clanging music played over him. He pulled up his right sleeve and showed the camera a tattoo on his shoulder—it was a black tattoo of a crescent moon and a star, a symbol of the former Ottoman Empire, and by extension, the Islamic world.

Arabic lettering appeared on the screen, superimposed over him as he spoke. Then he and all the other men were gone. It was just the girl now, kneeling, blindfolded, head down, the sign in Arabic still hanging behind her.

The video ended.

For a few seconds, no one spoke.

"I'm going to kill that guy," Ed Newsam said. "I don't mean I want to. I mean I'm going to. Don't matter how long it takes. Don't matter where he is. Don't matter who else is there."

"What does the banner in the back say?" Luke said.

"It says *Jama'at al-Tawhid wal-Jihad*," Trudy said. "In English, that means the Organization of God's Oneness and Holy War. It is a group founded by Abu Musab Al-Zarqawi, and has pledged its allegiance to Al Qaeda."

"Great," Luke said. "And what was all that wording at the end?"

Trudy shrugged. "That was a demand. They have a laundry list of individuals they want released from prison. The list is comprehensive, to say the least, and it makes it hard to get a sense of who is behind the abduction. It includes Palestinians held in Israeli prisons, numerous individuals held at Guantanamo Bay and at alleged black sites in Afghanistan and other countries—we don't have confirmation yet from the Pentagon or the CIA that some of these individuals are being held, or that they even exist. There are also terrorist leaders being held in Pakistan, the Philippines, Malaysia, and Thailand, not to mention Russia, Saudi Arabia, and Egypt, as well as right here in Iraq."

"How many people, in all?" Luke said.

Trudy glanced down at some paperwork in front of her. "Two hundred forty-eight, all men, thought to be held in twelve different countries."

"And if they're not released?" Luke said, though he imagined he knew the answer.

"The first thirty prisoners must be released by tomorrow morning," Trudy said. "As an indication of good will and acceptance of the terms. No preparation—simply open the gates and let them walk free. And they're right—in certain places this could be done. After that, at least another ten must be released or transferred to their home country every day, until they're all set free. The whole operation can take up to three weeks."

"And if it doesn't happen?"

"If the first thirty prisoners aren't released by nine a.m. tomorrow, Baghdad time, then Elizabeth Barrett will be beheaded, and the video will be released on Internet outlets and to news stations. If there is any stumble in the schedule after that, then the same thing will happen. Most outlets won't show the video, but of course within a short time a few will, then it will be copied, and then it will be everywhere."

"So…"

Trudy nodded. "Yeah. Twenty-six hours from now, more or less. The President's daughter will be dead, and the ultimate jihadi recruiting video will be released worldwide."

* * *

"Trudy, give us your impressions," Don's voice said.

They sat around the makeshift conference table—a slab of plywood balanced on two sawhorses. Don's voice came from the black octopus at the center. Trudy, Swann, Ed Newsam, and Luke formed a rough square.

Big Daddy Cronin and the British spy Montgomery stood at the edges of the rounded, stone room. Luke could hardly imagine why they were here—there must be a thousand other intelligence teams out there who were closer to the action.

"Well, Elizabeth Barrett is a kid," Trudy said, starting with something that couldn't be more obvious. "To some extent, because of her position, she's going to be more sheltered than the average eighteen-year-old. From what we have, her friend, the young woman from the Chadwick family, hooked her up on a blind date of sorts, and taught her how to sneak away from her security detail.

But the Chadwick girl was not, as far as we know, complicit in the kidnapping. It was a lark to her, a harmless escapade."

"Okay…" Don's disembodied voice said.

It seemed to Luke that Trudy was just speaking to get the feel for talking, that she was warming up to the real meat of this. Like she was priming the pump to get the water flowing. Trudy went on.

"The Turk, however, was not on a lark. Ahmet Kaya, his alias, is a person who does not exist. At this time, we have no idea if he really is a Turk. We do know that he spoke Turkish fluently, as a native speaker would speak it, or close enough that outsiders would think so. We also know he spoke English and French, both at a conversational level. So he has, or had, a lot of high-level language skills."

"Had?" Luke said.

Trudy nodded. "There's a good chance that Ahmet is now dead. He was planted in Geneva, close to the President's daughter, for at least the past year. He was put there to carry out a task, and once he carried it out successfully, he instantly became a liability. Unless he has another skill set we're not aware of, or he's a leader in the Islamic world, then to keep him alive is to take a risk. Half the intelligence assets on Earth are looking for him at this moment."

"Okay," Luke said.

"But let's get back to the language skills," Trudy said. "Excellent language skills, a good-looking kid, who according to all accounts, is a sharp dresser. What does this suggest to you?"

"I don't know," Ed Newsam said. "The camp?"

"Could be," Trudy said. "The camp you raided, or one very much like it. It's a long shot, for sure. But it's all we've got. There is ample security footage of Ahmet, entering the club, inside the club, and in the alleyway outside the club. There's security footage of him wandering around Geneva and the surrounding area for an entire year. It would make sense to match those images with the images that were taken from the camp, and see if anything comes up."

Big Daddy cleared his throat. Of course. Big Daddy Cronin didn't just hang around meetings.

"Hi, Bill," Luke said without turning around.

"Hi, everybody," Big Daddy said. "Thanks for inviting Monty and I to your little meeting. Of course we've already run the footage of Ahmet against images of students at the camp."

"What did you get, Bill?" Don said.

"We got fourteen possible matches. Seven of those fourteen are better than the others. None are perfect."

"You have to consider that the man named Ahmet may have had cosmetic surgery," Trudy said.

Big Daddy nodded. "We have. But we've hit a dead end. The individuals in those photos are identified by codes—series of letters and numbers—not names."

"Did you pass this intel up the line?" Don said.

Big Daddy didn't answer the question.

"Bill?"

"I think you know the answer to that, Don."

"Bill, I don't think this is the time to withhold information so you can build your little intelligence fiefdom. There are bigger issues at play here."

"Don, I'm not building a fiefdom. I'm about getting results. Too many times I've passed hard-won intel up the line, intel people have died for, only to see it get lost, stepped on, or squashed because it's politically inconvenient. That camp was given to us by a Sunni tribal elder, in confidence, and under pain of his own death. He's a source, and I'm protecting him. We pass this stuff up the line, and I guarantee you he's exposed inside of twenty-four hours. I don't do that, not here. Whisper the wrong word to the wrong person, and entire groups of people get snuffed."

Big Daddy let that linger in the room.

He was a strange and mercurial man. He was sitting on intelligence that might, or might not, save the President's daughter. He was not going to release it because he was protecting some Sunni tribespeople.

"We don't even know if what we have is relevant at all. Yes, the people holding Elizabeth Barrett claim to be aligned with Zarqawi's group, but putting a banner on the wall doesn't really mean anything. We have no identifying features in this video—no voices outside of Elizabeth's, no identifiable landscape features, or even internal architectural style. No faces of the terrorists. We have a tattoo, but nothing else. Any one of a hundred terrorist leaders and splinter groups could have taken that child. There is absolutely no reason to believe that we have an inside track on this. We could get people killed for a lead that's a dead end."

"If there's no reason to believe, then why even do it?" Mark Swann said.

Big Daddy shrugged. "We have to do something. We can't just sit here. There are a million investigations going on, and most of them are higher priority than this. But the vast majority of them will not bear fruit. This one also probably won't. But if we don't try, and the President's girl gets killed, I'm going to have a hard time living with that."

"What do you suggest?" Don said.

"I suggest we poke at it. Probe around a little. You know my motto—grab a loose end and pull. Let's see if we really have anything. We move fast, and in secret. If we do have something, then we pass it on. But only then."

"Monty?" Don said.

Montgomery shrugged. He was wearing a dress shirt that was soaked through with sweat. He looked ruffled, like he had slept in it. He was a very rumpled man. Even his face looked like it had come through some sort of clothing wringer.

He was drinking coffee and smoking a cigarette.

"I have access to a squad of blokes from the Special Air Service. If your lads and mine were all willing to go back out, I'd say we go and see our tribal elder Muhammad al-Barak at his family compound outside Tikrit. He brought that camp to our attention, which to me means he knows more than he's been willing to say. My feeling is he will be willing to cooperate, if it means he might save Elizabeth. Naturally, he would expect something in return."

"Naturally," Luke said.

Monty went on:

"We need to make a show of arresting him and his people, and then disappear them, so to speak. We get a name from him, someone who knows more, and who we can apply some pressure upon. Then we move up the line and acquire that person. We bring that person back here, not here to the Embassy, mind you, but somewhere nearby, and we have a little chat to them. A rather expedient chat, I imagine. There won't be much time for talking around in circles, if you see my point. We get a name, or a place, from that person. We keep doing that until we develop a real lead. It's a bit tedious, but I don't see any other options."

"And the elder?" Don said. "Al-Barak? What happens to him?"

"He's gone," Montgomery said. "For their own protection, we take him and his entire group and fast track their immigration to Britain or America. Overnight them, if you see my meaning."

"I do see it," Don said. "Luke?"

Luke stared at the octopus. He thought of Becca at home. Nine months pregnant. He had already told her he was leaving today.

"Don, Becca is going to give birth any minute."

"I know that."

"I need to get out of here. Can we go see the elder today?"

"My men can go as soon as you're ready," Montgomery said. "They've been awake since four a.m."

"If we do it, can you put me on a plane today?" Luke said. "Pretend I'm a journalist, give me a hardship pass, anything?"

There was a pause over the line.

"Don?"

"Yes. Go bring in the elder, and I will bring you home."

There was quiet for another moment.

"Ed?" Don said. "How do you feel about this mission?"

Ed shrugged. "I got a date with the man in that video. Other than that, I got nowhere to be."

A squeal of static came over Don's line. "Bill, do you have anything more to say about this?"

Bill nodded. "Yes. I would caution everyone in this room that given the current circumstances, and the danger to the people involved, the mission we've discussed here does not exist, and it will never exist."

CHAPTER TWENTY TWO

May 8
12:20 a.m. Eastern Daylight Time (7:20 a.m. Arabian Standard Time)
The Oval Office
The White House
Washington, DC

"David, I think you should go to bed."

David Barrett, the President of the United States, sat at the Resolute Desk. Although he was quite tall, well-built, and very nearly movie star handsome, somehow he looked like a small child behind there.

"I want to kill them all," he said.

"I know that," his Chief of Staff, Lawrence Keller, said.

Keller sat across from him, watching his boss carefully, analyzing him, assessing him. The desk, which had been a gift from the British people, was too big for David.

Not physically, no. But Franklin Delano Roosevelt had sat at that desk when dealing with the fallout from the Great Depression, the Pearl Harbor Attack, the darkest days of World War Two. John F. Kennedy had sat at that desk during the Cuban Missile Crisis, and also during the Bay of Pigs fiasco. Ronald Reagan had sat at that desk during the nuclear face-offs with the Russians of the 1980s.

David Barrett was too small for the desk. He was too small for the job. He was too small for the moment. Keller had always known this about him. Their relationship was a marriage of convenience—David had stumbled into the presidency through a confluence of family connections, money, good looks and grooming, and some rather glaring misplays committed by the opposing party. Their own party had installed Keller as David's Chief of Staff, with the hope that Keller could guide the man through the minefield of his own lazy mind and awful instincts.

"It's a crisis, Lawrence," Barrett said. He held his head in his hands, propped up on his elbows. His dress shirt was rolled back to his forearms. Until a few moments ago, he had been crying for a little while.

Keller nodded. "Yes. It is. And we're doing everything we can to manage it and see it through to a positive conclusion."

Barrett looked up. His eyes were red.

"They're killing me, do you know that? The press. They are killing me. My daughter is gone. The terrorists have paraded her on TV like a captured animal, making her say terrible, hateful things about me. They're going to kill her. I know that. You know that. If they've…"

He shook his head, unable to speak for a moment. "If they have hurt her in any way, I don't know what I'm going to do."

Keller was calm. "Sir… David… You can rest assured that when this crisis is over, there is going to be hell to pay. I am already in touch with every single decision maker who matters in the Pentagon, with the CIA, with the NSA, and a host of other organizations who safeguard our security. You do not have to worry about taking your revenge. I am going to take it."

Barrett nodded and began to cry again. "I know. I know. You're a good man. I trust you. If they hurt her, I want the entire world set on fire."

"And it will be," Keller said.

Barrett gritted his teeth. "And this media. My God, Lawrence! Can't we stop them? My daughter, my beautiful daughter, is under threat of death, and all these bastards can focus on is my military record. They're making me into a damn laughingstock. I hate them so much. I would bomb them, too."

Keller shook his head. There was nothing anyone could do about the media, or about David Barrett's military record. The man found it convenient to take five straight draft deferments during the height of the Vietnam War. At one point, during a period when his draft status was unresolved—meaning the Army felt he should report for duty, and his father and grandfather were frantically pulling strings to make the Army change its mind—David had spent four months in the French Riviera.

Keller himself felt no sympathy about this, or about the skewering a few of the newspapers were giving him. Keller had done two tours of Vietnam as a United States Marine, had been wounded on three occasions, and had seen many, many people die. He had fought street to street during the Battle of Hue. Afterward, his reward—his downtime, as it were—was to spend a year patrolling the DMZ between North and South Korea.

No. He didn't feel much sympathy for David and his military record.

The loss of his daughter was profound, and terrible. Keller would resolve that, if he could. But David being teased by a handful of resentful reporters? So be it.

"David, you should go upstairs to bed. Okay?"

"The things they're saying about me, Lawrence... it isn't fair."

"David!" Keller said, sternly now. "As your friend, not as your Chief of Staff, I'm telling you. I'm commanding you. Okay? Go to bed. Yes, Elizabeth has been taken. Yes, it is terrible, terrible news. But thousands of people are working around the clock, the best people on Earth, to save her life. Meanwhile, Caitlynn hasn't been taken, and she's still with you. And Marilynn is up there in bed, crying herself to sleep over the loss of her daughter. Be a man. Be her husband. Be strong for her, go upstairs and comfort her, and tell her that everything is going to be all right."

Barrett was shaking his head.

"But what if it's not going to be all right?"

Keller shrugged. "If that's what you believe, then lie to her."

Barrett stared at him.

"That's right," Keller said. "It's a time for comforting lies."

Finally, Barrett nodded his head. "Okay. I can do that. I lie all the time. I have to. It's part of the job."

Keller nodded, but didn't answer directly.

"Do it for her," he said. "Make her know that you're going to be a man for her. Try to get some sleep, and in the morning... I promise. This isn't going to look nearly as dark as it does right now."

"I can take a pill," Barrett said. "I can sleep some."

Keller nodded again. He stood, and now Barrett stood as well. Barrett was much taller than Keller. The two men shook hands.

"Promise me you'll go right now," Keller said. "I can see myself out."

Barrett nodded. "I will. I promise. And thank you, Lawrence. You're my rock. I don't know how I would ever get through any of this without you."

"It's my honor to serve this office," Keller said.

* * *

It was just after 1 a.m.

Lawrence Keller sat in his car, a black BMW 325i sedan, which he had bought new last year. It was a nice car, and he was proud of it. He was proud of what it said about him, as well. A lot

161

of people with high-level Washington jobs—and Keller had one of the highest of the high-level jobs—were driven everywhere.

But not Lawrence Keller. He wouldn't hear of it, partly because he was self-reliant to an extreme, and partly because drivers witnessed things. They saw things, and they overheard things. Washington, DC, was not a town where you wanted people to know what you were up to. The more people who knew, the more people who could (and almost certainly would, if the price was right) take you down.

Keller was parked in the south end of Georgetown. Now and then, a car rolled slowly past on the quiet streets. Keller liked Georgetown. Disasters came and went, scandals came and went, famous men and women sparked through the sky like Roman candles and then flamed out, entire governments ruled the city and the country for years only to see everything they worked for undone by the next group in power... all of that happened, yes. But Georgetown was eternal.

In his hand, Keller held a small Radio Shack digital recorder. He had been listening to the playback for the past twenty minutes or so, fast forwarding and rewinding to certain parts he wanted to hear again and again.

He listened to the President of the United States abjectly weeping in the Oval Office.

He listened to the President speaking certain lines, lines that were gold:

"I want to kill them all."

Keller had marked the spots that he liked best. He could go straight to them, with just the press of a button. He went to another one now.

"They're killing me, do you know that? The press. They are killing me."

And then another:

"All these bastards can focus on is my military record. They're making me into a damn laughingstock. I hate them so much. I would bomb them, too."

Those ones were all good. Together, they painted a picture of a small-minded man who was coming apart at the seams. Here was a person in command of the greatest armed forces the world had ever seen, with his finger on the nuclear button, who was sitting in the Oval Office crying, and who was expressing an urge to kill many people.

He was also almost laughably self-absorbed during a major crisis, worrying about his reputation, and the things the press were saying about him. And the self-incriminating things he said only got worse. The hole he dug only grew deeper.

For example, there was this:

"If they have hurt her in any way, I don't know what I'm going to do. If they hurt her, I want the entire world set on fire."

Keller nodded and smiled. David Barrett sounded unhinged, a man going through a personal tragedy, who was rapidly becoming a threat to everyone on Earth. Plus there was this:

"I lie all the time. I have to. It's part of the job."

The man seemed to believe that part of his job was to lie. Of course, this was true, but it wasn't something the American people would like to hear. And then there was this, a small subtle statement that was perhaps the most damning thing of all:

"I can take a pill. I can sleep some."

The President, who was weeping, raging about the media, and threatening to set the world on fire—something that was well within his power to do—was also dependent on medication to sleep.

Lawrence Keller took a deep breath. It was amazing. He and his allies had wanted David out of office from almost the time the tall dope had wandered into it. He was a weak, uncertain President. He was swayed by random conversations—Keller often met with him in the morning, got his stance on a particular issue, and couldn't be sure that it would still be the same by that afternoon.

It would be good to get David out of there. It would be good to replace him with someone stronger—someone like his current Vice President, Mark Baylor, for example. It would be good for the country, and it would also be good for Lawrence Keller, wouldn't it? Yes. It would. Being Chief of Staff to a weak President was a good job. Many people would kill for such a job. But it wasn't the best of all possible jobs, was it?

No, it wasn't. What was a better job? Chief of Staff under a strong President, certainly. But also, Secretary of State, let's say. Or Director of National Security. People made jumps like that sometimes.

Lawrence Keller was the type of man who could make a jump like that.

Admittedly, it was an unfortunate set of circumstances that were removing David from office. Keller would never wish anything like this on Elizabeth Barrett—he had met her several times, and thought her a fine young person. Attractive, but probably not beautiful. Smart enough, but certainly not a genius. Just a nice girl from a very rich family whose dad happened to be the President.

Elizabeth had done a very silly thing. And the Secret Service had probably been lax in their protection of her. They had relied too much on the school's security, and they had underestimated what a bored teenage girl might do to experience a little excitement and a little romance.

Keller hoped that they were able to retrieve Elizabeth safe and sound. But her antics had caused something of a disaster—which by the way, was likely to set off a chain of catastrophic violence that would impact thousands of innocent people, people whom irresponsible young Elizabeth would never meet or even imagine.

And her antics had opened an opportunity to remove from the highest office in the land a man who was unfit to occupy that office. In the end, this was a good thing, no matter what happened to Elizabeth. It was not an opportunity that should be allowed to go to waste.

Okay. That settled it.

Keller climbed out of the car and set out walking at a brisk pace. Within a few moments, he was at the bottom of the hill and crossing the Francis Scott Key Bridge along the pedestrian sidewalk, heading across the Potomac River toward the Arlington neighborhood of Rosslyn.

On the bridge, the six lanes were quiet. Now and then, a car passed. Up ahead, to his south, the tall office towers of Rosslyn loomed. Even this time of night, there were many, many lights on.

Halfway across the bridge, Keller stopped. He pulled out a small cellular telephone and flipped it open. It was a burner phone—he had purchased it anonymously for cash with prepaid minutes loaded on it.

It was breezy out here on the bridge. Someone with a camera and a high-powered telephoto lens could watch him, but it would be very hard for anyone to overhear him speaking. It would also be hard to intercept a phone call that no one was expecting, from a phone that had never been used before. And naturally, it would be impossible to trace from where the call had come.

He dialed a number, one that very few people had.

After a couple of rings, a voice picked up.

"Hello?"

"Hi," Keller said. "Do you know who this is?"

"Of course," the voice said. "I was staying up, watching the TV news, and waiting for your call. I was beginning to think it wasn't going to come."

Keller shook his head and smiled. "Here it is."

"Good. What do you have?"

"I've got everything we need. It's all on tape. He's cracked. This has broken him."

"Okay," the voice said. "You know what to do with it."

Keller nodded. "Right. But none of this comes back to me. Agreed?"

"Agreed. We'll have someone play the salient parts for him, but he'll think he was bugged. You'll have nothing to do with it."

"Good," Keller said. "I suggest you have someone play it for him after he's gotten some sleep, when he's a little more lucid. When I left him, he was barely making sense anymore."

"Very nice," the voice said.

Keller smiled. "Yes. It is."

After they hung up, Keller dropped the telephone on the ground. He stomped on it, three, four, five times, until it broke apart. He picked up the shattered plastic casing and tossed it over the protective fence and into the river. Then he did the same with the metallic interior, where the sensitive data might be.

He watched the silver metal hit the dark water and then disappear beneath it. Then he kicked apart the last bits and pieces of black plastic still on the sidewalk.

The phone was gone. The conversation had never happened.

And pretty soon, maybe as soon as later this morning, David Barrett would relinquish his duties as President.

CHAPTER TWENTY THREE

9:25 a.m. Arabian Standard Time (1:25 a.m. Eastern Daylight Time)
Al Alam
Near Tikrit, Iraq

"There's the river," one of the young British soldiers said.

To Luke's ears, it sounded like "Thay-uhs the rivah."

Four Black Hawk helicopters moved across the pale desert landscape toward an undulating line of green. The green marked a fertile area on either side of the Tigris River. In some places it was a narrow band. In others, it seemed a mile wide. It snaked on into the far distance.

Luke, Ed, and four guys from the British Special Air Service, or SAS, rode in the lead chopper. In the second chopper, there were another six of the Brits. A dozen men in all were on this mission. The Brits all wore black balaclavas across their faces and goggles on their eyes. It was hard to see who they were. The two last choppers were empty—they were meant to carry the arrestees. It seemed like it might be a little bit of overkill to take one man and his family into custody.

In the near distance, oily black smoke rose into the air. A narrow strip of road seemed to lead directly to where the smoke was coming from.

"Something's going on," Ed Newsam said.

He was right. As the chopper moved closer, Luke could see that red and orange flames were still burning, apparently out of control. The flames reached into the sky in several places.

"Attention," the chopper pilot said. "Estimated time of arrival to the target is one minute. Prepare for disembark."

"Oh, great," Luke said. "The compound is on fire."

"Looks like somebody got here first," Ed said.

The first two choppers touched down on the far edge of the compound, away from the river. The rotor blades kicked up minor dust storms. Luke, Ed, and the SAS clambered out.

They walked toward the center of the compound, rifles drawn.

Behind them, the helicopters pulled away.

The scene was apocalyptic. The main house, a sprawling twenty-room monstrosity, and two smaller outbuildings were burning. A cluster of large trees planted near the river were on fire, their flaming arms reaching toward heaven.

A tall, corrugated building which must have been a garage—there were several cars parked outside of it—was also on fire. That's where the dark black smoke was coming from. To the far right, the fields were on fire. The buildings and the trees could have been hit with mortars, but the fields must have been deliberately set, possibly with flamethrowers.

Near the gate to the road, a couple of large horses, brown and white Arabian chargers, stood together. They stamped their feet and their tails swung anxiously. At least the horses had been spared.

About a hundred chickens ran back and forth on the grounds. The sky above the compound was turning dark with circling vultures and birds of prey. Every few moments, a hawk would drop to earth, snatch a frantic chicken, and fly off with it.

Straight ahead, the corpse of a woman lay on the ground in a pool of blood, her white robes stained red.

Several more human bodies were scattered around, apparently shot while they ran.

A water tower had crashed over sideways, its tank ruptured.

A grain storehouse had been left intact. Also, a long chicken house was still standing, along with a barn. Luke glanced inside the barn. A few cattle lay on their sides, shot dead. Whoever liked horses didn't feel the same way about cows.

"Someone is a step ahead of us," Ed Newsam said.

Luke caught a flash of movement out of the corner of his left eye. He turned that way, MP5 already raised. He wasn't the only one. Two of the SAS guys had done the same. At high speed, Luke replayed the moment in his mind: someone in dark clothes and with dark hair had just dashed inside the chicken coop.

He and the men were moving quickly toward the long building, guns out.

They burst inside. It was dim inside the building, and motes of thick dust and feathers hung in the air. Weak light streamed down from high, narrow windows at the top of the building. Someone or something slid through a hole in the ground just as they came in. Small hands came up and slid a wooden board over the hole. The board was a cut-out of the wooden floor in an area where chickens would normally be fed their grain. Scattered piles of grain still lay on the floor.

When the board was back in place, it was hard to see where the hole had just been.

Luke, Ed, and two SAS men moved to the spot.

Ed reached down, pulled up the board, and darted backward with it.

The SAS guys stepped up, rifles trained down the hole, laser sights on, headlamps shining brightly.

Luke stepped up with them, hand raised.

"Wait!" he shouted. "Steady! Steady!"

In the darkness down at the bottom of the hole, two small children, a boy and a girl, were crouched, huddled together.

"Don't shoot."

* * *

"What is he saying?" Luke said.

A young SAS guy was translating the boy's Arabic. The SAS guy had removed his balaclava, helmet, and goggles, revealing a fresh-faced, blond-haired kid with pale blue eyes and fat cheeks. Hardly the fearsome storm trooper that the helmet and mask made him appear.

The boy, perhaps twelve years old, was being strong. The girl, maybe half that age, had given up entirely. She was being held by another SAS guy with his helmet off, hugging him tightly, pressing her face into his chest.

"He says a group of men came just before sunrise. They immediately set about killing everyone. They launched rockets at the houses, and shot down anyone who came out. There are more bodies down by the river of people who tried to escape out the back way. The elder imam, Muhammad al-Barak, was taken from the main house, forced to his knees, and shot in the head. The boy and his little sister had been trained to hide beneath the chicken coop if anything like this ever happened, and that's what they did. They made it there without being seen. When he heard the helicopters, he climbed out to see what was happening, and that's when we found him."

Luke was relaying the news to Trudy and Swann over a satellite phone. He winced at the news of al-Barak. The old man who had come to thank him and Ed personally had met a bad end. It was the kind of thing that happened all too often around here.

"Does he have any idea who the men were?"

The SAS guy said something to the kid in Arabic.

The kid nodded, his dark eyes hollow and empty. He said something and pointed to the north. He continued speaking for several seconds.

"Yes. He knows exactly who they were. They belong to a religious school and jihad training camp about twenty miles north of here, straight along the river. His grandfather the imam knew the school, and the teachers there, well. The boy himself has visited there with family members. His grandfather and father told him it would never be, but he imagined going there to train one day when he was older. Now he says he would never join them. Their betrayal is too terrible."

"Trudy?" Luke said into the telephone.

Her voice was there. "Yes."

"We need another quick meeting with Don, Big Daddy, and Monty. I want permission to go in there. We've got a dozen guys, although we're going to send two back with the kids. The boy believes the camp the killers came from is just up the river here. If we're going to hit them and get a prisoner who can give us some intel, we should do it before the trail goes cold. I think we can probably do okay with ten guys."

"When do you want to do it?" Trudy said.

Luke almost couldn't believe what he was about to say. Don had already given him the green light home. He wanted to go home, more than anything. He wanted to see Becca. He wanted to be there when their boy was born.

But he also wanted to finish what they had started here. He didn't like that these militia guys had come down and killed al-Barak and his entire clan. It wasn't right, no matter what al-Barak had done. If you had a problem with the man, then kill the man. Not the family.

"Now," Luke said.

* * *

Green light.

Three Black Hawk helicopters raced across the pale blue morning sky.

Big Daddy and Don Morris had been in agreement—move forward with an assault on the camp. Montgomery had been called away on some other business and had not been available for the meeting. But Luke had kept his SAS guys anyway.

Luke had Mark Swann patched through on his helmet radio. Swann had pored over the available satellite imagery, and seemed to have pinpointed a militia camp whose location agreed with what the child had described.

"What does it look like?" Luke said.

"It looks like a big piece of nothing," Swann said.

"Give me more than that, Swann."

"There is a road," Swann said. "It is marked as Unnamed Road. It hugs the Tigris River for several miles, on the west side. Just past a little piece of nothing called Salman Village, there's a bridge across the Tigris. There's a wide open dusty plain, and as near as I can tell maybe thirty tents. There may be a more permanent structure there, but if there is, I don't see it. It looks like there's an artillery range to the east of there, with some cannons lined up. On the imagery I have, which admittedly is old, there are about a dozen vehicles parked on the property. A few of them appear to be pickup trucks with rear-mounted heavy weapons. If I were you guys, I'd take those things out first, then hit the cannons."

"Can you get some more recent imagery?" Luke said.

"Not likely. I can't get control of a satellite in the next ten minutes, and I doubt there's anything better than what I have. No one has ever taken a high priority look at that place. It really is a slice of nothing in the middle of nowhere. This looks like a very local gang. What I described to you is from me pulling generic imagery in that region and then zooming in."

"Any place to land?"

"The whole place is flat as a pancake. I'd say land anywhere you like."

Luke shook his head and smiled. "Anything resembling a helipad?"

"No. Nothing like that. These people appear to be earthbound. When they go somewhere, they drive there."

"How recent is the imagery you have?"

"Uh… three months old."

"Swann!"

"It's all that exists. It's the best you're going to get."

Luke gazed out the bay door for a moment. The choppers were moving fast above the parched, flat landscape. They were about to assault a militia compound, but had no idea what it was going to look like.

"Ed? Are you hearing this?"

Ed was flying in the second helicopter. He and Luke had split up to each take command of a small squad of SAS operators. This was an Americans show, after all.

"Yeah."

"What do you think?"

"We got three choppers, man. These birds are loaded with Hellfire missiles and M60 machine guns. I say we come in and wreck the place. I doubt it's changed all that much. Go with Swann's priorities. Knock out the vehicles, then the stationary cannons. After that, if anybody still has fight left in them, we drop in and take them out, too. Shoot first, ask questions later."

Luke nodded. It made sense.

"Okay, sounds good. But let's spare a couple so we *can* ask questions later."

A few moments passed.

Luke looked at the young SAS men on his chopper.

"Guys!' he shouted. "America thanks you for your service on our behalf. We know you men are the best of the best. The mission today is smash and grab. We want to bag one or two of the leaders of this militia. If the foot soldiers lay down, that's fine. We let 'em live. If they want to fight, we give them a fight. No one stops us, no one challenges us. But we want the leaders alive and intact."

"What you gonna do with them, Yank?"

Luke shrugged. "We're gonna talk to them. Firmly."

The young guys laughed at that.

"Incoming," the pilot said. "Prepare for evasive action."

Incoming? That was quick.

"Uh-oh," Luke said. "The game's starting."

The men took seats and strapped themselves in as the chopper banked hard right and gained altitude. A few seconds later, a rocket whooshed by.

Then the heavy guns opened up.

Luke could hear it, though he couldn't yet see it—the metallic clank of automatic cannon fire coming from the ground up ahead.

Duh-duh-duh-duh-duh.

"Stone!" Ed said in his ear. "How do they know we're coming?"

"I don't know. I didn't tell them."

Luke went up and poked his head into the cockpit.

"What are you guys seeing up here?"

"Ahead and to the right," one of the pilots said. "Vehicles moving across open desert, mostly fast-moving pickups, maybe modified SUVs. Heavy weaponry in truck beds. Ahead and to the left, the same. I count at least a dozen vehicles. I see at least one lorry or heavy truck, maybe a mobile rocket launcher. They've dispersed to make it harder on us. But they're coming out to fight."

"Kill them," Luke said. "Fire when ready. Take the rocket launcher first. Tell the other choppers."

The helicopters raced across desert, four stories up. Luke poked his head out the bay door to the right. Ahead, to their right, trucks moved across open terrain. Luke could hear the rattle of their guns.

He looked at the folded-up door gun, an M134 Minigun. It had six rotating barrels powered by an electric motor. And it had a high rate of fire, usually thousands of rounds per minute without cooking off. He had barely glanced at it before. He wasn't expecting to need it. A long belt of 7.62 millimeter rounds hung from it.

He looked at the nearest SAS guy. The tag sewn into the man's jumpsuit said GILMOUR.

"You, Gilmour. You know how to work that gun?"

The guy looked at it. He looked back at Luke. "Naturally."

"Get to it. You're my door gunner. We're in a fight. Let's go. Rip it up."

The guy unclipped and went to the gun. Luke went to the other side. A pickup truck was running straight at them, broadside to the chopper, the cargo door wide open. A man was in the truck bed, working the heavy gun.

"Watch it! Incoming fire!"

Gunfire erupted all around them, like a swarm of angry wasps. Luke dove to the floor. Something cut a sharp path across his right shoulder. There was a slice, then stinging pain. Metal shredded. Glass shattered somewhere.

Luke crawled across the floor. He was hit in the shoulder. He could barely get a look at it. He looked at the three SAS guys who were still clipped in.

"How's it look?"

One of them shrugged. "Flesh wound, Yank."

The sudden roar of the Minigun was earth-shattering just above Luke's head. He slid away, ears ringing instantly. The SAS guy, Gilmour, rode the recoil, arms bouncing, his face a blank inside his face mask. A burst of fire came from the barrel.

Luke watched out the cargo door.

Gilmour was dialed in. The pickup had passed beneath the chopper. A line of bullets strafed the back of it. The man on the truck's heavy gun did a death dance and came apart like a straw doll. The back tires exploded and the welded metal over the back windshield punched in. The pickup rolled to a stop.

"Nice shooting, Gilmour."

Gilmour raised a hand in reply.

172

Suddenly, another burst of machine gun fire hit the chopper. It seemed to come from everywhere at once. THUNK THUNK THUNK. Gilmour's body jerked and he fell away from the gun. More glass shattered up front.

Luke hit the floor again.

Gilmour was with him, screaming. Luke crawled to him.

The rest of the SAS were already unclipping.

"Medic!" Luke shouted. "Medic!"

Instantly, the medic was there.

Gilmours's teeth were gritted in pain. His eyes were wild and mad. His breathing was fast. "I got hit," he said. "I got hit. Dammit to hell, man!"

"Where is it?"

"I don't know. Everywhere."

The medic cut open Gilmour's jumpsuit. He felt beneath Gilmour's body armor.

Gilmour screamed in pain.

"We've got to get this shit off him," the medic said.

Luke looked at the two remaining SAS guys. He pointed at one of them. "You! Next man up! On the gun! Don't get shot!"

Another burst of gunfire hit the chopper. More bullets ripped up metal.

"Stone!" the pilot yelled over the intercom. "We've got instruments down. We can't keep taking hits like this. We're going to lose this bird."

"Take evasive action," Luke shouted.

The chopper pulled up abruptly. It made a steep climb and banked hard to the left. The medic nearly fell over sideways. Luke clung to the floor, his fingers gripping metal slats. Another burst of gunfire came.

An alarm in the cockpit began to sound.

BEEP, BEEP, BEEP...

The pilot's disembodied voice said: "Too late. We've got mayday. A rotor's been hit. It's wobbling. It's not going to hold. We either land or we crash, but we're going down."

"How much time do we have?"

"Uh... none."

Gilmour was screaming.

"It's all right," the medic said. "You're hit, but it's all right."

The guy with him yanked away Gilmour's armor. There was blood everywhere. Something had been cut to ribbons.

"Aw, Jesus!" the medic said.

173

The chopper began to spin crazily. The pilot was trying to regain control—the chopper spun hard left, then spun all the way back again hard right. The desert was coming toward them with frightening speed. The chopper was spinning, but seemingly under the pilot's control.

"My rudder's going. It's shuddering. I'm about to lose it."

Everything seemed like a bad dream. The chopper moved horizontally at fantastic speed, maybe fifty feet above the ground.

"Stone!" Ed Newsam said in Luke's ear. "You guys are hit."

Luke shook his head. "I know that."

"Put it down!" one of the pilots shouted. "Just put it down!"

It dropped with a sickening lurch, three stories in one second.

The pilot's voice was resigned. "Mayday, mayday. Assume crash positions."

Luke stared up at the safety straps dangling. There was no way they could any of them could get there and tie themselves down in time. He reached down and hugged the floor as hard as he could. His fingers gripped metal slats. This was his crash position.

The world zoomed by with dizzying speed. They were twenty feet from the ground.

The pilot's voice: "Prepare for impact."

"Be cool," Ed's deep voice said. "It looks okay."

A burst of gunfire hit the tail of the chopper. Thunk—thunk—thunk—thunk—thunk. Bullets ripped up metal.

They were closer to land now, much closer.

The chopper dropped out of the sky.

It fell like a brick. SMACK. The impact was hard, the jolt going up Luke's spine and through his body. His face bounced off the floor.

Everything stopped.

Another burst of gunfire strafed the chopper somewhere.

That wasn't too bad.

"He's dead," the medic said, shaking his head. "Dammit!"

* * *

The fight had turned.

The militia had started with the element of surprise, and all the initiative. But in wide open desert, they were no match for the overwhelming firepower of the two remaining Black Hawks. Big Ed Newsam was the door gunner for his chopper, standing there like a mountain, tearing up the pickup trucks and jeeps.

Luke and the SAS men bounced out of the downed chopper. They ran from one ruined, smoking vehicle to the next, killing whatever opposition they encountered. Most of the militiamen on foot were running away across the desert to the north and west. They wouldn't get far.

The metallic rattle of the big guns from the choppers came from over there.

Duh-duh-duh-duh.

Luke's little squad was walking now, guns out. The cluster of tents was just up ahead, flaps billowing in the desert wind. A tall man in flowing brown robes and a head wrap stood at the doorway of the largest tent.

"Don't kill him," Luke said. "We need him."

The man's beard was dark, with streaks of gray in it. His eyes were piercing. He seemed angry, confident, and not at all afraid.

He said something in Arabic.

One of the SAS guys turned his rifle around and butted the man in the face. Instantly, the man fell to the ground. His hand went to his jaw. The angry look on the man's face only became angrier.

The SAS men looked down at him.

"That's for Gilmour," he said.

CHAPTER TWENTY FOUR

1:30 p.m. Arabian Standard Time (5:30 a.m. Eastern Daylight Time)
A Safe House
Baghdad, Iraq

Luke watched the militia leader from the corner of the room.

"In a moment," Big Daddy Cronin said, "if you won't give me the answers I'm looking for, I am going to hold your feet to the fire. Do you know this saying?"

The militia leader was sitting on a wrought iron chair. It looked like it might have had a seat cushion at one time, but that was long gone. Now there was just the rusty metal that made up the chair.

The man had black hair to go with his long black beard. Both were streaked with gray. His shirt and pants were gone—he was stripped to the underwear. He was thin and very fit, like a man who got a great deal of physical exercise on short rations of food. His boots and socks were gone—his feet were bare. The right side of his face was swollen from the blow with the rifle butt.

The man's hands were manacled around the back of the chair, the chain looped through the chair's openings, and was cinched tight. He was belted to the seat with a leather strap. His legs were out straight. His feet were bound together with heavy tape around the ankles, and were held in wooden stocks, making it impossible to move them. Moreover, the way he was strapped to the chair, and with his legs encased in wood, he had no leverage.

Big Daddy Cronin waited for the Iraqi translator to finish speaking. The translator was a slim, balding, middle-aged man in a nondescript, short-sleeved green uniform with no markings of any kind. He had a pencil-thin mustache. He wore heavy sandals on his feet. He could almost be a nurse, or a doctor, if doctors wore sandals.

There were five men in the room. Big Daddy, the translator, the heavily bearded mujahideen who had only recently commanded a militia, Ed, and Luke. Luke thought it better if Trudy and Swann missed Big Daddy at work.

Montgomery was not here. Apparently, he had run into trouble because of the death of the SAS man Gilmour. Monty had authorized them to go al-Barak's compound, but not on to the militia compound. Big Daddy and Don Morris had given the order anyway. As far as Big Daddy was concerned, the SAS men were on loan to the CIA.

Big Daddy and Monty were no longer on the same page about this. There was some talk of Monty being recalled to London. As far as his superiors were concerned, Gilmour's death was on his hands.

Luke was sorry that Gilmour had died. He hated that it happened. But the office politics surrounding that death was not Luke's major concern.

The militia leader began to speak.

"Yes, I know the phrase," the translator said. "But I remind you that any forms of torture or coercion are against the laws of war."

"Is murdering an old man and his entire family in alignment with your laws of war?" Big Daddy said.

The translator spoke for a few seconds, then listened to the bearded man's response before speaking.

"I'm afraid I have no idea what you're talking about."

"How did you know the helicopters were coming?"

The man shrugged. "People tell me things. How they know these things I cannot say. Spies, I suppose."

He glanced around the room. "The walls themselves have ears."

Big Daddy nodded. He looked around the room. It was a small, barren, empty place. The house was ugly, a squat structure made of cinderblock. This room was a perfect microcosm of the rest of the house. The walls were cracked and turning a sickly shade of green. Bare wires extended from the walls, attached to nothing. There was no electricity in here. The floors had been ripped up to bare cement. The room itself had no windows to the outside world.

The house stood nearly alone in a neighborhood that was mostly rubble. It had been bombed and strafed with automatic fire. Nearly all of the homes had been destroyed. Insurgents had held out in this area for a time. Now no one at all was here.

"Where do you think we are?" Big Daddy said.

The translator spoke. The militia leader shrugged his shoulders. It was one of the few movements still available to him. Luke was surprised at how confident he seemed. The man had seen a lot of death. Any Iraqi who had survived this far into the war was on an intimate basis with murder. He had dedicated his life to his god, and had probably done many horrible things in that god's name. Perhaps there was little left that frightened him. Perhaps he considered himself a martyr already.

The man smiled. "I was hooded when I was brought here. I could not see. I have no idea where I am."

"Well, let me fill you in then," Big Daddy said. "You're nowhere. You're not under arrest. No one has logged you in to any system. As far as anyone is concerned, you died in battle this morning with the rest of your men, slaughtered like a pig. You'll notice I haven't even tried to find out your name. That's because I don't care. Why would I care about the name of a dead man?"

He waited for the translation to reach the man. When the translator finished, the man nodded. Luke thought he saw a subtle change behind the man's eyes then.

"Did they all die?"

Big Daddy looked at Luke. Luke nodded.

"Yes."

The man stared straight ahead now.

"My name is Abu Ayyub Kamal. I was injured during the battle. I demand to see a doctor."

"You don't look injured," Big Daddy said.

"I have internal injuries. I have been mistreated during captivity. I would like to see representatives of the International Red Cross or Red Crescent. I want them to know I am a prisoner of war in American custody."

"You're not in American custody."

"Yes I am."

Big Daddy shook his head. "You're not listening to me."

He went to a small table in the corner. There were several items on the table. Luke hadn't looked closely at it before now.

Big Daddy came back holding a small metal canister with a spout.

"This is gasoline," he said.

He upended the canister and the amber green fluid began to flow onto the man's feet. The man tried to move his feet, but the stocks wouldn't move. They were weighted and bolted to the floor. Big Daddy also spilled some up the man's legs.

The stench of raw gasoline filled the room.

The man shouted. Then he began to scream.

"No! You must not do this!"

"Scream all you want," Big Daddy said. "There is no one to hear you."

Dutifully, wincing, the Iraqi translator repeated Big Daddy's words in Arabic. The translator, a Shiite working for the provisional government, in all likelihood had no love for Sunnis, but even so… Big Daddy's work, and the businesslike, matter-of-fact way he approached it, would make anyone wince.

The blank, expressionless look on his face made things even worse. Big Daddy wasn't even angry yet.

He took a large Zippo lighter from his pocket and clicked it on. A four-inch flame appeared, yellow-orange and blue at its base.

"This is what I meant when I said I would hold your feet to the fire. What did you think I meant?"

"No!" the man said. "Stop! Please stop! I will tell you. I will tell you anything."

Big Daddy looked at Luke and winked.

"Gets them almost every time," he said.

Luke raised an eyebrow. "Almost?"

Big Daddy shrugged. He glanced back at the militia leader. "Once in a while, you have to go through with it."

* * *

"I knew the boy, yes. The one you think of as Ahmet the Turk."

The militia leader Abu Kamal sat at a table in another room.

Luke watched from the corner. He had taken part in a lot of interrogations, and it had made him a skeptic. These guys *always* knew the subject in question.

They *always* knew the location of a secret hideout. They had incredible imaginations. They could spin fantastic stories with the when and the where and the why. They could describe high-level meetings that took place in cave complexes under inaccessible mountains, or at multimillion-dollar townhouses in London. And when you pursued the leads they gave you, it turned out to be smoke and mirrors.

Kamal's hands were still manacled, but the chain had been loosened. It looped under the table, and the table was also bolted to the cement floor. The effect was that it gave his hands much more freedom of movement than before. He used this freedom to smoke a home-rolled cigarette.

His legs were completely free, and his clothes were back on. His legs were folded. He seemed completely calm now. He spoke in a conversational tone.

"You think him a boy, probably, but he is older than he appears. He is from the village of Hajin, in Syria, just over the western border from Iraq. He is not a fighter. He is not strong, and he is not courageous. When he was in the camp, he failed most of

179

the physical tests demanded of him. He was useless with weapons. I'm not even sure that he has been called by Allah."

"What good was he, then?" Big Daddy said.

Luke had watched Big Daddy work before, too. He was still trying to decipher the man's approach. Sometimes he instantly rejected what the interviewee was saying. Sometimes he played along like he believed it, then suddenly jumped on an inconsistency. Sometimes he just listened and drew the interviewee out, completely trusting, like he didn't have any strategy at all.

There was a method to Big Daddy's madness, but Luke had no idea what it was.

Kamal shrugged and took a deep drag of his cigarette.

"Everyone brings their own gifts. Ahmet is thin and handsome, almost womanly in his way—he is a temptation to women. He is very intelligent. He is an engineer and a scientist, and he is very good at languages. He learned Turkish and French as hobbies when he was a teenager. I believe he had hoped to move to Europe one day, though the war dashed those hopes."

To Luke's ears, it sounded like a romantic story. *The war dashed the man's hopes.*

"Why would the war dash his hopes, if he is Syrian?" Big Daddy said. "Syria is not at war."

Kamal looked at Big Daddy. His face was calm but his eyes were hard. "I'm sure you well know that your war is a messy affair. It doesn't recognize borders. Two years ago, just after the war started, your special forces conducted a raid at Haditha, in western Iraq. Documents taken in the raid suggested that Syrian smuggling networks had turned their attention from oil, precious metals, and ordinary people leaving for Europe. They were moving fighters from Egypt, Tunisia, Algeria, and Saudi Arabia across Syria to Iraq. I can attest that this is true, as far as that goes."

Big Daddy nodded. "Go on."

"Your forces believed that the Syrian smugglers had set up a base of operations at Hajin, and were sheltering dozens of mujahideen there before they crossed into Iraq. That part was not true. It was, how would you describe it? Bad intelligence. A group of soldiers in helicopters conducted a cross border raid into Hajin. They found no fighters there, but killed at least a dozen civilians. This was one of your accidents. When your man Ahmet joined the mujahideen, he had just buried his younger brother and sister, who died in the raid. He was angry and broken, and he wanted revenge. He offered what skills he had. You might say these skills have proven very valuable."

"Where is the girl?" Big Daddy said.

Kamal shook his head. "That I have no idea. I merely met Ahmet in the camps. His name was Hashan at that time. He tried hard, but was a bit of a laughingstock. I knew nothing about the operation he was sent on. Since he couldn't fight, I assumed they would make a suicide bomber of him. You can torture me until I die, but I will save you the trouble by being honest. I rejoice that the brothers have taken your President's daughter. But I don't know where they took her, and I do not know what their plans are."

"Do you know where Ahmet or Hashan is?"

Kamal shook his head. "No. Dead, I would guess. But I suppose you could ask his parents."

Luke perked up at that. "His parents?"

"When I met him, he was concerned about his parents in Hajin. They had lost two of their three children to the Americans, and soon they would lose their last child. They were in mourning at that time. I assume little has changed for them."

"You believe Ahmet's parents are still in Hajin?"

Kamal nodded. "Yes. I think so. Where else would they be?"

Big Daddy eyed the man closely.

"Wouldn't someone move them from there? The most important of all the mujahideen on Earth is their son. It seems risky to leave them there."

Kamal took another drag on his cigarette. "You make a lot of assumptions, don't you? Who said Hashan is the most important mujahid? You say it, because you are blind. Your President's daughter is important to *you*. Her taking is sensational, yes. It will give hope to some who were wavering. It will recruit new soldiers. But true believers don't need a sensation to sacrifice their lives to Allah, and we have more important goals than slaughtering this young cow."

He paused for a moment, to allow that word to sink in. *Cow.*

Big Daddy stared down at his own hands. His fingers made a strange, wavelike motion. They looked like the tentacles of an octopus. He was showing remarkable restraint. Again, Luke wondered at his interrogation strategy. He had seen Big Daddy break men's teeth for less than what Kamal just said.

Kamal continued speaking. "Anyway, who believed Hashan would ever complete this mission? I told you he was an incompetent. I thought he would die in an explosion in a Shiite market square. They sent him to Geneva, to kidnap the daughter of the President of the United States? Who would dream such a thing would work? I can only guess they did this out of pity. Hashan is a bright young man. He is very kind. He has no business in a war zone."

"What are you saying?" Big Daddy said.

Kamal shrugged. "This kidnapping took place last night. It is a surprise to everyone."

"Yes, and?"

"His parents are still in Hajin. I'm certain of it. But if you wait much longer, perhaps they won't be."

Big Daddy looked at Luke. He raised an eyebrow.

"Can't hurt to check it out."

Luke looked at Ed Newsam.

"Let's go," Ed said.

CHAPTER TWENTY FIVE

7:05 a.m. Eastern Daylight Time (3:05 p.m. Arabian Standard Time)
The Oval Office
The White House
Washington, DC

"It's a disaster."

David Barrett, the President of the United States, was back behind the Resolute Desk. If anything, he looked even less resolute and smaller than he had the night before. His eyes were dark and hollowed out. He looked like he hadn't slept at all.

Lawrence Keller nodded. He was once again standing in front of the desk. "I know it. These people are barracudas. They have no mercy."

An hour before, David had received the audiotape of himself coming unhinged the night before. He said he wasn't sure where it came from. A young interoffice messenger, already at work at 6 a.m., had brought him the tape in a manila envelope.

"What do you want to do?" Lawrence said.

Barrett shook his head. "I don't want to step down."

Lawrence nodded. "No. Of course not."

"But I think I should step aside for now." He clenched his fists. "I had no idea that Mark was this... ambitious. That he would go to these lengths to unseat me." He shook his head again. "Maybe it's for the best. Mark is a tough man. No one has stolen his daughter. Maybe he can... help me... get her back."

"I think Mark Baylor will make an exceptional Interim President," Lawrence said, feeding David the term.

For a second, David's eyes showed confusion. "Interim..."

Lawrence nodded. "Of course. David, you're my friend. I've never seen you like this. I've never seen you so indecisive. You can't simply take a leave of absence when you're President of the United States. If you're going to leave, even for a week, even for a couple of days, you've got to appoint Mark as the Interim President. Mark will need the power that comes with the title—do you think the Joint Chiefs of Staff are going to obey a substitute teacher?

Also, the American people need to have confidence in their leadership. They need to know they have a President. They need to know someone is in charge. When we get Elizabeth back, after you have some time with your family to recuperate, then maybe…"

Now David was staring at Lawrence. He stared for what seemed like a very long time. Lawrence did not look away. There was a light of recognition in David's eyes.

"Did you… did you do something to me, Lawrence? Were you in on it with them? I mean, I figured they bugged the Oval Office. That made sense, but…"

Those eyes stared and stared, imploring him.

Keller shook his head. Now that the secret was out, there was no sense dancing around the topic. Still, it was best not to confirm or deny anything. You never could tell who was listening.

"David, whatever I did or didn't do, all of my actions have been for the benefit of the United States of America. Please trust me on this. We're going to get your daughter back. Then we're going to demonstrate to some people who the boss is around here. There's going to be a show of power."

Barrett was hanging his head now. "Please, Lawrence. Please get her back. That's all I really care about."

Keller nodded. "I know that, David. And we're going to do everything we can to make it happen. This is for the best. You're not thinking clearly right now. You wouldn't have been able to manage. No one would. There's no way to have objectivity in a situation like this. There's no way to make decisions. Mark is fresh and alert. He can step up to the plate for you."

Barrett's shoulders slumped. He seemed to be withering right in front of Keller's eyes. He sighed heavily.

"I am so tired."

"I understand, David. There's only one thing left for you to do. Then you can go back to bed for a few hours. Wake up, maybe feel refreshed a little, and be with your family. You can go to Camp David and stay secluded for the duration. No prying eyes. No questions. No decisions to make."

Barrett looked up. "What do I need to do?"

Keller slipped a piece of paper on the desk in front of him. "I drafted some very brief remarks for you. All they say is everything we've discussed. For the good of the country, you're stepping aside indefinitely. You are appointing Vice President Mark Baylor to the role of Interim President on your behalf. President Baylor should be considered to have all the powers of the Presidency until further notice."

Barrett picked up the paper. He stared at it, but didn't seem to read it. It seemed like it could have been upside down for all he cared.

"We can tape the segment right here in the office. No reporters. No questions. A simple statement from you. Twenty minutes later, Mark takes the Oath of Office."

Barrett slid the paper back onto the desk. He gazed around the Oval Office for a long moment.

"Okay," he said.

* * *

The surge in confidence was palpable. Even a jaded old hand like Lawrence Keller, a man who had been through decades of political infighting in Washington, could feel the difference.

A new group moved through the hallways of the West Wing. At the head of the pack, aides and assistants double-stepping to keep pace, was Interim President of the United States Mark Baylor. Keller the long-distance runner moved along fluidly beside him.

Baylor was tall, like they all were. He was broad, a little broader now than was probably healthy. His hair was white. He was from a rich family, like David Barrett, but somehow it was a different kind of wealth.

Eight generations before, a hardscrabble male ancestor of Baylor's had stepped off a sailing ship from England, and immediately set about acquiring vast areas of northern wilderness, regardless of how the people who already lived there felt about it. The Baylor family were lumber barons, and had been for two centuries.

Mark Baylor had attended East Coast prep schools, just like any other member of the ruling class. But he took no military deferments—his family wouldn't hear of it. He deferred his entry to Yale instead, and joined the Marine Corps as a raw recruit on Parris Island. He took his lumps, served in Vietnam, and came back with two Purple Hearts for his troubles. Then he went to Yale.

It had seemed all along to Keller that Mark Baylor wasn't the Vice President. He was the President in waiting. The shadow President.

Circumstances had proved him right. Keller was not technically Baylor's Chief of Staff, not yet, but he had long been a confidant of his, and he was very much on the man's team.

"Lawrence, after this briefing, I'm going to want a smaller, private meeting in the Oval Office, where we can speak frankly with relevant parties about what needs to happen, and who should do it. You'll know better than I who those parties are."

Keller nodded. "Consider it done."

The group piled into the elevator. They pressed shoulder to shoulder as the elevator descended into the Earth.

"We owe it to David Barrett to bring his daughter home safely," Baylor said. "I want to focus like a laser on that outcome."

The doors opened and the entire Mark Baylor entourage stepped into the egg-shaped Situation Room.

Lawrence Keller glanced around the room.

The plush leather chairs at the table all looked like the captain's chair on the command module of a spaceship crossing the galaxy. Big arms, deep leather, high backs, ergonomically correct with lumbar spine support. Nearly all the chairs were filled with thick bodies.

The seats along the walls—smaller, red linen chairs with lower backs—were filled with young aides and even younger assistants, most of them slurping from Styrofoam coffee cups or murmuring into telephones.

Mark Baylor took a seat in a leather chair at the closest end of the oblong table. Keller stood by his side and a little behind him. People continued to talk among themselves as if the President of the United States hadn't just entered the room.

"General Stark," Baylor said.

The chatter went on.

"General Stark!"

At the head of the room, Richard Stark of the Joint Chiefs glanced his way. His face was jagged and hard. He smiled when he saw Baylor.

"Mr. President," he said.

Baylor nodded. "I took the Oath fifteen minutes ago. Can you please bring this room to order? We have a lot to go over, and I feel like I'm playing catch-up."

Stark stood. He clapped his hands. "Order, everybody! Come to order, please."

The place went silent. Almost. A couple of young men in suits along the wall continued to whisper to each other, heads leaned in close.

Stark looked at them. "You two! Either shut up or get out."

Startled, the two men looked up. Their eyes were wide.

Now the room went dead quiet.

Stark nodded. "Good. Welcome, President Baylor. We are very glad to have you here."

To Lawrence Keller's ears, the general lingered on the word *very*. People at the Pentagon were no fans of David Barrett. Baylor, on the other hand, was a frequent visitor to the Pentagon. As a senator, he had been a consistent advocate for increased military spending, increased recruitment, and the pioneering of new weapons systems.

Baylor nodded. "Thank you, General. Get me up to speed. Where are we with the search for Elizabeth?"

Stark stood. He referred to some papers he had on the desk in front of him.

"We are moving along at a very fast pace, uncovering, then following up on leads. In the past eight hours, special operations units have raided dozens of known and suspected militant compounds throughout Iraq—both in Sunni- and Shiite-held areas, in the mountains of northern Syria and western Iran, in Libya, Egypt, Lebanon, Tunisia, Algeria, and Yemen, as well as Afghanistan and Pakistan. Turkey, Saudi Arabia, Kuwait, and the United Arab Emirates all assure us they are doing the same within their own borders—for obvious political reasons, we cannot make incursions on their territory.

"Thus far, we have inflicted enemy casualties in the many hundreds, possibly thousands. I regret that we have also already lost over thirty men in these raids, with at least another ninety wounded. We have managed to keep these casualty tallies out of the newspapers for now, but eventually that information is going to be leaked."

"What is the upshot of all this?" Baylor said.

Stark shrugged. It was an oddly ineffectual movement. "It's a needle in a haystack, Mr. President. Countless intelligence agents are poring over data, seeking to find a clue as to where she may be held. There are hundreds of suspected militant sites. For obvious reasons, each one needs to be approached in a sudden, unexpected, and surgical fashion. So while we are moving fast, we also have to move carefully. Whoever has Elizabeth, if we set them off, they are going to kill her."

"They are likely to kill her anyway," Baylor said.

The general nodded. "Yes. That's true. In the meantime, we proceed as best as we can, and as fast as we can. Across Europe, police and intelligence agencies are doing the same. They are raiding known and suspected terrorist safe houses, on the chance that the kidnappers never left Europe. In particular, French SWAT units have hit at least eighty homes since the abduction."

187

"And we're not putting any information together from this?" Baylor said. "I find that hard to believe."

"It's not that we're not gleaning information. It's that we're moving so fast, we are generating a massive pile of information. We are being flooded with data. It could take weeks or months to make sense of it all. We have hundreds of people detained, many of whom have been trained to resist interrogation, or have memorized false narratives designed to make us chase our tails.

"Meanwhile, entire networks are being taken down or destroyed, including ones that have been under surveillance for years. A who's who of rogues and baddies have been killed or captured. If there is an upside to this unfortunate situation, it's that it has lit a fire under everyone, and a lot of house cleaning that should have been done long ago is getting done now. But not without cost, as I indicated."

"How long before Elizabeth is killed?" Baylor said.

The general glanced at his watch. "A little over seventeen hours. But I caution you, Mr. President, not to take the word of terrorists as bond. Elizabeth could be dead even now."

"And where are we with the prisoner release?"

An aide whispered in Stark's ear.

Stark shook his head. "For reasons I can't get into here, there are numerous people on that prisoner list who we cannot even consider releasing. Some of them are among the most dangerous men on Earth. There are others we have no control over whether they'll be released or not, because we're not the ones holding them. The horse trading involved, for example, in getting terrorists released from prison in Egypt, Tunisia, or Malaysia would be long, protracted, and probably not worth our while in terms of what we would have to give. I'm sorry to say that as far as the intelligence community and the Pentagon are concerned, trading prisoner releases for Elizabeth's life is a non-starter."

There were a few quiet gasps around the room at that pronouncement.

Baylor only nodded.

"Are you saying that we are forfeiting Elizabeth's life?"

The general shook his head. "I'm saying that we are in a very difficult position, and our longstanding policy is not to negotiate with terrorists."

Baylor took a deep breath and then sighed.

"Here's what I want," he said. "I want a list of the five or six most likely countries or territories where Elizabeth could be held.

Then I want to know how we can apply the most amount of pressure to the populations who might be harboring the terrorists."

"Pressure, sir?" General Stark said. "On the civilian populations?"

"General, you seem to believe that David Barrett's daughter Elizabeth is going to die, and there isn't much we can do about it," Baylor said. "Would you say that's an accurate assessment of your position?"

"I wouldn't necessarily phrase it that way, sir."

"How would you phrase it, General?"

"I would phrase it that Elizabeth is very likely to die, and we are doing everything in our—"

"I'm not interested in semantics, General. What I want after this meeting is a menu of options available to us. If Elizabeth dies, I want the people who harbor terrorists—their mothers and fathers, their neighbors, their children and loved ones, their entire communities—to feel our collective pain."

* * *

"What are your ideas, General Stark?" Mark Baylor said.

The men were standing in the Oval Office. Lawrence Keller was there, along with a few others. The tall blue drapes were pulled, shutting out the natural daylight. Two big Secret Service men stood by the door. David Barrett was nowhere to be found. There was no sign of him. It was almost like he had never existed in the first place.

This was not a "let's settle down, everybody get comfortable" meeting. Baylor hadn't offered anyone a chair. There were no sandwiches or coffee coming from food service. It was clear that Baylor was going to be no-nonsense.

The general referred to three sheets of paper his aide handed him. "Mr. President, we have an entire menu of options available to us."

Keller liked that the general was already referring to Mark by his new title. Generals in the Pentagon were nothing if not political animals—Stark had clearly smelled which way the wind was blowing.

Baylor nodded. "Let's hear them."

"There are quite a few," Stark said.

"Journey of a thousand miles," Baylor said.

The general nodded. "Of course."

189

He looked at the papers again. "In general, we assume that none of these options bring Elizabeth Barrett back alive. That's an unfortunate side effect of the situation. As I indicated in the briefing downstairs, special forces units of all kinds are conducting raids throughout the Islamic world as we speak. None have borne fruit thus far. We have no idea if Elizabeth is still alive, and as more and more contact is made with terrorist cells, militias, and enemies of all stripes, the odds of her survival decrease rather than increase. They decrease dramatically, in fact."

"Why is that, General?" Baylor said.

Stark shrugged. "Good question, sir. Mostly, it's because we're blundering around like a wounded bull in a china shop. Working at this speed, we have no way of vetting the intelligence we are getting. A lot of it is bad. Most of it is incomplete. Whoever has Elizabeth sees what we're doing, and if we appear to be getting close, they will likely become spooked and simply kill her. Or they may kill her because right now the eyes of the entire world are watching. For the terrorists, an Elizabeth Barrett beheading video is a powerful recruiting tool."

"Wonderful," Baylor said. "So where does that leave us?"

"If I may be frank..." Stark began.

Baylor nodded. "Of course."

"It leaves us with an opportunity. We are the angry bull, and justifiably so. If Elizabeth dies, and even before she does, we are now free to engage and destroy many of our enemies with complete impunity. Does Hezbollah have Elizabeth? We don't know. They might. We are free to punish Hezbollah for any role they may have played in this fiasco. What about the Assad regime in Syria? The Taliban? Muammar Qaddafi in Libya and the Muslim Brotherhood in Egypt. We could decide to pacify the Sunni Triangle from the air, rather than on the ground. We know that the Iranians have previously allowed Al Qaeda operatives to cross their territory unimpeded."

Baylor listened, but didn't say anything.

"The beauty of this, if you will, is we can issue an ultimatum to all of our enemies in the Muslim world. Either they are with us or against us. The groups and places I named earlier must pull any and all strings they have to gain Elizabeth's safe release, or we will begin a campaign of open warfare the likes of which they have never seen."

He paused. "Whoever did this has sponsors. And we can make anyone we suspect of being a sponsor pay dearly."

Baylor took a deep breath. "Correct me if I'm wrong," he said. "But isn't Saudi Arabia the most likely sponsor of whoever carried out this kidnapping?"

Stark shrugged. "I don't know. No one can know that for a fact. Does Saudi Arabia the state, and wealthy individuals in both Saudi Arabia and the other Sunni states of the Persian Gulf, sponsor Al Qaeda and other Sunni terrorist groups? Almost certainly. You know that. I know that. But Joe and Jane Sixpack don't know that. And what's more, they don't really care. They just want someone to pay for this. We can decide who that is. Obviously, we're not going to attack the Saudis. They're allies of ours. But Iran? Syria? Hezbollah? Libya? It's open season. Or can be, if we want."

"And so," Baylor said. "The options?"

"Many," Stark said. "As you know, we have a great many military assets in the region. Tens of thousands of troops on the ground in Iraq. Tens of thousands of troops stationed at Doha. Jet fighters and bombers that can leave from Iraq, from Doha, and from Saudi Arabia. The Fifth Fleet controls the Persian Gulf, and the Sixth Fleet has destroyers and cruisers on standby in the eastern Mediterranean Sea. Central Command has drones in the air twenty-four hours a day. I would suggest that we publicly give whoever is holding Elizabeth a twelve-hour deadline to release her unharmed. At the same time, we indicate to several bad actors in the region that they are also responsible for her well-being."

He paused. "At the end of twelve hours, if Elizabeth hasn't been released, or if she has turned up dead by then, we unleash an all-out assault from the air. We destroy, as much as is possible, Hezbollah fortifications in southern Lebanon. We destroy Shiite training camps the Iranians have set up in the northwestern mountains of Iran. We also wipe out the Iranian fast boat navy in the Persian Gulf. All of them. Wipe them off the map. We fortify the whole thing with missiles locked on air force and naval bases in southern Iran, along the coast. If they even try to fight back, we destroy those assets, with impunity. We can do the same in the north, to their assets on the Black Sea."

Stark flipped over a page and scanned the next one.

"Last but not least, we bomb Bashar al-Assad's presidential palace in Damascus, and other compounds he has throughout Syria. Bomb them to dust. We can do the same to Qaddafi in Libya, if we want."

The room became quiet. Lawrence Keller considered that, far from eliminating problems that had been bedeviling the United

States for some time, what General Stark was describing was the beginning of World War Three.

Keller had bum-rushed David Barrett out the door. He was beginning to have an odd feeling about that decision. Stark never talked like this in front of Barrett.

"What about the Russians?" Mark Baylor said.

Stark shook his head. "The Russians are a shadow of their former selves. They're weak. They're focused on rebuilding their economy and their military. Yes, they are allies with the Iranians, with the Syrians, and with Hezbollah. But our intelligence indicates they won't risk a shooting war to protect those allies. Not now. Not yet. Ten years from now, they might. All the more reason to take these steps now."

To Keller, it was clear that the general was not speaking off the cuff. He had come to the meeting with these ideas in his pocket. And he wasn't speaking for himself. The Joint Chiefs of Staff had probably cooked up this plan years ago. Keller had to admit it had a certain grim logic. Except...

"The Russians have nuclear weapons," Keller almost said. But didn't.

Mark Baylor, the new President, was nodding. All eyes were on him. The ghost of a smile appeared on his face. He didn't hesitate.

"I like it," he said. "Let's do it. Start putting everything into place. Begin to lock on targets, and make it obvious that we're doing so."

Baylor glanced around the room. His eyes fell on Lawrence Keller.

"Let's get a video team in here, and alert the media that we're going to want airtime. We've got an announcement to make."

"What about allies and strategic partners?" Lawrence Keller said. "England, France, NATO, Japan, Australia... these people might want a little bit of a..."

Mark Baylor waved that away.

"I don't want to hear a lot of debate about this, no matter how well intentioned. Let them all watch it on television."

CHAPTER TWENTY SIX

4:30 p.m. Arabian Standard Time (8:30 a.m. Eastern Daylight Time)
Hajin
Eastern Syrian
Near the Iraqi Border

"My kind of place," Ed Newsam said.

The village was dusty and remote, a cluster of shacks and cinderblock one-story houses built along a narrow tributary of the Euphrates River. The water flowed dark brown here, and green reeds and scrub brush grew along the stream's edge. The ground was a deep, dull orange fading to brown and tan. Chickens chased each other across the dirt paths. Tidy vegetable gardens were planted in rows behind people's homes.

To the north, in the far distance, rose rugged mountain peaks. Closer to the village, the surrounding area was as flat, and as hot, as a frying pan.

"You can move here after we're done," Luke said.

Luke and Ed walked through the village, catching the stares of the locals. They were accompanied by an Arabic translator, a cheerful young guy from the suburbs of Chicago named Greg Welch. Greg worked for the "State Department."

He made the little crow's feet with his fingers when he said the words *State Department*. He thought that was funny.

In Luke's experience, CIA office people who rarely or never saw combat seemed to think a lot of things were funny, especially their own status and their cover stories. Undercover CIA agents and special operatives, and the people who staffed black site prisons, tended to think nothing was funny.

"How's your Arabic, Greg?" Luke said.

Greg smiled. "It's awesome. I'm fluent in the Mesopotamian dialect, as though I grew up here. I can speak Levantine, but some of the slang phrases are a little dicey. I've got some Middle Eastern blood myself, and I tan really well. There's been talk of sending me undercover at some point."

Luke thought of his own time undercover as a Western jihadi in Iraq. The bloodstained images passed through his mind in a flash. He glanced at Greg again.

"I don't know if I'd recommend that."

The three men wore casual TV reporter war zone clothes as they entered the village—utility vests, heavy boots, cargo pants, and T-shirts. Greg Welch wore a floppy sunhat. They all carried sidearms, even Greg Welch, although he was just an "embassy staffer."

The chopper had dropped them off on a flat sandy plain a quarter mile outside town. What they didn't want to do was drop in suddenly, fully armored, and possibly retrigger the trauma of the original raid. They wanted this to go as smoothly as possible.

They were in Syria now, and Syria was not part of the war. They walked in, moving slowly and deliberately, not trying to hide or defend themselves. They were not invading or infiltrating a sovereign nation.

They were just visitors, policemen actually, here to ask a few questions.

Everyone knew already.

People stood in front of their small homes, as still as statues, watching them pass. In the best of situations, Ed Newsam's sheer size would bring stares, but this was more than that. It was as though the people of the village had been waiting for someone to come.

It was as though they were ghosts, the ghosts of their former selves, the people they were before the raid. Those people were gone and these ghosts were here, and the ghosts knew what the young man from their village had done, and they were waiting for the hammer to drop again.

They came to the house. It was a small cinderblock home, painted pale blue. The paint was faded and chipped. The plants in the front yard were dried out and dead. Much about the house seemed shabby and rundown, as if the people inside of it had given up. A rusty metal chair sat near the front door. An old man had just risen from it.

The man was small and bald. He was thin, and probably only in his fifties, but something about him seemed ancient, and heavy. His skin was dark. He wore a light gray jacket over what looked like a T-shirt, and some kind of thick bandaging. He moved his upper body gingerly, as though his back had been injured and he was in terrible pain.

Down below, his right pant leg was cut off above the knee. A very basic metal prosthetic device was attached with leather straps at his knee and thigh. He leaned on a wooden crutch. His right leg was gone from the knee down.

He waited for them to walk up the path.

"Abbas Antar?" Greg Welch said.

The man nodded and waved his hand toward the open door.

"Come in," he said. "Come in."

* * *

"The drinks are sweet hot tea," Greg Welch said. "The pastries have almonds and honey. Very nice, very traditional Syrian hospitality."

Luke and Ed sat in the small living room of the modest house where Hashan Antar—the man now known across the world as Ahmet—had grown up. The furnishings included an upholstered love seat with two matching chairs. An intricate red and gold rug hung on one wall. On the other walls were family photographs. Luke noticed with a twinge the framed photos of two young teenagers, a boy and a girl, featured prominently.

Just before Luke sat down, his eyes scanned a shelf of porcelain and ceramic figurines, cups, and jewelry boxes. It was a high shelf, one of two. The one below it had numerous hardcover and paperback books on it, all with titles in the Arabic alphabet. The upper shelf was better. Among the various knickknacks and paddywhacks up there, things that normally wouldn't catch Luke's interest, was something unusual. Lying on its back, screen upward, was a flat, dark blue mobile telephone in a plastic casing.

If Luke had to guess, he would say that it was a satellite phone. He would like very much to pick up that phone and scroll through the recent incoming and outgoing calls.

Abbas Antar's wife, a heavyset woman in a black headscarf who they knew to be Eva Antar, but who Abbas had not introduced by name, had brought out a folding table and placed a ceramic teapot and tiny tea cups upon it. A moment later, she had returned with a plate of small, flaky pastries. Then she went out again. She did not smile, make eye contact, or speak at any point.

Abbas took a seat in one of the chairs.

Greg Welch stood near the corner of the room.

"Please," Abbas said, indicating the food and drink.

Luke sipped his tea. It was hot and very, very sweet.

195

"We are here because we want to ask you a few questions," Luke said. He waited for Welch to translate.

The old man nodded. "I know. You are Americans?"

Luke nodded. "Yes."

Abbas Antar spoke for several seconds. He spoke without pause, but his voice was calm and his face impassive.

"You will forgive me," Greg Welch said in English. "The Americans came in the darkness before sunrise one day. Big men, much like you. They came in battle helicopters, with heavy weapons, screaming and kicking down doors. They took my son and daughter away from me, and away from their mother. They also took my leg. They took our hope, and our futures. They broke us, and broke our village, and then they left as quickly as they came. There was never an explanation, and never an apology. And now they—you—are back. And you wish to ask me questions. Which is good, because I wish to ask you questions as well."

"I am sorry for your loss, and your pain," Luke said. "I will answer your questions the best I can. But first, I am in a great hurry, and I must talk to you about your son Hashan."

Abbas Antar nodded. "Yes, I know. It appears that my son, who I love very much, is the most wanted man on Earth. I am a little surprised that it has taken this long for you to come to me."

"Has anyone else come?"

Abbas shook his head. "No. I think that no one has identified him before now."

"How did you know it was him? Have you spoken with him?"

Abbas made a face of exaggerated surprise. "No. I have not spoken with Hashan in more than eighteen months. Nor has his mother. You must understand that, after the American attack, he left here on a suicide mission. He would gain his revenge, not for Allah, but for himself. He was never a religious boy. He believed in science! He believed in enlightened thinking! The Greek philosophers, the Arab and European astronomers and mathematicians. Never the religious sages. He had no patience for it. But when his beloved sister and brother died, he went to die as well."

Antar's voice choked and trailed off for a moment. He looked at the floor between his left foot and the simple metal platform that functioned as his right foot.

"His mother and I did not agree with what Hashan wanted to do. We do not believe in war. We believe in peace. We wanted the best for all of our children. But with only one left, of course we did not want to lose him. We had hoped he would go to Jordan, and then perhaps to England. We told him this, and he became very angry. He broke away from us, and he cut off all contact."

Luke's eyes nearly strayed to the phone on that top shelf, but he controlled them. He focused on Antar instead. The man was telling a compelling story. It was heartbreaking. It was beautiful, in its way.

The wayward son, a tragic figure, who went away to die in war.

When Antar looked up again, there were tears in his eyes.

"We thought he was dead until today."

"How did you find out?" Luke said. "How did you know it was him?"

The old man shrugged. "Our neighbors have satellite television. His face is all over the TV news. The cameras in Switzerland captured his image. They came and told us. Hashan is alive! He has done a great thing! When we saw what a great thing he had done, his mother wept for two hours. That poor girl. Now she will be killed by fanatics, and it will be shown on the television. Because the scripture commands it. An eye must be taken for an eye, and a tooth must be taken for a tooth."

He paused again and looked directly at Luke.

"A life for a life. An important life for many unimportant ones. The life of your President's daughter, for the lives of my son and daughter, and so many countless others. Don't you agree that this is very wise? You, of all people, a soldier, must agree."

Luke didn't know how to respond. Yes, he had been a soldier, but he had always thought of himself as in the business of saving lives. Kill these ones now, to save all these other ones later.

How could he phrase this to make this man understand?

"We are sad that Hashan did this," Antar said. "We are ashamed of our only son."

Luke nodded. "I understand." He gestured with his head at the shelf.

"I am sorry to ask this. You have been so welcoming already. But may I borrow your satellite telephone to call my base? I have an account that will make the call free of charge for you. I just…"

He raised his hands as if to show how silly it all was. He smiled awkwardly.

"I left my own phone at the base by accident."

"Satellite telephone?" Antar said.

"Yes," Luke said. "There is a satellite telephone on your top shelf."

Antar eyed Luke. He followed Luke's gaze.

"Oh my! Hashan left that thing behind. Is that what it is, a telephone? I thought it must be a computer game. I have never even looked at it. I have no idea if it works. I imagine its batteries died long ago."

Antar smiled. It was a smile that looked brittle, like it might crack in half.

"Do you mind if I take a look? The batteries might still work. I really do need to make a call."

Luke glanced up at Greg Welch. Welch translated what Luke had just said. He stood there, watching Luke. It was almost as if the temperature in the room had just dropped twenty degrees.

Welch looked at the phone on the shelf.

A long pause drew out. Antar's demeanor had changed. His brow was furrowed, like he was thinking. Then he seemed angry. He waved a hand. He spit something in Arabic. It sounded vicious, like a curse.

"Do what you like," Greg said.

Luke looked at him.

Behind Welch, Eva Antar lingered in the doorway. Suddenly, there was a small black pistol in her hand. She pointed it at the back of Welch's head.

"No!" Luke shouted. "Greg!"

BANG.

The noise was loud, but not deafening. It was a small gun, after all.

There was a moment, an instant, when Welch grimaced, his eyes squinting shut, probably not in pain, but in anticipation of what was about to happen. Then his face seemed to *bulge* for a split second, before spraying outward in a shower of blood and bone and flesh and gore.

Luke looked back at the old man. He had ripped open his jacket. What had appeared to be bandages earlier was a suicide vest. His shaking hands worked to pull the cord that would ignite the explosives. Luke noted a string of them working their way around the man's torso—enough to blow the house apart.

Luke felt oddly frozen. It seemed impossible that this man, who had been quietly airing his grievances and his heartbreak and his tragedy a moment before, was going to...

Then Luke had his gun out. It happened automatically, animal instinct, with no conscious input from him. He fired, without taking aim.

BOOOM!

Antar's head blew apart, much if it spraying out to his right. The noise was loud. The man's face went blank, his hands slack, and he oozed bonelessly to the floor.

Then Ed Newsam was on his feet. Now he had a gun in hand.

He turned and faced off with the wife.

She pointed her small gun up at Ed.

BOOOM!

Ed fired, the shot hitting the woman's chest. Her arms flew upward, her gun dropping from her hand. She fell to the floor, her back coming to rest against the wall. Her mouth hung open. For a moment, she sat there, her face blank. Then her upper body slid sideways onto the floor, leaving a trail of red on the wall, like a snail leaves behind a trail of slime.

Luke stood, surveying the carnage in the tiny living room. The smell of gunpowder hung in the air. Three people dead, and it could have easily been five.

"Oh my God," he said.

Ed looked at him. "We better go."

Luke walked across to the shelf and grabbed the telephone. He glanced down at it. Of course it was a satellite phone. It was on. The battery power was full. The satellite connection was good.

He breathed deeply. His racing heart skipped, then slowed down the tiniest amount. "We better call the chopper to land right here," he said. "That made a lot of noise. I doubt we could walk to the rendezvous site and make it there alive."

"Shouldn't we search the house?" Ed said.

Luke looked around. The rooms were spare. There wasn't much to search. More concerning was that the house was small. A rocket attack would probably blast through and bring the whole thing down on top of them.

"I'm worried about the neighbors. In a minute, we're going to be in a shooting war just holding onto this place."

Ed had pressed himself against a cinderblock wall, away from the windows.

"Have you noticed?" he said. "Everybody seems to know when we're coming."

Luke looked out a window. There were already a dozen people gathered outside. Children were running in the alleys between houses, calling out. Luke wasn't sure, but he thought he might have seen an AK-47 in someone's hands, which disappeared quickly. Luke also pressed himself against a wall. It was getting ugly out there.

He got on the radio to the chopper pilots.

He had met the pilots for the first time today, but he had heard of them before. They were an odd couple, a woman and a man, Rachel and Jacob. They were US Army 160th Special Operations Aviation Regiment, and they'd apparently flown together for years. Luke liked that about them. The 160th SOAR were the Delta Force of helicopter pilots.

Rachel was thick and muscular and as tough as they came. She looked like a Rosie the Riveter poster. You don't join an elite group of Army special operations pilots as a woman. You brawl your way in. Meanwhile, Jacob was thin and reedy, but as steady as a rock. His calm under fire was legendary, almost surreal.

"Guys, we're gonna need an extract down here," Luke said.

Rachel's voice: "How did the interview go?"

"Uh, not quite as planned. The translator is dead. The subjects are dead. The natives are growing restless."

"Okay, we've got a visual on your location. Seems like a crowd is gathering."

"Yes."

"Not good."

Luke nodded. "My thoughts exactly."

Jacob's voice came on, calm as always.

"Luke, we'll be there in thirty seconds. I'd suggest we make this a just-in-time thing. Touch and go. We'll drop into the front yard, guns facing the bulk of the crowd, you guys come out, jump on board, and we're gone in five seconds. Sound okay?"

"We're bringing a body out," Luke said.

"Okay," Jacob said. "Then make it six seconds."

They could hear the chopper already.

"Sounds good."

Ed Newsam kneeled and slung Greg Welch's body over his shoulder. Welch's head was dripping blood and gore. It didn't matter. The rule was you didn't leave a man behind. It was a rule that you couldn't always follow, but in this case...

"Got him?" Luke said.

Ed nodded. "Let's go."

Just before the helicopter landed, Luke came out of the house first, his own gun in his right hand, Ed's gun in his left. He pointed them directly into the crowd. No one moved or even flinched. Hard eyes stared at him.

Behind him, Ed Newsam came out, carrying his tragic cargo.

The chopper barely touched down before it was back in the air. Luke looked back at the crowd. Upturned faces watched the helicopter flying away.

Luke was already on the radio again.

"Swann? Swann, can you hear me?"

The Little Bird chopper banked hard left and headed south and east, away from the village and back toward Iraqi territory. If they were lucky, they would make it across the border before anyone in the Syrian government knew they were here.

"Three minutes to the border," Jacob said. "Three minutes. Hold tight and send a little prayer to whoever or whatever you believe in."

The remains of Greg Welch lay sprawled across the tiny passenger cabin. Ed Newsam was working to zip Welch's corpse into a body bag. Welch's head was ruined. His face seemed as though a giant fist had punched a bloody hole in it.

Swann's deep voice: "Luke? I'm here."

Luke felt breathless, like he had just run ten miles. "Swann."

"Yeah. How did it go? Did you get any information from the parents?"

"There was a problem with the parents," Luke said.

The radio crackled. "A problem? How so?"

"Don't worry about that right now. I don't want to get ahead of myself, but it seems like these really might have been the kidnapper's parents. If so, that's a big break, buddy. And there's a way we might confirm it. I have with me a satellite phone that I confiscated. Is there any way you can access it without my having to come all the way back to Baghdad? It has a number that it called repeatedly over several months in its log, and I need to know where that number was located, and where it is now."

There was a pause over the line. Luke looked at Ed. Ed pulled the zipper, closing the black bag over Greg Welch's head.

"Yeah. I can do that. No problem. I'll need you to use the phone to call a number I give you. You'll be calling my laptop. Once we're connected, I can look at the call record and trace where those calls went. It shouldn't take me very long."

"Okay," Luke said. "Give me the number."

Luke punched the digits in as Swann read them off to him. The phone was quiet for a long moment, then made a buzzing, humming sound as it connected to the computer.

"Luke, I'm going to cut you off for a moment."

"Don't make me call you back," Luke said.

"I won't. Just be patient for five minutes, okay?"

Luke checked his watch. It was 5:35. Maybe two hours of daylight left. "Five minutes, man."

Ed Newsam was at an open bay door, scanning the skies for enemy activity.

"Anything?" Luke said.

Ed nodded. "Yeah. Black spots on the horizon, coming low and hard. Three of them, by my count."

"Gentlemen," Rachel said over the intercom, as if to confirm their worst fears. "I suggest you strap yourselves in. Syrian fighter planes approaching from the west. They should overtake us in less than a minute."

Luke poked his head into the cockpit.

"How soon until we cross the border into Iraq?"

"About the same," Rachel said. "One minute or less."

"If we make the border…"

Jacob shrugged. "Doesn't guarantee a thing. We encroached on their airspace. And anyway, they have missiles that could take us out right now, if they want. They could fire on us and take us out when we're twenty miles into Iraq. We're moving like a bumblebee compared to them."

"Dammit," Luke said. He gazed through the cockpit windshield. It was wide open desert in front of them.

"I'd strap yourself in, Stone. This could get interesting."

Luke went back, sat down next to Ed, and strapped in. Ed was craning his neck behind them, watching out the bay door.

"Anything?"

"I can see one. He has us right on his nose. Coming hard like a missile."

Luke took a deep breath. This was going to happen faster than the speed of sound.

Ed turned around and faced front. "Here he comes."

Luke looked to his right. Through the bay door, behind him, he saw the Syrian plane. It was a dark shadow, a blur, coming almost too fast to see. An image of a pterodactyl appeared in his mind.

His heart skipped in his chest.

"Oh man."

The fighter zipped past, just over their heads, way too close. The shriek of its jet engines was LOUD. For a moment, they were everything. Both Luke and Ed plugged their ears with their fingers.

An instant later, the turbulence hit them and the tiny chopper shuddered. The Little Bird rode the unsettled air, then simmered down. A second passed, then another jet went screaming by. Another second, another jet.

"Ahhhnnnnh!" Luke shouted. He hated those fighter pilots.

The chopper bounced across the turbulent airfield. It was like being caught in the churn after a monster ocean wave breaks.

Out the bay door, Luke saw all three of the planes banking hard in single file, heading back the way they had come.

Luke let out a long breath. He felt his heart now, thumping steadily, thumping hard, but already almost like normal. His ears were ringing.

"Congratulations, gentlemen," Jacob said. "We just crossed the border into the loving arms of Iraq."

A long moment passed. Ed and Luke sat still, straps still holding them.

"This has been a day," Ed said. He stared down at the body bag holding the former CIA translator.

"Amen," Luke said. "Yesterday was bad, but this…"

"Brutal," Ed said.

A burst of static came from Luke's radio. He picked it up. Swann was back.

"Luke?"

"Yeah, Swann. What's up?"

Swann's voice was shaking. Just a guy doing some data mining, and yet he was nervous. He was lucky he wasn't out there. Syrian fighter jets hadn't just buzzed over his head.

"I ran the locations of that phone number. It's also a satellite phone, and for most of the past year it barely moved, stationed in Geneva, Switzerland, the entire time. It seems that the parents were probably calling their son. This could be the real thing."

Luke realized what was making Swann's voice shake. He looked at Ed.

Ed's eyes lit up. "Pay dirt," he said.

"Where is the phone now?" Luke said into the radio.

"For the past twelve hours, it's been located in the Sinjar Mountains, on the Iraq side of the border. The phone you took from the parents called that location twice."

A feeling began to swell in Luke's chest. Suddenly there was a chance. That was all he ever wanted, was a fighting chance.

"Sinjar Mountains?" Luke said. "Can you be a little more specific? The Sinjar Mountains doesn't tell me a whole—"

"About a hundred and twenty miles due north of your current position," Swann said. "Give or take a few miles."

Luke did the math in his head. The Little Bird topped out at about 175 miles per hour, but would burn fuel like crazy at that speed.

"What's it like up there?"

There was chatter behind Swann. Trudy Wellington was saying something. Suddenly she was on the radio.

"Luke, it's Trudy."

Luke smiled and shook his head. "Yes. I know that."

"The Sinjar Mountains are steep and rugged, difficult to access. There's a patchwork of interests there. Kurdish militias control much of the region, but some areas of the mountains are wild, and up for grabs. The most inaccessible parts are thought to be hiding spots for Sunni terrorists and militias. There are also minority groups living up that way, like the Yazidis, who try to stay out of all this."

A new shriek of static interrupted her voice.

"In a nutshell, I'd say those mountains are cold, hard, and heavily armed."

Luke looked at Ed Newsam. Ed shrugged.

"You know what to do," Ed said.

Luke undid his straps and jumped up. He poked his head into the cockpit again.

"We need to go north," he said. "Sinjar Mountains."

"North?" Rachel said. She looked at the indicators in front of her. "Sorry, Stone. We don't have that kind of flying time left. We have to go back to base to refuel. We can't go to the Sinjar Mountains and expect to make it back. We'll be just about out of fuel by the time we get there."

Luke shook his head. "Guys, I'm sorry. We've got new orders. We have to go north. We'll find fuel along the way. Or we won't. If we have to, we'll set this bird down and walk."

Jacob was uncharacteristically concerned. "This is untamed country," he said. "We don't have a lot of friends out here."

"I guess we'll have to make new friends."

Luke went back to his radio.

"Trudy, I need you to talk to Big Daddy and have him pull as many people as he can into this. This could be a breakthrough, but it's going to take us about forty-five minutes to get up there. We're going to have to ditch this chopper at some point. I'm sure Big Daddy could have a drone over those mountains twenty minutes from now. We could have a drop team jump in from a plane, if need be. If they start scrambling now, they can get there before us."

"There's a little bit of a problem here, Luke."

Luke rolled his eyes. "There's always a problem. Which problem is this?"

"It's the problem where we commandeered British Special Air Service troops this morning without permission, and one was sent home in a bag. Apparently, Montgomery's a cowboy, plays things fast and loose, and this was a breaking point for his bosses. They called him back to London. Big Daddy's got a reputation similar to Monty's. There's been what the British would call a diplomatic row, with some finger pointing going on. There may be a problem gaining access to more—"

"Trudy, don't anticipate it being a problem, okay? Tell Big Daddy we have a satellite phone that's been calling another satellite phone, which was located in Geneva for months. The person at the other end might be Ahmet, the man who kidnapped the President's daughter. If we can get to him before someone else does, he might know something about where she is now."

"Luke, do you have any idea how tenuous that lead sounds? The terrorists probably stationed a dozen satellite phones in Geneva as blind alleys. How hard would that be? Even if it is the right man, he could well be dead. If he isn't, he should be. Someone else probably took his phone. Satellite phone locations are notoriously bad intel. We're always making drone strikes on satellite phones and killing the wrong people. If through some quirk of fate, Ahmet's somehow still alive and holding that telephone, he probably handed Elizabeth over to others and immediately went another direction. The odds of him knowing where she is are slim, to put it mildly."

"Are you playing devil's advocate?" Luke said.

"No. I'm telling you what the official response is likely to be. Especially after what happened this morning, and the rift it caused between Big—"

"Trudy, this is a lead. A man died to get it. Do you have a better one?"

"No."

"Then tell Big Daddy I need some troops in the Sinjar Mountains. A strike force, preferably special operators, fast and light and silent. Don't send a battalion. I also need a spy drone, at least one. Get me these things, please. If it's a problem to get them, then try harder."

"Got it," Trudy said.

"Good. Thank you. Is Swann still there?"

"I'm right here," came the skinny man's deep voice.

"Swann, I need you to pinpoint that location as exactly as—"

"I'm already working on it," Swann said.

CHAPTER TWENTY SEVEN

10:05 a.m. Eastern Daylight Time (6:05 p.m. Arabic Standard Time)
The Situation Room
The White House, Washington, DC

Lawrence Keller was beginning to regret his decision.

He had known Interim President Mark Baylor for two decades, or thought he had. Now he was starting to wonder who, and what, he had known.

Keller was all for a strong military. He felt there should be a fierce American response to the Barrett girl's kidnapping and what looked like her inevitable death. He could even see the logic in taking advantage of the situation to move some pieces forward on the board.

Mark Baylor, on the other hand, was prepared to ignite the Apocalypse. And it didn't seem clear that anyone in this room was prepared to stop him. If anything, General Stark was even more eager for it than Baylor.

Keller looked around the conference table in the center of the room. People seemed nervous. But they were careerists who wouldn't rock the boat, or were junior advisers who would speak only when spoken to. In a few cases, they were people who didn't have an original thought in their heads. It would never occur to them that advice coming from someone at the Pentagon could be wrong. They didn't make it to this table by questioning things.

Keller glanced at the young aides and assistants lining the walls. They offered no hope. They were here to do exactly as they were told. Not one of them could stop this unfolding train wreck even if they wanted to.

No. If this was going to stop, it was going to fall on Keller himself. The ultimate political animal, the sly operator, was going to have to put his own neck on the chopping block. He didn't relish that thought.

On the screen at the front of the room, there was a large map of the Middle East. General Stark stood in front of it with a laser pointer. He indicated various spots of interest with the pointer.

"We have B-2 bomber sorties, along with fighter escorts, flying at the limits of Iranian airspace over Iraq, over Turkey, and over Afghanistan. They are prepared to make deep runs into Iran at a moment's notice. We're also flying fighter patrols at the edge of Iranian airspace in the Persian Gulf. We are coming into contact with Iranian fighter planes, but no provocations have happened as of yet."

The red dot of his pointer made a squiggle on the Persian Gulf, then settled on the narrow Strait of Hormuz.

"American destroyers and aircraft carriers in the Gulf are at a high state of readiness. We are prepared to engage Iran with a massive, overwhelming attack that will significantly degrade their ability to respond, and will set their infrastructure back decades. We can also call in a targeted decapitation strike aimed at their leadership in Tehran."

"What do you recommend, General?" Mark Baylor said.

"Personally, I would go with the decapitation strike, for starters. We have a network of moles, agitators, and if need be, guerrilla cells, that are salted through Iranian society. Some of that network has been rolled up in recent years, but some of it is still functional. Once we hit the leadership, the Supreme Council, then I would call for acts of sabotage and the organization of street demonstrations. Through a fairly narrow attack, combined with support for the resistance in-country, we may be able to destabilize Iranian society to a surprising degree."

He paused.

"What is the Iranian response to our preparations?" Baylor said.

The general shrugged. An aide leaned over to him and whispered something in his ear. "Well, we do have vulnerabilities. As you know, Iran has issued threats against the American airbase outside Doha, in Qatar, as well as our embassy in Baghdad. We have ten thousand servicemen and women stationed at the Doha air base, along with another twenty thousand family members living on the base and nearby.

"To be fair, Iranian missiles could reach Doha in minutes. And CIA and NSA listening stations are reporting advanced states of readiness throughout the Iranian military—including their fast boat navy in the Persian Gulf, their air force, missile command, and the Revolutionary Guards. Missile silos are preparing to launch, with more reporting a state of combat readiness all the time. They're on a bit of a hair trigger. That's what we're hearing."

"Does that concern you, General?"

Stark shook his head. "Not really. The Iranian air force is more of what I'd call an air farce. And as much as they have a robust arsenal of conventional missiles, despite a lot of saber rattling in the past, they have never used it. My hunch is that their reluctance stems from knowing the kind of overwhelming, Biblical response they would get from us if they did dare to launch. I'm confident that we can engage in a surgical strike against them and receive almost no reply."

He waved his hand in dismissal. "Other than, you know, an appeal to the United Nations and some hand wringing and condemnation from the usual suspects. China, Cuba, Venezuela, a few others."

Keller's breath was taken away by the man's offhand confidence in his own assessments. He was suggesting a massive attack against a large, well-armed regional power, and expecting nothing in return. Meanwhile, he would nonchalantly put more than 30,000 American lives at risk.

"In fact," the general said, "I feel so good about this that I recommend the exact same approach in Syria, and I say we launch the attacks simultaneously. Bashar Assad is a squirrelly character, to put it mildly. He is good at being elusive. But we might get lucky, and Syrian society is especially brittle. Assad is part of the Shiite Alawite minority in a country that is predominately made up of Sunnis, and he holds his grip on power through violence and intimidation.

"We are currently flying sorties over the Mediterranean near Lebanon, over Israel and the West Bank, over southern Turkey, and over Western Iraq. We enjoy vast air superiority and have Syria completely surrounded. Our ships in the Mediterranean are on standby to launch missiles at the Presidential Palace in Damascus, as well as half a dozen other known hideouts that Assad uses. If we hit Assad, then lend some encouragement to Sunni extremists on the ground during the ensuing confusion, there is a chance that Syria will devolve into chaos."

"I like it," the Interim President said.

Lawrence Keller resented this. He hated it. He felt a tide of anger rising within him. They were going to force him to risk his career by stating facts that should be painfully obvious to every single person in this room.

"General," he said.

"Yes? Mr...."

"Lawrence Keller. I'm President Barrett's Chief of Staff."

"Well, Mr. Keller, I think your team might have left the locker room."

Mark Baylor spoke up. Thank God for that. "Lawrence is an old Washington hand, General. He's valuable in any administration. He's staying on to ease the transition of power, if it comes to that. In the meantime, he's currently President Barrett's representative in these meetings."

The general nodded. "I see."

"General," Keller began again, "aren't Sunni extremists the ones who attacked us on September eleventh?"

"I believe so, yes. But they weren't Syrians, as far as we know."

"Aren't Sunni extremists also the ones who bombed the USS *Cole*? Aren't they an existential threat to the future of Iraqi society? And considering that the video we've seen of Elizabeth Barrett being held bears all the hallmarks of videos previously made by Abu Musab al-Zarqawi, the legendary Sunni terrorist, isn't it likely that Sunni extremists are the ones holding Elizabeth?"

General Stark shrugged. "I don't know if I'd describe Zarqawi as legendary. Infamous, maybe. Despicable, certainly."

Everyone in the room seemed to be staring at Keller now. With just one short sentence, he had outed himself. One of these things didn't belong, and he was that thing. It was almost like he was giving off a bad smell, the smell of someone who had just soiled their pants.

Nevertheless, he plunged on.

"Regardless of how you might describe Zarqawi, if Sunni extremists are the ones who kidnapped Elizabeth, who destroyed the World Trade Center, who bombed the *Cole*, and are making Iraqi society ungovernable, then why in God's name would you support them in Syria?"

The general's response was not at all what Keller expected. Stark pointed at him and smiled. "That's a good question, Mr. Keller. And it's a question with the answer already embedded in it. The reason we would support Sunni extremists in Syria is because they do such a good job of making Iraq ungovernable. We want Assad out. We want Syria ungovernable. If that means supporting Sunni extremists, so be it."

"Sunni extremists are our enemies," Keller said.

Stark nodded. "Assad is also our enemy. And he's the enemy of Sunni extremists. And the enemy of my enemy is my friend."

"Our friends are the same people who attacked on September eleventh?"

The general shook his head. "Those were Saudis, for the most part. I'm talking about Syrians. You're comparing apples and oranges."

"And you, General, are suggesting that we attack two Shiite-dominated societies, even though the attacks against us have come almost exclusively from Sunnis, and it's very likely that the people who kidnapped Elizabeth Barrett are Sunnis."

He stopped and took a breath. He hadn't realized he was going to have an outburst like this one. And it occurred to him that he was only halfway done.

"During your planning, have you considered for one moment what effect all these attacks will have on the life of Elizabeth Barrett? We don't even know if she's alive or dead. What we do know is that a heavy-handed response is going to put her life at risk."

Suddenly it came to him that earlier, in his rush to move David Barrett out of the way, he had been callous about Elizabeth and her chances of survival. But now the sense of her humanity seemed to flood his system. She was a real person, young and certainly naïve, but she was not a pawn in a game.

General Stark stared at Lawrence Keller for a long moment. He seemed confused, as if he didn't quite know what to make of everything Keller had said. Did they let traitors in the Situation Room now? The general looked over at the Interim President, as if Mark Baylor was a referee and Stark was hoping for an objective ruling.

Baylor, in turn, looked at Lawrence Keller. He furrowed his eyebrows a little bit.

"Are you okay?" he said.

"I don't know," Keller said. He thought about it for a moment. "No, I suppose I'm not okay. Instead of talking about all the ways we can attack Iran and Syria, I'd suggest we talk about all the ways we can find Elizabeth Barrett."

General Stark lifted a stack of papers on the table near his elbow. "Do you know what this is?" he said.

Keller shook his head. "No. Why don't you enlighten me?"

"This is pages and pages of leads about Elizabeth's possible location. This is lists of more than two hundred high-level detainees with ties to Islamic extremists who are currently being questioned. This is seven dozen covert operations that have taken place just today in an attempt to find her. This is frozen bank accounts and police raids in Switzerland, in Brussels, in Paris, in Madrid, all over Germany, and in London and Manchester, not to mention in

Brooklyn, Baltimore, and Minneapolis. This data is an hour old. There's more flooding in all the time."

"What are you saying, General?"

"I'm saying Elizabeth Barrett is one person. Yes, she's an important person, but one person nonetheless. And many, many competent people are working to find her, whether she's dead or alive. In the meantime, we have bigger fish to fry."

"So we, the people in this room, have no responsibility to her?" Keller said.

"Sir, we do have a responsibility to her," Stark said. "In all likelihood, she's already dead. And when the video turns up of terrorist savages beheading her for the world to see, our job is to avenge her death with a firestorm that no one will ever forget. We need to have a plan in place to do that."

Stark paused, and nodded at the truth of what he had just said.

"That's our responsibility."

CHAPTER TWENTY EIGHT

6:25 p.m. Arabian Standard Time (10:25 a.m. Eastern Daylight Time)
Sinjar Mountains
Nineveh Governorate
Northwestern Iraq

They were both running out of time.

Ahmet sat on the dirt floor across from the girl Elizabeth. They were inside an old stone building, which was very badly deteriorated, and left over from some distant past that had long ago faded from memory. There was no longer a door, and most of the roof had collapsed. There were large chunks of broken rock all over the floor.

They were high up on the western edge of the mountain ridge. By Ahmet's guess, there was less than half an hour of daylight left. Once the sun set, it was going to become cold up here. The night would be frigid, probably with a biting wind.

The mujahideen planned to execute the girl in the morning, after prayers. Ahmet thought she might not survive that long.

"You have to get me out of here," she said, in a low voice.

She was still wearing the orange jumpsuit in which they had dressed her for the video. She wore a black scarf over her head. The clothes were not warm. She had no gloves, no hat, and she was wearing open-air sandals on her feet.

Her wrists were bound with leather straps attached by a short chain. A sturdy chain was wrapped around her waist and attached to spikes, which were driven into the stone wall on either side of her.

It was a makeshift arrangement, which gave her some small freedom of movement. Indeed, it almost looked like she could squirm out of there, but what then? She was high in the mountains, far from any civilization, with dozens of Sunni fighters outside that door, holding this ridgeline. There was nowhere to run.

The militants had not fed her at all since she arrived. They had given her nothing more than a few sips of water. It was not out of cruelty or spite—they had very little food, and barely any water, for themselves. And with Kurdish fighting units roaming much of the lower reaches of the mountains, protecting the villages to the north, the east, and the south, it was unlikely the mujahideen were going to obtain more food any time soon. They were free to head west, except there was nothing but more barren wasteland that way—no villages or farms to raid.

Ahmet had also eaten nothing, but like the holy warriors, and unlike the girl, he was accustomed to the feeling. In the camps, they often made you go without food for days. It was done to toughen you. He supposed it worked. He had spent a year eating well in Geneva, whatever and whenever he liked. Now he had not eaten since the day before, and he wasn't hungry at all. He was a little lightheaded, but he thought it was more from exhaustion, from stress, and from the altitude, than from lack of food.

He realized that he might never eat food again. The thought didn't trouble him.

"They're going to kill me," the girl said now.

Ahmet nodded. "Yes. There's nothing I can do about that, I'm afraid."

But was it really true? Was there nothing he could do for her?

An odd thing had begun to happen. Before he had really met her, he had thought of her mostly as a thing, a prize, a goal to be reached. She was the daughter of an imperialist, someone to be targeted, taken, and killed. She should be slaughtered as an animal is slaughtered for the table.

But his feelings had begun to change. She was a person. She was a person adapted to comfort and fine things, who suddenly found herself in an alien environment, surrounded by people who hated her and planned to kill her for the whole world to see. And yet, she was trying to be brave. She was trying to adapt. She had not completely collapsed in the face of these things.

He realized now that her death would in no way avenge the deaths of his sister and brother. It was a tragedy, it was a crime, but another tragedy would never fix it.

Perhaps there was something more he could do for her.

"They're probably going to kill me, too," he said.

That part was true. He was a little surprised it hadn't happened already. The men of this militia unit were savages. Uneducated, ignorant, vicious, and traumatized by combat. They were religious fanatics, yes, but they were also like dogs that had been beaten too much. Whatever affection or friendship that had once been in them was gone. Now, they knew only how to bark, and to bite.

Far from a hero, they saw Ahmet as a stranger, and as a liability. He was well-educated in the sciences, and he spoke four languages. He had spent time in Europe. He was not a guerrilla fighter. His body was not built for the rugged terrain here. If it came to fighting the Americans on these hillsides, or the Kurds, he would be useless, possibly worse than useless.

"They only keep me alive to communicate with you. After that…"

He shrugged.

"I don't care what happens to you," the girl said. "You did this to me, so it only serves you right if you die."

She said it calmly and without spite. It was a simple statement of the facts, as she understood them. The girl, who was raised surrounded by opulent wealth and power in the Western world, could not know the circumstances of Ahmet's life. She could not imagine the forces that had brought them both to this place. He did not feel a strong need to try to explain them to her.

Nevertheless:

"American special forces raided my village at daybreak two years ago. They killed my brother and my sister, ages fourteen and eleven. They killed numerous other people. Then they left. There was no explanation for their actions."

She shook her head and started to cry again. She had cried a lot today. He was surprised by her capacity for it. He would have thought that by now she would have gone numb and been beyond tears.

"I don't believe you," she said. "I don't believe a word you say. You were supposed to be a nice, normal guy from Turkey. You had a migraine headache, remember? Everything about you was a lie."

He nodded. "Okay."

He glanced around the room. The afternoon was really fading now. Night was coming on. The last yellow light of day played against the concrete walls. It was beautiful. For an instant, he had a thought, a wish…

But it was elusive, and gone before it even formed.

"Ahmet," a harsh voice said.

A mujahid stood in the doorway. He was a large man, and strong. He had a thick black beard and piercing eyes. He was carrying an AK-47 rifle. He had three or four grenades hanging from his vest.

He had been introduced to Ahmet as Siddiq Jara'a, a *nom de guerre* if ever there was one. Siddiq meant truthful. Jara'a meant daring. But Siddiq wasn't really supposed to be used as an actual name. It was an honorific, first conveyed on men of high integrity by Muhammad himself.

This man, calling himself Siddiq, was an idiot.

"Yes?" Ahmet said.

"Do you have a satellite phone?" the man said in Arabic.

Ahmet stared at him. Siddiq was mostly a silhouette looming in the doorway, as day slowly turned to night. Ahmet was not certain how to answer that question. He hesitated to say anything. No one had asked him this before, and he had not volunteered any information.

"Do you?" Siddiq said.

"Yes. Do you want to borrow it?"

Siddiq shook his head. "You fool."

Without warning, he marched into the room. He took the rifle from his back, turned the butt of it to Ahmet, and struck him hard in the ribs.

The girl screamed.

Ahmet raised a hand. "Wait!"

Siddiq pulled the rifle back and struck him again. Then again.

Ahmet curled into a ball, and Siddiq hit him in the back. The hit was harder than the others, and Ahmet felt a searing pain. The man had broken something, maybe a rib. Ahmet rolled onto his side, breathing heavily.

Siddiq hit him again.

"Uhnh."

"Stop!" the girl said. "Stop! You're going to kill him."

Again Siddiq hit him, in the side this time. Something else broke. The pain was unreal. Siddiq hit him yet again.

He leaned in close.

"I should smash your skull, you idiot. Do you not hear the helicopter buzzing the hillsides? Of course you don't. You are not a warrior. You don't hear anything. You don't see anything. You know nothing."

He grabbed Ahmet's jaw in one viselike hand.

"Look at me."

Ahmet turned his face to Siddiq's. The man's hard, bloodshot eyes glared at him. They almost seemed to give off their own light. They were like lasers.

"A runner came up the mountain with news from our spies in Baghdad. He risked his life to come here. The Americans are dropping commandos on the lower slopes. Why? Because they know we are here. They traced a satellite call from your parents' house to this very spot. Your parents are dead. Are you happy? They were killed by the Americans. You have destroyed your family and jeopardized everything with your own stupidity."

Ahmet didn't respond. He simply stared at the man. Was it true? Of course it was. He saw now how this mission, this adventure he had gone on, could never have turned out any other way.

His beloved parents...

"Give me the phone."

Ahmet reached into his pocket. It hurt to move. His hand came out with the satellite telephone in its black plastic casing.

Siddiq snatched it, dropped it on the ground, and smashed it to pieces with the butt of the AK-47. He looked down at Ahmet.

"You never should have had that."

He turned away from Ahmet and faced the girl. He turned the rifle around and placed the barrel against her temple. She closed her eyes. She was trembling.

"You're a pretty girl," Siddiq said to her in Arabic.

Ahmet shook his head. Of course she wouldn't understand a word the man was saying. Siddiq probably didn't even care.

"We should have kept you, used you for ourselves, and then sold you into slavery."

Tragedy upon tragedy. Ahmet's entire family was dead. Now Siddiq was going to kill the girl. Once the Americans knew the girl was dead, they would kill all the mujahideen on this mountain. Some of the Americans would die. Oaths of revenge would be taken on both sides. The cycle would begin again.

The girl.

The girl. Her death would lead to the deaths of thousands. It would rain fire on innocents everywhere.

More oaths. More revenge. More dead girls.

Where Ahmet had fallen, there was a large chunk of broken rock. He reached his hand to it. He could barely get his fingers to grip it. It was solid, with sharp edges. Yes. He picked it up.

Silently, he worked his way to his feet. He was scorched by pain. Siddiq had broken his bones. There must be internal bleeding.

Siddiq still held the gun to the girl Elizabeth's head. He was still taunting her in a language she couldn't understand. His back was to Ahmet.

"Goodbye, American dog," Siddiq said.

Ahmet raised the chunk of stone and slammed it across the back of Siddiq's head. One hit cracked the man's head open. Siddiq turned slowly around. His eyes were large and already vacant. His mouth hung open.

Ahmet smashed him across the face. Teeth flew.

Siddiq fell to the floor, making no attempt to slow his fall. His head bounced off the hard ground.

Ahmet went to where the girl's chain was driven into the wall. He gathered himself for a great effort. It was going to hurt, he knew that. Still, he would do it. He would force himself.

He yanked on the heavy chain, a test pull.

The spike slid easily out from the wall and clattered to the floor. Just like that. A child could have pulled it free.

He looked at the girl and shook his head. Then he laughed.

* * *

Elizabeth could hardly make sense of what was happening.

"Run," Ahmet said. "Go west, toward the last of the sunlight."

Elizabeth nodded. "West, okay."

Her head was swimming. She was hungry, she was thirsty, and she was tired. She had been terrified of dying, but now she was much less so. They had made her say terrible things about her father, things she didn't mean, things she didn't even remember. She knew they were horrible, and that was all. She hated them for doing that.

She tried to focus on what Ahmet was saying, on what it meant, but it was hard.

A fighter had suddenly walked in, spoken to Ahmet in their language, and then started killing him. Then the fighter had turned his back on Ahmet, and Ahmet had killed the fighter instead. Ahmet was a slippery guy. Who could trust him?

But Ahmet had also saved her life.

"If I go west, is there a way down?"

Ahmet shook his head. "No. I don't think so. But west will take you away from the mujahideen, who are mostly deployed to the east. They will try to hold the line against the enemy coming uphill. The terrain here is harsh. There is nowhere for the Americans to land."

"So what's to the west, then?"

"The cliffs."

She stared at him.

"You are wearing bright orange," Ahmet said. "If you are lucky, your friends will see you from the sky. If you are unlucky, you can still choose your own death, and not the one the militants would choose for you."

It took a few seconds for that idea to sink in with her.

"Jump?" Elizabeth said. "From the cliffs?"

Ahmet nodded. "Yes."

Elizabeth didn't love the sound of that. Maybe there was another choice here, one that Ahmet wasn't thinking of. She had learned that in a business class once. Look for the third option, the one that was being overlooked.

"What are you going to do?" she said.

He had picked up the other man's gun and was checking the ammunition. Now he was taking what looked like hand grenades from the man's vest.

"I'm going to die protecting you," he said.

She gestured at the gun. "Do you even know how to use that thing?"

He patted the barrel. A ghost of a smile appeared on his face. "Of course. I was trained in the jihad camps."

He put the gun down and began to go through the dead man's pockets. There was blood soaked into the dirt near the man's head. It was shocking to her, a little bit, the businesslike way Ahmet killed someone, then went about looting the corpse. Ahmet was cold-blooded. All of these people… they just…

She didn't have words for it.

Ahmet came out of the man's pocket with a fold-out knife. He opened the blade and slid it under the leather strap that held her left hand. He sawed at it, and within a few seconds, the knife cut through, popping out away from her body. Then he did the same with the right wrist.

She put her hands on her wrists, getting the feeling of freedom into them. The ghost sensation of the tight leather straps was still there somehow.

Ahmet looked at her. He took her face in his hands.

"Run," he said. "Run west."

* * *

"The shooting has started."

Ed Newsam had spoken. He was crouched near the open bay door of the Little Bird, peering out into the gloom with a pair of high-powered binoculars. The chopper banked hard right, flying eastward high above the ridgeline of the Sinjar Mountains. Behind him, the body of Greg Welch lay where he had zipped it into a bag and fastened it to sturdy metal eye hooks in the flooring.

Luke was on the radio.

"Swann? Swann, come on!"

The radio crackled.

"The signal went dead, Luke. That's it. I don't think it's coming back. They must have figured out the satellite phone attracted us, and they destroyed it."

Luke looked up and shook his head. They had gotten here five minutes ago. They had gone straight to the area where the phone seemed to be, and right away they had spotted militia activity. The militia had spotted them, too. They were based in the highest reaches of the mountains. Their location was along a sharp ridgeline, a dragon spine of jumbled rocks. There was nowhere to even consider landing. And if they dropped altitude, they were going to catch hell from militia guns.

This was a Little Bird. It was fast and as maneuverable as choppers came. It could land in the tightest spots. But it couldn't land on a razor's edge while taking enemy fire.

"Where was the signal again when it went dead?" Luke said.

"I told you. I plotted the location on a satellite map of the area. I also plotted it on a topographical map. It was near the highest altitude on the ridge, thirty miles from where the mountains cross into Syria. There's some kind of old settlement up there. There's a small building of some kind, which is the same color as everything else, and was probably built from local stone. It fades into the background very easily. It looks like somebody tried to do some terraced farming there once upon a time, but the terraces are too narrow to land. It looks like there might be an old well and a small freshwater spring. All of this is about half a mile east from some sheer cliffs. Find that building. The signal was coming from inside, or near, that building when it went dead."

Luke glanced at Ed. "Are you hearing this?"

Ed shrugged. "I don't know, man. We went out and around. Looks to me like we're coming back in, approaching some cliffs from the east. Talk to the pilots. They have Swann's coordinates. Somebody just started a shooting war up ahead, and it looks like it's starting to get hot."

"Guys," Rachel said over the intercom. She and Jacob must have overheard them up front. "We can't play this game anymore. There's nowhere to set this thing down. We are almost out of fuel. That firefight he mentioned is directly in front of us—practically on top of the coordinates Swann gave me. We need to get this bird to Kurdish territory or we are going to crash. I don't know about you, but I'm not in the mood for a chopper crash in the middle of an Al Qaeda hideout."

Luke raised a hand to no one. "Okay, Rachel. Okay. Swann, who is shooting at whom?"

"Two platoons of Marines dropped in from Hueys near some friendly Kurdish positions on the lower slopes about ten or fifteen minutes ago. I'd assume they got their bearings, geared up, and they're starting to fight their way uphill."

"Big Daddy sent those Marines?"

"Yes. He's trying to wrangle some Navy SEALs, but he doesn't have them yet."

Luke shook his head.

This didn't sound right. It was going to take those Marines all night to push uphill against positions held by even a handful of religious fanatics.

Luke had an idea. He ducked his head into the cockpit.

"I'll strike you a deal."

"Name it," Jacob said. Both he and Rachel were staring through the windshield and monitoring controls at the same time.

"Put me right over Swann's coordinates, even if there's shooting. Hold that position for ten seconds, and let me get a peek down there. Then we'll go anywhere you want. Sound okay?"

Jacob glanced at Rachel. She shrugged.

"Sounds good," Jacob said. "Just don't blame us if we get our skin shredded."

Luke looked out the cockpit windshield. There were flashes of light up ahead.

"I won't blame you," Luke said. An image of the disastrous Afghanistan mission flashed through his mind. "I'll blame me."

"Fair enough," Jacob said. "We'll be over those coordinates in thirty seconds. Let's make this quick."

Luke ducked back into the cabin. "Eyes sharp, Ed. We'll be there in half a minute."

"We're already there, white man. Passing over those cliff faces... now."

Luke pulled a long metal box out from under the bench. He shoved the body of Greg Welch out of the way. He turned a silver knob on the left, then on the right, and opened the box. More weapons in here. An MP5 with a three loaded box magazines. An M-79 grenade launcher. Half a dozen grenades.

Not enough. Not nearly enough.

"What's the armament configuration on this bird?" he shouted at the cockpit.

"One M230 chain gun, two Hydra rockets," came the reply.

"What about Hellfire missiles?" Luke said.

"They weren't loaded," Rachel said. "You were just going to interview someone, remember? We weren't going to need all that muscle."

Luke grunted. Lesson learned. Always load up the weapons. Overload them if necessary. Too much was better than not enough.

"Oh, man," Ed said. "Stone, you better see this."

Luke went to the bay door. Ed pointed at the ground toward their right. In the last of the fading daylight, Luke saw a tiny figure in bright orange go running by, headed toward the cliffs. Just behind that figure was where the shooting began.

Another figure was firing back the way the orange figure had come. From that direction, at least two dozen others were approaching. Some were running fast, some were stopping and shooting. The bright muzzle signatures of automatic weapons lit up the night like fireflies. The faraway blat of machine gun fire came to Luke on the wind.

"Oh my God," he said.

"The girl," Ed said. "Elizabeth."

It was. It was a girl in an orange jumpsuit. Just like Elizabeth had been shown in an orange jumpsuit in the video.

It took Luke a long second to process the information. A wave of unreality washed over him. All this time, he had been focused on the telephone, finding it, capturing the person holding it, and then asking more questions. The right questions, put to the right person, could bring them closer to Elizabeth. He never thought, not for one second, that Elizabeth would be in the same place as the phone.

Luke jumped up and poked his head back into the cockpit.

"You gotta put us down there. Did you see that? The President's daughter is down there, running for the cliffs. They're right behind her. You gotta drop us. Somehow, you gotta put us on the ground."

The two pilots turned and looked at him.

"What?"

CHAPTER TWENTY NINE

11:05 a.m. Eastern Daylight Time (7:05 p.m. Arabic Standard Time)
The Situation Room
The White House, Washington, DC

The insanity rolled on. Lawrence Keller watched it unfold with increasing alarm.

"The Russians are overreacting," General Stark said. "And they're overplaying their hand."

Stark was a madman, and Mark Baylor was just a step behind him. How did this happen? How had Keller himself gotten this so wrong?

They were better off with a do-nothing like David Barrett.

NSA and CIA listening stations had started picking up chatter from inside the Russian strategic command. Instead of simply allowing the United States to attack its allies in Syria and Iran with impunity, Russia was ready to go the mat. They had emerged from the disastrous 1990s in a weakened state geopolitically, militarily, and economically, but they did have one last card up their sleeves.

They had nuclear weapons left over from the Soviet Union.

Keller pointed at a military aide sitting to Stark's left. "Can we hear that assessment again, please?"

Stark shook his head and sneered. "Mr. Keller, you have no authority here, and you have no military experience. I'm not sure we need to—"

"Incorrect, General," Keller said. "Do your homework. I am the authorized representative in this room of the duly-elected President of the United States, David Barrett. I served in the United States Marine Corps, Second Battalion, Fifth Marines, from 1967 to 1971, with two tours of Vietnam. I spent the month of February 1968 in Hue City, taking it back from the NVA. I probably have as much combat experience as you do, General, if not more."

Lawrence Keller was all the way out on a limb now. The situation was nuts, and as a result, he had lost his mind. Mark Baylor was watching him closely. Everyone was watching him. It was impossible to put the genie back in the bottle. It was impossible to fade back into the woodwork.

"Now let's hear that assessment again," he said.

The aide looked down at the paper in his hand. The paper had been passed to him from a runner who had come downstairs with the latest printouts.

The aide cleared his throat.

"Uh... as of eleven hundred hours Eastern Daylight Time, May eighth, Russian Strategic Command appears to have mobilized far-reaching military assets in response to American activities in the Middle East. Russian bombers and fighter planes are patrolling at the edge of American airspace in the Bering Strait, and have penetrated across the Arctic Ocean, testing British RAF response in the North Sea, and buzzing Canadian airspace over Newfoundland and Labrador.

"Russian bombers and jet fighters have been sighted over the Sea of Japan, and are moving eastward across the Mediterranean Sea toward the Levantine coast, hugging the contours of North Africa. Russian MIG-21s have entered Iranian airspace, at the invitation of the Iranian Supreme Islamic Council, and in an unprecedented provocation, are patrolling the borders between Iran and Iraq, as well as Iran and Afghanistan. American fighter jets have made visual contact—repeat, visual contact—with Russian fighters in both of these regions."

The aide turned over the page, and skimmed the next one before reading aloud. He appeared to be a man of about thirty-five. His face had blushed red while reading the first page of the intelligence report. He cleared his throat again and breathed deeply.

"Perhaps most worrisome, more than two hundred missile silos across the Russian heartland and Siberia are reporting states of combat readiness. These include launch silos for nuclear-equipped intercontinental ballistic missiles targeting the United States. Russian Strategic Command has issued a communiqué stating that any American or NATO attack on Syria or Iran will constitute an act of war against the Russian Federation, and will be treated accordingly."

He looked up from the paper and stared at Lawrence Keller. He raised his eyebrows as if to say: *Satisfied?*

"Thank you," Keller said.

"They're bluffing," General Stark said.

"What makes you think that, General?"

Stark raised a bound sheaf of paper from the table in front of him. Stark was a man who was fond of paperwork.

"I've brought a Pentagon intelligence assessment of Russian strength relative to our own, which was developed over the past eighteen months. I brought it because I anticipated the possibility that they would pull these kinds of antics in an attempt to get us to veer off course. I'd like to summarize its findings, if I may."

Mark Baylor nodded. "Please do."

Stark nodded. "Thank you, Mr. President."

It irritated Keller to hear Stark calling Baylor by that title. He should call him *Mr. Interim President*, as unwieldy as that might sound. David Barrett was the true President of the United States, and as soon as this meeting was over, Keller was going to get started on a plan to reinstall him.

"Fact," Stark said, raising a finger. "Russian Air Force, naval, and ballistic missile capabilities have degraded significantly since the collapse of the Soviet Union. As of December 2003, more than fifty percent of the MIG fighters in their arsenal are legacies left over from before the collapse. Maintenance on them is suspect, and we believe that at least five percent and possibly as many as ten percent are not even flight-worthy as of this moment. In any event, MIGs, new or old, are no match for our modern F/A-18 fighter jets. Their pilots are no match for our pilots. The Russian jets patrolling the skies are so much window dressing."

Stark barely paused for breath. He raised a second finger.

"Fact," he said. "The Russian Navy is in worse shape than their Air Force, if that's possible. Many Russian ships and submarines are rusted hulks that can barely leave port. In August of 2000, less than five years ago, gentlemen, the Russian nuclear submarine *Kursk* exploded and sank during naval exercises in the Barents Sea, the first major exercises the Russians had attempted in ten years. All one hundred eighteen crew were lost. Russian communications systems, and command and control, were so poor that for six hours the Russian Navy didn't even realize the ship had gone down. An internal assessment conducted by the Russian Navy, which we intercepted, suggests that sailor morale is as low as it's been at any time in the modern era."

He raised a third finger. "Fact. Russian infantry units performed so poorly, and so chaotically, during the two recent Chechen Wars, that we do not anticipate them being deployed against us in any theater at the current time. We would welcome it if they were. Their leadership corps are some of the same people responsible for the humiliating debacle in Afghanistan during the 1980s. The vast majority of their foot soldiers are either young, inexperienced, and poorly trained, or have gone through adverse experiences in Chechnya, with the attendant psychological damage that suggests."

He stopped speaking. It was quiet in the room.

"Thank you, General," Mark Baylor said. He looked around at the faces gathered there. The last face he reached was Lawrence Keller's. "I like it," Baylor said. "I think we need to strike while the iron is hot. Let's go forward with the attacks."

Lawrence Keller sighed.

"Mr. Interim President," he said, trying the title out. It sounded fine to his ears. It sounded almost emasculating, as though Baylor was the caretaker of a small nonprofit organization for children, while the executive director was recovering from hip replacement surgery.

"Mr. Interim President," he said again, more forcefully this time. "That's all well and good, and I'm certain we can defeat the Russians in any conventional theater of combat. But we haven't heard anything from the general about their nuclear and ballistic missile capabilities. General?"

"You already know what I'm going to say about their ballistic missile capabilities," Stark said.

"Well, a few moments ago this gentleman to your left told us that more than two hundred Russian missile silos are reporting full combat readiness. I'd like to hear more about that, if I might, before we launch a war against the world's other major nuclear-armed power."

General Stark's voice suddenly rose in anger. "In what capacity are you acting that you think—"

Keller pointed at Stark. "I already told you what capacity. I am the representative of the duly-elected—"

Stark looked at Baylor. "Mr. President?"

Baylor shrugged and nodded. "Just give him the assessment," he said. "So we can all get out of here."

"Okay," Stark said and sighed. He turned to a new page.

"Give us all of it," Keller said. "Don't hold back."

Stark stared at him.

"Russian ballistic missile capability is a shadow of its former self," he said. "Many of the weapons systems have not been maintained or upgraded since the late 1980s. Command and control has degraded, as have general communications system-wide. We believe that some silos are reduced to making telephone contact with Russian Strategic Command. Their missile defense and distant early warning systems are Cold War–era leftovers, and may be nonfunctional by any modern standard. However, the sheer size of the original Soviet arsenal is a matter of some concern. If even fifty percent of the original arsenal is still operational, and we believe it is, then it's clear that an even, toe-to-toe nuclear exchange would be a disaster for both them and us."

Keller shook his head. "And you would like to instigate a war with them, General?"

Stark's face turned red. He raised a single finger. "The Russians are not going to risk a nuclear war over Iran and Syria."

"Is that a fact, or is that your opinion?"

Stark's eyes were on fire.

"Sir, if it comes to that, we can win a nuclear war against the Russians. My intelligence shows that a massive preemptive first strike on the Russian mainland, with simultaneous launches from our ballistic missile silos as well as our nuclear equipped submarines and destroyers, would overwhelm—"

"General, are you insane? Should we really risk a nuclear war just because you want to attack Iran? I remind you that the President's daughter has been kidnapped. We should be sifting through intelligence data about her whereabouts, rather than—"

Stark's voice rose almost to a shout. "Completely overwhelm their missile defense capabilities, resulting in the loss of more than ninety percent of their—"

Keller didn't know what to say. He stood and pointed at the general again.

"Behold a pale horse!" he shouted, quoting the Book of Revelation. "And its rider's name was Death, and Hades followed close behind! And the two were given dominion over the Earth, to kill by sword and famine and plague, and by the wild beasts."

Stark stopped. He gaped at Keller.

"Did you just ask me if I was insane? Listen to what you're saying."

A man at the conference table stood. He was a tall man with wire-rimmed glasses. He wore a light blue dress shirt and khaki pants. A dark blue blazer was draped over his seat. A wire hung from his right ear, suggesting he was listening to information coming from somewhere else. He was clearly not military, but he was also dressed a little bit casually for normal government work. He had been sitting there quietly this entire time. His appearance was utterly nondescript. He was not a man who stood out or would be easily remembered. He could be anyone.

"Gentlemen," he said. "If I may interrupt, I'm Special Agent Smith with the Central Intelligence Agency. I was sent here to participate in these discussions, but I haven't felt I had anything to offer until now. I'm receiving real-time updates indicating that in the past several minutes, the President's daughter may have been located. No one is sure yet. But if it's really her, she is in the mountains of northwestern Iraq, she is alive, and ad hoc rescue attempts are already underway."

He paused and looked at Mark Baylor.

"Sir, I'd like to suggest that we stand down from a nuclear war footing for the time being, and focus our deliberations on…"

Baylor nodded, not even missing a beat. One minute he was ready to bring about Armageddon, the next, he was ready to discuss a rescue operation. He was a chameleon. They all were. It made Lawrence Keller sick.

"Yes, of course," Baylor said. "That's very good news. Let's get Elizabeth out of there."

A silence drew out. It seemed to last a long moment. Keller was still standing, frozen in place, his finger pointed like a gun at General Stark. Stark's mouth was open as if he was about to speak.

"Are you gentlemen okay with that?" the CIA agent said.

"I'm fine with it," Keller said. "Of course. I welcome it."

"General Stark?" the agent said. "We need to act fast and assist the rescue attempt in any way we can. At the very least, we need to put the assets in place to secure the region where we believe she might be. We need to do that now."

Stark shrugged. He turned the paper over in front of him.

"Okay," he said. "But I think we're losing an opportunity."

CHAPTER THIRTY

7:12 p.m. Arabian Standard Time (11:12 a.m. Eastern Daylight Time)
Sinjar Mountains
Nineveh Governorate
Northwestern Iraq

Run!

The thought repeated itself like a mantra.

Run!

Over and over again. It was all she could think.

She had lost the sandals that were on her feet. They had been too big, and now they were gone. She ran as fast she could in bare feet, stumbling over sharp rocks. Her legs pounded, her arms churned, her lungs screamed for air.

RUN!

It was cold out, but she was hot. They were right behind her. Her feet screamed in pain, cut to ribbons on jagged stone. It was dark out. The cliff was up ahead somewhere. She would run straight off the edge, rather than let the men catch her again.

Ahmet was dead. She was sure of it. She had seen it happen. After he freed her, she ran out of the stone building and immediately headed west. But the men saw her right away. There was a group of them down the ridge. They chased her, but then Ahmet came out and started shooting at them.

She turned and looked back, just as the men started shooting at him. In the last of the dying light, she saw...

It didn't matter.

Ahmet didn't matter. He didn't make sense. He had helped them capture her, and then he had died helping her escape.

She couldn't think about that. She had to run.

That was all she could do.

Suddenly, a burst of light zipped by her from behind. She heard it whistle as it passed. She tripped over something sharp and fell to the ground.

"Annhhh!"

It hurt. She tore up her hands, her forearms, her knees.

BOOOOM!

228

An explosion rent the night maybe a hundred yards in front of her. They were shooting missiles at her! Oh my God. They would blow her up rather than let her kill herself. There was a sound above her now, in the sky, loud and growing louder.

"Get up!" she said to herself through clenched teeth. "Get up and run."

A burst of machine gun fire passed over her head.

It was too late. They were shooting now. She couldn't stand or they would blow her head off. So she started to crawl. She squirmed over the rocks like a snake. It was too slow. She was never going to make it.

A strong hand grabbed her by the collar of her jumpsuit. The collar was tightened by his grip, choking her. The man spun her over onto her back. She hit her head on the hard ground as she landed. It was a man with a thick beard. His eyes seemed to glow.

He said something but she couldn't understand.

He raised a pistol to her face.

"No!" she screamed and kicked at him.

Suddenly, a bright blinding light enveloped them both.

* * *

"Kill that guy!" Ed Newsam shouted. "Kill that guy!"

The man was illuminated in the bright front light from the chopper. He stood over Elizabeth Barrett, gun pointed at her.

Luke leaned out the bay door onto the outside bench. He let it rip with the MP5.

He sliced the man in half just above the waist. The two parts, upper and lower, separated and fell apart.

"Nice," Ed said.

"We gotta get down there," Luke said.

"Incoming!" Ed shouted.

It wasn't the response Luke had hoped for. He dove back inside the chopper, even as it whirled away, banking hard, taking evasive action. A rocket zipped out of the darkness, hit the chopper with a solid metal GONG, and bounced away.

Luke was on the floor of the cabin, next to the former Greg Welch.

"What the hell was that?"

"I don't know," Ed said. "Must have been homemade."

"Gentlemen, we can't be here anymore," Jacob said. He sounded almost calm, but not quite. "The next one's going to put a

229

hole right through us. You wanted a peek, and you got one. I hope you're satisfied."

"Negative!" Luke shouted. He clambered to his feet, despite the sharp angle the chopper was taking. He stumbled to the cockpit.

"We have to go down there. She's there. Elizabeth Barrett. I know it's her. The place is crawling with Al Qaeda."

"Tell me something I don't know," Rachel said.

The chopper was moving fast, very close to the ground.

"Okay, Stone," Jacob said. "Okay. We're going to put you down, but you have to meet me halfway. We're nearly out of fuel. I don't like that terrain."

"That's fine. Get us close. We'll jump. Then get out of here. But do me a favor and launch those Hydras and squirt those guys with your cannon before you go."

Jacob nodded. "Okay. Good luck. Ten seconds."

Luke stepped across the cabin to Ed. Ed was crouched in the bay door with the M-79 grenade launcher, looking for a target.

Luke clapped him on the back. "Come on, man. We're going in."

"Out of sight," Ed said. He went out the bay door and clambered over the outside bench. Already the chopper was hovering. An instant later, Ed was gone.

Luke followed him out. His MP5 was still in hand. He slipped over the bench. The chopper was hovering right at the cliff's edge. The ground was five or six feet below him. Just ahead, Ed Newsam was running in a low crouch, toward the action.

A rocket came screaming out of the night, headed straight for the chopper.

The chopper lurched away and banked hard, just as Luke was about to jump. His foot got snagged, and he tumbled off the bench. The rocket zoomed by. His gun clattered away. He grabbed for anything; he was falling. The chopper was out over nothing. Upside down, he caught the landing gear of the chopper with one hand and swung wildly. The cliff face was way *over there*. Below him the sky fell away into the darkness.

"I'm still here!" he screamed. "Jacob! Rachel!"

A blat of machine gun fire hit the side of the chopper, tearing up metal.

"Jacob!"

The chopper banked again and raced back toward the mountain. Luke dangled, hanging free by one hand. His body swung crazily. He reached to get his other hand on the landing gear. The chopper zoomed toward land.

Suddenly, they were past the cliff and over hard-packed earth again.

Another rocket came sizzling toward the chopper.

Luke let go. His legs hit hard, and he bounced into the air, his momentum carrying him along. He hit again, tucked his body, and rolled over the stony ground. He lay there, breathing hard. He tried to do a body scan, but everything hurt right now.

Had his head hit? No.

Could he feel his legs? His arms? Yes?

Okay, he was operational. All he had left was his sidearm. He got up and ran, heading toward where he thought the girl might be, north along the cliff face.

Behind him, the Little Bird launched its Hydra rockets toward Al Qaeda. Whoooosh! They screamed across the night, just above the ground, throwing insane shadows.

BOOM-BOOOOM! Double explosions as they both hit. Luke though he saw the remains of a body fly through the air.

An instant later, the chopper opened up with its M230 chain gun. The ugly metallic blat of automatic cannon fire was music to his ears. The thing fired armor-piercing, explosive thirty-millimeter rounds, designed to shred on impact—three hundred of them a minute.

Duh-duh-duh-duh-duh. Duh-duh-duh-duh-duh.

Luke ran, gun in hand.

Somewhere ahead and to his right, he heard the telltale hollow bonk of the M-79 grenade launcher. Ed Newsam.

Doonk!

The gun made a launch sound all out of proportion to its destructive power. It sounded like it had just served a tennis ball. The grenade skidded across the dark on a nearly flat trajectory.

BOOOM!

Another bright explosion. The ground shook from it.

But the bad guys weren't done. A missile fired, whistling this way.

BANG!

It hit somewhere behind him. He turned. The helicopter was hit.

"No," he said.

An image came to him, the bad thing, all those guys in Afghanistan. Wayne. Martinez. Luke had convinced Jacob and Rachel to stay. Always, he was always convincing people to stay. That was Ed's whole point, wasn't it?

Jesus.

The auto cannon stopped firing. The chopper spun. It came down with a heavy metal crunch in the darkness, somewhere behind a low ridge.

Luke turned and kept running. There was nothing he could do for the chopper or the pilots. Up ahead, to his left, there was a spot of bright orange on the ground. He made for it, humping it over loose rocks and jagged edges.

There she was. It was her. She lay sprawled out, her body in an odd position, the kind of unnatural position Luke had seen too many times in war zones.

"Elizabeth! Are you alive?"

Her eyes popped open.

"American?" she said.

Luke nodded. "Yeah."

"I'm playing dead."

Luke's shoulders slumped. All the breath went out of him. He nearly laughed.

"Good idea," he said.

There was a sound behind him, breathing, feet running on gravel. He turned and it was a man—skinny, bearded—running with a rifle. Luke shot from the hip and put one in the man's chest. The man kept coming, crashed into Luke and they tumbled to the ground. For a moment, they wrestled for the gun, but the strength ebbed out of the man.

He lay on his back, mouth hanging open. He might have been twenty years old. That thick beard was probably his proudest possession. He reached a hand to his chest. It came away bloody. He looked at Luke, mouthed something, and then died.

Luke picked up the man's rifle. It was an old AK-47. He checked the magazine. Loaded. That was a bit of a gift. The kid should have fired instead of charging like that. Luke shook his head. His loss.

Anyway, Luke was back in business.

"Elizabeth, I need to move you. I'm going to hide you somewhere."

She shook her head. "No. I'm not going anywhere. I should stay here with you."

"There's going to be shooting here any minute, and if that happens, you're going to get shot. Not once, but a lot of times. I need to move you somewhere safe, so I can fight to protect you. It will be easier for me to do that, and much safer for you, if you are nowhere near me."

She stared at him with big eyes. "Where will I go?"

He shook his head. "I don't know. We'll find a place."

Somewhere to his left, Ed launched another round from the M-79.

Doonk!

Luke checked his watch. 7:35 p.m.

It had been a long day. It was going to be a long night.

BOOOM!

Ed's grenade hit somewhere behind Luke.

A man started shrieking. He sounded almost like a siren.

There was a fire off to Luke's left, where the chopper must have crashed. He didn't want to think about that right now.

He held a hand out to Elizabeth. She took it and he pulled her to her feet.

Luke had an idea. He walked Elizabeth to the cliffs. They were only another fifty yards further on. Sometimes cliffs were totally sheer, sometimes they weren't. He looked over the edge. It was a long way down.

But just below, maybe four feet down and to the left, there was a narrow ledge several feet long. A stunted tree stuck out from the wall there. Its root system was exposed, thick and gnarled.

"Elizabeth, I'm going to need you to be brave. You've been very brave so far, but you're going to have to be even more brave, as brave as you've ever been. Can you do that for me?"

"I don't know," she said. "What do I need to do?"

"You need to slide down to that ledge, get a good strong grip on that tree trunk, and wait. I will help you get down there."

Elizabeth gazed down at the ledge. Luke could see what she was looking at. Just behind the ledge, the cliffs fell away from a dizzying height. It was dark now, but the truth was clear enough. The fall from here would be endless.

"Oh my God," Elizabeth said.

* * *

Luke crouched low and moved to a ridge of stone thirty yards from the cliff face. He took cover and aimed his gun at the bad guys.

Two men were moving slowly across the rocks, guns out, stepping carefully. Their heads swiveled back and forth, looking for the girl, looking for the enemy.

Luke fired on them, killed them both.

An instant later, a rocket came screaming out of the night.

233

Luke ducked and rolled away just before the rocket hit his ridge.

BAM!

The sound was more than deafening. His ears rang. He went deaf for a long moment. Fragments of stone flew into the air and showered down on him.

Doonk!

From somewhere to the left, Ed had fired back at them.

BOOOM!

Machine gun fire strafed the spot where Ed's muzzle signature had been. Hopefully, Ed wasn't there anymore.

And so it went, tit for tat.

Luke crawled forward, like a worm, and shot another Al Qaeda in the head.

From somewhere ahead of him, a flare launched. Luke was silent. The militia was going to probe with that flare and see if they could spot Ed's or Luke's location. In the brief glow of the launch, Luke thought he saw perhaps a dozen men crouched by a low stone wall.

The flare began its slow ascent, lighting up the night.

An instant later, a line of bombs dropped from somewhere in the heavens. They came screaming down, a violent rain, invisible, pounding the place where the flare had just gone up.

BOOM! BOOM! BOOM! BOOM! BOOM!

A hundred yards of fire and fury, a field of death, briefly turned night into day. The explosions echoed across the mountains, and back. In the aftermath, there came the crackling of flames as something burned, possibly a small building, and possibly the bodies of whoever had just been positioned there.

Drone strike. Beautiful.

Hours passed.

In the first bleak light just before dawn, a squad of United States Marines appeared like ghosts out of the mist. They moved carefully across the rocky terrain.

Luke ducked behind the ridgeline again. This was when people got shot by accident.

"Americans!" he shouted. "There's Americans over here!"

Luke threw the rifle away. He heard them running toward him. He kept his empty hands in the air, where everyone could see them. Two helmeted Marines came around the ridge, rifles pointed at Luke.

"I'm an American!" he shouted again.

"Don't move!"

The Marines charged him, flipped him over onto his stomach, and began to search him. A heavy foot was planted on his back. The muzzle of a gun was at his neck. Rough hands roamed his body.

"Agent Luke Stone," he said. "FBI Special Response Team. The President's daughter is thirty yards or forty yards from here, on a ledge hanging off the cliff. She's wearing a bright orange jumpsuit. Don't shoot her."

From the corner of his eye, he saw more Marines running past.

"Boy, am I glad to see you guys."

* * *

Ed Newsam picked his way across the jagged rocks.

He was tired. He was dirty. He was scratched up.

If he raised his gaze, the morning view across the mountain range was astonishing. If he looked down, the view was also astonishing, in its own way. Dozens of terrorist fighters littered the ground. They were skinny, they had thick beards, they wore head wraps. A few were alive and moving. Most were dead.

Many eyes were open and staring, seeing nothing.

He didn't care about these guys. They had an unmistakable look about them. They were foot soldiers. Ed had a date with someone else.

Up ahead, a guy was sitting on the hard, dusty ground. He was one of the few without a serious injury. He sat cross-legged. The Marines had shackled his wrists behind his back.

"You," Ed said.

The guy looked up. His eyes were exhausted. He didn't have any fight left in him.

"Where's your leader?" Ed said.

The guy stared at him, his eyes round and concerned. He shook his head.

"*Ayn hu zaeim?*" Ed barked.

Ed knew a little Arabic. The words were right. The grammar and syntax could go to hell. The man on the ground understood well enough. Light dawned in his eyes. He was careful not to speak in response. Silently, he gestured to his left with his head. The move was so subtle, it hardly qualified as movement at all.

Over there, perhaps twenty yards away, was another man on the ground. This man was also manacled, and he leaned back against some rocks. He had a leg injury, which the Marines had been kind enough to patch up for him. His right pant leg was cut

235

away below the thigh, and the leg was wrapped in a bloody bandage.

Ed walked over to him.

The man looked up at Ed. He had jet black hair and a handsome face. His eyes were hard and unafraid. Oh well. There were a lot of hard guys in a war zone.

"You speak English?" Ed said.

The man nodded. "Little."

"Who are you?"

The man smiled. "Who are you?"

Ed reached down and ripped the right sleeve of the man's shirt. There, on the man's round shoulder, was a tattoo of a crescent moon and a star, the symbol of the Muslim world. The man looked at it as if seeing it for the first time.

How did that get there?

Instantly, he realized his mistake. The one identifying feature in the video was that tattoo.

Ed pulled his sidearm. He pointed it at the man's head. Still, the man showed no fear. If anything, his smile broadened.

"I should have gutted her like a pig," he said.

BANG!

The shot rang out, echoing across the rugged hillsides.

The man's body slumped on the stony ground. A halo of blood began to spread around his ruined head.

"Yeah," Ed said. "Whatever you say."

* * *

A Black Hawk helicopter hovered overhead, its basket lowered to the ground.

In the near distance, three Apache helicopter gunships patrolled the skies, moving in slow circles. Further out were more of them. In fact, the sky was black with American helicopters. Luke began to count them but stopped at fifteen, because there were plenty more than that.

If there were still Al Qaeda militants alive on this mountain, or anywhere nearby, they were not going to challenge those choppers.

"Thank you for saving my life," Elizabeth Barrett said.

She stood facing Luke. She was a head shorter than him.

"It's okay. I was just doing my job. That's all any of these people were doing."

She stood on her tiptoes and kissed him on the cheek.

"Who are you? What is your name?"

236

"Luke Stone," he said. He thought about who he was, and how to express it. He wasn't a soldier, a commando, a special operator anymore.

"I'm an FBI agent."

She nodded. "Stone. I'm going to tell my father about you."

She turned and limped to the chopper basket, two Marines helping her. They would have carried her, but she insisted on walking. Her bloodied feet were wrapped in thick bandages. Her hands were ripped up pretty badly. She walked with her back straight and her head held up.

She was a trouper.

From the low ridge where he stood, Luke could also see the remains of the Little Bird. It looked like some sort of modern art sculpture. The landing gear had bent on impact, dropping the chopper over sideways. A rotor blade had wedged itself into the ground, its opposite number sticking up, pointing skyward. And the whole chopper itself had burned. Its burnt out frame gave the impression of a human skull.

Jacob and Rachel stood not far from it, looking at the remains. Somehow they had gotten out. That was a very nice development. He wouldn't call it a surprise, though. Those two had been surviving combat together for a long time.

Ed Newsam walked across the ridge, the M-79 over his shoulder. He had gone to keep his date with the man in the video.

"You find him?" Luke said.

Ed shrugged. "I think so."

"Well, you can still try to beat me up, if you want."

A light went on in Ed's eyes. It was if he had forgotten about that, and he was glad that someone reminded him. He looked at Luke, squinted, and grinned.

"Nah," he said.

CHAPTER THIRTY ONE

May 9
8:35 a.m. Arabian Standard Time (12:35 a.m. Eastern Daylight Time)
The Embassy of the United States in Iraq (aka the Republican Palace)
The International Zone (aka the Green Zone)
Karkh District
Baghdad, Iraq

"Every single time," Ed Newsam said.

Four men stood in a rounded room of polished stone. As much as they spoke just above whispers, their voices seemed to echo off the walls. Big Daddy Bill Cronin was there, in dress slacks, suspenders, and a dress shirt with sleeves rolled to the forearms. Mark Swann was there in jeans and a T-shirt, ponytail pulled tight to his head. Ed and Luke were there, still dirty and rumpled and scuffed up from combat.

Both Ed and Luke were like the Pig Pen character from the old *Peanuts* cartoons. They were walking dirt hills.

Big Daddy looked at Luke.

"Yeah?" he said.

Luke nodded. "It seemed that way to me. Every time we went somewhere, they knew we were coming. That SAS guy got chewed up... But those were his own guys. I don't think he would..."

He shook his head.

Big Daddy nodded. "Yeah, he's been acting a little weird the past couple of months. I wouldn't put anything past anyone. It's a temptation over here. There's a lot of money floating around. You've seen it."

No one said the word, but they were all talking about the same man: Montgomery.

"Now he's been shipped back home," Ed said. "He's out of reach. There's no evidence he did anything. What are we supposed to do?"

Suddenly the door opened with a bang. The person didn't even knock.

It was Trudy.

"Luke, I've been looking all over for you. I just got off the phone with Don Morris. Your wife went into labor thirty minutes ago. Don sent the SRT chopper to your house to pick her up and bring her to Fairfax. They can land at the hospital. He says you should come home right now. You might get lucky. Sometimes these first labors take—"

Luke was already up and headed for the door.

"Oh, man. It's fifteen hours in the air. There's a stopover in Germany. I'm never going to—"

"There's a State Department Lear jet fueling up at the Baghdad Airport. It's waiting for you. Direct flight to DC."

Luke was nearly out the door. He looked back at Big Daddy.

"What about…"

Big Daddy shook his head and waved Luke on. "Monty? Don't worry about it. I'll talk to him."

Luke looked at Ed and Swann.

"See you guys around."

CHAPTER THIRTY TWO

6:05 a.m. Eastern Daylight Time
Camp David
Catoctin Mountain Park
Thurmont, Maryland

"It's a beautiful morning."

Lawrence Keller walked the quiet, wooded path with David Barrett in the first light of day. The sky was pale blue, with shades of pink and yellow where the sun was rising. There was a slight chill in the air, which would soon burn off. It was shaping up to be a very nice day. Somewhere, a crow cackled, and further away, another one answered.

Since the days of Franklin Delano Roosevelt, Presidents had used this as their country retreat, and as a place to host foreign dignitaries in a relaxed atmosphere, and Keller could see why.

He mused that it would be just like a Robert Frost poem, except for the six big Secret Service men spread out behind them, and in front of them, and off to their sides. The men murmured into their collar microphones as they moved along. Their voices could be the sound of a small stream.

David Barrett walked slowly and thoughtfully.

"I'll never forget what you did, Lawrence."

He said it pleasantly enough. But he left the statement there, and left Keller to wonder about its meaning. It was fitting to walk in nature like this, and to have the President drop a mysterious Zen koan on him.

What had he done, in David Barrett's eyes? Taken control during a bad situation, when Barrett was clearly out of control? Put Barrett on the sidelines until his daughter was safe, and he could pull himself together? Derailed a misguided attempt to start World War Three?

Or was it that he had betrayed David, taping him in the Oval Office during his most vulnerable moments, and then using that tape against him?

Keller had done all of these things. But what did Barrett think he had done?

"What are your plans, David?" Keller said.

Barrett took a deep breath. "This is the happiest day of my life, so first of all, I'm going to enjoy it. I'm going to thank God for my many blessings, and take stock of what the future holds. They've flown Elizabeth to a hospital in Germany, and she's still en route there, but everyone assures me she's doing fine. Later this morning, Marilynn, Caitlynn, and I are all going to fly out there to be with her. It's going to be one heck of a family reunion."

He stopped and looked down at Keller. "Is that what you mean?"

Keller shrugged. "Sure. That, and when do you think you'll be coming back to work? You are the President of the United States, after all. The country needs you. I'm not really sure Mark Baylor is cut out for the job."

There was a mischievous twinkle in Barrett's eyes. He started walking again. "Some people are meant to be President, and some people are meant to be Vice President," he said.

"I couldn't have put it better myself," Keller said.

"I think I'll be in Germany for a few days until Elizabeth is ready to come home. Then I'll take a couple more days here at Camp David with the whole family. My mom and dad will probably come up and stay, too."

"That's nice."

"So, I'll be out of commission for another week or so. I talked to Mark late last night, and he's willing to hold the reins for a bit longer."

"Good," Keller said. "And I'll be there to look over his shoulder."

Barrett shrugged. "Well, that's why I bring it up. Mark would like to move you over to Legislative Affairs for now. He thinks you're a bit of a hothead. And he's got his own Chief of Staff, as you know. He's concerned that having you around will be stepping on his guy's toes, and I told him that would be fine."

Keller nodded. "I see. Okay."

"Yeah, I'll be honest with you, Lawrence. I've been contemplating a similar move for some time. How are you doing? I mean, you seem a little burnt out to me, like you're just not enjoying this anymore. I've been worried about you, and I was going to do something about it, but then this whole Elizabeth fiasco happened."

Keller felt his heart speed up. A flush began to creep up his neck.

"I'm feeling fine. Never better, really."

Barrett went on as if Keller hadn't spoken at all. "You know Kathy Grumman from State? She's a real whip. I'm going to bring her on to tidy things up a bit."

"As Chief of Staff?" Keller said.

Barrett nodded. "Think of Legislative Affairs as a lateral move, Lawrence. You'll keep the same salary as you have now, with all the same benefits. And the hours will be better. They're regular nine-to-fivers most of the time, unless we're trying to push a bill through. I'm going to need you to ride herd on a few of our reluctant friends in the House. You'll be reporting to Mike Donovan. Do you know Mike? He's been working Capitol Hill for about a decade."

"I'll be reporting... to Mike?"

Lawrence Keller had never met Mike Donovan, but he knew who he was. He was about thirty-seven years old, the son of the obnoxious, bulbous, alcoholic former Congressman from Massachusetts, Mickey Donovan.

Mike Donovan was a prep school jerk. He had strolled into his job because of nepotism. And he was fifteen years younger than Lawrence Keller.

Barrett nodded enthusiastically. "Yeah. Mike's the Director of Legislative Affairs. I like him. You'll be his Assistant Director."

They walked along the path in silence for a moment.

"What do you think?" Barrett said.

What did he think?

Lawrence Keller thought one thing was for certain: he was NOT going to work for Mike Donovan at Legislative Affairs. If David Barrett wanted to push Keller out because he made a tape of an Oval Office conversation, so be it. But he'd better watch his back. Keller hadn't gotten where he was by nepotism—he'd clawed his way there. And he would claw David Barrett's eyes out.

"What do I think? I think your daughter Elizabeth is a very irresponsible young woman, who caused the needless deaths of dozens of people, and who almost sparked a world war."

* * *

Beautiful.

David Barrett was feeling such a surge of joy that even his early meeting with Lawrence Keller couldn't drag him down. Keller was a problem, that was true. He was untrustworthy. Apparently, he'd had an outburst during deliberations in the Situation Room, and had yelled at a general.

Lawrence Keller did not fit the suit. Short, angry, uncultured, that was Keller in a nutshell. He was banished to Legislative Affairs for now, but he would almost certainly try to claw his way back into relevance. David would have to keep an eye on him.

No matter. Elizabeth was alive, the birds were singing, and David was President of the United States. All was right with the world.

Forget about Keller.

This next meeting was the one he was really looking forward to. He sat in the rustic, sun-dappled great room of the main house. When he was a child, he would stare at photographs in magazines of Dwight Eisenhower and Jack Kennedy entertaining foreign heads of state in this very room, and he would think:

"That's going to be me one day."

Amazing. He shook his head at the wonder of it.

His guest walked in and David rose to meet him. David was a bit taller than the man, but it didn't matter. The guest was so impressive physically, that David almost felt diminished in his presence. The man was broad and muscular. His eyes were sharp and intelligent and aware, in a face that looked like it had been carved from granite. His body seemed to radiate electricity. He looked like a man who never slept and who never needed to sleep. The only concessions he'd made to age were the gray in his flattop haircut, and the crow's feet around his eyes.

He was Don Morris, decorated combat veteran of many wars, pioneer of the very concept of military special operations, and the Director of the brand new FBI Special Response Team. His agents had saved Elizabeth's life.

He wore dress pants and a dark blazer. His light blue dress shirt was open at the collar. He was meeting the President of the United States, and he dressed down! It was perfect. The man was a legend.

"Mr. President," he said, extending a hand. "It's an honor to meet you, sir."

Barrett took Morris's hand. He noted that Morris's handshake was firm, but not too firm. There was the sense that the man was holding back tremendous strength, which could crush David Barrett's hand to mulch.

Barrett shook his head. "Ah, Don. Call me David, please. Won't you sit down? What can we get for you? Anything at all. Water, soda? Beer? I know it's early, but if you want something, you can have it. We can have them make us lunch."

Morris shook his head. "No sir. I'm fine. Thank you. That's very kind."

They sat down.

"I know we've talked once before, haven't we?"

Don nodded. "Yes sir. We talked briefly on the phone just a few weeks ago."

"That's great," David said. "I remember that." He felt foolish. These pleasantries were not at all what he wanted to come out of his mouth.

"I want to tell you how grateful I am, how grateful my wife is, and our parents. I think we are the most grateful family in America at this moment. We owe you a debt that we can never adequately repay."

Don shrugged. "Sir, I appreciate that. But I had very little to do with the operation that saved your daughter. It happened because of the initiative, and frankly, the guts, shown by our field agents Luke Stone and Edward Newsam. And they had a big assist from our intelligence team, from a covert CIA agent it's better if I do not name, crack helicopter pilots, and dozens of on the ground troops. A lot of people made this thing happen."

"I know. I know that," David Barrett said. "It's wonderful the people who do these dangerous jobs. But I'll tell you, I'm fascinated by the career you've had and the work you do. I'm very excited that you've started this new agency, and I want to meet your people. The best of the best, isn't that what you told me? Like a civilian Delta Force?"

Morris nodded. "That is exactly what I said. You have an excellent memory."

"Well, Don, I'm hoping we can all work closely together going forward."

Don Morris smiled.

"I would like that, sir. I hope we can, too."

CHAPTER THIRTY THREE

It was time to go.

Andrew Montgomery came out of his pale blue Victorian-era terrace house, carrying two suitcases. There were no clothes in the suitcases. His clothes were already in the car. No, the suitcases held nothing but cash, and a lot of it.

His time in Iraq had been well spent.

At first, he had been called on the carpet for the death of that Special Air Service lad. But now that it turned out the man was a hero who had not died in vain, but who had been instrumental in helping discover the location of the American President's daughter… well, the winds had blown back in Monty's favor a bit.

Even so, there were worse things than career setbacks to worry about. Bill Cronin had called him three times today from Baghdad, wanting to chat about the operation. Bill's voice had a funny tone in it. It was a tone that Monty did not like. Monty guessed that his little intelligence partnership with the CIA agent Bill Cronin might be coming to its conclusion.

They were never friends, he and Big Daddy, and work relationships eventually ended. Sad, really, but just part of the life.

Monty placed the suitcases flat in the trunk of his old Porsche 911 Targa, next to two identical suitcases, also flat, making four in total. He put his clothes bags and his badminton rackets on top of the suitcases, obscuring them. It wouldn't survive a search, of course, but who was going to search his car? No one suspected him of anything, nor should they.

Bill Cronin was calling him a bit, of course, you might even say harassing him, but that meant nothing. Bill probably just wanted to tie up a few loose ends. He could be rather pushy, in his way.

Unfortunately, Monty was not available. He was leaving right now for a few days' getaway to his country house on the Welsh coast, near Caernarfon. There was a telephone at the house, but Monty was very careful about sharing that number.

No, Monty was unreachable for the time being. In fact, he was thinking of extending the amount of time involved. A period abroad, maybe in some far-flung, anonymous place, might be what the doctor ordered after so much time spent in war zones.

The Seychelles? Maybe.

The South Pacific?

The coast of Nicaragua?

It was hard to imagine a place on Earth where Big Daddy Cronin might not eventually find him.

But it wasn't like he was on the run, was it? No, of course not. Big Daddy might have a few questions, but they were easily answerable.

Monty slammed the trunk closed and slipped in behind the wheel. It was a beautiful cockpit for a car—they didn't make them like this anymore. It felt like driving an airplane. This was his favorite car, one of the best he had ever owned.

He turned the key in the ignition, but there seemed to be something wrong with the starter. It was an old car, and these things could be tricky.

He turned it again and gave it a little gas.

A spark ignited under his foot, and then flames shot upward.

He knew, even before he knew what it was. He reached to open the car door and get out before…

Ga-BOOOM!

The ground trembled.

Someone screamed.

Afternoon strollers on picturesque Portobello Road in London's fashionable Notting Hill suddenly dove to the street and took cover in shops as a beautifully restored Porsche 911 exploded. A ball of black smoke and orange flame rose into the sky. A moment later, the fire reached the gas tank, and a secondary explosion went up.

"Help!" a young woman shouted. "There's a man! I saw a man!"

People ran toward the site of the explosion, but no one got too close. The flames crackled. The fire raged. It was intense.

"There's a man inside that car!"

CHAPTER THIRTY FOUR

"Okay, Rebecca," said the doctor, a woman of about fifty. "I think this is it. One last time. Give me a big one. Push!"

Becca screamed, a loud, shrieking wail.

Her hand crushed Luke's.

"Oh God, Luke, I love you so much!"

"I love you, too, babe. You're doing great."

Luke, in surgical scrubs, mask, and gloves like the doctors and nurses, stood watching. He had raced halfway around the world for this. He had dozed on the plane, but poorly. He never imagined he would get to this operating theater in time, but somehow he did. He was nearly out on his feet.

Thank God for a long labor.

He placed his head right next to hers. She was sweating. Her face was red. She was in pain. She was exquisite.

"You're just doing so good. I am very proud of you."

Every word he said was true. He was in awe of what Becca's body could do and the strength she showed. She was never more beautiful or powerful. Luke had seen a lot in his time, but he had never seen anything like *this*.

He saw a small patch of blond hair pushing its way out. The baby was starting to crown.

I will not freak out. I will not freak out.

"One more, Rebecca. One more big one. Come on. Push!"

"Ahhhnnnhh!"

She crushed his hand again.

What he had thought was the crown was the smallest tip of the tip of the iceberg. The head was emerging, like the moment a giant superheated bubble rises to the surface of a geyser. The head was massive, enormous. It couldn't be. Something had to be wrong. It was like a cannonball was coming through a drinking straw.

"Is that…?"

He could barely speak. He could barely breathe.

"One more. Push!"

Suddenly, the boy was out. But he was blue. The child was blue.

Is he alive? Why is he blue?

The nurse was wiping off the afterbirth as if nothing was wrong.

"Gunner."

The baby started crying. He was alive. Oh my God, the baby was *alive.*

Someone pressed a pair of scissors into his hand, and guided his hand to the place where he should cut the cord. He did it. He did his job like a good soldier. The baby was crying.

It was wrapped in a blanket. Someone put the baby in his arms, just for a second. Luke was terrified, never more vulnerable. Then the boy was gone, and placed on Becca's chest. Her eyes were closed and she was breathing deeply, the baby on top of her. Luke fell in love with her all over again, but in a different way this time. He could not describe the feeling.

At some point, he was out in the hallway. His gloves were off. He had pulled his mask down. But he was still wearing the scrubs.

A nurse put a hand on his shoulder. "Good job, Mr. Stone."

"Thanks. It was nothing."

He stared out a large window at the hospital grounds. It was daytime, and for some reason that surprised him.

Strange thoughts went through his head, a mad jumble of disconnected thoughts. Sometimes, things didn't seem to make any sense. He was a killer, he knew that. He had killed a lot of people, even in just the past few days. The world often seemed like a horrible place, and yet, he had just witnessed a miracle.

He thought of a short conversation he'd had with Don Morris, what, maybe an hour ago? Don had commended him on the mission, had wished him luck in the birthing room, and told him he was sure it was going to be easy.

"There's nothing to it," Don said. "I've done it three times."

Then Don told him the mission had put the SRT on the map. He'd met with the President that morning. The President was thrilled. There were more missions right on tap. As soon as Luke and Ed were ready.

Luke didn't know if he'd ever be ready again. The thought of going back out there... But he didn't tell Don that.

248

Luke wanted more miracles, like the one he had just witnessed. That's what he realized. He wanted this life, with this woman, and this little boy. Maybe there were more miracles out there to be discovered. And maybe there was something else he could do for a living.

He shook his head. It didn't even matter. Becca's family was wealthy. That was the true, unspoken thing. For some reason, they never talked about it. Luke probably didn't need to work again. He probably didn't need to risk his life, or kill anyone, ever again. Not for money, anyway.

But he never did it for money in the first place.

Why?

That was the question on his mind today.

No. Not why did he do it?

Why was he here? Why was everything here? Why was there something rather than nothing? Why was there a strong, beautiful woman in that room, and a new baby boy, instead of no woman and no boy and nothing else?

Life was a mystery. What was the reason for it?

"Love," he said, surprising himself with the answer. "It's love."

He nodded silently. He looked around to see if anyone had heard him. There was no one here. The hallway was empty.

"Love," he said again, stronger this time.

PRIMARY COMMAND
(The Forging of Luke Stone—Book #2)

"One of the best thrillers I have read this year."
--Books and Movie Reviews (re Any Means Necessary)

In PRIMARY COMMAND (The Forging of Luke Stone—Book #2), a ground-breaking action thriller by #1 bestseller Jack Mars, elite Delta Force veteran Luke Stone, 29, leads the FBI's Special Response Team on a nail-biting mission to save American hostages from a nuclear submarine. But when all goes wrong, and when the President shocks the world with his reaction, it may fall on Luke's shoulders to save not only the hostages—but the world.

PRIMARY COMMAND is an un-putdownable military thriller, a wild action ride that will leave you turning pages late into the night. The precursor to the #1 bestselling LUKE STONE THRILLER SERIES, this series takes us back to how it all began, a riveting series by bestseller Jack Mars, dubbed "one of the best thriller authors" out there.

"Thriller writing at its best."
--Midwest Book Review (re Any Means Necessary)

Also available is Jack Mars' #1 bestselling LUKE STONE THRILLER series (7 books), which begins with Any Means Necessary (Book #1),

Jack Mars

Jack Mars is the USA Today bestselling author of the LUKE STONE thriller series, which include the suspense thrillers ANY MEANS NECESSARY (book #1), OATH OF OFFICE (book #2), SITUATION ROOM (book #3), OPPOSE ANY FOE (book #4), PRESIDENT ELECT (book #5), OUR SACRED HONOR (book #6), and HOUSE DIVIDED (book #7). He is also the author of the new FORGING OF LUKE STONE prequel series, which begins with PRIMARY TARGET.

Jack loves to hear from you, so please feel free to visit www.Jackmarsauthor.com to join the email list, receive a free book, receive free giveaways, connect on Facebook and Twitter, and stay in touch!

BOOKS BY JACK MARS

LUKE STONE THRILLER SERIES
ANY MEANS NECESSARY (Book #1)
OATH OF OFFICE (Book #2)
SITUATION ROOM (Book #3)
OPPOSE ANY FOE (Book #4)
PRESIDENT ELECT (Book #5)
OUR SACRED HONOR (Book #6)
HOUSE DIVIDED (Book #7)

FORGING OF LUKE STONE PREQUEL SERIES
PRIMARY TARGET (Book #1)
PRIMARY COMMAND (Book #2)

KENT STEELE SPY SERIES
AGENT ZERO (Book #1)

Manufactured by Amazon.ca
Bolton, ON

30727533R00142